QUANTUM HEIGHTS

BOOK ONE
OF THE
DEAD PATH CHRONICLES

BY
R.A. VALICEK

Visit online at www.richardavalicek.com

Copyright © 2015 Richard A Valicek
All rights reserved.

Book layout by www.ebooklaunch.com

Intro

THEIR WORLD HAS CHANGED. None will live; none now will rest. The evil forces have risen to conflict chaos and destruction upon the free people of Alamptria. The rise of the knight masters of Petoshine will challenge the monstrosities and sinister plots. The great elf wizard, Grongone, and the spirit of Felicia - the Golden Fleece will guide and strengthen the knight masters. The power of the vim must triumph over the darkness of the lands. Let me tell you a tale… once, in a far off land called Alamptria.

Chapter 1

Something Wicked Comes This Way

THE YEAR WAS 2255. In the privacy of his candlelit room, Confidus Seaton, King of Elysium, sat in his rocking chair engrossed in a book. Still dashing and debonair in his mid-fifties, he had long grey hair, a moustache, and short beard and wore thin-rimmed spectacles that gave him a wise, handsome air. Apart from his warmth and the ease with which he carried himself, his most distinguishing feature was that his left hand bore six fingers.

Noting a smudge on his glasses, Confidus reticently set his book down on the mahogany side table, took off his spectacles, and reached for a small bottle and cloth. He carefully huffed on the glass and sprayed his lenses before buffing them. He turned them over and over in the burnished light from his reading lamp until he was convinced they were clean. Once again content, he settled them onto his nose and resumed reading.

Only five minutes later, however, someone knocked on the door. "Oh, now what?" he muttered.

He set his book down again and placed his spectacles on top. The knocking continued. "Coming. Coming. These old bones need time to get to the door," he said. The person knocked again. "You certainly are tenacious," he chuckled to himself.

When he opened the door, his youngest son, Dragus, greeted him. "Hello, Father!" he smiled brightly and held out a bottle wrapped in colored paper. "For you."

"I don't recall it being my birthday," frowned Confidus.

"No, not yet, but I thought you might enjoy a little brandy to soothe your throat and give you comfort in this dark hour," said Dragus.

Confidus accepted the gift. "My son, you spoiled the surprise. Why bother wrapping it if you're going to tell me what's inside," he playfully chided his son. He set the bottle on the étagère by the door and pulled off the wrapping. It was a premium bottle of brandy, very exclusive and hard to find. "Soothsayers' Brandy, Dragus? You shouldn't have."

"See, it was a surprise after all," said Dragus.

Confidus handed Dragus the bottle. "Here, why not pour us a drink." He sat down on the sofa. Dragus went to the cart where Confidus kept drinks, glasses, and ice and poured two shot glasses full. He brought the drinks to the sofa and sat beside his father. The two of them clinked their glasses and wordlessly watched the deep blue Begonia Ocean as it roiled and pitched. Dragus sighed and set down his drink. He reached into his shirt pocket and pulled out his silver cigarette case, slid out a cigarette, tapped it on the outside, and retrieved the matches from the box in his coat pocket. He lit the cigarette, inhaled, and let out a plume.

Confidus stared at his son with one eyebrow raised. "I thought you quit," he said.

"Father, the dark hours are upon us. The Dark Lord Makoor is standing behind his vampire minions planning his next move." He let out another stream of smoke. "*These* are the least of my worries."

"Or the most; if the vampires don't get you, the nicotine will," said Confidus. They both sipped their brandy and set the glasses back onto the coffee table. He chuckled. "I remember years ago, when you and your brothers were just boys, and I caught the three of you smoking. Do you even remember? You were only six. You'd crept out to the shack behind the apple orchard. I heard the coughing, and when I opened the door, I was nearly knocked over by the wall of smoke." He smiled. "I thought you all needed to be punished, but your mother, God rest her soul, knew that the foul air you'd all inhaled would be punishment enough. And, she was right; the three of you were sick as dogs for the rest of the day. But,," he frowned with fatherly concern, "it seems you didn't learn, and here you are, twenty-six years later, smoking again."

"May I remind you, Father, that it was your smoking that influenced us and not just cigarettes but cigars. Mother kept telling you to put them out in front of the children. I know you still smoke periodically."

"Dragus, you're still young enough to quit. I don't want you taking after my bad habit."

Dragus ground out his cigarette in the ashtray and went for his case again. "Would you care for one?"

Confidus looked at the cigarettes, feeling the urge. "No, thank you. I'm going to stay strong to show you how I can control my cravings," he said.

Dragus smirked and returned the case to his shirt pocket. "Would you like to wager a bet? Fifty shillings says within ten minutes you will ask me for one."

"I only have to hold out for ten minutes?" said the king, chuckling. "You're on." They shook hands.

"Care for another drink?" asked Dragus.

Remembering the heavy feeling that had been haunting him all day, Confidus said, "Yes, actually, I think I'd like another."

Dragus poured another two fingers of brandy into their glasses. "You know, a cigarette would go fine with a shot of brandy." He cocked his head.

Confidus held out his hand.

"Don't think I don't remember that today is the day Mother died. Eighteen years isn't long when you're still in love. That is the real reason I called this the dark hour. I miss her. I miss her every day, but I miss her today even more acutely."

Confidus closed his eyes against the pain of his loss. Memories of his beautiful wife began to stir. "Your mother was a wonderful woman, everything I wanted in a wife and a best friend. She was always smiling and was so kind and considerate, always putting everyone else first. And, so even tempered, always maintaining control. We had our little squabbles, like all married couples do, but she was always so reasoned, so clear-headed. That is why people called her the 'Iron Lady.'" Confidus sighed. "Those were good days," he said sadly.

There was another knock at the door. Confidus stood and slowly headed toward the door, wiping his eyes. "Senator Vijas," he said when he opened it, "what brings you here on this Sunday afternoon?"

"I thought I'd stop in to see how my old friend is doing," said Vijas, cupping the king's arm warmly.

"Well, my bones feel like they're eighty today, but my heart is young," he laughed. "Do come in, Vijas," said Confidus.

Vijas pointed to the wrapping on the table by the door, "Someone brought you something?" he asked as they went to the sofa. He immediately saw the brandy on the table. "Soothsathers'! Dragus, where on earth did you get a bottle of that?"

Dragus laughed. "I have my ways," he said. He fetched a glass from the cart and offered it to Vijas.

Vijas poured himself a shot. He sat back on the sofa and enjoyed his drink. "Beautiful. Thank you. In this lovely room in the castle, there's no better place in which to drink it," said Vijas.

"Alright, Vijas, you didn't really come for a visit, did you?" said Confidus, eyeing his advisor. "What brings you here?"

Vijas smiled. "You know me too well, Confidus. Very well," his face grew instantly serious. "I'm sorry to report that the board of council has denied your request to refurbish the council chamber. They say that the spending would be an unnecessary drain on the budget at this time."

Confidus' nostrils flared. Why interrupt his weekend—quiet time he was spending with his son—and calm afternoon to deliver this bad news? "May I remind you that it was the Elysian council who convinced the council of Koriston to expand the railway system into much of Alamptria. And, how much did that cost?" demanded Confidus.

"Confidus, we needed the railway expansion," said Vijas, leaning back.

"Father, Vijas is right. Our spending needs to be reduced," said Dragus.

"You knew about this, Dragus?" Confidus raised his voice.

"Father, please try and understand," said Dragus.

"Not all is lost. It was decided that we can still proceed with plans for a new facility in ten years," said Vijas. He shot the king a placating smile. "The council does understand that the chamber needs to be modernized. But, now is not the time."

"Ten years? You want to wait ten years?" asked Confidus. He glowered at Vijas and then sat up and went for the bottle. "Now I know why you brought over this bottle of Soothsathers', Dragus. It was a low blow."

Dragus pulled out his cigarette case. "Smoke, Father?"

"Why the hell not; I'll be dead anyway before the chamber is updated." Confidus pulled out a cigarette. Dragus lit the cigarette for him and smiled.

Confidus puffed angrily and stared at his son. "This was all planned," he said. "Do you seriously need fifty shillings that badly?"

"A bet's a bet, Father," said Dragus, shrugging.

At this, Vijas began to smirk. Then, Dragus began to smirk. They looked at each other and started laughing. Dragus reached for the bottle of brandy and topped up everyone's glass. "I suppose we should tell him," said Vijas.

Dragus giggled. "Yes, I guess we should." He put his hand on his father's shoulder. Confidus glowered at him, not at all impressed by the other men's mirth.

"Confidus, Dragus and I are both here because the council has, in fact, unanimously agreed that it is more than high time to renovate the council chamber and update all the equipment."

"You mean this was all a big joke?" Confidus smiled.

"Yes, your son Caprius put us up to this," said Vijas still giggling. "The brandy is our way of saying thank you to our great king and to celebrate the future to come."

Confidus stood and went to the window. He watched the deep azure water toss about and admired its wild beauty. Below, the citizens of Elysium were walking about the castle grounds enjoying the lovely afternoon sun. A shadow crossed his sight, and he looked up far into the mountains of Drone. Lightning from dark grey clouds flashed with vigor. "A storm is coming," said Confidus calmly.

Dragus joined him at the window. "Indeed," he murmured peering out the window. "Something truly wicked is coming this way." Confidus looked down to the right at a train whistling its way out of the station.

***

In the Garden of Meadow-lie, Caprius Seaton was standing on the Bridge of Vows with his wife Melina Hampshire. The river flowed avidly beneath them.

Caprius tucked a lock of hair behind his wife's ear. "I remember when you were so madly in love with me. You could hardly keep your hands off me," said Melina as she took his hands and held him.

"To think I won your heart, and poor Fenison Torrington had his heart broken."

"You know perfectly well he got what he deserved," she said.

"You know as much as it was his fault that we had a role to play in his departure," said Caprius. "And, you, my sweet, were the object of his affection."

"So, you wish to put the evil eye on me, don't you?" She folded her arms. "Remember, Caprius, we did something we may regret some day. Fenison Torington may have been a high school student with much more on his mind, and should he return to Elysium, I think you and I will be in for more of his escapades." They began to walk off the bridge and onto snowy land. They walked along the waterbed.

"As mischievous as he was, I don't think you and I have anything to worry about. Fenison was in love. It is only natural for a man to fight for a woman. That is why I forgive him. Despite what he intended to do."

"He was a fowl breed, with no thought to his devious intensions," she said. "But, I must admit, he did have charm. You know, if I hadn't met you, Caprius Seaton, Fenison and I would probably be together."

"Yes, shacking up in your love nest and making wild noises in the night, enough to wake up the dead," said Caprius. "Raising rug rats by the many and being a full-time mother with no time for anyone but you and him. You would be totally disengaged from the public eye."

"I don't imagine him in that way. I thought of him as a person who only had an interest in a serious career as a teacher. You know his marks were extremely high. He was quite intelligent, you know. I was merely his hobby—someone to share in his adventures with."

"Every man has his passion. But, he was deranged. You were his main ambition, not his schooling," he said.

"Oh, let's not talk about him anymore. I do wish him well. And, he did move on. So, let's just leave it at that," Melina insisted.

"Yes, he is just a memory. We'll leave it at that," Caprius agreed. They continued to walk.

"I was in the sacred garden having words with the Golden Fleece. She told me you visited yesterday," said Caprius. "What did you talk about?"

"I merely wanted her advice on motherhood. How to be a good mother to a new born child," she said.

"Is that all you talked about?" he asked.

"That, and..." she trailed off.

"You talked about me constantly going on missions," he said seriously.

Melina bit her lip and shook her head. "Felicia is a tattle-tale. She shouldn't have told you."

"Melina, you must understand that I am bound to the *'holy council of sacred deeds,'* and my work is very important. I know you like me to be at your side at all times, but these are really important missions. The Dark Lord is sending his vampire minions across the lands; he is eager to destroy humanity. He means to take control of Alamptria. The powers of Petoshine sense a great attack upon us. There's no telling where Makoor will strike next."

"Is that supposed to mean that I am to be second fiddle?" asked Melina concerned, crossing her arms.

"Second fiddle?" Caprius raised his voice. "Melina, I'm not on your becking call!" He stopped her as she tried to walk. They stood still looking into each other's eyes. "If you wanted someone who would be by your side at all times, then perhaps you were meant to be with Fenison Torrington. These are hard times. We live in a very dangerous world. The society is filled with corrupted individuals."

Melina pouted. "No, I don't want to be with Fenison." She put her arms around him. She laid her head against his chest. "I want to be with you." Caprius put his hands upon her cheeks. He cupped her face and laid a sweet kiss upon her.

"You know, being a man who is in the service of his majesties ongoing missions, I think I deserve the pleasure of a night of courtship. I'll make like a wild cat," said Caprius jokingly.

Melina backed slightly away. Then, with her hands against Caprius' chest, she pushed him away. Caprius lost his balance, falling onto the snow.

Caprius sat upon the snow-covered ground. He looked up at his beautiful wife. "All right, I guess I deserved that."

Melina walked toward him. She held out her hand to her husband. As Melina tried to pull Caprius, helping him up, Caprius pulled her hand and she tumbled onto the snow. She gingerly held onto Caprius, pulling herself up. As Melina now looked away, her eyes caught a familiar little girl wearing a yellow dress staring at them. "Run along, Tabetha. There is nothing to see here," she said to the little girl. "Tabetha, it's not nice to stare," said Melina. A woman called out to the little girl. "Tabetha, your mama is calling." The little girl ran off.

They walked the garden trail. "You look so radiant, Melina. Our child will be born to the most beautiful mother there is," he said, looking down at her belly with love.

"The birth is still nine months away. But, I am already very excited to bring your child into this world," said Melina, cupping her hand around her husband's.

"Our child," corrected Caprius.

"Yes. Yours and mine," said Melina. "Do you still believe we will have a son?"

"You needn't worry. You have even heard it yourself from Felicia - the Golden Fleece. The prophecy states that it will be our child, Lantrinon Seaton, who will destroy the Dark Lord Makoor and the undead creatures of Mount Drone," said Caprius. "We can rejoice, Melina. His days on this earth will soon come."

Melina abruptly pulled away from Caprius. "How can you say rejoice when we are faced with such darkness?" she asked.

She was right in more ways than she'd meant; at that very moment, the sky darkened and the birdsong stopped. Dark clouds rolled in and settled above the garden. Lightning flashed inside the dense clouds.

"Indeed, you are right. These dark clouds are foreboding. It seems something stirs from the mountains of Drone," yelled Caprius over the wind. "Come, Melina, I must get you home."

The pair, now bowed against the wind and rain coming down in sheets, made their way off the bridge and quickly left the garden.

***

A man rode a wagon. He was hauling wooden coffins. His name was Bombidus Barons, and he had been a member of the Elysian council. He had been secretly importing these cassettes. He had just arrived at Hotel Quantum Heights. As he rode up the trail, he approached a gate. He halted his horse, pulling on the reigns. A man approached him. "State your business here at Quantum Heights," said the man.

"I have three parcels that I am to deliver to Mr. Willy B. Pinkles. He is expecting me. My name is Bombidus Barons."

"Oh yes, Mr. Barons. We've been expecting you. But, first, I need you to open up one of the wooden boxes. Inspection you know. Nothing gets past these eyes."

"Certainly," said Bombidus, getting off the wagon. Bombidus and the man climbed onto the back of the wagon. Bombidus opened the crate. The man looked in. Six other men stood on the trail near the wagon observing.

"Dirt? What does Mr. Pinkles want with dirt?" asked the man. The man stuck his hand into the dirt feeling around. "Open up the others," the man said to Bombidus. Bombidus opened them. "More dirt," said the man looking at it. Bombidus began to feel nervous.

"Mr. Pinkles has a keen interest in botany," said Bombidus. The man got off the wagon. He wiped his hands free of the dirt.

"Okay, Mr. Barons. You may go in," said the man.

Bombidus closed the crates. "Thank you, my good man." He got off the back wagon and got in the front. "I say, my lad, would it be possible for me two borrow two fine gentlemen to help me carry these crates? There quite heavy, you know, and I do have a bit of a back problem."

"Sure, I suppose so. The two of you, help Mr. Barons out." The two men got onto the wagon sitting beside Bombidus.

"Are you staying for the hotel anniversary party, Mr. Barons?" asked the man.

"Ah, no. I'm afraid I can't. But, I'm sure you'll get a big kick out of it. It's going to be a night to remember."

"Ha, ha, carry on," said the man.

Bombidus smiled and drove toward the rear of Quantum Heights.

Beneath hotel Quantum Heights, in an unguarded and dismal basement, were two bodies laid to rest in crates filled with dirt.

The two men who had helped Bombidus had left. Bombidus took his sword out of his sheath. With the sword, he loudly tapped the wooden crate. Bombidus backed away from it. As the lid cracked open, his eyes widened and he peered inside. The finger of a creature bearing a sapphire, and he pushed the lid to the side. The creature's hand was large and menacing, larger than any man's. He was covered in dirt. He gave Bombidus chills. Now, fully outside the coffin, the creature's hand began to take on human form. A tall man stepped out of the coffin. He looked down at Bombidus. Then, from the other coffin, the other man stepped out. They both gazed down at Bombidus. A man had entered the basement. As he turned the corner, he saw the three men by the caskets. The man looked at them in fright. Be began to run. Suddenly, one of the vampires materialized in front of the man with swift speed. The man pulled his sword out of his sheath. He swung his sword swiftly, and the vampire drove his body into the sword. The man backed away looking at the sword within the vampire's belly. The vampire pulled the sword out of his belly. He held the sword in hand and slowly walked toward the man. "Oh, that should have killed you," said the man.

"What is your name?" the vampire asked him in a soft, pleasant voice.

"Dryfus. My name is Dryfus."

The vampire had a small smirk on his face. "Come to me, Dryfus." The vampire held out his two fingers in front of the man. Dryfus suddenly felt dizzy and drawn to him. He began to walk toward the vampire. He was face to face with him, still feeling dizzy. The other vampire arrived with Bombidus. Then, Dryfus tilted his head to the side. The vampire slowly came to his neck. It bit Dryfus on the neck. The vampire sucked hard, extracting the blood from the man. It wasn't long before the man fell into the vampire's arms. The vampire gently held him. He began to carry him toward another part of the basement. The vampire came across a large room filled with wooden coffins. These coffins were all empty. The vampire used his mind to open up the lid from one of the coffins. He placed Dryfus' body inside gently. "I give you a new life; the life of everlasting hunger for living blood. You will never see the sun rise and set through countless centuries. You, Dryfus, have endured the Monisar. Now, sleep, Dryfus."

***

"As so, I made it perfectly clear to Caprius, that just because he is two years older than you, Dragus, he hasn't the right to speak to you that way. I would like all my four boys to have respect for one another. I don't like anyone having the upper hand," said Confidus.

"Try telling that to Andromin. He is the oldest. His ego is his pride. And, he thinks he's the gem of jules. He is expecting to take the thrown after you step down," said Dragus.

"Well, he will be very surprised to learn that your brother Caprius is in line for the thrown."

"He won't take that very lightly when he finds out," said Vijas.

"When will we tell him, Father?" asked Dragus.

"When the time is right. I will be the one to break the news to him," said Confidus. Seeing the clouds swirl about with such violence made Confidus excuse himself from Dragus and Vijas so he could go see Felicia. He went to the basilica near the Garden of Meadow-lie and began to read the sacred words aloud from the book of Bivion. The golden statue of the elf queen in the center of the pond began to glisten. The clouds above billowed, and lightening struck fervently above the golden statue. Finally, light streamed out from the statue's eyes and mouth, and the elf screamed, her transformation complete. Felicia - the Golden Fleece, now standing before Confidus, a living, breathing soul, used her magical powers to walk over the lily pads with her bare feet.

She came to Confidus. He closed the Book of Bivion and returned it to its column.

"The undead have devised a new plan to overtake the powers of Petoshine," he said.

"Yes. I have foreseen this," said Felicia. "Calista will be conflicted, so tempted by the dark forces. She will accept an invitation from a Goncool."

Confidus shook his head. "Oh, no. Not Calista."

"Don't worry. It will be short lived. She will ask Caprius for forgiveness. At first, he will banish her from his life, but he will come back to her. Their bond will be strong, virtually unbreakable. But, she must first go through what will be a difficult time."

"You know this to be true?" asked Confidus.

"I have seen it," said the Golden Fleece, bowing her head.

"What is it you see?" asked Confidus.

"I see a church tower, with its bells chiming. And, a great battle with Caprius and Calista standing victorious, scores of vampires at their feet." Confidus smiled, his shoulders relaxing. "You need not fear what is to come," said Felicia. "The vim of Petoshine will shine brightly."

"What of Melina?" he asked.

"No harm will come to her yet. Before the birth of your grandson Lantrinon, Melina will be escorted to Petoshine. There, she will be protected by the vim. Grongone will watch over her and keep her safe."

"When will this happen?"

"Nine months from now," said Felicia. "That will be your greatest challenge. But, for now, focus on the present mission." Felicia looked into Confidus' eyes. "I see that your mind is troubled by other thoughts."

Confidus smiled sadly. One couldn't keep a secret around Felicia. "My thoughts are on my late wife," he said.

"I know it pains you to think of her past travesties. Talk to her. Go to the Triplonion simulator and see her. Your burden will be lessened once you confront her spirit."

"I will do as you say. I will speak to Evelyn," said Confidus.

Felicia turned and went back up onto the mound, which was surrounded by water and lily pads. Her bare feet hardly graced the floating plants, so light she was upon them. As she situated herself on the mound, she crossed her arms over her chest. "Burry your burdens. Don't let the travesties of Evelyn wear upon you." She spoke the words of Bivion, looked down into the waters, and with her body glistening gold, she metamorphosed back into the statue she was.

***

A day later, Confidus strolled along the cobblestone road. It was a lovely day. Snow was falling lightly, and the mood among all the people on the street was cheery. Merchants called out, hawking their products and trinkets. As Confidus passed, a merchant handed him an old copper chalice. "Most beautiful and rare of all the chalices in Elysium," he said, grinning beneath his moustache. Confidus shook his head, smiled, and kept walking.

Among the goods were colorful stylish blankets and shawls and samples of food. "Confidus! Confidus Seaton," a cook behind his cast iron pot called out in greeting. Confidus stopped to chat with the man, whom he'd known for years. The chef handed him a skewer of spiced pork. "Sire, do try this," he said.

Confidus bit into the morsel. "This is quite good, my man. Very good," he said admiringly.

"A special blend of spices. Handed down from my great grandfather. He was a master chef, you know. My only goal is to follow in his footsteps," said the man.

"Well, you definitely have talent," said Confidus.

The chef bowed. "Thank you, sire. Someday soon I shall be opening my own restaurant: Franky's Gourmet Eatery." He beamed at the king.

"That sounds splendid, Franky. I'll be looking for it," Confidus said. He nodded at the friendly cook and went on his way.

"A good day to you, Your Majesty!" said Franky. He didn't know that the king was not only a lover of good food, but he also truly appreciated an entrepreneurial spirit, and later in the day, Confidus would send Franky a large anonymous donation to help with his new restaurant venture.

Confidus continued his walk through the winter festivities. He came upon a table stacked with copies of books. The author sat behind the table. "Ah, Morbius Moldrige," said Confidus.

"A good day to you, Confidus Seaton," said Morbius. The men shook hands.

"I must congratulate you on your success," said Confidus. "Your last book did very well. I thoroughly enjoyed reading it."

"Why, thank you, sire!" said Morbius.

"Is this your latest book?" asked Confidus picking up a copy and turning it over in his hand.

"Hot off the press," smiled Morbius.

Confidus read the title aloud, "*The Flagships of Hollandres.*" Confidus reached into his satchel and handed

Morbius a number of gold coins. He put the book into his satchel. "I'll look forward to this one. A good day to you, Morbius."

"Thank you very much, and a good day to you, as well, Confidus."

Confidus resumed his walk but was now feeling the chill of the day enter his bones. He put his hands into his jacket to keep warm. All around him, the streets teemed with people brightly dressed in woolens and knitted scarves, happily enjoying the afternoon. He turned onto a smaller side street on which only a few people were scattered. A few houses down stood a gate. Confidus went through the gate, and down at the end of the long path stood a magnificent tower. At its top, the clouds parted, and pure yellow sunshine poured over it. Confidus went in and admired the great hall: the tall gold ceiling gleamed, and the walls were a pure clean white. He felt an instant peace fall over him. This was the hall where people came to make contact with the dead. Here, they could awaken the spirits and communicate with them in a Triplonion Simulation Chamber.

"A good day to you, Mr. Seaton," said a lithe young woman with heart-shaped lips. She wore a yellow tunic and a headband with a porcelain oval at its center that was painted with a floating angel.

"I wish to communicate with my late wife," said Confidus.

The woman at the desk handed Confidus a chip card. "Seventeenth floor, chamber six," she said. Confidus accepted the card and walked down the aisle toward the elevators. When he came to the chamber, there was a gentleman standing by the control monitor. He was escorted to a chair within a large glass tube. He settled into a plush chair. The man put rubbing alcohol onto a small spot on Confidus' forehead. He attached a wire with a small rubber suction used to monitor a traveler's brain waves. A tube came from above that let in oxygen.

"Who is it you wish to contact?" he asked.

"My late wife - Evelyn Sandra Seaton." Confidus rested his arms to the side leather hand bars.

"Enjoy your travels," he said and walked to a stone positioned in his corner, where he rested his hand atop the rough surface. The tube door closed shut. Confidus could hear the man's voice as he spoke from a microphone. He pushed a few buttons on a monitor. At the top of the tube Confidus was in, a metal circular cylinder vibrated up and down by a foot surrounded by a glass tube. It went faster and faster. "Now, Mr. Seaton, close your eyes, relax your spirit, and concentrate on Evelyn." He slowly pulled down on a leaver. There was a humming sound that came from the tube.

Confidus let his eyes close and soon began to have visions of deep space. Tiny white stars raced across the darkness, going faster, then faster still, until soon, the dark gave way to a light blue sky filled with clouds. The clouds parted, revealing light shining down on a great city. A lone cloud that had remained came toward him. It lifted, and inside stood the spirit of his wife, Evelyn Marry Seaton.

The spirit spoke. "My husband, you have come back."

"I miss you, Evelyn. I had to see you," he said. "A day ago marked the eighteenth year of your passing." He paused. "We need to talk."

"Speak, my husband," she said.

"Your granddaughter Melina Hampshire will give birth to her son, Lantrinon, in eight months time," said Confidus.

"It will be a blessing. He is the chosen one," said Evelyn.

"But, the dark forces are at work once again. The man who slayed you is still at large. And, he plans his greatest threat against us," said Confidus.

"Indeed, Cambrozes Genesis must not succeed. Both he and the Dark Lord must be destroyed if Alamptria is to survive," she said, her brow furrowing. "Caprius Seaton's child must endure. He must be protected. Melina must be protected."

"Yes, we will make sure of that. She will travel to Petoshine. There, Grongone will protect her. Our council senses that there is great danger. With each passing day, the dark forces are growing stronger. But, we will prevail. Felicia - the Golden Fleece foresees triumph. It will be a battle hard fought, but in the end, we will succeed."

"And, what does Grongone foresee?" she asked.

Confidus frowned. "I do not know, but I am certain he shares Felicia's optimism," said Confidus.

"All in good time, Confidus. Remember that the vim of Petoshine is stronger than the dark forces."

"Yes, Felicia said the same. Yet, I can't help the feelings I have, especially for you. Cambrozes Genesis has made my heart heavy for eternity. I fight to overcome your absence from my life every day."

The spirit's face was mournful and filled with love. "Don't dwell on the past, my husband. What is done is done. You cannot change what has happened, but you can overcome the pain you feel by giving your love to those who matter to you. Seek the light of Petoshine. There, you will find the answers. Now go, and be safe." There was an instantaneous flash of white light that was so fierce, Confidus screwed his eyes against it and shielded his face.

When he opened his eyes, he felt somewhat dizzy and disoriented. His forehead was sweaty, and he was breathing hard. The glass tube door opened. Confidus waited to feel himself again, then rose from his chair and headed toward the exit. His guide met him there. Confidus stepped out of the chamber. "Were your travels to your satisfaction?" he asked.

"Yes, thank you," said Confidus as he walked past him and headed toward the elevator. When he came to the main floor, he gave the woman his chip card and went out of the Triplonion Simulation Chamber.

Chapter 2

A Vampire's Love

WITHIN THE VOLCANIC UNDERGROUND LAIR sat the very large, undead creature Makoor by a deep gorge, which went down four hundred feet. Stalagmites and stalactites surrounded the flaming gorge from top and bottom. The Dark Lord was in thought and grimaced with a smile. He was eager to fulfill his long lust for dominating the lands of Alamptria. He looked down at an egg, which lay upon the ground. His hope was on a young beautiful woman, which Titanis Clore longed for—a woman so pure in heart and without any sin or thought of being tempted by the dark world of Mount Drone. "The dark world is my oyster," said Makoor. "I have so mercifully longed for the moment when all would accept my offering. What is in light that the darkness has to offer? The sour fruit, which I plant upon the tree will spread over the dominion, and all will know that I, Makoor, am the way. Today, the seed, which I plant, will grow to my desired needs. All this will begin with a young innocent girl that has been chosen. Here me, Parthalius! I send onto you that which I am so anxiously eager to give you. My heart is for you. My soul is for you. All this, I bestow upon your inheritance." His will was strong. His hunger grew.

***

Melina trotted on horseback through the woodlands of Meadow-lie with her friend Fetrona feeling blissful. It was a gorgeous late afternoon. The trees were bare, the few leaves present waved gently in the breeze. A light blanket of snow covered the landscape like powdered sugar, delicate enough to be almost translucent.

Fetrona didn't seem to be in tune with the harmonious environs, though, and, unprovoked, began a rant. "Andromin can be quite aggressive. He has to have everything his way. And, I think he uses me as his security blanket." She snorted. "He chats up other women everywhere he goes—even when we're together. But, when I try to break up any conversation he's having with them, he always smiles, shrugs, and says to them, 'Thorns and roses, whatever comes my way—it's all nature!'" She sighed, her breath clouding up around her face. "I often wonder whether Andromin actually does love me," she said. "He says he does on occasion, but I've started thinking he only says it to keep me around and keep me quiet."

Melina rolled her eyes. She felt sorry for her friend, but Fetrona had a way of complaining that made Melina want to stick a sock in her mouth. "I understand," said Melina sympathetically. "But, it is certainly a beautiful day, isn't it? Hard to think about negative things in such a divine setting," Melina said sweetly, trying to change their conversation.

Melina's horse snorted and shook its mane. "That is a beautiful horse you have there, Melina. A fine white stallion," said Fetrona.

Melina smiled and patted the steed's neck. "He was a gift from Caprius. A token of love," she said. "And, last night... was wonderful. So wild!" she smiled impishly.

"Oh, Melina, I see what's happening here," Fetrona said somberly, nodding her head. "Did he melt your wintering frost and set your heart aflame with his passion only to throw you to the cold like a spurned cat?"

Fetrona was smirking, but Melina widened her eyes, and her face grew hot. "Fetrona! My husband would never cast me aside, and he certainly wouldn't reject my loving affection. You take that back this instant!" Melina huffed.

Fetrona laughed loudly and waved her hand. "Oh, Melina, you should know me by now. I'm only teasing."

"Sarcasm is something I'm not accustomed to hearing in my station, Fetrona. You should be more careful about the things you say."

"Alright, alright, I'm sorry, Melina. No harm intended." Fetrona smiled sincerely. They continued riding along the trail. After Fetrona's remark, their conversation grew as cold as cast-aside porridge. Ten minutes went by without a word. Fetrona grew bored and figured Melina needed some time alone. "I'll see you in a bit, Melina." She clucked her tongue and turned her horse around. "Don't wander off too far. See you at dinner. And, watch out for potholes!" She trotted away back to Castle Elysium.

Melina continued to slowly ride along the trail. She loved her friend, but sometimes, she was just too much to take. Now on her own, she felt lighter and unencumbered. She began to sing. "Through wind - and rain - and sleet - and snow, he travels so far - he knows where he goes. He journeys by night - he travels by barge. Love has him calling - heaven so far. In my bed, I'm slee - ping. I'm so sad I'm wee - ping..." she let the words trail away as she hummed the tune.

When she came to a clearing, she got off her white stallion and stood beside a large rock. She decided to sit down. Glancing around, she hummed the same tune. Suddenly, a red cardinal bird approached hovering near her. As the bird now was in front of her, Melina noticed the bird had a bobble head of Caprius Seaton. This was Caprius' flight communicator, which he had sent to find Melina and have a word with her. It was also capable of transmitting visuals. It was customary for many people in Elysium to have one of these flight communicators. It was the latest gadget, and people were purchasing them. When one would place an order for it, they would send photographs of themselves to the Department of AI Flight Communicators, and they would assemble the device for the purchaser. It came with a wrist watch, where one could see and communicate with the other person.

The flight communicator hovered in front of Melina. "Oh, hello Caprius," said Melina. "Are you keeping an eye on me, again?"

"Just wanted to have a word with you. I'm going into mission headquarters. I'm having a combat assessment. So, I'll be late for supper. It will take about two hours for this assessment. But, I'll see you when I get back."

"Why this assessment so late in the day, Caprius?" asked Melina. "Couldn't they have had this test done earlier?"

"It's out of my hands. The agency makes the arrangement, and I have to show up when they ask me to. Every agent is taking these assessments. They do these tests every once in a while."

"I understand, I just hope this doesn't happen often," she said.

"Like I said, it's out of my control. If I don't show up, it goes on my record."

"Well, I don't want to see you get a point deduction," said Melina.

"Thank you for understanding, Melina. I'll see you when I get back." The Caprius bobble head flight communicator flew into the sky toward castle Elysium.

Melina sat down in the sunshine. She held her face up, enjoying the warmth. "In my bed, I'm slee - ping. Woke up to be gree - ted," she sang again.

When she opened her eyes, she saw to the east, marring the otherwise perfect day, some dark clouds were forming. A crow flew across the horizon and disappeared into the grey mass. She realized then that her shadow had disappeared and clouds were roiling in the sky, approaching quickly. Their speed is odd, she thought, since there is only this light breeze. Her hair, which had been playing gently about her shoulders, began to whip violently across her face. Lightning flashed close enough so she could hear the sizzle of electricity.

In the now fierce wind, she heard a foul voice, something dark and sinister, call her name. "Melinaaa…"

Melina waited, small prickles of fear beginning in her chest, but then just as quickly as the clouds had arrived, they vanished. The sky was suddenly as blue as the sea and the sun ever as vibrant. Melina looked up, wondering if something had driven the odd weather away or even if she'd imagined the whole thing.

Out of the corner of her eye, she saw something move. A tiny creature had hopped out of the bushes and approached Melina. Suddenly, Melina's horse began digging dirt on the ground with its hooves. It became frantic. On closer look, she realized it wasn't a creature at all, but a man, a tiny variety of man known as a trot. Melina stared at him, and when he caught her eye, he furrowed his brow. Melina tried to calm the horse. The trot came closer. Just then, wild as the horse was, the stallion scooted off toward castle Elysium. "Oh no! Come back!" she said to the horse.

The trot put his hands to his mouth frightened at the scene. "Oh, I beg your pardon," Melina said, blushing.

"No, I'm the one who is sorry. Did I frighten you?" asked the trot.

"Well, you did startle me, but I'm not so easily scared," she said, laughing. "I must ask, though, if you don't mind, what a trot such as yourself might be doing in this part of the woods?"

The little man sighed and let his arms flop to his sides. "It seems that I'm lost. I was trying to get to the Mogo ridge," he explained.

"The Mogo ridge?" she asked. "I know exactly where that is, but it is quite a far way off from here."

"As I said, I'm lost. But, since you know where it is, would you be able to show me the way?"

Melina started to say, "Oh, I was on my way back to the castle, so I'm afr-"

"Oh, please," he interrupted, "I'd be ever so grateful." He smiled winningly.

Melina hesitated. The little trot was indeed charming, and he looked so cute and bewildered that she felt sorry for him. "Well, all right," she said. "But, we had better go quickly. It will be dark in a few of hours, and I would like to be back to dine with my husband."

"Not to worry," he said, linking arms with her. "You'll get home right on time. I promise you!"

"Let's go then!" she said, feeling excited suddenly for the promise of an adventure. Melina and the trot walked deep into the forest. "What is your name, little one?"

"I may be small, but I got heart. My name is Grom."

"So, Grom, you haven't told me what you're doing all the way out here," said Melina.

Grom shrugged. "I went wandering off. There's a wagon at the Mogo ridge that has all sorts of ice creams and candy."

"I do love ice cream!" laughed Melina. "Strawberry is my favorite."

"If you get me to the wagon, there's a treat in it for you," he winked.

Melina looked about her in the dense wood. "Let's see now, I believe we should go this way," she said, pointing to the left-most path. They veered onto that path and were delighted to see that it was lined with bluebells. "Isn't it so pretty here," she murmured. They continued to walk, making their way deeper and deeper into the forest. The sunlight was all but blocked for the tall spruces stretching into the sky above them.

Melina had wandered far off. She heard the rush of water before they saw the river running beside them. "Ah, yes," said the trot knowingly. "I know where we are. Wonderful! My ice cream wagon is just across this stream. There's a bridge just further down the shore."

"I don't recall there being a bridge around here," said Melina, looking upstream.

"Oh, there is. Just a little further down," said the trot, waving his hand. And, indeed, as they approached, there was a bridge. "Here it is!" the trot said excitedly. He hopped toward it and then turned to Melina. "Hold my hand," he said. For as lovely as the day was, the bridge was covered in ice, which glinted in the sun.

Melina began to approach the trot, who was standing at the edge of the bridge, and had to shield her eyes from a sudden piercing light. Her head swam, and she felt dizzy. "What's happening," she muttered. Around them, the landscape began to change, and a castle appeared at the other side of the bridge. "Where am I?" she asked woozily. "This isn't the Mogo ridge. I don't recall there being a castle here."

The castle loomed tall, its spires reaching so high the tips were shrouded in dark grey clouds. This was not Castle Elysium, her home, but Castle Plaphorius. The trot held Melina's hand firmly and brought her across the bridge to the castle doors, which were made of solid ice and taller than three men standing atop one another. Melina was trembling terribly.

The door cracked open, and a large hand, covered in frost with ice for fingernails emerged. It reached out and grabbed Melina's other hand, yanking her toward the door. She tried to struggle, but the hand held tight and pulled her to the door. When she hit it, she felt it give way, and suddenly she penetrated the door as if it were made of freezing cold water and found herself on the other side. She heard an ugly giggling outside of the door: the trot. Within seconds, he too came through the door and then, before her eyes, transformed into his true self: a gruesome changeling, a creature able to adapt its size, shape, and overall appearance into anything it wanted. It looked at her and laughed. A gust of wind appeared along with black smoke, which began to circle the changeling's body. Something from inside the tornado of black wind spoke. "You have done well, trot. You will be greatly rewarded." The tight circle of smoke blew faster and faster until it created a thin tail that blew into an open window high up one of the castle's turrets. Watching with horror, Melina then felt as though she were falling. Light encircled her and suddenly she was careening backwards through an icy ceiling.

Her fall, however, was soft and cushioned. Melina cracked an eye open to see where she'd landed and realized she was on a large bed with a satin coverlet and pillows, all bedecked in a fierce bright white. The large opulently furnished room smelled of the most fragrant camellias and was cozy warm. Exhausted and confused, Melina lay back on the bed and, within seconds, drifted off into sleep.

The room may have been lovely, but evil lurked inside. From above the bed where Melina lay, the ceiling began to bulge until it cracked. Through the fissure appeared a very large face wearing a black shiny mask. It stared down at Melina with eyes of glimmering gold. It narrowed its eyes admiringly as it took in her beauty, then dissolved, the ceiling returning to its unblemished state.

When Melina awakened, she was alone. She looked around at the room, which now was dark and desolate in contrast to how warm and inviting it had been earlier. She wished she knew how much time had passed. A chill ran through her, and she hopped up, with the hope that she could get herself out of this place and back to Elysium.

Melina rubbed her eyes; noticing a stone basin in the corner, she went to it, hoping there was water inside. A folded white towel was set beside the basin, so she splashed the cool water over her skin and paused over the water a moment. There, suddenly, was a masked man staring at her. Melina recoiled in fear and looked around. "Am I dreaming?" she thought. She peered back into the water and saw only her own reflection. She waited for her heartbeat to calm before reaching for the towel to pat her face dry. But, when she looked down at the towel, it was covered in blood.

Melina screamed, dropping the towel on the floor. Frightened and angry, she flipped the stone basin over. It crashed onto the marble floor, shattering into pieces, water streaming everywhere. She ran to the door and tried to open it, but the knob wouldn't turn. Terrified, she turned back to the room. The basin's rim was still intact, and on it lay the white towel, again perfectly folded. "Now, I know I'm dreaming," she said. Again, she tried to open the door, and this time, it opened easily. She fled the room and went out into the great hall, the walls twice the height of those in Castle Elysium. The ceiling was gold and reflected a pure light into the otherwise gray and sodden-looking hall.

Lining the hall were bronze statues of winsome men and women striking elegant poses. Though she was very frightened, Melina couldn't help but admire the artistry as she ran past. "How real they look!" she muttered. She didn't notice one of the statues she'd gone by turn to look at her.

Melina ran down the hall until she came to another that intersected the first. After looking in both directions, she went right, again walking quickly past statues evenly spaced along the side of the hall. Another turned to watch her.

The black marble floor was cold on her bare feet, and Melina shivered, wrapping her arms around herself. The statues all looked so young, so sylph-like. Toward the middle of the hall, Melina saw one woman whose resemblance to herself was striking. She paused and put her hand on the statue's face to touch the contours. It was simply so life-like that she couldn't stop herself. A hissing sound started up around her. Startled, she tried to pull her hand away, but her hand was stuck, as if glued.

Suddenly, the floor beneath her cracked, tiny black fissures webbing out in all directions. Vines began to grow up from the cracks and wrapped themselves around Melina's feet, then up her legs. Melina squirmed but stopped at the sound of a loud roar, fierce, as if from a tiger. In the noise, she was able to wrench her hand free, and when she did, the vines withered and released their hold on Melina, retreating back through the floor as quickly as they'd come. Melina looked down, and the floor was normal again, the marble unblemished.

Another noise from behind Melina startled her: this time it was footsteps. Slow and methodical at first, then faster and louder, as if whatever it was was coming for her. Melina didn't bother looking to see what it was; she broke into a sprint. Her gown bunched up around her legs as she ran, but she pushed on. When she came upon another hall, she turned left and continued running. With one more step, though, her foot became tangled in the abundant material of her dress, and she tumbled to the floor. When she got up, she saw the tear in the fabric. Realizing this wasn't a time to worry over her appearance, she tore the rest of the material off, freeing her legs.

Then, out of the corner of her eye, she saw something scarlet shimmering beneath the gold ceiling. A mannequin in the corner was wearing a deep red dress and a pair of lovely red shoes. Melina turned to check on the thing following her. Not hearing anything, she paused and caught her breath. She stared up at the outfit. "These are beautiful," she whispered, captivated by the attire. Melina approached the dress, as if propelled by an outside force. She touched the fabric and stood, stroking it as if there were no urgency or anything were amiss at all. At once, as if the fabric were responding to her touch, a bright red light flashed from within the dress, and inside of a few seconds, the dress was on Melina. She looked down and saw the dress on her body and the shoes on her feet and smiled.

The sound of the footsteps then came into focus and seemed headed directly toward her. Melina looked down the hall, and all together, every one of the bronze statues turned to look at her. Melina gasped and put her hands to her mouth. "What is this place," she said to no one, backing away. After a few steps, she bumped into something alive. She turned and was face to face with the man wearing the shiny black mask from the water basin, a black cowl over his head and shoulders. The man grabbed Melina's wrists with a fiercely strong grip. Melina trembled, "No, no," she said, trying to fight. After letting her struggle a moment, he released her and took off his mask. It was Melina's husband, Caprius Seaton. "Caprius! But, how…" she stopped when Caprius' handsome face transformed into that of a horrific vampire. Melina screamed and instantly fainted, falling right into the creature's arms. It stood, alone in the hall among the all-seeing statues, holding her in his arms before carrying her off.

The creature brought Melina into another decadently furnished room filled with mahogany and walnut pieces topped with velvet and satin brocade. He laid her on a plush ottoman. Melina had been expected: the room was scrubbed and perfectly appointed in preparation for her arrival, with maids and servants standing at the ready to ensure her every need be taken care of. The masked creature had been on hand to personally inspect every phase of the preparation.

Melina woke up to find herself in a familiar room. She quickly sat up looking around. The masked man came over to her. "Here, drink this," he said to her. Melina refused to take it, shaking her head. "It's just ice water, I assure you." Melina accepted the glass and began to drink. And, sure enough, it was water. Melina gulped it down. She handed him the glass.

"Take off the mask," Melina said to him. "I want to see who you are." The man slowly took off his mask, revealing his face. He stared down at her. He put two fingers of his right hand in front of her. She began to feel dizzy. "I'm beginning to feel woozy." She swayed her head from side to side. "You bastard. You put something in the drink." She tried to stand. And, seconds later, she dropped onto the ottoman fast asleep.

Titanis stood and slowly went to the piano. He sat down and touched a few keys lightly, then looked at Melina. With his eyes on her, he began to play. The melody brought a smile to his face. Titanis playing a haunting tune, filling the room with music.

Finally, Melina stirred and slowly opened her eyes. She blinked and turned her head, focusing on Titanis' playing. The music was exquisite. She sat up and looked around, bewildered. "Who are you?" she said. "I seemed to have forgotten things. I'm not even sure of my name."

"Your name is Clarisse. You were involved in an accident. I found you unconscious and brought you here." Titanis stopped playing the piano and walked over to her. "You, Clarisse, are by far the most captivating woman I have ever set my eyes upon," said Titanis.

Two human vampires rose from the couch, which lay not too far away, and left the lounge. Now alone, Titanis peered closely at the helpless Melina.

Titanis could feel her beside him, but he did not look at her. "Sir, who are you? And, what is this place?" she asked.

He smiled at her. "My name is Titanis Clore. I am prince of Plaphorius."

"But, I don't understand. How did I get here?"

Melina realized the room was terribly dark and wondered why the curtains were drawn.

Titanis continued to smile at her. Melina stared at his handsome face.

"Something lingers to my mind. Something I seem to have forgotten," she said.

He came closer to her. He held her by both hands together. "All that you must know is that you and I were very close. The fall has taken away your memory, Clarisse. And, because you do not remember me, my heart is aching. When you hurt... I hurt," said the devious Titanis Clore.

Melina's eyes watered at his beautiful words. "You must be a great and respected man. You say such nice things, Mr. Clore."

He put his hand to her cheek, gently caressing her. "No one should ever be alone. I will always be with you. Come, let us sit down on the couch." He took her in hand, and they walked over. Titanis sat down.

Melina stood momentarily before sitting down with him. He immediately sat up. "Oh, I'm sorry. A woman should always be seated first. Forgive me." He took her hand, giving her a kiss. Clarisse smiled warmly. She sat down.

"Sit, my dear prince," she said. The handsome vampire sat down. "Tell me more of who you are. And, my involvement with you," she said sweetly.

The vampire began to put out a performance of his life to win her heart. "My story is an unhappy one. I have been tormented by being left alone. Growing up…" he put his hand to his chin rubbing it, thinking of what to say, "… I was the ugly duckling. Pushed aside by my family. Ignored and laughed at for my differences. Many times, I've tried to fit in, but the harder I tried the further they pushed me away." Titanis put his finger to his eye and drew a tear.

"No," she said softly, falling for his story. "It's all right. I am here," said Clarisse.

Titanis sniffled. "I cried almost a lifetime. Alone in my bed, with no one to comfort me." He paused and drew a breath. "I thought I would spend my life searching for her. And, after many years, centuries it seems, I had given up. I went to a nearby river to drown myself. I stood at the edge of a dock, looking out to the sea. The moonlight was full. And, it would be my last night."

"Oh, no!" she said humbly, drawing a tear. The vampire continued to lie through his teeth. Clarisse looked at him sadly. She was taken in by his delusions. She put her arm around his back. She lightly patted him. "It's okay. Go on."

"It was a chilly autumn evening. I wasn't wearing heavy clothing. I knew the cold water would get to my bones. With no more optimism for life, I jumped." Clarisse put her hands on her mouth. "The cold water was chilling to the bone. I did not fight it. I let the water into my lungs. I saw flashes of my life before my eyes. Something happened at that instance. I found my courage. I began to climb onto the dock. I managed to pull myself out. I lay on the dock momentarily coughing up water. I consumed much of it. I dragged myself to the nearby bench. I sat down. As I sat, I trembled. Then, the most wonderful thing happened. A beautiful young woman approached me. She sat down beside me.

She put her hand on my shoulder." And, Clarisse, feeling his sorrow, put her hand on his shoulder. "She said to me that she saw the whole thing from the start. We talked and got to know each other. Soon, we held hands."

"I can feel the love," said Clarisse.

Titanis looked at her humbly. He put his hand onto hers. "She spoke of her life. And, it seems her life was an unhappy one, too." Titanis sniffled and rubbed his nose.

"What was her name, Titanis?" she asked softly. "I want to be her. I want to connect."

"She was a victim of abuse. And, I cried for her. We sat on the bench until three am in the morning, holding each other, comforting one another. We talked of ships and how they crossed the vast ocean waves. In search of a new home. We spoke of children." He sniffled again. "And, how they play." He smiled at that. "We talked of many things."

"I feel the love. I can see now you mean what you say, and it is true love." Again, Clarisse smiled warmly.

"She spoke of her mother, who she lost at a young age. Her mother was very sick." He drew a tear. Clarisse put her finger to his eyelid to wipe it.

She nodded her head. "It is a sad story indeed," she said humbly.

"We became one. We married," he said smiling warmly. Clarisse nodded her head happily.

"We lived together for a number of years. Then, tragedy. She had an accident."

"No, what happened?" she asked.

"She was diagnosed with a serious kidney problem. She had very little time to live." He paused and stood up straight. "I was forced to make a decision. I would give her one of my own kidneys." he looked at Clarisse. "She lives now."

"What was her name? Who was she?" she looked at him with puppy love.

Titanis held both her hands firmly. "That woman, Clarisse... is you." He looked at her tearfully, saying it very humbly, almost breaking down. Clarisse put both her hands to her mouth; her eyes were wide open. "And, now because you hurt your head in an accident, you don't remember. You have forgotten who we were."

Clarisse drew a tear. She stood to her feet, putting one hand to her mouth. "Oh, I wish I could remember. I want to be her so much—the love." Her mouth trembled.

Titanis stood and went close to her. She turned and looked into his eyes. "I can see the truth in your eyes. And, I want to remember."

Titanis put his arms around her. She held him close. "I will help you remember. Clarisse, your memory will return in time." He gestured with his hand. "Take it slow."

At that moment, Lydia, the vampire sorceress, barged into the room, her long red skirt swirling about her ankles like snakes hanging down. "Oh, such an adorable young girl, Titanis," Lydia gushed with a smile. "So alluring and seductive." She fingered Melina's flowing hair.

"Excuse me, ma'am, but I don't count myself as being seductive. I'm more in count of being in the presence of an array of flowers, and..." she smiled warmly at Titanis, "my husband. Well, at least I think so."

"Yes, Clarisse. You are remembering," he said.

"Ah, yes, of course. And, I shall watch the flower as it germinates. Come, my dear. Let us hold hands and see how we can dance and show Titanis what we as woman are accustomed to a night's pleasure."

Lydia took Melina's hand. Suddenly, there was music. It was light and gentle at first, but soon, the tune became dark and gothic. The piano was playing without anyone touching the keys. And, then out of nowhere, an orchestra appeared playing violins. Melina danced with Lydia. Lydia was a lighthearted dancer; their dance mirrored the music, their movements more unusual to match the low male vocals accompanied by atonal string quartets. A choir of female opera singers gave the sound of music a shear elegance. Lydia swung Melina around and around over the black and white checkered floor. The music was lovely. And, when it ended, Melina stood gazing at Lydia. "My dear, you dance so divinely." Melina looked at Titanis. He held out two fingers, and Melina felt woozy again.

Titanis walked over to her. "My sweet, Clarisse, perhaps you'd like me to take you to a room where you can get some sleep."

"Yes, I actually would like that. I'm feeling rather nauseous."

Titanis used his powers and floated a glass from a table filled with water. As Clarisse watched it float across the room, she was amazed. The glass gently came into Titanis' hand.

"How did you do that?" asked Clarisse.

"My dear, we do this all the time. You have simply forgotten. In time, you will learn who you are," said Titanis. "Come, Clarisse. Let me take you to your room."

Melina arrived in an elegant bedroom. Titanis tucked her into bed. "I will set your glass of water onto this night table. Should you get thirsty, it will be here for you."

"Thank you," said Clarisse.

"Don't worry, by tomorrow's noon, it will all come back to you. Just drink your water; it will help."

Titanis left the bedroom. As Clarisse lay on the pillow, she observed the room. "It does look familiar. Just drink my water, and it will all come back to me." She sipped her water from time to time. Eventually, she drank the whole glass. She began to feel woozy. She struggled to set the glass back onto the night table. But, eventually, she did. Clarisse' eyes began to squint in a state of fear. She began to pull off the covers as she entered a dream. She saw herself walking bare foot on soil. Her feet stepped down on earth and worms. She wore a red elegant dress, and it swayed in the wind. She was in a barren landscape surrounded by nothing but a deep stretch of land. The land was dehydrated and cracked. As she looked up, the sky was blazing with storm clouds. As she continued to walk, she came across Titanis Clore in his black outfit and shiny black mask. She came close to him. The wind rustled and blew Titanis' black cowl. His cowl wrapped around Melina like arms. Titanis held her close. "My love. My sweet love," said Melina.

"You do not know what it means for me to hear you say this," said Titanis.

"It is of my own accord," said Melina. Melina reached for Titanis and took off his mask. She looked into his eyes. "I want to live for countless centuries by your side."

"Then, it shall be given to you. I give you the kiss of eternal life." He grabbed her gently, and Melina put her hands upon his shoulders. They kissed passionately. Melina felt awe.

"Hold me, Titanis," And, he did just that. "I can hear the sweet music ringing in my ears. The song of sadness and the emptiness. It is only you and I." Then, the earth beneath them began to crack.

As Melina slept, Titanis had come back into the room. As her head lay on the pillow, Titanis looked down at her with admiration. He wore his shiny black mask, which covered his face. He sat down on the bed. He looked at her hand and her finger, which wore a wedding band. He took off her ring and held it in the palm of his hands. He looked down at it. Suddenly, the golden ring turned into a pile of black ash and disappeared. "There will be no memories of Caprius Seaton," he said. He looked upon her and stroked her face with two fingers. Her skin was a blossoming white. Her lips were of lush red glossy lipstick. Her mouth was partially opened, revealing some teeth, and she blew a warm breath. Titanis was enchanted by her. "So beautiful," said Titanis. "Like a red flower blossoming." Then, he bent down and kissed her lips. As he bent away, looking at her, he put his fingers on her lips. He looked up at the ceiling, where the carvings of two angels extended their arms to hold hands. "Grant me this one wish, Makoor. If I am to die, Melina be given a seat by your side. To rule as queen and to live an eternal life. For my life is hers. And, all will bow down to her."

Melina had woken. She slowly sat up to find Titanis Clore sitting in an elegant chair beside her. Titanis had taken off his mask and looked at her warmly and smiled. Melina stared at him. "I had a dream. It was pleasant." She drew a breath.

Titanis walked to the bed. He sat down beside her. "It is here that you will find peace," he said. He held out two fingers in front of her, trying to penetrate her mind. Melina suddenly felt joy.

"Are you my dark angel? The one who will chase all my bad dreams away?"

Titanis put out his hand toward her. He reached for her. Melina held out her hand, touching his. They touched each other's fingertips. Titanis lay a kiss upon her lips. Soon afterwards, they embraced each other. They both slowly lay down on the pillows holding each other in comfort. As they held each other, they felt love. They closed their eyes and slept.

Two hours had passed and Clarisse awakened. She had her face upon his chest. She put her hand upon his chest caressing him. Titanis opened his eyes. Minutes later, Titanis stood to his feet. "Won't you join me," he asked her.

Melina's mind was poisoned. Her heart told her this man who called himself the dark angel was a man of noble intentions. The water, which she had consumed, erased her memory and her homeland of Elysium. The dark angel's hypnotic effect had confused her, and she accepted his offer. They walked out of the bedroom hand in hand.

Clarisse found herself with Titanis in a lavish room filled with different kinds of flowers. There was a beautiful set of French chairs by a small white elegant table. As the flowers besieged the room, there were French windows surrounding it. Titanis walked over to the table with Melina. They sat down on the chairs. Melina looked around staring at the beauty of the place. "This place, it's beautiful," she said. The room had resembled slightly the conservatory from back home in castle Elysium. Melina could not put her finger on it. She had forgotten. A butler came in. He set down a glass of drink beside Melina. The butler set down a drink of aged blood beside Titanis.

"Is Melina's drink to my liking?" Titanis asked.

"Yes, my lord. As you requested," he said.

"Thank you, Birus. That will be all."

Melina's mind was lost. "I feel like I belong here. Like, like…" she began but could not finish her sentence. She sat back. "Come to think of it, I don't remember anything of my past." She looked at Titanis. "Seems to me you are all I remember, Titanis."

"Clarisse? I have been with you a long time. This is your home. You were born and raised here. You have been here a very long time." Titanis puckered his lips. "You will see, you will remember everything as it should be."

"Yes, I suppose I will," she said. "Something clings to me, like a bee on a flower bud extracting its nectar," she said.

Titanis edged closer to her and held her hand. "Try not to think about it. You are here, and that's all that matters."

"Yes, I suppose you're right. No sense in banging my head against the wall," she said. Clarisse took a sip of her alcoholic drink.

"Mmm, it is quite good," she said.

Suddenly, Lydia came into the room. She walked slowly toward them. "Happy are those who cherish what they are given," she said to them.

Melina looked at her. "Hello, Lydia," she said warmly.

"Melina is starting to remember who she is," said Titanis.

"Clarisse, darling! Don't you worry. It will all come as it should be," Lydia said kissing her on the forehead. "My dear, why not join us tonight. There is a great party at the main hall."

"Yes, Clarisse. You need to be among our people more. Then, you will understand who you are," said Titanis. "Clarisse, why don't you go ahead. I will join you in a minute."

"I don't know where to go," she said.

"I'll be right behind you," said Titanis. Melina began to walk toward the doors.

"She has forgotten Elysium," Lydia said smiling. "Your story was very convincing. I heard it all. You're quite the actor, Titanis."

"There is no need for more drugs. I don't want to pollute her blood," Titanis said. He walked out to catch up to Melina.

Melina smiled, and she and Titanis rushed to the entrance. Titanis kissed her gently on the cheek. He held his hand out for her, and they walked together into a large room filled with human vampires. Titanis' smile extended from one ear to the other.

Titanis escorted her to a lavish dance hall where an orchestra played beautiful, haunting music that resonated throughout the hall. Couples danced together very closely.

"Come, let me get you a drink," Titanis said.

They made their way to the bar, moving to the sweet music. Titanis left Clarisse on the dance floor and leaned into the bartender.

Titanis brought the drink to Clarisse, and they clinked their glasses together.

"To us!" Clarisse said and gulped down the drink.

Titanis laughed. "And, there is more where that came from."

"If you don't mind, Titanis, I would like to just sit down and watch," she said.

"Certainly." Titanis and Melina sat at a cozy table.

Looking at Clarisse, Titanis chuckled. She was not yet a disciple of the devil, but her time would come.

"Tell me, Titanis, tell me more of who I am," said Melina.

"We are vampires. As you are yourself. Though you are not fully grown into who we are, you are transitioning. It comes with age. Your time has come. Soon, I will give you the Monisar," he said.

"The Monisar?" she asked bewildered. "Vampires?"

"It is what you are. And, what you always have been." He gestured with his hand. "Don't worry, it will all come back to you, Clarisse."

Clarisse was shocked. *"Is this true?"* she thought. *"Am I a vampire?"* she paused. "Oh, I see," she said to him, biting her lip.

Titanis looked at her and held her hand. "Your life is the most precious to me—over my own. I would sacrifice a thousand Droges in your honor."

Melina put her hand to her lips. "A thousand Droges sacrificed in my honor." She shook her head; it sounded familiar. She put her elbow on the table, her hand to her chin, trying to remember. Melina just sighed.

***

Confidus sat in the conservatory enjoying a cup of Earl Grey tea. While slowly sipping it, he read the book he had purchased from Morbius Moldridge. And, now as his eyes were affixed to the forty-seventh page, a guard approached him with great urgency. "You have something to report?" asked Confidus.

"Sire, one of our men rounded up a horse running the field," said the guard.

"A horse running the field is really not my concern. The horse trainers should keep a watch on the horses that are let loose," said Confidus.

"I wouldn't be that concerned ordinarily, but when the stallion belongs to Melina Hampshire and she is not riding it, it strikes me as odd. Melina knows better than to have her horse running loose. She has not been seen," said the guard.

"Not seen?" asked Confidus bewildered.

"Sire, she should have been back at the castle by now."

"Perhaps, she arrived unannounced. Maybe taking a hot bath before dinner," said Confidus. "We need not worry just yet."

After Caprius was informed of the situation, he went knocking on doors and talking to people. He stumbled upon Confidus and exchanged words.

"Father, I've asked around. Fetrona says Melina was with her last. I can only think that something terrible has happened."

"Good god. We must see the Golden Fleece at once!" said Confidus.

"Yes, Father, we'll go at once!" Caprius stood, the muscles in his face rigid.

They arrived at the stables and saddled their horses. They led the horses to the water trough before taking off in a gallop through the hills of Meadow-lie to the basilica.

They rode madly across the trails of Meadow-lie, the horses' hooves sounding on the ground like thunder. They shouted at civilians in their way, leaving them coughing in the kicked-up snowflakes, wondering what all the excitement was that had the king and prince in such a sprint.

The evening had darkened, the meadow thickly cast in a melancholy shade. Both Confidus and Caprius looked to the east and noticed how black and thick the clouds were that hung over the mountains of Drone. They rode onward until the night was dark, but soon, blazing in the distance, they saw the fires of the basilica on the hill and its belfry gleaming in the moonlight. Moments later, they were in the forest. They rode through and headed to the entrance of the basilica. At the gate stood a friar.

"Good evening, Friar," said Confidus.

"Good evening, my king," the friar said and bowed.

"We are here because Melina has gone missing."

"I haven't seen her. Perhaps Friar Basil can be of better service to you. Please, come in." The friar opened the gate and let them in. They dismounted their horses and tied them to a post. "I will take you to Friar Basil."

In the basilica, Friar Basil sat at his writing desk reading the word of God. He was startled by the men entering his library but quickly smiled and stood to welcome them. "Good to see you both again. What is it I can do for you?" he asked.

"Melina has gone missing. We must speak with the Golden Fleece," said Caprius.

"Missing?" he asked concerned.

"Friar Basil, there is no time to explain," said Caprius.

"Yes, of course, of course," said the friar, frowning slightly. "I will do anything to help find her."

Caprius and Confidus entered the small room where sacred texts were housed. Basil opened the chest where the Book of Bivion lay on its pillow, untouched. He picked up the book.

"Felicia will know where she has gone," said Confidus.

Basil closed the chest and held the sacred book. "I will take you to see the Golden Fleece. Come, this way."

They rushed from the sacred room, out of the library, and through the garden. There was no time to waste. The monks in the halls and garden saw them running. "What is it? What's going on?" asked Friar Flavius.

"Melina has gone missing," Confidus said discreetly as they passed him.

The men entered the garden on the hill, which shone in the moonlight. Basil quickly began reading the sacred words of Bivion to the statue. Instantly, light burst from high above the statue and swirled around her. After a few words more, white light shot from Felicia's eyes and mouth. Caprius and Confidus gasped as the Golden Fleece came to life.

The moment Felicia was animated, she dropped to her knees, terrified by a prophetic vision of Melina being abducted by Titanis Clore. She stood and left her pedestal, walking toward the men with her hand on her heart and tears coming down her face. "Melina is…" Confidus comforted her while Caprius looked on, his face taut with worry.

Felicia righted herself and spoke, "I know why you have come and what you seek," she paused. "I'm afraid Melina has been abducted. She has been tricked. She is in the hands of Titanis Clore and will enter the world of darkness." Confidus bowed his head and pressed his eyes tightly together. Not his Melina.

"I'm afraid you may be too late."

Confidus whispered, "Felicia, has Melina transformed to the undead?"

Felicia closed her eyes and pressed her hands to her heart. She smiled and opened her eyes. "Melina is alive. She will soon taste the blood of Makoor, and she has will endured the Monisar. It will still be in its early stages. She will willingly become his concubine."

"We must leave at once," said Caprius.

"Plaphorius is a long way off. It will take two days and night," said Confidus.

"Go into the forest. You need to go toward the Mogo ridge. Follow the river until you get to a bridge," said Felicia.

"Felicia, there is no bridge there," said Confidus.

"There is. It was built by the undead. To cross the bridge you enter another realm," said Felicia.

"An assault force is to be prepared, and you are to come to Plaphorius with me!" said Confidus to Caprius.

"Melina is not lost, and Titanis Clore has no means of transforming her at this moment! Now, both of you go. Prepare for war and leave immediately. Now go! I am Felicia - the Golden Fleece - and I have spoken."

Caprius, Confidus, and Friar Basil left the garden of the basilica. Caprius paused and looked back. He watched Felicia walk onto the mound and return to a statue.

***

Within her dark chambers, Lydia stood overlooking a cluster of red-lit candles. The candles burned brightly, and she looked upon them with worry. She had just had a vision of Titanis Clore's failure. She had seen the outcome of what will happen on Jethro. The slaying of vampires by the Seaton knights. Titanis Clore will send a small army of vampires to destroy the Seatons and will fail. Titanis Clore wanted to gain his respect but would fail to do so. "Damn!" she cried out.

"Titanis will fail." She put her hand above the candles six feet away, and with her powers, she drew a wind and blew out an array of candles. She walked out of the room and headed to a deep underground chamber.

She arrived in a dark chamber, which was again lit with many candles. These were white candles. To the side of the candles was a thrown. Sitting on the thrown was the corpse of her late husband, Orphius Clore. As she gazed into his face, she peered at his decayed bony jaw. She held her hand above drawing a force of energy. "I summon you, Orphius. Come forth to me and tell me what you see. What is in the future you see?" Suddenly, Orphius' bony wrist began to move. In front of the corpse was a small table. Upon the table were five tiny bones. Orphius picked up the bones with both bony hands and shook them in his palms. He diced the bones onto the table. Lydia walked closer to the table, looking at the bones. "What is it you see, Orphius? Speak."

Orphius' head began to move. The corpse began to speak. "Our dark powers are under threat. A powerful knight will join the Seatons. The knight will grow strong. These knights must be eliminated."

"Who is this knight? What does he look like? Where do we look?" asked Lydia.

"I sense she is female. And, much more aggressive than Calista Genesis. In time, you will know it. Titanis will send a small force of twenty vampires to Jethro. The knights will defeat us. The time will come when you must go to hotel Quantum Heights. It is there that these knights will confront you. And, there you must destroy them." Lydia disengaged the dark forces and put down her hand. The corpse sat still and lay dead. Lydia left the chamber.

She stormed into Titanis' chambers. As Titanis had his back to her and sat down in a chair, Lydia came from behind him. She pulled out a dagger on him, held out her hand, and came around him slitting his throat. Titanis put his hand to his throat as he bled. He gasped. With his powers, he healed his wound and stood to his feet looking at Lydia. The bloodstains upon his hands and throat had disappeared. She looked at him intensely then through the dagger on a table near her. "Are you brain dead?" she asked him. "Orphius has looked into your future. This girl, Melina, should not have been abducted from her homeland. You bring us death and destruction!"

"I sought to get retribution for Jengon Crumps' death," said Titanis.

"By sending out a mere small force of twenty? It's suicide!" she exclaimed.

I sent no such force," said Titanis.

"Not yet. But, you will. I don't want you making the same mistake over again. This act of vengeance will only cost more of our kind. I need you to focus on getting results, not making more mistakes. Makoor has probably seen this, as well."

"Jengon was a leader. He had greatness," said Titanis.

"Your foolish sentiments will only make you weaker. I need you to grow up. If you are to be king of the undead one day, I need you to take a greater course of action. When the time is right, we will send out a great force." Lydia crossed her arms. "I have heard the words from the world of none existence. Your father has spoken to me. The Seatons are to be confronted by a knight who will join them, and they will grow stronger. Orphius also states that this knight will confront us at Hotel Quantum Heights."

"Quantum Heights? Why there?" asked Titanis.

"I don't know. For some reason it is to be there." Lydia put her hand to her chest. "But, I for one don't intend to see it end over there. I want these knights out of the way before that." She crossed her arms again. Lydia put down her arms and walked out of the chambers.

***

They came out of their rooms and walked into the hall together. They entered an elegant room. Caprius closed the door behind him. Dragus swung open a painting of Castle Elysium, which was hinged to the wall. There, he pushed a large brick. At the far end near the painting, after the brick movement triggered a mechanism, a large wide column emerged from beneath the floor. It was oval in shape. As it came to a halt, at the top center appeared a large circular surge of energy, rotating. It was light purple in color with sparkles of gold. It twinkled and rotated. At that instance, from the globe of energy, a voice began to speak. "Welcome, knight masters. You are about to embark on a mission. The vim of Petoshine is active." This was the voice of the elf wizard Grongone. A beam of white and purple light shown on Caprius' forehead, which beamed out from the ball of energy. "Please state your name and code," said Grongone's voice.

"Caprius Seaton. Code 472556."

"Name and code recognized. Permission granted," said the voice. At that moment, beside and in front of the column, a sword of power emerged from the floor incased in a field of purple energy. Caprius took his claymore of power in hand.

Then, a beam of light shown upon Dragus' forehead. "Please state your name and code," said the voice.

"Dragus Seaton. Code 723446."

"Name and code recognized. Permission granted," said the voice.

Again, from the floor, a sword incased in energy appeared. Dragus took his sword in hand. From the ball of energy, the lights scanned the room for more knight masters. The energy recognizing two knights said, "Good luck, knight masters." Caprius and Dragus stood side by side with their swords in hand. The floor, which they stood upon, began to move back. As it moved back, the darkness of night shown. As the two knights looked to the bottom, they could see the castle from beneath them.

"Ready, at my signal," said Caprius. At that instance, Caprius jumped followed by Dragus. As they were falling down to the earth, the two knights channeled their powers and a force of energy came from the swords, which lit up the night and brought them safely down to the ground. The bottom of their boots had air compression, which helped soften the landing. The knight masters came down to the ground landing with a thump and ready for combat. They both headed for the nearby stables. When they came to the stable, they harnessed their horses and rode off. They had joined with the rest of the army to meet Andromin and Confidus.

Like thunder rumbling the skies, Confidus and his small army stormed across the forest. The moon shone brightly. They traveled far. They now went passed the fields of bluebells. The forest was thick with birch trees. They approached the stream. "This way!" yelled Confidus. They ran the shore line with their horses. It wasn't long before they came across a bridge. "I don't recall there being a bridge here," said Confidus.

"This is it. Felicia said it was a bridge near the Mogo ridge," said Caprius.

"There's a whole lot of nothing across the bridge," said Dragus.

"No, this is it," said Caprius. Caprius began to ride his horse slowly across the icy bridge. The thirty-five soldiers followed. On both sides of the bridge was the river beneath. The river seemed to go for miles across. And, further up was a dense fog. As they now trotted through the fog, they were transported into a different realm.

"I feel strange," said Confidus. As the icy fog cleared up, they saw a great castle. The soldiers sat on horseback gazing at the solid large doors.

"We must have been transported into a far off land. This bridge is a gateway to this world," said Dragus.

"When our mission is over, this bridge must be destroyed," said Confidus. "Break down the doors," said Confidus quietly and with controlled strength. He motioned to the men with the battering ram.

"No, a battering ram won't work," said Caprius. Suddenly, as Caprius was on his knees, from within Caprius grew a great power. His sword of power shone a bright white color. Caprius' eyes were keen and focused. He rose to his feet and pointed his sword at the tall icy doors. Dragus now channeled his powers, as well. A great burst of energy came from the swords of power. The doors were engulfed with the light of Petoshine. Moments later, the large doors blasted open.

Andromin motioned to his men to enter the castle. "Kill everything in sight. We are going to take them by storm. Show no mercy!" he yelled.

The soldiers expedited Andromin's orders and stormed the castle grounds. But, once inside, many of them stopped short. In the main courtyard, an uncountable array of wood and stone coffins lay scattered.

A vampire emerged from a coffin. The soldier forced down the sword, cutting through the vampire's hands. The creature, nonetheless, tried to hold the sword back, blood pouring through her fingers. The vampire rose from her coffin to get a better grip on the sword and began pulling on it, but Caprius was faster. He lunged forward and drove his claymore deep into her heart.

The vampire cried out. Her ghoulish face shrank, and the tiny red veins in her eyes turned blue as her eyes rolled back into her head. Her fingers went stiff, and she slowly laid back. Caprius dislodged his sword and decapitated her. The head toppled to the floor. He backed away in horror, leaving her once beautiful face pressed into the earthen floor.

The knight masters and their army quickly went around the castle grounds setting the wooden coffins ablaze. The fire consumed the vampires quickly. The soldiers silenced their squealing with their swords. In moments, the castle grounds became a crematorium littered with bodies.

Caprius grabbed a hold of a vampire by the throat. "Where is she!" he yelled to the creature.

"Sorry, I can't help you with that," the creature gurgled. Caprius lunged his sword of power into the creature, slicing him upward to his chin. Caprius grabbed a hold of another and another, destroying them all. "Where is Melina Hampshire!" Caprius grabbed a vampire by the chin.

"You're too late, Caprius. She's down in the cave of the sacred forest. By now, she's one of us."

Caprius drove his claymore into her belly and with his powers, he set her a blaze. The creature burned rapidly on the floor.

***

Beneath the castle grounds, Titanis walked the forest cave with Clarisse. She had accepted her life of the undead with him to be her husband. The life she once cherished was forgotten. And, it was now that she would fulfill her dark destiny; a life never to walk in sunlight and never to see the sun rise and set through countless centuries. They stood in a crypt within the forest. torches were lit, which nested upon columns. There were two caskets made from glass and gold trimmings. The two caskets were upon a large flat concrete tablet. Down upon the tablet, snakes slithered and hissed. Clarisse didn't seem to be frightened. Her mind was lost, and she was a follower of the underworld. As she looked into his eyes, she felt love and welcome. "Now, my sweet Clarisse, I give you the first of three blood transfers. In three days, you will be in full service to the Dark Lord Makoor. Let the blood of everlasting life after death enter your soul," he said to her.

"I give myself to the Dark Lord Makoor. It is of my own accord," said Clarisse.

"Then, so it shall be," said the vampire.

At that moment, Titanis held his mouth over her neck. Sharp fangs protruded from within his mouth. The moon began to turn red, and a wolf who sat near them began to howl. Clouds moved rapidly. Within the clouds, Felicia - the Golden Fleece's face appeared. "No, Melina," she said. As the vampire's fangs drew closer, Clarisse's heart began to beat faster. The wolf continued to howl. As the vampire held her in his arms, his eyes turned ruby red, and he bit into her neck. Clarisse felt pain and began to shake. She breathed heavily. Her blood was now polluted with the vampire's. She held him tight. Bats flew the caves as they sensed a presence. From within the tunnel, the Elysian knights appeared.

Caprius immediately noticed Melina. "Nooo!" Caprius yelled out as he watched the vampire bite into her neck. At that moment, Titanis drew his head away from Clarisse and, staring at the knights, growled—his eyes a menacing ruby red. His teeth were stained with blood. The knights rushed in, and the vampire set Clarisse, who had fallen in a state of sleep, into her coffin. The vampire approached the knights. With his powers, he drew a force, which threw the knights in the air. They tumbled to the ground. The snakes began to slither and enter Clarisse's coffin. Clarisse lay sleeping with snakes slithering across her body. The knights again attacked. Caprius rose to his feet. Holding his claymore in hand, he channeled his powers. He drew a large flame from his sword at the vampire. The vampire held out his hand and created a force field. The fire went in all directions. When the fire was extinguished, the vampire looked at Clarisse in the coffin. He gestured with his hand, and the lid closed the casket. With his mind, the vampire jammed the casket handle, twisting it and trapping the helpless Melina inside. Calista drew her bow and arrow, sending an arrow near the vampire's head. The vampire caught the arrow in hand, growled, and threw it to the ground.

The vampire came closer to the knights; with his power, he lifted one knight off the ground and forced him back. The knight flew across, landing on and through a tree stump. Its pointed end cut through the knight's body, sticking out from his chest. The knight spilled blood from his mouth and widened his eyes. He slumped over dead. As Dragus and Andromin rushed to the creature, the vampire again drew a force pushing the knights back. Dragus and Andromin fell into the stream with a splash. Calista speared another arrow across the air. The vampire noticed it and moved his head to the side. Dragus lunged swinging his sword, and the vampire swung his arm hitting Dragus in the face. Dragus flew back. At the same time, as the vampire wasn't looking, Calista threw her sword into the air. The sword spun around. The creature saw it in time and jumped into the air. The sword struck a nearby tree with the handle embedded into an open stump. Calista immediately went to her bow and arrow and let out an arrow. The arrow pierced the vampire through his left collar bone. The vampire grimaced. He dislodged the arrow. At that moment, Caprius lunged at him with super speed. The force sent the vampire against a tree. The creature fell dazed. Caprius wasted no time, and with great speed, he came at him swinging his sword. The sword severed the vampire's left hand. The vampire, now injured and angry, picked up Caprius by his chest and pushed him high up. Caprius somersaulted and landed on his knees. The vampire cringed and laughed. Andromin drew a powerful flame, and now the vampire turned into a hundred bats and flew away.

The snakes continued to slither across Melina's body. Her face white as snow and eyes closed. The vampire bats merged into human vampire form near Dragus. The vampire, who's eyes were fierce, held Dragus by his wrists with great strength. Caprius lunged at them both, kicking the vampire back toward a tree. The vampire was on his knees, and both Dragus and Andromin drew great balls of fire, which engulfed the creature. Dragus ran to Melina looking at her in the casket. Melina opened her eyes and snarled. Fangs in her mouth. The creature used his powers to extinguish the flames. He was burned and revealed his fangs. The vampire's eyes glowed a ruby red; he snarled. Caprius ran toward the vampire, striking with his claymore but missed. At that moment, Calista drew another arrow, which sped through the air, and as the vampire's eyes widened, before he could do anything, the arrow pierced him through the forehead. His eyes opened wide.

Caprius came at him swinging himself around and thrust his foot into his abdomen. As the vampire flew back into the tree, he struck Calista's sword embedded in the open stump. The vampire was pierced through his heart. The knights stood looking at the dead vampire. Caprius immediately went to Melina. Again, her eyes were closed. Her face turned a normal color, not pale and white. Caprius tried to open the casket, but it was jammed. He slammed his sword handle against the end of the glass near the handle. He could not break it. He tried again and again.

"Wait, Caprius," said Dragus. "Step aside." The snakes continued to slither upon Melina's body. Dragus channeled his powers to his sword. He drew a great heat of light upon the door handle. The handle melted. Caprius swung his sword up from the bottom hitting the edge of the coffin lid. The casket blew open. Caprius and Dragus began taking the snakes in hand and tossing them out of the coffin. "She has better color in her face now," said Dragus. Dragus opened Melina's mouth, moving her lips. "The fangs have retracted. The spell has been broken."

"With the vampires death, the Monisar was reversed," said Calista, who stood by their side.

"Will she be all right?" asked a soldier.

Caprius took her hand. "She has a pulse." He put his hand upon her chest. "I can feel her heart beating."

"That would mean that the vampire baptized her only once," said Calista.

"That means we got to her right on time. She will be all right in given time," said Dragus. They all glanced back looking at the dead vampire pinned to the tree; his head slouched down.

"Let's take her home now," said Caprius. They came out of the castle and stood at the entrance.

"This bridge must be destroyed," said Dragus. Dragus took out a small flat circular explosive device from his side pocket. He set the detonation and put the device onto the bridge. "Let's go! It's going to blow!" Caprius held Melina's body in front of his as they both sat on the horse. The small army trotted across the bridge away from Castle Plaphorius. They approached the land and began to ride off the bridge. Caprius halted his horse. "Wait, I want to see this," he said. Seconds later, the bridge exploded. The bridge rumbled and cracked. A great light dispersed, and the bridge vanished. The gateway to another land had been shut. In the distance, there was no castle Plaphorius.

"Well, we had best be off to Elysium," said Caprius. The army was full of gratitude for being able to escape the evil that was Titanis Clore and happy to live another day.

***

When the knights arrived back in Elysium, Caprius set Melina's body down on the bed. He lay her head gently on the pillow. He watched her sleep. He sat on the bed by her side, and after being with her for nearly four hours, he got to his feet. Melina was still fast asleep. Caprius looked at her one last time, then left the bedroom.

Chapter 3

Cold-Hearted and Driven

CONFIDUS RECALLED SOMETHING HE HAD read in the sacred Book of Bivion, a prophecy written by Felicia - the Golden Fleece, that he suddenly needed to see. Confidus decided he would visit the basilica in Meadow-lie to check the Book of Bivion at once.

He went into the library, where the mahogany walls flickered in the candlelight. The Book of Bivion rested on its stand, as with its more than one thousand pages, it was too large to hold. All of Felicia's writings from before her passing were contained in the book: scriptures, diagrams of ancient Elysium, and much more. He flipped through the pages until he found what he was looking for. He centered his glasses on his thin nose and began to read. "Here lie the shocking words as written over a thousand years ago." He continued until he came to a passage Felicia had written: "It is through my vision I glimpsed the future. Before the chosen one, whom they will call Lantrinon, is born, the king of Elysium shall send forth his son, whose name will begin with the initial C, on two journeys, which shall involve the slaying of the Dark

Lord's vampire minions. This knight shall be joined by an outsider who will embrace the light of Petoshine and too become a knight master. This knight shall be female, and her name will also begin with the letter C. After some months, the two will join to form a lasting bond in the light of Petoshine. During their journey, they will be joined by yet a third companion, another female, whose first name again shall bear the first initial of C. The three will join forces to form a larger, stronger bond. The three knights, known as the 'Three C's,' shall ultimately help destroy the Dark Lord and his vampire minions. This is my vision, for I am Felicia - the Golden Fleece."

Confidus closed the book and considered her words. "Three C's... my son Caprius and Calista...," he murmured. He sat back in his chair and touched his beard absently. "But, a second female? I cannot imagine who that would be." He sat up. "I know what I must do," he said, this time aloud, his voice ringing out into the large room. Confidus closed the golden Book of Bivion. He strode out of the basilica.

***

Two days had passed. Jethro was riddled with hoodlums, bums, and grifters. The few who tried to live an honest life were burned out, and the only way anyone got any money was to cheat or steal. The downtown area was thick with the worst kind of action; looting and burglary were commonplace, but recently, things had heated up, and the murder rate was creeping up to an all-time high. In the last years, the crime had gotten so bad, people didn't like to leave their homes, knowing a simple walk down the street could mean a mugging, a beating, or worse. The western part of Alamptria was the opposite: safe, clean, congenial; its lawmakers ensured the police were in fine form and out in force, keeping their streets secure. But, in the east, cowards were beaten alive, and only those who could defend themselves kept their heads above water. This nasty social climate turned most toward taking up some kind of self-defense: martial arts, krav magna, capoeira. So long as a person could thrust a kick into an attacker's windpipe or carve him out at the knees, he could go about his business in town. Child or grandmother, it didn't matter; it was all about survival.

Downtown in Jethro, the honest work opportunities were scarce, so those who could fled to the north of the city where the more upright folks lived; those who couldn't because they didn't have the means stayed, but eventually, like the many who came before them, these desperate people inevitably turned to darker pursuits, stripping or gambling or worse, to stay afloat. Those who lived in northern Jethro were, by and large, able to avoid most of this seedy life; there, the families and the elderly lived in well-cared-for homes with manicured lawns and ran decent businesses. But, the action, the mystery, the opportunity to make a quick buck, these were downtown. Anyone who ventured to that part of the city knew he had to get his fists ready.

Cynthia Davenport was a strikingly beautiful woman in her late twenties. Her almond eyes were fringed by a wave of waist-length chestnut hair, perfectly manicured nails topped her long fingers, and toned muscles made up her slender shape. Her job as an agent working undercover for a small organization paid her decently enough so she could maintain a cheerful two bedroom apartment in the northern part of the city. While she believed it was important to keep herself up physically, she budgeted her finances for all her other expenses to be able to give her adopted sixteen-year-old son, Henry, anything he needed. He meant the world to her, and she truly would do anything for him. She ardently wished she could have a better life in a city like Elysium, where good fortune and opportunities were plentiful, but her job was all consuming and prevented her from doing much else, including spending the time she wished she could with her son. They had only been together for four years, when she rescued him from living on the streets, bone thin and shivering. She took him in, taught him how to defend himself, and loved him like he was her own. When she was out in the field, Henry was on his own, but he was clever and knew how to take care of himself. He learned to cook and keep the house tidy.

The only concern Cynthia had, which she would never talk to Henry about, was that one day he might sense the dangerous excitement in downtown Jethro and try to make his way there. He knew how to fight, so if he got into trouble, he could at least defend himself, but she didn't want him to enter into that world, one she knew very well herself. As a child, she'd seen her mother die at the hands of a mugger, who shot her through the neck, killing her instantly. Sensing his daughter's deep psychological trauma, her father, a war veteran, embarked on a rigorous training plan that gave Cynthia all the combat and training she needed to fend off any attacker. And, she did from that point onward, getting herself into trouble just to beat her way out of it. She was a fierce fighter in both hand and sword combat and won all of her battles. But, after killing some young thugs just for the sport of it, she realized she had deeper emotional scarring than she'd been willing to admit and went to a psychiatrist. She confessed to hearing voices and having visions that taunted her into fighting. When she met Henry, she felt complete in a way she hadn't since her mother's death. In him, she found she could love and care for someone fully. She also began teaching other young people martial arts so they could productively avoid criminals, not beat them to a pulp. Privately, she found agency in helping out the community; if she saw any scourge trying to steal or bother anyone, she stepped in to help. It became second nature to be on guard.

***

On this bright and sunny day, she donned a skin-tight outfit with a sword tucked into each of her thigh-high boots to continue her hunt for a man named Colburn who had been eluding the authorities and gone into hiding. He was a dangerous villain, secretly planning a mass production of a serum used to genetically enhance animals, turning them into super intelligent and dangerous predators. Her previous attempts to stop Colburn had failed, and she vowed to continue to search for him until he was either captured or exterminated. She'd gotten a lead, and though all she wanted was to stay home and read with Henry, she left, determined to snare this monster.

After a long day and night yielding nothing, early on Monday morning, she crept back in exhausted. She started the kettle before going to check on Henry in his bedroom. She opened the door gently, then stopped. His bed was made and his pillow was fluffed. Henry always pulled his covers up in the morning but never so neatly and never with his pillow so centered and nicely propped up. She knew he hadn't slept at home during the night. Her heart sank as she suspected it had to do with her mission. Cynthia had not only taught him combat fighting, but she had also mistakenly gotten him involved in her dangerous world. She cursed herself for ever having confided in him about her involvement in the dark world. Since taking in Henry, she'd managed to keep him safe, away from the danger of downtown Jethro, but now, because of who she was and what she did, she'd inadvertently gotten him involved in an exponentially more dangerous and sinister world.

Cynthia numbly shuffled back to the kitchen and plunked down onto a chair. She began to weep, her voice mingling with the whistling tea kettle. She wiped her face on her sleeve and prepared a cup of Earl Grey. As she dunked the tea bag, she thought about Henry and what a mistake she'd made. She hoped that he had gone for a run or had slept over with a friend. Even a girl would've been preferable.

She sipped her tea, but it was so hot, she scalded her lip and jostled the cup, spilling tea onto her lap and the table. "Shit!" She brushed away the hot liquid from her pants and stood to get the dishcloth. As she wiped up the mess, she sat back down, filled with sorrow. She sat, immobile, for over an hour until finally she stood and put her tea, now ice cold, in the sink. She went to the bathroom, filled the tub, and took off her clothes; she sank into the steaming water. She laid there a long time before dressing in large soft pants and a woolen sweater, taking to the sofa with her head on a pillow and arms over her head to wait for her son.

The room was silent. The wind picked up, and the snow slowly patterned down, but inside was still. Cynthia squeezed a small rubber ball over and over. As the minutes passed, with no sound of footsteps approaching the door, she became more frustrated. She sat up and whipped the ball across the room.

Cynthia clasped her hands in prayer and glanced at the gilt crucifix on her wall. She clapped her hands to her knees and stood, unable to bear it any longer. She was going to go look for him. She dressed again in black, sheathing the swords at her thighs, and headed downtown.

Cynthia headed straight to the shadiest part of Jethro and walked through, aware that all eyes were on her. A cluster of greasy looking men at the corner paused in their raucous banter as she approached. She recognized them from playing the horses. They didn't play fair, either. A tall one with stringy hair and dungarees stepped away from his mates and glowered at her. "You're the one," he said. "I recognize you. You took me for my money."

Cynthia raised an eyebrow and shrugged. "Of course, I did. It was a bet, and I won," she said.

"Ya, well, I got rules. And, I say you cheated," he said.

"Hmm," she pretended to size him up. "It was fair. Pity for you that you're a sore loser."

"There was nothing fair about it, and a real lady would challenge me to a rematch," he said, his lips twisting into a sly grin.

"What's the matter, Neddy, your mommy put you out in the cold for losing her nest egg in the race?" asked Cynthia feigning sympathy. She fingered his dirty lapel and matched his smile, which he dropped in sudden seriousness.

"Listen, give me a chance to win my money back, and I'll lay off for good," he said.

"And, if you lose, then what?" she asked.

"I'll never bother you again. All I want is a chance." Ned held out his hand. "What do you say, Cynthia?"

"All right, but under one condition. Tell me where Henry is."

Ned sneered. "I haven't seen your son. He don't hang out with us," he said, then grinned again. "Maybe he's out putting in a hard day's work at the strip bar. Even he likes to watch."

"You know, I don't think I want to bother with a rematch. And, you can tell your mommy you've been beaten by a woman," Cynthia said, turning around.

Ned's eyes went wide and desperate. "Henry may not make it alive," he blurted out. "I ain't going to tell you nothing," he said.

"Fine. Let's race," said Cynthia. "But, you promise me you tell me where Henry is whether I win or lose."

"Man, you're gonna lose. You're going down," said Ned, grinning wildly.

At the edge of Jethro stood a hill in the center of a snowy forest. The four men and Cynthia sat astride their horses on the rugged path at the ready. Cynthia knew full well this would not be a fair ride and that these men would pull every punch they could. She knew her life was at stake. She bent forward and patted her horse's firm neck, steeling herself to beat these low-life deadbeats. With her thighs gripping the saddle and the reigns firm in her hands, her thoughts flashed to Henry, but she shook them off, knowing she needed to be focused in order to win. At the sound of a gun, their five horses took off down the rocky path, riding fast and furious. Above them, the trees arched into a snowy canopy all but blotting out the sun.

The horses rode perfectly in sync until suddenly the one beside Cynthia nudged hers, and its rider began punching Cynthia's arm. Cynthia took the blows and held steady until they came to a bend in the road, and Cynthia backhanded the man in the nose. He yelped and flew off his horse landing in the snow, rolling backwards over and over as if he were a snowball. They left him behind and kept racing. Cynthia was neck and neck with Ned. Suddenly, someone reached around her waist. She teetered, off balance, which caused her to yank her horse to the side and veer into the horse beside her. Cynthia reared back and elbowed whomever had been behind her. That man lost his balance and fell off his horse, bouncing off a cluster of snow-covered branches. Cynthia looked back to see the man cursing and dusting himself off as he sluggishly got up. The remaining three horses were weary and frothing, but they kept on.

In an upcoming dense thicket, Cynthia noticed two men crouched beside tree stumps on either side of the path. Each held a length of rope that was tied to their stump. As they passed, they threw their ropes, and the stumps came swinging down onto the trail. Cynthia saw one headed straight for her, so she ducked and went down to her horse's flank, hanging on sideways. The stump went over her saddle and struck the man riding just behind her to the side, knocking him off his horse. He flew into a tree and lay still in the snow. Now, it was Ned and Cynthia. Ned jammed his heels into his horse and took a good lead. Cynthia sat back up in her saddle and dug in, too. They were approaching a steep slope that led to a cliff. They rounded the corner at such a great speed, both riders fell off their horses, sliding down the slope on their backs over the ice toward the cliff. The adrenaline racing through Cynthia was fierce. She reached out and grabbed hold of the back of Ned's jacket. She managed to get her other hand down to her thigh and yanked out her dagger. She raised her arm and plunged it into the snow, which slowed them down. But, not slow enough; they kept racing down the hill until they hit a clump of brush. Ned had too much momentum and sailed over and off the edge; Cynthia was able to stop herself by activating the spikes within her finger part of her gloves. Instantly, the tips of her fingers and palms shot out a number of one inch spikes on her left hand. With a grip on the icy snow, she held on. Ned dangled over the side, his hand gripping her right hand. "Where's Henry?" she yelled.

"Pull me up and I'll tell you!" screamed Ned.

Cynthia pursed her lips but decided she had to trust him. If he knew anything at all, she needed to know. She used all her might to pull Ned up from the edge. He gripped some rocks and hoisted himself up. He clambered up onto the hill. Cynthia looked at her spiked glove and retracted the spikes. Ned sat beside her, both of them breathing hard. She looked at him. "Where's... Henry?"

He shook his head. "I really don't know. I told you. I haven't seen him. I'm telling you the truth."

Cynthia saw in his eyes that he was being honest with her. This chase was just a game to recoup his money. They stood and began to climb the hill that led back to the trail. When they reached the top, they paused at the overlook and glanced at the view. Ned chuffed the dirt with the toe of his boot and looked sheepish. "So, um, thanks for saving my life. I owe you." Ned held out his hand. Cynthia looked down at her feet and then at Ned before swinging her fist wide and cracking him in the jaw. Ned fell to the ground.

"You took me for a ride, Ned. I win again," Cynthia said as she walked away.

***

The city of Jethro was sodden and heavy from the slushy rain that fell thickly over the streets. It was warm for a winter's day, and the cobblestone shone from the wet. Upon nightfall, the citizens slowly made their way into their homes and bunkered themselves in for the dark. Night in Jethro was a fearsome time, and the people who lived here were scarred by their memories.

In a suite of a small apartment building, Cynthia was grieving for the loss of her brother, her best friend. It was one year ago on this night that the dreaded vampire had taken her brother's life. For Cynthia, it was a year of pain and desperation; she ached to find a way to destroy the entire vampire cult that continually persecuted their great land of Alamptria. The people of the kingdom had to spend their time and precious limited resources to defend their homes from these wretched creatures of the underworld, who flew by night out from Mount Drone, which stood at the base of Plaphorius, and flooded the skies, turning them black. Elysium and Koriston had joined forces to eradicate their land of these horrid creatures.

Cynthia sipped a glass of red wine. She was a beautiful woman who worked undercover, but her current investigation looked like it had come to a dead end. She downed the last of her wine and checked her watch again. She felt in her bones that something was wrong, but she tried not to worry and poured another glass of wine to take her mind off her fears. She wasn't losing hope just yet. "Come on, Henry," she muttered.

In another hour, she was feeling thick in the head, and Henry had still not arrived. Thunder rumbled in the distance, and the rain started up again. Cynthia lay down on the couch and dozed off fitfully. Not long later, thunder clapped and lightning sizzled as if the storm had leaped up with a vehemence, and she jumped. This, she knew, was the bewitching hour: the time when the one you expected to come home did not and was either simply delayed or undergoing the

Monisar, the transition one went through as he became undead.

***

In the pit hall of a dark warehouse stood three of the dark lord's most notorious henchmen. Cambrozes Genesis, the Dark Lord Makoor's chief henchman in charge of subsuming the land of Alamptria, was in a heated discussion about his complicated scheme for stealing Caprius Seaton's claymore of power. The claymore was a sword of power harnessed by the great wizard Grongone and his mighty Vim. The undead feared the Vim over all else: a power so intense, it could cripple the vampires and potentially destroy them.

It was a scheme that had made strong headway now that they had captured Caprius' good friend and were torturing him to get him to cooperate and do Cambrozes' bidding. He writhed and spat in the corner, and Cambrozes watched, a thick, evil smile smeared across his oily face.

Carcass Doom, the other henchman helping administer the torture, grabbed the prisoner by his now bloodied and torn shirt, dragged him to a nearby chair, and threw him into it. Henry Hudson, who had been captured and was being forced to watch the other man's suffering, was restrained by the third of the group, Lavender Frikiseed. Henry noticed a tattoo of a snake on the man's wrist as he pinned him down. He gathered from the conversation that Lavender was going to be the one responsible for obtaining the claymore of power. "Look up," hissed Lavender who grabbed Henry's head and forced him to watch. "Your good friend here is about to die."

Lavender pushed him into a chair, and two Droge creatures scurried forward and began wrapping him to the chair with lengths of rope. They bound his torso to the chair but mistakenly left his arms free. Henry smiled to himself but clasped his hands behind his back and said nothing.

Carcass Doom then straightened up and walked over to a chain, which was wound around a wheel attached to a steel beam. He hooked one end to the chair. "I don't know what you want from me," said the man. Carcass Doom glanced at the stagnant pool of freezing water that lay beneath an opening in the wooden floor before grabbing the chain and pulling it so the man was lifted off the ground. The Droges helped position the chair and the screaming man over the water before Carcass Doom lowered him into it. Down he went, deep, deeper into the cold water. The man struggled to get a last breath of air, but he was submerged too quickly, his eyes bulging with fear. There was nothing he could do. Carcass Doom's strength was no match for any mortal.

"Carcass!" yelled Cambrozes. "That's enough!" Carcass rolled his eyes and pulled the man out of the water. He lifted him in his chair, sputtering, his head lolling about on his neck, and put him brusquely back onto the dry floor.

"Why are you doing this to me?" the man got out between fits of coughing.

"Now, Mr. Brandon Peasley, we're going to have a little talk," said Cambrozes.

"But, I don't know anything!" Peasley yelled.

"It's not what you know that we're interested in; rather, it's what you're going to do for us." Cambrozes took a step closer to him. "I want you to write a letter instructing Caprius Seaton to meet you in the dining lounge of hotel Quantum Heights."

"Why would Caprius Seaton want to meet with me there?" asked Brandon. "It's way out of the way."

Cambrozes slapped Brandon in the face so hard it knocked Brandon and the chair to the ground. Carcass pulled on the chain and lifted him gently back up. "Don't talk to me like I'm stupid!" Cambrozes peered into Brandon's eyes. "I know all about the work you do for him. I also happen to know that he trusts you. And, this is why I know Caprius will show up."

"Take heart, Peasley; soon, we Goncools will run all of Alamptria," said Lavender.

Cambrozes stared intently into Brandon's eyes. "Now, write the letter." Carcass and the Droges moved the chair in front of a small writing desk.

"What's the letter for? What is it exactly that you want?" asked Brandon.

"That isn't any of your concern. All you need to know is what you already know and nothing more," said Cambrozes.

"Well, I won't write it!" yelled Brandon. "You're going to kill me anyway."

"Write the fucking letter!" yelled Cambrozes.

"I won't do it. You'll just have to kill me," said Brandon.

"Frikiseed, soften him up," he said. Lavender gave a small whoop and began hitting him across the head and abdomen. Brandon shrieked with pain, but that seemed only to enliven Lavender, who punched him even harder.

After several minutes, Cambrozes put up his hand. "That's enough!" he said. "We don't want him to swell up just yet. He needs to be able to use his hand, and I need him alert—just enough for him to finish the job." Cambrozes grabbed him by the chin. "Write the letter." Brandon shook his head and spat a mouthful of blood onto Cambrozes' face. "Carcass!" Carcass Doom picked up the chain and lifted the chair and Brandon off the ground. He kicked Brandon to the side, where he fell back into the frigid water. Brandon tried to struggle, and bubbles came up as he became more and more frantic.

After a moment, Cambrozes held up his hand. Carcass lifted Brandon out of the water and plunked him down at Cambrozes' feet. Brandon choked and coughed. Off to the side, Henry Hudson's expression became more terrified. He'd always known the Legion of Doom was something to fear, but now, faced with it, he was petrified.

After Brandon had caught his breath, Genesis pulled back Brandon's hair. "You're making this more difficult than it needs to be," he said gently. "There is an easier way." He leaned forward, his fetid breath on Brandon's neck. "But, you should know, we have stamina beyond what you can imagine. We're happy to play this little game all night."

Brandon stared at him through unfocused woozy eyes. Cambrozes puckered his lips and whistled. "Okay, you're right. We're going to kill you. But, no more torture. I promise you a quick death. You have my word. Now, write the fucking letter!"

Brandon nodded slowly. "Thank you. I appreciate that. But, no."

Cambrozes' expression hardened before a sweet smile broke out and showed all his rotten teeth. "Perhaps, you haven't thought this through. What about your lovely lady friend here in Jethro?"

Brandon's face crumpled. "How do you know of Elizabeth? You wouldn't harm her."

"You see, Mr. Peasley, we didn't get involved in this little endeavor until we were sure we knew everything there was to know about you," said Cambrozes. Off to the side, Carcass squeezed out a horrible laugh.

"And, if I write the letter, you'll leave her and her kids alone?" asked Brandon.

"Of course! She's just a local peasant. We have no use for her."

Brandon looked down at the blank paper in front of him. He picked up the pen with a shaking hand and began to write as he was instructed. When he finished, he threw the pen and shoved the paper toward the cold-hearted bastard. Cambrozes picked up the letter and smiled as he read it.

"Are you satisfied?" asked Brandon angrily.

"You have done well, Brandon Peasley. It sounds very authentic." Cambrozes turned. "Carcass!"

Carcass strode over and picked up Brandon and the chair. "Killing me isn't going stop the Seatons! Whatever your plan is, it won't work, Genesis! Caprius will come after you!"

"I'm counting on it, Mr. Peasley," said Cambrozes. Carcass threw the chair containing Brandon into the pool of cold water. It swung heavily from the chain like a clock pendulum.

In the commotion, Henry had used his free hands to untie himself. When Lavender was busy laughing at Brandon, struggling again beneath the water, he shook off his ropes and began to back away.

"You said you were going to give him a quick death," said Lavender.

"Whatever. He'll die soon enough," said Carcass, flapping his hand.

Underwater, Brandon continued to struggle as he tried to untie the rope binding his chest. He gasped, and bubbles erupted from his mouth, his lungs instantly filling with the icy water. He took one last look at the predicament he was in before silenced with death.

Henry, now with several feet of distance between him and his kidnappers, began to run. He ran for his life. When Lavender turned around to check on his captive, Henry was gone. "Hudson!" yelled Lavender.

"Get him, you fools!" Cambrozes screamed at the two Droges creatures. He turned to Lavender. "After you're sure that boy is dead, too, take this letter and send it to Caprius Seaton in Elysium."

In the water, there were a few last valiant bubbles that rose to the surface before the water was glassy and still. Not able to spare a last look at his dying friend, Henry bolted from the warehouse and made it outside. He quickly headed for the dense forest ahead. As he ran, echoes of eerie laughter filled the forest, yet he had no choice but to try to survive there. He entered a patch of meadow that was bathed in moonlight, and Lavender and the Droges spotted him and ran toward him. Henry had a good head start, though, and was able to make it into the cover of forest. He dodged trees and hopped fallen logs, running faster than he ever had in his life.

Lavender was more familiar with the forest and saw best at night, so even though Henry had an advantage, it was lessening by the moment. The Droges who accompanied him were even faster. This was their element. These superior Droges, far more deadly than ordinary Droges due to the injections they'd received of the Dark Lord's own blood, smelled and wanted more blood.

Henry turned around to see them closing the gap and stumbled; he fell and hit his face on the wet earth, but the pain felt like nothing since he was flooded with adrenaline from fear. He got back up and continued to run. He could hear the lathering breath of a Droge behind him. Henry hopped a small boggy marsh thinking he'd lose the creature, but he was wrong: he'd come to the edge of a cliff, a raging river below. Off to the side were some boulders, so he quickly climbed down the rocks. Ahead was a fallen tree that seemed to bridge the gap to the other side. He climbed down and began walking across the tree trunk. It was not a very wide river; he talked himself through it and kept his chin high. It looked like he was going to make it.

On the cliff's edge, the two Droges spotted Henry and easily clambered down the rocks. But, when they came to the fallen tree, they chittered among themselves, too afraid to walk across. All Droges were terrified of water. They, instead, jumped nervously, snarled, and growled at Henry, who was inching his way to the other side and away from them. Having to give up on their desire for his blood but still having a job to do, the Droges took their bows and arrows and began to fire at Henry. Arrows whisked by him. Henry was just a foot from the edge, he'd nearly made it, and he was smiling, when an arrow struck him directly in the back near his spine. He lost his footing and fell into the river. Behind him on the cliff, Lavender arrived. He watched Henry's body get swept away in the current.

The Droge creatures turned around and gave Lavender the all clear. "Heesa dead," yelled over a Droge.

"Well done, my friends. Let's go," said Lavender.

***

Henry's body was swept downriver, but he was not dead. He managed to turn himself over onto his back and let the chill water numb the pain. The current soon subsided, and he drifted toward shore. When he was close enough, he helped himself by swimming, though he had to fight against screaming in pain. The arrow was still sticking out of his back. He knew, however, if he didn't keep moving, he would die.

When he was close enough to shore, he felt the rocky land beneath his feet and stood, clutching branches as he stumbled onto the sand. Dazed, he looked around. "I know this place," he muttered. He began to walk. The river had wound around into a near circle, bringing him back to the village of Jethro. Henry staggered past the trees and now arrived at a familiar road. "I have to make it. I'm so close," he thought optimistically. He walked about four miles in the dark. He didn't see a soul for the late hour; he guessed it had to be near two o'clock in the morning.

Another hour had passed. When he finally made it to the heart of the village, he went another two blocks to a small apartment building. He squinted to see the sign. "The Melbourn," it said. He opened the door and tripped on the threshold, catching himself on the stairs. He climbed, laboriously, painfully, up to the fifth floor, then limped down the hall to 511. He knocked gently, but there was no answer, so he used his last bit of strength and pounded on the door.

Cynthia had fallen asleep on the sofa and was startled awake by the noise. "Henry!" she said aloud. She quickly leaped up and went to the door. When she opened it, Henry fell into her arms. "My god, what's happened to you!" she said, looking with horror at the arrow sticking out of his back and feeling his soaked clothes. She helped him over to the sofa and lay him down on his stomach. After propping up his head on her pillow and smoothing back his hair, she whispered, "What happened to you? I was worried sick!" She examined his wound. "Don't worry. I'm going to get this arrow out." She filled a small basin with hot water and got a few clean cloths.

Cynthia looked at the arrow. It was deep inside his back. She touched it, and he yelped. She paused and then took off her belt and folded it over. "Here, put this in your mouth." Henry gripped the leather between his teeth. "This is going to hurt," she said. She slowly pulled on the arrow, with Henry screaming into the pillow through the belt, but it actually came out fairly cleanly. "There. That wasn't so bad."

"You're funny," Henry said, tears coursing down his face.

She tended to the wound, sterilized it, and bandaged it tightly. "There, that's better." She touched his forehead. "You seem rather warm." She got to her feet and looked down at him. "Rest now. It will be morning in a few hours. We'll talk then." She left Henry and went to her bedroom, lay down on her bed and went to sleep, so grateful he was still alive.

When the morning sun broke through, the light penetrated the room and awakened Cynthia. She got out of bed and went in to check on Henry. He was still sleeping deeply. She made breakfast for the two of them and sat down with some hot coffee. When she came back into the living room, Henry was awake but distraught. "Good morning, handsome," she said. Henry sat up higher on the cushions and winced. "How are you feeling?"

He tried to chuckle but winced again. "I guess I've had better days," he said. "I'm actually kind of weak." He brushed his hand through his short hair. "Cynthia, we need to talk."

"Do you know how worried I was about you? You were due back here yesterday afternoon."

"I got a little side-tracked. That investigation on Mr. Colburn didn't turn up much. But, I did run into someone who would have given me ample information on Colburn. A Mr. Brandon Peasley."

"Yes, I know him," she said. "What did he tell you?"

"Not much, unfortunately. Just as things were going to come into play, we were ambushed by three of Makoor's henchmen. It was Peasley they wanted. I was merely at the wrong place at the wrong time."

Cynthia looked horrified. "Makoor?" she whispered.

"We were taken to a warehouse here, just past Jethro, where they tortured Peasley and made me watch. In the end, they drowned him. Brandon Peasley is dead."

Cynthia was shaking. "What did they want?"

"They forced Brandon to write a letter to someone named Caprius Seaton saying they needed to meet in the lounge of hotel Quantum Heights."

"You mean *the* Caprius Seaton? As in the Prince of Elysium?" she asked, bewildered.

"How do you know about him?" he asked.

"I don't just know about him; I went to school with him. I actually had a terrible crush on him, but he didn't show much interest in me, the louse," she chuckled ruefully. "He ended up marrying Melina Hampshire." She was up on her feet now, pacing back and forth. "Melina has a sister named Selene, and it just so happens that she works at the hotel in one of the concourse shops." Cynthia stopped pacing and looked intently at Henry. "What else did they instruct Brandon Peasley to write in that letter?"

"That's all I know," said Henry.

"Is there anything else that can help us?" she asked.

Henry nodded. "As I said, the letter was meant specifically to have Caprius Seaton meet Brandon at hotel Quantum Heights, though…" he paused and tried to remember any other details. "Wait a minute. There is something else. One of Makoor's Henchmen, Lavender Frikiseed, he's a member of a dark cult. They call themselves the Goncools. And, now that I think about it, Lavender had a strange tattoo on his wrist of a snake with a spike through it." He shook his head. "But, that's really everything I can remember."

Cynthia rubbed her forehead. "I need to go to hotel Quantum Heights and warn Caprius." She glanced at the clock. "I'll leave right away."

"I'm going with you," said Henry firmly. "I'm not letting you go alone."

Cynthia shook her head. "Oh, no, you're not. If you can remember, only a few hours ago, I removed an arrow from your back. You're in no condition to travel."

"It's a miracle; I feel much better," he said, getting up.

Cynthia had to admit she would've been very happy for his company. But, the risk was too great. "No, now it's too dangerous. Lavender Frikiseed knows you, and should the Goncools recognize you, our mission would be compromised. This now goes beyond our investigation of Mr. Colburn. The Goncools don't know me from Adam, however, so I can travel around undetected." She started gathering up some things into a satchel. "The Dark Lord has spun his web of malignancies. You, Henry Hudson, must not interfere. You stay here and wait for me. I want you to rest and take care of yourself. I will be all right. The Goncools won't suspect a thing."

Henry sat back down, his face showing relief. "Be careful, Cynthia. They will be watching for any suspicious activities," he said.

"They won't suspect a thing. As I said, they don't know me. And, I know just how to get to Caprius Seaton." She folded her arms. "Now come, I'll warm up your breakfast." As she reheated his eggs, she thought about the Colburn affair. 'I'll get back to that later,' she thought. 'I wonder if Caprius Seaton will remember me.'

Chapter 4

Quantum Heights

HIGH UP IN THE NORTHERN mountains at the eastern edge of the forest stood the prestigious Hotel Quantum Heights, a resort for Alamptria's most illustrious citizens. Christmas had just past, and the gala to celebrate the new year had brought the house down. Everyone's spirits had been high: dancing girls flirted with the men, whose wives were too busy flirting with other women's husbands to notice. All the revelers sang, drank, and ate until well after dawn.

On the morning of January 7, 2256, the hotel was quiet, as all the guests were still recuperating from the party days. Those who drank heavily needed the rest. There were a number of people who had to deal with their hangovers. But, bright and alert in his office, Mr. Willy B. Pinkles, the hotel's manager, whistled at his books, grateful the hotel had come through unscathed. Previous years' repairs from the party had been expensive, indeed.

He rifled through the receipts and felt satisfied. He could already see how the profits outweighed the expenditures by a great sum, and thus heartened, he looked that much more forward to the hotel's 10th anniversary celebration taking place later that month.

Looking a bit rough around the edges, his assistant, Arnie, shuffled in. Pinkles still had his eyes on the books. "This was a fine event, Arnie. We exceeded even last year's winter festival celebration profits," said Pinkles.

"Yes, and, Sir, it was a wise investment to build a railway stop at the hotel. I'm sure that will bring in a whole new flood of visitors," said Arnie eagerly. "Just think, Mr. Pinkles, with the renovations you did last year, you'll probably make your money back within, perhaps, even four years or so."

Pinkles snorted. "Four? I expect two years, no more." He sighed. "I'm just relieved the Seatons were able to control themselves this year; no damage to the hotel due to their antics, and," he muttered, "their stupid claymores of power."

"Sir, certainly you can understand that the damage the Seatons caused in the past was due to their being on missions for his majesty's secret service."

"Missions or no missions, the Seatons were responsible. Arnie, if you want to take over as manager of Quantum Heights one day, you're going to have to learn to put your foot down." Pinkles pushed his chair back and walked over to the large window. He gazed outside into the wilderness. Snow had fallen in thick white clumps overnight, and the view from atop the mountain was breathtaking.

"I have eight years until I retire, Arnie. In my remaining years as hotel manager, I want to continue to make improvements to this establishment." He spread his arms out. "I want people all over Alamptria to remember this as the most prestigious hotel in our land

and, maybe one day, the world. I want people to remember the name 'Quantum Heights.'"

Just then, there was a knock on the door. "Enter!" yelled Pinkles. The concierge manager entered. "Brunt, what is it?"

"It seems we have a problem with one of the tourists, Sir. A Mr. Brandon Peasley," said Brunt.

"What is this problem?" asked Pinkles, frowning.

"There are a number of expenses on his account that are still outstanding, and Peasley is nowhere to be found. I last saw him on the 2nd of January, so this morning, I had a porter go to his suite to check on him. All his belongings are still there. We found some bloodstains on the carpeting. But, no Peasley. We checked the room with a fine-toothed comb," said Brunt. Pinkles raised an eyebrow and folded his hands. Then, he sat back down in his chair. "Sir, I think Brandon Peasley is dead and have reason to believe this was a professional hit."

"Where was the blood found, Brunt?" asked Pinkles.

"By the sofa, near the coffee table," said Brunt.

Arnie jumped in. "Sir, should we call on the Seatons to investigate?"

"No, Arnie, we'll leave this to the local police," said Pinkles.

"Mr. Brandon Peasley had been involved in some sort of business with the Seatons in the past. Shouldn't they be informed of what has happened?" asked Arnie.

"Yes, they will be. But, this needs to be a police matter now," said Pinkles, sneering. "Brunt, I want you to get a messenger to deliver a note to the police and inform them as to what has happened," he said. He went to his desk to dash off the note and handed it to Brunt.

Quantum Heights was situated within the city of Alba May. The city looked as beautiful in the daytime as it did in the twinkling light of dusk. At this time of year, reflected off the snow, the hotel, with its glowing yellow lanterns, looked warm and festive.

On horseback en route to Hotel Quantum Heights, Caprius Seaton approached a waterfall cascading down from the mountain into a pond that fed into a larger lake. Above, the water had slowed to a trickle from the large icicles hanging down, and where Caprius rode over a curve of stones beneath the falls, the road was thickly carpeted with snow. His white stallion blended in, his footfalls dampened but for the crunch of snow beneath his hooves. The storm of the previous evening had caught everyone off guard. There hadn't been a single cloud in the sky, and then, at 6:00 a.m., the winds picked up, and sinister clouds roared in, dumping several meters of snow.

Caprius looked up and saw a passenger train arriving to the new station at the hotel, steam blowing off its back. He rode up the mountain to the hotel and went around back to the stables, where he handed his steed over to the groom. He patted the horse before turning to leave. "Take good care of her, Charley."

"Like she was my own, Sir."

Unlike the city streets at the bottom of the hill, which, despite the additional manpower and hours of shoveling, remained thick with snow, the roads impassable, the road leading to the hotel was pristine. Horse-drawn carriages went swiftly to and fro. Caprius waited for a break, then dashed across the road and went into the hotel, his claymore of power by his side. Caprius was eager to meet his contact—Brandon Peasley. Caprius knew Brandon well; they went back many years.

He found his way to the concierge and plunked his sack on the wooden counter. Although Dragus, Confidus, and a few other council members from Elysium had come there for the New Year's Eve party, Caprius had spent the evening in Elysium with his wife, Melina Hampshire, and her family. This was his first visit to the hotel since New Year's Day in 2247. He'd always liked coming here; it was elegant and serene, a place to rejuvenate his spirit. He hoped the new railroad station wouldn't bring too many people to the place and spoil it.

"A good day to you, Mr. Seaton. We have been expecting you," bowed the concierge.

"A good day to you, as well," said Caprius. "You have my usual suite?"

"But, of course. Here is the key and your room number, Sir. I'll have the porter take up your sack."

"That will not be necessary. I will see to my room." Caprius tipped the concierge a few shillings and turned to scan the lobby.

"As you wish," smiled the concierge. "Can I send any lunch to your room, Sir?"

"No, thank you. I have a table waiting for me in the dining lounge and am expecting someone," said Caprius. "But, first, I shall have a hot bath. I am quite chilled and stiff from the long journey."

The concierge winked. "Ah, yes, I know just the thing for that. Perhaps, you would like me to send up a girl to give you a massage."

"That won't be necessary. But, you can send a woman up to fill the bathtub."

"Right away, Sir."

"I shall be up momentarily," said Caprius. "I wish to check on something. And, actually, I have changed my mind. Please have the porter take this sack up to my room." Caprius turned and went down the large hall into the concourse. In the flower shop, he saw a woman he knew. She was bent over watering the lilies when he snuck up on her. "Hello, Selina," he said teasingly.

"I know that voice," she said. She stood and turned to face him. "Caprius Seaton," she announced and gave him a hug. "How is my sister?"

"Melina is doing fine. Did you know we are planning to have a child?" As he spoke, he became aware of a beautiful brunette over by the bouquets eying him. Caprius glanced over at her, and for a moment, they locked eyes.

"Good God, you're going to be a father!" she exclaimed and kissed him. "When is the big day?"

"Well, she isn't pregnant yet," he said. "But, I'm afraid I will not be witnessing the birth of my child. Melina will be leaving Elysium to live with Grongone, the wizard, in Petoshine. She will live where the child can be protected."

"Protected from what?" she asked, alarmed.

"It's a long story. But, the baby will be in good hands. I must take my leave now; I just stopped by to say hello. I'm going upstairs to my room for a while, and then I have a meeting to attend." He smiled at her, then recalled seeing several police in the lobby. "By the way, any idea what is going on out there?"

Selina lowered her voice. "I don't know all the details. But, I heard a hotel guest has gone missing and is presumed to be dead."

"That is terrible news." He kissed her on the cheek. "Goodbye, Selina."

"Caprius, it's always a pleasure. When will I see you again?" she asked.

"I don't know. Maybe if the meeting doesn't take too long, we can have dinner. I'll let you know."

When he arrived in his suite, he checked the bathing room to see that the tub was filled with steaming water. He returned to his sack, which was sitting on a table in the living area, and checked the time on his pocket watch. He undressed, laid his claymore on the floor beside the tub, and submerged himself in the hot bath, feeling the tension in his muscles falling away.

He closed his eyes and laid a hot cloth over his face. He became so relaxed, he didn't notice a woman enter his bathroom and remove all her clothes. It was only when she entered the water and sat across from him did he throw off the cloth and sit straight up. It was the woman from the flower shop. "How did you get in?"

She smiled like a cat. "I told the porter I was Melina Hampshire."

"I'm not accustomed to finding naked women in my bathtub who aren't Melina Hampshire," said Caprius.

"I'm sure. I work with Brandon Peasley," she said.

"And, Brandon thought he could send you here? Why, to break the ice?" said Caprius archly.

"Not exactly. I'm afraid Brandon won't be attending the meeting," she said.

"Why the hell not!" he said. "I came a very long way to see him."

She looked straight at him with pure blue eyes. "Brandon Peasley is dead. I came to warn you."

"Dead?" Caprius said astonished. "And, what's to warn me about?"

"You know that letter you received from him asking you to meet him here? He was forced to write it."

"By whom?" Caprius asked. "What did this person want?"

"There were actually five men. They belong to some sort of cult. I came to warn you that you should go back home and forget about Peasley," she said. "These men are dangerous. Forget this meeting was ever to take place."

"I can't do that. I have to find out who's behind this."

"You're in over your head. They will take your claymore, and they'll kill you."

"Not if I kill them first," said Caprius. He made to stand, but the girl quickly sat up and crawled over to Caprius. Her breasts were right in his face. She curled her legs around Caprius' waist and peered into his face, deeply, with concern. She slowly bent to him and kissed him on the mouth. Then, she stood and looked down at him.

"I'm not getting involved in this. They don't know me. If you choose to go to the meeting, these men will kill you," she said. "You'll know it's them by the tattoos on their wrists: a snake with a spike through it. If that means anything to you," she said.

Caprius' eyes widened. "The Goncools."

"That's the name! I couldn't remember it at first." She got out of the bathtub. "If you value your life, you won't go to that meeting." She grabbed a towel and wrapped it around herself. "I warned you, and now I'm leaving."

"Wait a minute. I don't even know your name," said Caprius.

"That's right. And, you never will," she said. She walked out, paused, then leaned back in. "But, I remember you, Caprius Seaton. You always ignored me in school when I was young. I'll let that be your hint."

Caprius thought for a moment. "Please, tell me. Who are you?" he asked again.

"Still the same old Caprius," she said from the living room. Caprius got out of the bathtub. He took the towel from the bar and wrapped it around his waist. As he came into the living room, the girl opened the door to the suite. "Goodbye, Caprius." Cynthia closed the door behind her.

Caprius got dressed and went to the table. There, before his sack, was a note with a bottle of wine and one glass. Caprius picked up the note; the paper bore the aromatic scent of pine. "This scent. It is familiar." Caprius said as he sat down in the chair, his thoughts consumed with the mysterious woman—a woman who seemed to care about him enough to give him this very personal warning, probably at her own peril.

Caprius opened the bottle of wine and poured himself a glass. He sat back sipping it, thinking of the note, which read, 'Stay in the room and drink yourself to sleep.' Caprius found the wine to his liking, redolent of berries and tobacco, and made to do as the note stated. He pulled out his pocket watch, looking at the time: 1:05 p.m. He sipped his wine and sat back. Every ten minutes, he checked his watch, weighing the Goncools and all he knew of them against this very sincere warning from the woman.

By 2:05 p.m., Caprius had drunk two full glasses of wine. Again, he thought of the Goncools and of the mysterious woman. He paused in his sipping, feeling woozy. When Caprius checked his watch next, it was fifteen minutes before the meeting was to take place.

He couldn't take it any longer. "I'm sorry, pretty woman, but I have to know. I have to find out what this is all about." He set the third glass of wine on the table and pushed it away. He stood, retrieved his claymore of power from the bathing room floor, recalling the taste of her kiss but turned his focus to the Goncools. The thought of them caused an anger to grow inside him that burned with a fierce light.

Caprius had a lengthy history with the Goncools. Years ago, his brother Andromin had become involved with a group of men in a cult without knowing their true intensions. They had plotted to take over the Council of Koriston, get close to Queen Amenova, and kill her. In the battle that ensued, many good men from Koriston's Taughtenslotte army lost their lives.

When the whole plot was foiled, the Goncools were arrested and sentenced to hang. Andromin was among those to be hanged. But, his father, Confidus, came to Andromin's rescue. Confidus had bargained with some of the Goncool members, asking them to confess, reasoning with them, saying that Queen Amenova was willing to spare some of their lives, which would allow them to go to prison rather than be hanged.

Nine held true to their mission and were, thus, hanged. Eleven Goncools confessed, and their lives were spared. One man's confession vindicated Andromin, saying he'd only been a pawn used by the Goncools to get to the queen, and he had had no knowledge of what he was doing. The noose around Andromin's neck was loosened, and Andromin was made a free man. But, the damage was done: Andromin's image was forever tarnished. This whole incident became known as the "Goncool Affair."

Caprius closed the door to his suite lightly behind him and headed toward the entertainment lounge. Going to the meeting meant he was about to play a game with the Goncools, but he had no idea what the result would be or who would be the winner.

In the entertainment lounge, Caprius was seated at his reserved table, now fully aware that the men who killed Peasley were watching him. He quietly watched the belly dancer sway to the music. Much time passed, and he began to wonder whether these men would actually approach him. Caprius finally decided, Goncools or not, he was hungry. He signaled the waiter and ordered; then, he saw the drinks menu. "And, a glass of your finest bourbon would be nice," said Caprius.

"What room should I charge it to, Sir?" asked the waiter.

"To 2111," said Caprius. The waiter left. More time ticked away, and Caprius began to feel that waiting for these assassins was like waiting for a cold meal to warm itself. The belly dancer made her way around the front tables and now approached Caprius. She shook and wiggled her voluptuous body, and Caprius allowed himself to be mesmerized by her beauty. His eyes traveled over her body, finally arriving to her face. It was the woman from his bathtub. She rolled her hips around, and he noticed a small slip of paper was tucked into the waistband of her beaded skirt. He reached forward and took the paper. She glided toward other tables as he opened the note. "Leave before it's too late. Leave now." Caprius tore the note up into little pieces and placed it in the ashtray. He took up the complimentary cigar on the table, put it to his nose, and breathed in the heady tobacco smell. He struck a match and lit it, puffing until it had a nice glow at the end. He wondered whether these men would ever make their move.

In a moment, there was a scuffle at the end of the dining room by the kitchen. Caprius' waiter tumbled from a closet and collapsed onto the floor dead. Some commotion ensued, but the entertainment continued. Caprius didn't leave. Clearly, this was another note, meant just for him. When his meal arrived, Caprius looked up at the new waiter.

"Your meal, Sir," he said gruffly. "What's the room number?" Caprius wrinkled his nose at the foul, musky scent of the man's aftershave.

"Room 2111," said Caprius.

"Enjoy your meal, Sir," said the waiter.

Caprius realized this waiter was one of the men who'd previously been sitting at the far end of the table—certainly one of the assassins. Caprius pretended to eat the meal, regretfully letting none of the food pass his lips in case it had been poisoned, while he kept an eye on the remaining men. As they stood to leave, Caprius signaled his new waiter.

"Is everything fine, Sir?" the waiter asked looking around.

"Could you bring me a bottle of bourbon? And, don't open it."

"You want a whole bottle of bourbon, Sir?" the waiter seemed puzzled.

"Yes, an unopened bottle," Caprius said.

The waiter returned momentarily. Caprius chuckled to himself at the good service. "Your bottle of bourbon," said the waiter. "Sir, you hardly touched your meal."

"I'm afraid this meal won't do. It stinks. Like your aftershave," said Caprius.

The man sneered at Caprius, and Caprius, tired of the games, got up and met the man's eyes. He said nothing but swept up his bourbon by the neck of the bottle and walked calmly from the entertainment lounge.

The waiter watched Caprius disappear through the doors. He went into the back and took off the stolen uniform.

When Caprius approached his suite, a cold vibration was coming from his claymore of power. He took another puff from his cigar and shook the bottle of bourbon thoroughly. He opened the door and entered his suite. There, seated on chairs, were the four men from the entertainment lounge. Caprius' hand instantly went to his sword, but before he could grasp the hilt, a man standing behind the door hit Caprius over the head. Caprius fell to the floor, dazed and bleeding. The man took Caprius' claymore from its sheath. Caprius struggled to regain his focus and stand. Behind him, the door to the suite opened, and another man came in. Caprius' vision was fuzzy, but he could smell that it was his second waiter. That made it six men against Caprius, and he didn't have his sword of power. The fake waiter bent down to Caprius and drove his fist into his stomach. "Incidentally, I happen to like this aftershave."

The waiter spied Caprius' bottle of bourbon and grabbed it before joining the others. "You won't be needing this anymore," the waiter laughed and grasped the bottle to his chest.

The man who had hit Caprius from behind came around to join his cronies. Caprius saw his face. "Lavender Frikiseed. Are you behind all this? What does a Koriston Taughtenslotte want with the Goncools?"

"When I get out of this, I'm going to apprehend you, bring you back to Elysium, and make sure you see a cell of Zaderack prison." The Goncools began to laugh.

"Immortality, my dear Caprius, immortality," said Lavender.

Caprius peered into their eyes. Then, his gaze fell to their tattooed wrists. "The Goncools have new followers, I see," said Caprius.

"Yes, but soon they'll be joining us," said Lavender.

"They are in prison, and there they'll stay," said Caprius. "And, you intend to continue where they left off? If so, you know that their fate will soon be yours. And, God will condemn you for what you do."

"My fate is to serve Makoor. And, your belief in your religion is what makes you weak," said Lavender. "Your God is a very poor advisor. Do you think such prayers and worship will protect you from what you are about to face?" He smiled. "But, I am a kind man. I will give you your moment of prayer." He leaned in to where Caprius could smell the man's fetid breath. "In the end, you will see that the dark powers are the only real religion. But, please, go ahead, have your senseless prayer, Caprius."

Caprius hadn't waited until he was told; he'd been silently in prayer since his arrival, knowing he'd need all his resources to get out of this. "I gather you're responsible for Brandon Peasley's death," said Caprius.

"I know nothing of what you speak; I only requested he write to you, and I took the liberty of sending the letter on his behalf," smiled Lavender.

"What do you want with me?" asked Caprius.

"All we need is your claymore of power. Beyond that, how we get rid of you is entirely up to me," said Lavender.

"My claymore is of no use to you. It only works for me," said Caprius.

Lavender took the claymore and balanced it on his open palm. "This sword of power is what we need to bring the Prince of Darkness to life again," he said. His eyes misted over in reverie.

"You think you can harness the sword's power and bring Titanis Clore back from the dead? It will never work. The power comes from Petoshine. And, the vim cannot be forced to work against it," said Caprius.

"Well, Caprius, I'm not going to tell you how it will be done. But, I assure you it will work," said Lavender. "Nick! Malory!" Two large men approached Caprius and grabbed his arms. "Pray to your God now, foolish mortal."

"You do realize that killing me won't stop the rest of the Seatons," said Caprius.

Lavender gave the sword to one of his men. "Take the claymore of power down to the stables. We will meet you there as soon as we take care of Mr. Seaton." The man took the claymore and left the suite.

"Mind if I open the bottle of bourbon for a final drink?" asked Caprius.

"Not a chance," said Lavender.

"At least let a condemned man finish his smoke?" asked Caprius, holding up his cigar. Lavender nodded to the men. They let go of Caprius. He put the cigar in his mouth and puffed on it slowly. "Say, this may take a while. Why don't you gentlemen pour yourselves a drink. The bottle's on me."

Lavender looked skeptically at Caprius but nodded to the man who had posed as the waiter. "Go ahead, Ronen."

Caprius chuckled. "You're good at waiting on people. The drink is on you, Ronen," said Caprius puffing his cigar. Ronen pulled on the cork, but it didn't budge. He pulled harder, and he stumbled backward, bourbon splashing all over his face and torso. Caprius took a last hard puff of his cigar before throwing it at Ronen. Ronen burst into flames. He screamed and ran about the room, crashing into paintings and knocking them off the walls.

While the horrified men were stunned, watching their comrade, Caprius punched the man closest to him, which allowed him to grab the dagger on the inside of his boot. He took a running start and crashed through the large window across the living room, landing on the awning. It bounced gently, and two men leaned out through the shards, preparing to go after Caprius. He punched his fist through the fabric, and it tore in half. He grabbed the two sides and leaped like a parachute glider down the mountain's side.

Up above, Ronen, still aflame and running in circles, fell out the window and smashed into the rock face. His body fell heavily to the gorge beneath.

Caprius had his eye on the man running to the stables with his claymore. The man turned, saw Caprius approaching from above, and ran faster. He entered the stable and went to his horse. It was tethered firmly to a post. He struggled with the knot, clearly aware he didn't have much time.

He made it out, mounted, and began galloping down the mountain through the forest. Caprius landed quietly, got his stallion, and went into a chase. Bombidus Barons, who got on his horse, had fled. The snow was thick, sodden tree branches slapping at their faces. The canopy was dense, blocking out the sun and shrouding them in semi-darkness.

They followed the main path until, suddenly, the man veered left and careened down a hill. Caprius followed and soon was within a horse's length of him. Caprius spurred his horse on to go faster, then caught up to the man's horse's hindquarters. He reached out at full gallop and grasped his claymore sticking out of its sheath at the back of the saddle. The man reached back and grabbed Caprius' hand. They struggled, the horses jostling into one another on the thin path.

Suddenly, the man's horse lost its balance on a patch of black ice and fell, bringing Caprius and his horse down on top of it. Caprius was launched down the hill and slid on more ice, catching stones and brush in his face as he went. The man was close behind, grunting and howling when he hit the stones.

At the bottom, they landed in a fast-moving river dotted with ice. The men were carried by the current quite a ways until Caprius caught a hanging branch and hefted himself up and out of the water. The man, just meters behind Caprius, caught hold, as well, of an adjoining branch and Caprius' leg. He was a burly brute, close to three hundred pounds and too much for the one tree. It snapped, sending the men back into the water with a great splash, the two of them still clinging to the thick branches. Caprius used his as a raft, and the man followed suit. When the water moved the man close enough to Caprius, he struggled to reach the claymore. Caprius punched him in the jaw, sending him reeling, but he recovered and lunged at Caprius. They tousled on the single branch, too thin to hold them in the churning water. The rapids had increased in intensity, white water cresting and peaking around their bodies as they fought.

They stopped at the sudden sound of violent, rushing water. At the end of the river was a waterfall. The man panicked and clung to Caprius. Caprius used his last reserve of strength to kick the man in the face and send him into a cluster of boulders just off to the side by the waterfall. Caprius clung to his branch with one hand and his rescued claymore with the other.

He neared the falls and thought he should pray again, but he realized it wasn't prayer he needed. Caprius stuck out his arm and unleashed a lasso rope, which wrapped itself around a tree. Caprius pulled away from the falls. The man following him was not so fortunate; he plunged, screaming, over the falls and crashed onto the rocks below.

When Caprius met the shore, he grabbed hold of another set of branches and climbed up onto the snowy riverbank. The foliage was thick, and the snow had an icy crust over it. He shivered but was relieved to be on dry land. He made his way back up the hill, sheathing his claymore of power.

***

Caprius walked a very long time, stopping only to eat some snow to quench his thirst. After some time, he came to a clearing. There in the center of it was a squat, spry fellow with white hair and twinkling eyes, tinkering with a deflated hot air balloon.

Caprius approached him. "Mechanical problems?" he asked affably.

The man turned and looked at Caprius. He didn't seem surprised to see another person in this wilderness. "Hello," said the man pleasantly before returning to the balloon with his wrench.

"That's quite a contraption you have there," said Caprius.

"Yes, if only I can fix this throttle..." murmured the man as he sweated over his work.

"My name is Caprius Seaton. And, who might you be?"

"The name's Nero," said the man.

"Nero what?" asked Caprius.

"Just Nero. That is what I like to be called," he said. Suddenly, a blast of fire erupted from the base of the balloon as helium began to blow. "Ah, there we go. All set to fly."

"Can you really fly this thing?" asked Caprius.

"Yes. I'm off on another adventure," said Nero, tightening the ropes.

Caprius scratched his head. "I say, Nero, how would you like to take me to Elysium? If you get me to his majesty safely, there's a reward in it for you."

"Ah, yes," said Nero thoughtfully. "I thought your name sounded rather familiar."

"What do you think?" Caprius asked again. "You would be doing his majesty a great service."

"Well…" Nero began, "I had been planning on heading in a different direction. But…" he scratched his chin, "yes, alright. Hop in," he said and opened the gate for Caprius to enter the basket.

"Thank you, Nero," said Caprius. He grinned. "When we get to Elysium, it would be my pleasure to host a luncheon in your honor."

"That's splendid!" Nero said smiling brightly. "I've never been among royalty before." A minute later, with both men safely inside, the basket began to rise gently into the air. As they took flight and soared over the great white forest into the vast blue sky, the two men warmed their hands and spirits on some hot mead Nero produced from a large flask, sat back among pillows and blankets, and chatted like old friends.

"Off we go, Nero," said Caprius. The hot air balloon rose from the ground.

Chapter 5

Escape from Zaderack

DEEP IN THE WATERS OF Lorgania sits the island of Moldern. Upon this island is the prison of Zaderack, the prison where Alamptria's most notorious criminals were living out their sentences. The nine Goncools imprisoned by King Confidus and Queen Amenova of Koriston languished as they served out their two life sentences. Even if they were to survive imprisonment enough to see their eventual release, it would be when they were too old to enjoy the taste of freedom.

As they lay in their cells, they thought about the events that had brought them there and ruined their lives. Their thoughts were focused on revenge, specifically aimed at the Seatons and Queen Amenova. They wondered about the dark angel who had promised them freedom and vengeance.

One winter's day, one of the Goncools, named Gabriel, who had been vigilantly marking the days on the wall since their incarceration, slashed in the 1825th day of their arduous, grim confinement. He trailed his fingers over the marks, wondering why this particular number sounded familiar. When it hit him, he broke into a cold sweat. This was the night the dark angel had said he would set them free. "This is it." Gabriel bounced around his tiny cell with a devious grin on his face. "The dark salvation to Makoor's word of truth begins TONIGHT!" he babbled. He turned to his Goncool cellmate. "Tonight we shall be set free, Bendrum."

"How do you know this?" asked Bendrum from his cot.

"Did you forget, you idiot? Lavender Frikiseed promised that on this night he would come for us. I tell you, tonight is the night!" said Gabriel.

Just then, the lights for the cellblock snapped off. Within a few minutes, snoring reverberated off the cold stone prison walls, but Gabriel's and Brigadier's eyes were wide open with excitement. Was this really the night of their salvation or just a false promise? Minutes turned to hours. Judging from the position of the moon, they knew the midnight hour was approaching.

Indeed, their benefactor was not going to disappoint them. Outside the prison, beyond the island of Moldern, on the rocky seas, a small ship was slowly approaching. Standing portside was Lavender, who kept his steely vision on the prison as they neared. Beside him was the vampire Smogolous and the tall, gruesome creature known as Carcass Doom, the vampire Makoor's henchman, who loomed over the others with his tall, reedy frame and scaly skin. Once they came up onto the sand bar just outside the island, Smogolous lifted off and flew into the night. The sound of his wings flapped against the hush of the surf until he disappeared through one of the darkened prison windows—one where a Goncool lay.

In the dark, with midnight approaching, Brigadier began to have his doubts. "He's not coming. That's all just a story they fed us," he groused. But, Gabriel remained optimistic and was too filled with anticipation to sleep. All around, the night was exceedingly quiet, more quiet than usual.

At the stroke of midnight, in their adjoining cell, came the gnashing sound of metal bars bending and stone crumbling. Brigadier and Gabriel looked at each other in the dark, their eyes terrified and excited. The sound stopped abruptly. Then, it came again. And, stopped. And, again. Then the bars of their windows began to bend. A large menacing hand was bending the bars. Once all four bars were bent apart, Smogolous emerged and extended his arm into the room. He slowly pointed at Gabriel and gestured that he should come forth.

"The Dark Lord," croaked Gabriel. "He has sent for us." Gabriel walked over to him as if in a trance. The vampire grabbed him and put him on his back. Gabriel hung on as the creature scaled the wall back down. Brigadier stood on his tiptoes trying to see out into the night, but he could see nothing. He began to wonder whether he'd imagined the whole thing until moments later, the creature returned. It placed Brigadier on its back and scaled the wall down to the sand outside the prison. No alarm had sounded, no lights had gone on. The night was black as ink.

The creature dropped Brigadier on the sand. Smogolous went back to get the others. Only one person could have remained to tell of what had happened, but he was not a Goncool, and the creature snapped his neck, leaving him dead on the floor. The creature and the Goncools quietly walked over the wet sand down the slope to the docked ship. Once the men were aboard, the ship set sail toward the city of Elysium on the island of Alamptria.

It wasn't until the next morning that the prison guards discovered the Goncools had escaped and a man was dead from inexplicable wounds in a prison cell.

***

Andromin walked the forest of Tithenro. His vision led him to this point of the forest. The forest was old and eerie with a sense of death. As he walked slowly, stepping on small branches, he heard the sound of wolves yelping. There was now a low bared fog he came across. As he walked through the mist, he saw a corpse rise onto its knees, holding out its hand as if it were seeking help. The corpse wore black clothing, which was torn and floating in the air. Andromin ignored it and kept walking. As he walked past it, the corpse lay back down upon the misty ground. But, as Andromin turned away, another corpse rose from the fog, it too extending its arm out seeking help. Again, Andromin ignored it, turning away, and the corpse lay back down in the fog. As Andromin continued to walk, there was another and another corpse that rose with their arms extended out in friendship. He passed them by ignoring them. It was then that five corpses at once stood to their knees. Again, they extended their arms out. Moments later, they disappeared in the fog. "What is this place? Where am I?" Andromin spoke. He continued to walk. Now, he stood before a small white tree. It had colorful red leaves, which swayed in the gentle breeze. Andromin felt drawn to it. As he stood ten feet away from it, he heard a soft voice.

"What is it you seek?" asked the voice. The voice was that of Calista.

"Calista, my love, I seek to find out who I am—the purpose of my life," said Andromin.

"Come closer, Andromin Seaton," said the voice. Andromin stepped closer. "I am the path to immortality. I know all. I am here to give you the chance to find the way to the truth."

"What truth?" Andromin asked.

"The reason why you were born."

"And, what reason my that be?"

"You are here for a purpose." Suddenly, ten corpses rose from the fog to their knees. Each holding out their hands at Andromin. "Death awaits you. And, with your death, you will be born into a life of service to the great Makoor. Upon your death, these ten Trothcorpse will live once more to serve you in your needs. You will help in our conquest in Alamptria. With your honor and devotion to Makoor, you will be seated on the thrown of mount Drone."

"What must I do?" asked Andromin.

The tree said not a word. In an instant, the red leaves from the tree sprung to life, flew from the branches, and latched onto Andromin. The leaves absorbed Andromin's body as if they were eating him. Andromin screamed contorted.

Fetrona awoke to her husband's screams. He was sitting up in bed, obviously asleep, with his eyes open wide and his breathing jagged.

"Andromin, what is wrong?" She rubbed his back until he slowly came out of his dream. He slowly lay back down onto his pillow breathing heavily.

"Bad dream," he said.

"Andromin, you were talking in your sleep. You referred to Calista as your love," said Fetrona.

"Oh, I didn't mean…" Andromin began.

"Andromin, I think we need some time away from each other so you can get straight in your head who you're married to. It's either me or Calista. I don't like you spending your time with her. And, I don't want her around you. I think you need to take a vacation to give you some time alone to think."

"I've had this dream before," said Andromin.

The castle was silent. Outside, there was no wind or rain or howling of wolves. All seemed at peace. The candlelight on the table beside him put out a soft glow. He turned to watch the candle's flame flicker. Andromin closed his eyes exhausted. He sat up in bed and faced the flame. He hesitated for a moment, then blew it out. Darkness filled the room. He closed his eyes, and soon, he fell asleep.

***

The next morning in Castle Elysium, Confidus stood in a room inside the great hall looking down at a crate that had just arrived by the post carriage. Two of his men pried it open to reveal another crate, casket-shaped, inside. Some dirt was escaping from cracks in the seams, and when it was opened, they were not surprised to see much dirt and a man dead. Confidus frowned. A week prior, another similar crate had been delivered.

Confidus edged closer to see the man's face. He felt anger in his throat. "Just as I expected. Another of our agents killed and delivered to us," he said.

"We cannot afford any more mistakes. Send no agents to investigate this. The Seaton brothers must be called upon instead," said Vijas, dusting himself off.

"Yes, there is something far more sinister going on here," said Confidus. He bent down and lightly touched the man's hand. Inside his clenched fist was a pocket watch on a chain. Confidus took the watch and opened it. "Just like the other one. The time stands still at precisely 8:10 p.m." He put the watch in his pocket.

"This has the makings of a serial killer, and our agents are targeted."

"Whoever is doing this is sending us these bodies as a warning to back off," said Vijas.

"Four days ago, I received a note from Thomas Humphries saying he was making progress. Then, he winds up dead. Just like Simmons. Humphries' last stop was in a hotel, where he was to meet with a woman. An artist, if I'm not mistaken."

"How could a woman be responsible for any of this? Such a sinister plot can only be orchestrated by a man and a devious one at that," said Vijas. "A female artist can only-"

"I know about this artist. She is not directly involved in this transport of bodies. But, she does play a part," said Confidus.

"The powers of Petoshine must rise again," said Vijas.

"Yes, the claymore of power is needed." He paused. "I don't want to do this, but I will have to send my son Caprius to investigate. And, he will not be going alone."

"Whom shall you send with him? Andromin is on holiday and Dragus," Vijas laughed a tight little laugh. "Well, he's not up to the task. Remember how he let himself get bitten by the undead," he said scornfully.

Confidus glared at Vijas. "You know as well as I do that my son Dragus performed valiantly in that battle, and anyone in his position could have been compromised." Confidus sighed. "However, the fact is he is not as strong a warrior as Caprius. The other person I have in mind will be an excellent partner for Caprius, and I know she will take good care of him."

"She?" asked Vijas, sneering.

"Yes, she. This she saved my life." Confidus looked down at his dead agent. "I will inform Thomas' wife of what has happened. It will not be easy." Confidus laid his hand on Thomas' forehead. "That poor woman. Thomas had a very young daughter. And, now she is fatherless. Much like Melina was when she came into my life, so young and fragile. It will be very difficult. I've known Thomas for sixteen years. I remember when his little girl was born. He was so happy. He ran to tell me like a boy running home from school." He sighed. "How did it come to this?" Confidus closed the lid of the coffin. "I will make the proper funeral arrangements." He looked at the two men. "Seal it shut."

Chapter 6

Win, Lose, or Die

GRIMY SNOW COVERED THE DISMAL land of Plaphorius. The gloom of the falling night blanketed the lost souls lurking in the dim light. The vampires, however, rejoiced at the dark, and as it crept in, their spirits rose.

At a dim pub riddled with mice and spider webs, the vampires were having a marvelous time. At one round table, six vampires were so immersed in their poker game, they didn't even worry over finding fresh blood to feast upon. Yet, there was one worry they all shared, which was the arrival of Carcass Doom, chief henchman to the dark lord Makoor. Accompanying him would be his right-hand man, Cambrozes Genesis, a man greatly feared among the undead for his power and strength.

The six Goncools at the table knew one of them was going to be disintegrated. They had to answer for their bungled attempt to steal Caprius' claymore of power. It had been so decreed by Makoor himself that Carcass should take whatever action he felt was appropriate against the Goncool responsible. The men threw down their cards, dealt fresh hands, and anted up high and higher amounts, each feeling superior to the others, believing he couldn't possibly be the one held responsible.

"Alright, gentlemen, show me your cards," said Lavender, fanning out his four aces and a queen on the table before him. The others groaned as they threw down their cards. "So, you see gentlemen, why it would be pointless for you to play another game," he smirked. "Unless you like handing over your money."

One of the Goncools stood up, his face red with rage. "I think you cheated! You've been playing us," he said waving a finger in Lavender's face.

"My friend, I don't have to cheat. I'm simply talented, unlike yourself," scoffed Lavender. He scooped all the chips over to himself and began separating them according to their worth. "Surely, there are far worse things in life than losing a poker game?"

The one Goncool who had folded early spoke, his voice shaking. "You may gamble as you wish, but to lose your life, that would be a greater tragedy," he said, eying everyone at the table. "Who's it going to be?"

"Not I," said another of the Goncools, a large, burly fellow with a great head of dark curls. "I was not among the four of you when you failed to deliver the claymore of power," he said.

"Neither was I!" said another Goncool raising his thin, frail voice.

Lavender sat back and crossed his arms. "A-ha, and that gives Carcass Doom even more reason to select one of you fools as the ultimate loser in this game. If you're a minor player, you're of no consequence. Those of no consequence," he paused to dramatically pick at his teeth with a long fingernail, "are not needed. By anyone. And, certainly not the Dark Lord."

"Lavender, you're drunk as a sow. You know what they say, 'The bigger they are, the harder the fall,'" said the burly Goncool.

Lavender grinned and shrugged. "Speaking of which," he said, "I see my glass has become empty." He snapped his fingers at a passing waiter. "The drinks are on me, boys. May I say it was a privilege. And, since for one of you it will be the last time you set your eyes upon this life, I say you drink up!" The waiter arrived. "My good lad, bring us a round of young blood, well aged. And, doubles for these two."

"Yes, Lavender," said the waiter. Lavender smiled and rubbed his hands together. "I'm feeling very lucky. The moon bleeds red on this night." Then, he edged closer to the two and said in a whisper, "but it isn't *my* blood that will be spilt." He leaned back in his chair and laughed heartily. Moments later, the waiter came by with a tray of goblets containing aged blood. "To your health!" said Lavender. "And, may I make a toast to the chosen one. May he rest in peace," he grinned.

They clinked glasses and downed their blood, each one eyeing the others over the rim of his drink, except for Lavender, who seemed more than sure of whom the victim would be. Outside in the dark, a foul wind rattled the shutters. "Oh, good. Carcass Doom is making his approach," said Lavender. "Might I make a suggestion to the two of you?" he raised an eyebrow. "The more you prostrate yourselves and beg for mercy, the better your chances of survival." He took a sip of his drink.

Suddenly, the front door blew open, bringing in gusts of snow and icy wind. From inside the blizzard's gateway, the dark phantom's shape became clear. He entered the pub spinning like a cyclone in a fog of darkness. Chairs skidded across the floor; poker chips flew off tables; playing cards were tossed into the air. The spinning cyclone of dark fog moved toward the Goncools. The wind was so fierce, it pushed the flesh back from the bones of the patrons' faces. Everyone's eyes were plastered open. Men grabbed at their eyes, trying to protect them from the flying debris.

From inside the cyclone of wind and the fog surrounding them like a cocoon, there appeared the great Carcass Doom. He brought his hand up, and instantly, all was still. His height was formidable, his head nearly grazing the wooden ceiling. His clothing was black, an aged tuxedo and tails shredded from time and use. When the dust settled at the table, the Goncools got a close look at Carcass' face: skin like tree bark had become embedded in his flesh. His eyes were a liquid yellow, his lips cracked and black, moldy at the corners from rot. When he spoke, they saw his teeth: decayed stumps, the same dark yellow as his eyes. "Playing cards and drinking on this blood moon night. Can one of you feel the chill of your doom?" he said, his voice hard and cracked like aged ice.

One of the two Goncools who feared Carcass most stood, his legs quaking beneath him. "It is he who orchestrated the plan at Quantum Heights!" he said pointing at Lavender. "I was not among them. I was not a part of that ordeal. Have mercy on me, Great One."

"Mercy, you say?" Carcass said, pretending to be bewildered. "This is no time to be merciful, for I must acquire a soul for the Dark Lord."

"I had nothing to do with it either, Doom," the other Goncool stood to defend himself.

"Impudent fool. Do not call me Doom. I am Carcass Doom," he said, pointing to himself.

"Forgive me, Your Greatness. But, as I said, we were not at Quantum Heights. We were both here in Plaphorius the whole time. We did nothing."

Carcass Doom showed his teeth. "Nothing you say? You did not contribute to the conquest of Alamptria?"

"Well, I mean…" The vampire drank calmly from his glass while the man floundered. "I didn't mean it that way."

"Your Greatness, the two of them are right. They had nothing to do with it," said Lavender. "I solemnly swear on their lives."

"Enough said!" Carcass yelled bringing down his fist, breaking the table in two. The table crashed to the floor, spilling the glasses of blood and toppling the men who had been leaning on it.

One of the two Goncools who had managed to hold on to his glass before it fell to the floor held it out to Carcass. "Th-thirsty? Are you thirsty?" he asked Carcass. The hand that held the goblet was shaking so hard, blood was sloshing out the top.

Carcass grabbed it and drank the whole goblet down. He wiped his sour mouth with the back of a scabbed hand. "The Dark Lord thirsts, too, and he has made his request. I think we have found our winner." Carcass reached out and snatched the nervous Goncool from where he stood beside the phantom. "You see, the Dark Lord and I share something in common." He leaned in, and the Goncool, terrified, leaned back. "We both don't like squabbling and simpering begging for mercy. You did not contribute to the conquest of Alamptria. You will pay for your lack of contribution." He tightened his grip on the man's throat and, with his vampiric powers, transformed him into a statue of hardened dust. Carcass set the statue down and blew on it. It crumbled like dust. Carcass laughed a deep booming laugh that penetrated the soul of every person in the room.

Still seated, Lavender leaned back in his chair. He rolled his eyes and puckered his lips. "Tut tut tut," he clucked.

Carcass turned to him and pointed a rotten tree-root finger at his chest. "Make no mistake. We will get that claymore." Without another word, Carcass Doom stepped back, and twirling around like a spinning cyclone of dark fog, he crashed through the front doors and swirled out of the pub.

Once Carcass was safely out of earshot, Lavender leaned in to the dust now scattered over the floor. "You really should never beg," he said to the petrified Goncool. "Very unbecoming."

Chapter 7

Menate' el Demore'

OUT AT QUIGLEY'S PUB, at the border of Elysium and the bay of Begonia, Caprius sat at a table with his brother Dragus and their new friend, Nero Fergus, the high-flying adventurer. The place was full of lively chatter and good cheer, and Dragus and Nero cracked jokes and whistled at the woman on stage singing her heart out. This wasn't the kind of pub women frequented, and the men were thrilled to see her soft round body and flashing blue eyes.

Caprius, however, was in a sour state. He was terribly worried about Melina. He wondered if her memory would return. His disappointment was eating at his heart. He kept his head down and scratched at the surface of the wooden table with the tip of his sword's blade.

"Don't worry, Caprius," said Dragus. "Melina's memory will return in time." Caprius kept his head down.

Nero felt the dynamic between the brothers and was somewhat annoyed. This was hardly the grateful welcome Caprius had promised him.

"You want another ale, Nero?" asked Dragus.

"Two is my limit. I'll be flying off soon and need to have my wits about me," said Nero.

Dragus looked disappointed. "I thought you wouldn't be leaving until tomorrow morning," he said.

"I am. But, I need a clean system before I go," Nero remarked. "At that altitude, you want to stay focused. I had once a near-death experience that scared the living daylights out of me. I vowed never to drink so much before flying again."

Dragus looked over at Caprius, wishing his brother would snap out of his gloom. At that moment, Calista walked in and made her way toward the Seatons' table. "Good afternoon, gentlemen," Calista smiled and pulled up a chair. A barmaid came over. "One ale, please. I'll take it with some nuts on the side."

"The nuts are already there on the side, honey," said the barmaid, pointing at Dragus' elbow.

"Dragus, you're hiding them. Here, let me take that bowl off your hands," said Calista. She pulled the nuts toward her. She was still smiling as she glanced around the table, since grown somber. "What, am I not welcome here?" she asked. "And, what's with Caprius chewing up the table?"

No one said anything. Caprius' eyes were red. She didn't want to pry, so she smiled, looked over at Nero, and held out her hand. "Who's your friend here?"

"The names Nero Fergus, ma'am," said Nero. "A pleasure to meet you."

"I haven't seen you here before. Are you from out of town?" asked Calista.

"I'm originally from Alminite. But, I get around," he said.

"Nero brought Caprius all the way from Quantum Heights in a hot air balloon," said Dragus.

Calista hooted. "I've heard of those crazy contraptions! They seem to be the hottest thing these days," she said. "I wouldn't mind having a ride in one of those... but only so long as you fly it ten feet off the ground."

"Ha ha!" Nero laughed. "It may seem a little scary at first. But, you get used to it. I remember the first time I flew one. My heart was racing! But, after about the fifth time, it was like second nature. It's like when a baby first tries to walk. It seems a little challenging, but eventually you overcome your fear."

"I don't know. Being two thousand feet off the ground can be pretty scary," said Calista.

"Two thousand? It isn't that high. I would say I go about six," said Nero.

"That's awfully high," she said grinning. She stole a glance at Caprius and then Dragus. "Listen, I can't take it anymore. What's going on? Maybe you just need a woman's touch."

Dragus shrugged. "When he isn't up for talking, I guess neither am I. After all, we're twins," he said.

Calista looked at Caprius. Dragus finally said, "Melina has lost her memory. She remembers no one."

"I'm so sorry Caprius," said Calista.

"I feel like I'm losing her," he said.

"You know, carving up that table isn't going to bring Melina back. And, what will the pub owner have to say about it," she said gently.

"I'll buy him a new table," replied Caprius.

"And, will you carve up that one, too?" she asked.

"I got money. I'll buy another," he said.

Calista got off her seat thinking Caprius should be left alone. She stood and lifted her chair, as if to bring it down onto Caprius' head, when she heard from behind, "Not so fast, Calista!" King Confidus, who had just entered the pub, said quietly. "Have a seat." Confidus waited until Calista returned the chair to the floor, then he put his hand on her back to guide her into it. He pulled up a chair himself. "Caprius, I need you on a mission. I need you on the train tomorrow. And, Calista, I want you on this mission, as well."

"What? You want me to go with him?" Calista was not pleased. Grief-stricken or not, Caprius had just been extremely hurtful to her days ago. The barmaid came by and tried to ask Confidus if he would like an ale, but before she could speak, Confidus waved her away. "I need you on this mission," said Confidus, his gaze never wavering from Calista's face.

"Why can't you send someone else with him?"

"Because I think you are best suited for this job. You would fit right in," said Confidus.

"I don't want to do this one," said Calista.

"Calista, you are an agent now. Your loyalty is with the council of Elysium. And, I want you on this mission. Is that understood?" Calista's face remained skeptical. "Further," Confidus said, "it is urgent. And, to be frank, I need you and your skills desperately."

Calista felt her well-trained warrior's body respond to the call. "Okay," she said, crossing her arms. "I'll be there."

"Good! I will see you both at precisely 11:00 a.m. tomorrow morning at the Menate' el Demore'." Confidus stood and departed Quigley's pub.

The table was again silent. Calista stood. Her voice was flat, her face twisted in a grimace. "Nero, it was nice to have made your acquaintance. Hope to see you again. Good bye, Dragus." She turned and walked out.

Dragus looked at his brother's nearly untouched ale. "Are you going to drink that?" he asked.

Caprius shoved it at him. "Go ahead," he said. "I think I'll leave as well." Caprius threw down some money and stalked out.

"Well, Nero," said Dragus, "looks like it's just you and me." They clinked glasses and enjoyed the last of their ales. Unfortunately, they went down more bitterly than when they had started.

***

Caprius entered his bedroom. He walked over to the bed where Melina lay sleeping. A caregiver was looking after her. Melina awakened and looked around. When she gazed at Caprius, she was confused. "Who are you?" she asked. Caprius did not understand.

"She still doesn't remember. She has no recollection of who she is. She calls herself Clarisse. She doesn't remember me. Dragus and Setra were here earlier. She doesn't remember them either."

"What has happened?" asked Caprius. "What's wrong with my wife?" Melina stared at him confused. "I have a pink lady here for Melina. But, I see she is in no condition to drink. I will set it down here. I am hoping the drink helps jog some memories."

"I'm so sorry, Caprius," said the caregiver. "She thinks she is involved with a man named Titanis Clore. She talks of a woman, Lydia, and of her homeland Plaphorius.

Caprius ran his hand through his hair. "Titanis Clore is no man. He is a vampire. And, he has been destroyed. But, he has left his mark on her. Poisoned her mind."

"Give it time, Caprius. Her memory will return," said the caregiver.

"I have to go on a mission. I must leave her now. Take good care of her, Sandra."

***

Confidus boarded the train *Menate' el Demore'* and headed toward the last car in the back. *Menate' el Demore'* is a term meaning 'Light of Petoshine' in the language of elf. He opened the steel door. From the instant he opened it, opera music filled the area from a gramophone, which lay upon an elegant gold table in the left corner in the back. The door was solid and heavy. It closed with a clank. It was an elegant looking car: golden trimmings on red-painted walls. He walked toward the end, where he was met by Zafrodius Clemenzie, who served as the head of the treasury. Senator Vijas sat on a cushioned black chair in the corner quietly rubbing his chin. Clemenzie and King Seaton each took a seat at the council table and launched into the difficult discussion of how Caprius had mishandled the kingdom's affairs at Quantum Heights.

Calista entered silently and stood to the side while the men grew heated. She worried about her future mission with Caprius and felt despair; he had grown so unpredictable of late. Clemenzie was enumerating the damages to the suite, "… an expensive vase imported from China, smashed… paintings on the wall," he riffled through the pages of bills, "seven paintings, to be exact, were knocked down, broken glasses, and a crystal bowl from Vienna, strewn everywhere. The floor was stained from liquor. The window was smashed to pieces," said Zafrodius, scowling at the pages over his glasses.

"A window was broken?" repeated Confidus.

"Yes, and an awning hanging above the lower-floor's window was torn clean through. And, the fire damage! We're lucky the whole hotel didn't catch."

"Hmmm," said Confidus scratching his chin.

Zafrodius threw down his pages. "Tell me, Sir, is your son deranged? The damage Caprius caused to the hotel is beyond excessive. The hotel manager calls the Seatons a 'force of destructive nature.' They're having a big celebration on February 2 to mark the anniversary of their first decade. Pinkles has made it clear that under no circumstances are there to be any surprises. This is the second time the hotel has gone through such extensive damage due to the Seatons. Confidus, as your financial council, I must advise you that we're laying out far too much in compensation. We need to focus on holding our assets, not throwing them away on broken windows." Zafrodius was leaning in toward the king, his voice loud and angry. The opera music continued to play loudly. "And, what's with the loud music!" Zafrodius raised his voice.

"Sir, you will watch your place. Your business is to put the money of this kingdom where I tell you to. And, I appreciate the fine culture of music." He paused. "We have much larger issues to worry over, and as you say, a broken window is hardly the most of it. Do you not recall the lives of our men, women, and children lost in the destruction of Elysium centuries ago? When we were victims of a city that crumbled before our very eyes? You know nothing of this. My son's efforts are to prevent such a thing from ever happening again." Confidus smiled curtly. "So, write the promissory notes and leave my chambers."

At that moment, Caprius arrived. When he saw Calista standing quietly off to the side, he averted his eyes.

"You're bloody late," said Zafrodius to Caprius. "Trying not to make it seem like you were with your girlfriend beforehand, were you?"

"I was detained," said Caprius, turning red.

"And," snapped Calista, "I don't take kindly to such insinuations. There is certainly nothing going on between me and Caprius," she said.

The whistle blew, the steam hissed, the engine roared to life, and soon the great train surged ahead . A fine white smoke puffed out into the clear sky from the steam engine.

"Enough, you have crossed one too many lines today, Zafrodius. I am now seeing that not promoting you to agent was a wise decision. You may go." Confidus' gaze was steely. "Enjoy your train ride."

Zafrodius bristled. "I need to discuss the sums for the damage with Caprius," he stammered.

"That is between me and my son, our agent," Confidus said coldly.

Zafrodius grabbed his papers and sauntered out. "Seems you get away with everything, Seaton," he murmured to Caprius before closing the door.

Caprius shrugged. "What was that all about?"

"It seems there is significant damage at the Hotel Quantum Heights. They're not pleased, Caprius," said Confidus, raising an eyebrow. "Your work couldn't have been done more quietly?"

"Father, as I said, the mission was compromised. Lavender Frikiseed was the one who forced Brandon Peasley to write the letter asking me to come to the hotel. It seems Alveron Goncool is in charge of this."

"Yes," said Confidus. He scratched his chin and looked at the floor. "Caprius, I have something to tell you." He paused. "Marcus, would you turn off the music? We are to begin with the board meeting." He motioned that Caprius should sit down at the table. Caprius plunked down, looking puzzled. Confidus sighed. "The Goncools have escaped from Zaderack prison."

"What?" Caprius said, bewildered. "But… that means all the Goncools are at large," he said.

"Yes, nine to be exact," said Confidus.

"And, then there was that one Goncool who had escaped in Koriston, never to be seen again," said Caprius, "which puts it at ten at large." He thought for a moment. "Do you think he is the one who orchestrated the escape?"' asked Caprius.

"Yes, I do. He fled, breaking free from the clutches of the Taughtenslotte army and hasn't been seen since. He must have known the other Goncools who confessed to the ordeal were sentenced to Zaderack prison. Vernon Goncool, who, as we know, is the most dangerous Goncool of all, is eager to continue where he left off. And, so the terror will begin all over again." Confidus' face grew long, deepening in shadows. "But, this time, not in Koriston. It will be in our beloved Elysium."

Calista began to tremble. She put her arms around herself and swallowed. "Do you think he is here now, watching us, waiting to strike?" she asked.

"Yes, I think they're all here. Planning their next move," said Confidus.

"We better put our men on extreme alert," said Caprius, standing.

"Warrants are already out for their arrest, and their pictures will be posted everywhere to keep people alerted," said Confidus.

"You do have to marvel at the timing of all of this," murmured Calista. "With the Seaton brothers gone, Elysium will be in great danger."

"Calista, you're quite right. I will double our efforts and mobilize a second battalion to search for them," said Confidus.

He turned and nodded to Vijas, who was scribbling on a parchment with a quill pen. "We will find them, your majesty," Vijas said.

"They will be easy to spot. They cannot hide," said Confidus.

"Koriston must be informed of what has happened," said Caprius.

Confidus nodded. "I have already sent a messenger with a letter to Queen Amenova."

Caprius scoffed. "Their mother must have been one busy woman."

Calista glared at him. "They're not all actually related," said Calista. "Five of them were outsiders who joined the Goncool brothers for the sake of immortality. They were obsessed with the dark cult."

"Father, this definitely means they could be in Elysium. And, remember Nigel Goncool's threat: if he ever escaped from prison, he would come after the Seatons. His eye is on you, me, and Andromin."

"I suppose that since I'm a member of the Seaton family, he'll be after me, too," said Calista trying to make a joke.

"He doesn't know you. You're in no danger," said Caprius, waving a dismissive hand in her direction.

Calista drew in a big breath. "There is something you must know. I was once involved with Nigel." She looked down and blushed. "Romantically. Then, when I found out that he was a Goncool, I fled. He never saw me again. But, I returned to Koriston to watch the nine Goncools hang. It brought me some comfort knowing that a part of him died that day when he watched his kin being killed. Later, when I heard that Nigel was sentenced to prison for two counts of life, I was very relieved to know that monster would die in prison." She paused. "See, he raped me. But, I left a mark on him. A scar. I defended myself with his dagger. But, he made it public that I'd stabbed him, and as a result, I became an outcast. So, I joined the Bramonian cult, and, of course, you all know how that turned out." She paused and smiled. "And, now I'm here in Elysium, hoping I could start over, live happily without ever having to worry about the Goncools or Platasus Cremiss and his men." Calista shrugged. Her face was clouded over as if she would cry. She thought about the secret she was keeping from them and how she ached to share it.

"What is it, Calista? Is there something else?"

Calista shook her head. "No, I have nothing more to say."

Caprius put his hand on Calista's shoulder. "She's been through enough. Let's use her story as further flame for the fire. We will capture these Goncools and send them back to prison... for good." Calista felt Caprius' firm hand on her shoulder, aware of its warmth and compassion and thought that despite his erratic behavior of late, he was a good man, one whom one day she might be able to confide in.

Confidus sat in his chair. "Please, be seated," he said to Calista and Caprius. "Senator Vijas, you may proceed with the briefing."

Senator Vijas had remained silent all throughout the conversation among Confidus, Caprius, and the secretary of treasury and didn't know the circumstances that had led Caprius to have such a tumult at the hotel. His job was to identify what had happened. He began to debrief Caprius. "Caprius, how was your mission compromised and for what reason?"

"Lavender Frikiseed was after my claymore. He said he would harness the sword's power to resurrect Titanis Clore. If he were to succeed, Titanis Clore would most certainly launch a full-scale attack on Elysium, leaving every last Elysian citizen a member of the undead. I had come there believing I was merely having a meeting with Brandon Peasley. The letter was definitely in his handwriting, but it turns out, he was forced to write it, and Frikiseed mailed it." Caprius stopped. "Doesn't matter, anyway. He did what they asked, and they still killed him. Brandon is dead."

"Or undead," said Calista.

"Yes, precisely," said Confidus.

"I don't understand how it is possible for the undead to harness the sword's power. From what I understand, only you, Caprius, and your brothers are capable of that," said Vijas.

"There is one other," said Senator Marcus, who was just letting himself into the chambers. "Maximus Seaton is a knight master himself and also possesses this power." He took a seat and poured a glass of water from the pitcher on the table. "Nobody has seen Maximus in years. Who knows, perhaps he has fallen to the dark side. If so, they could very well mean to use him to bring Titanis Clore back from the dead."

"But, Maximus has a claymore. Wouldn't the undead just use his?" asked Confidus.

Marcus shrugged. "Maybe it takes the power of two claymores to bring the Prince of Darkness back from the dead?" he asked.

"I don't buy that. The Seatons' powers grow stronger by the day. They are invincible. There's no way any Seaton can be forced to turn to the dark side of immortality," said Calista.

"So, then, how would Makoor bring Titanis Clore back without the use of the Seatons?" asked Marcus.

Confidus sat back in his chair. "We'll have to attend to that more fully later. For now, we need to move on to another unpleasant point of business." He opened up a file lying on the table before him. "Two days ago, a coffin filled with dirt was delivered to me here in Elysium. Buried in the dirt was the body of Thomas Humphries. This is the second agent to be killed and delivered to our doorstep in such a way in the last six days, and we still have two agents in the field whose whereabouts aren't known. We've lost contact," said Confidus grimly. "That is why I have chosen you, Caprius, to go on this most delicate mission."

"Lost contact?" said Caprius. "Is there no way to determine if they're still alive?"

Confidus shook his head. He felt helpless in uncharted territory. "One of our most experienced agents, Lylin Chiles was assigned to this case a week ago. He is missing, but there's no reason to presume he's dead. We received this note from him, which leads us to believe he has been making progress," said Confidus, handing his son the rumpled piece of paper.

"It says here that a Seaton should be assigned to the case." Caprius looked up. "That in and of itself is suspicious. Might be a trap. Also," he looked back at the letter, "look here. The note ends oddly. He began to write the last sentence, but the tone shifts abruptly, and it ends by stating some sort of involvement of exportation of coffins. Chiles says very little about it, and it's not much to go on."

"We do have one lead," said Vijas. He pulled a small box out of his pocket. Inside was a pocket watch. "This watch was found with one of the bodies." He handed it over to Caprius who turned it over, examining it, before giving it to Calista.

"Did you read the engraving on the back?" said Calista. "It says… 'warning: death to those who follow.'"

"Clearly a warning to the council not to send any more agents or they, too, will wind up dead, delivered in a casket," said Vijas.

"If that is so, then it is only a matter of time before Lylin Chiles is murdered," said Calista.

"Yes, that is what we fear," said Confidus. "Tilly Croft has also gone missing. We haven't seen a body, so we simply don't know-"

"Father, I know Tilly Croft. She is a good agent," said Caprius. "We should have some faith."

"I know her, as well. We've had drinks together," said Calista, feeling nervous at the number of people who'd been involved already.

"We cannot afford any more mistakes." Confidus put his hands on the table and looked at his son and Calista. "And, that is why we have turned this assignment over to the Seatons. The powers of Petoshine are needed," he said.

Caprius scratched the back of his neck roughly. "I'm curious... did the bodies delivered to us have any puncture wounds?"

"No, which is why I do not believe this is the work of the undead. But, nonetheless, something sinister is afoot, no question. Their bodies were, in fact, stabbed by what look to be knives," said Vijas. "Or," he paused and rubbed his eyes, "more grimly, it could very well be that they fell from a great height onto tall spikes, and that's what killed them."

"I'm sorry, Senator, but I do believe the undead are behind this. One of their signatures is to bury bodies directly in dirt. May I ask what the dirt looked like?" asked Caprius.

Vijas thought a moment. "It was dark but... it had a bit of a red tinge to it," he said.

"Just as I suspected. That is the dirt found in the bowels of the castle in Plaphorius and Mount Drone. But," Caprius paused, "I do not think these deaths are related to what happened at Quantum Heights. This means we have two separate instances in which the undead are taking control."

"What I don't understand is why those bodies had no puncture wounds at the neck," Confidus said. "Their blood had clearly been drained but it seems not by vampires."

"As you said earlier, those agents were delivered here dead as a warning to us not to send any others. Their blood was drained to prevent their bodies from decaying so we could see them intact," said Calista.

"That makes good sense, Calista," said Confidus.

"But, why didn't they infect the bodies with the blood of Makoor and have them transform into the undead?" asked Vijas. "That's the curious part."

"They must have felt it was more important to call us off than to bring over the bodies to their side," said Calista.

"Senator Marcus, why don't you inform us of what you found," said Confidus, gesturing to Marcus and leaning back in his chair.

"Thank you, Your Highness." Marcus cleared his throat. "We know that these two pocket watches were purchased in a store in Koriston. The proprietor is a well-respected businessman in the city, so to imagine him involved in this dark scheme is a bit farfetched. I believe he and his business are being targeted and used. We want you to find out who is behind all of this and learn what they are up to. Koriston was the last place of Chiles' whereabouts just prior to his disappearance. The two bodies delivered to us were sent from another city, but the driver of the carriage bringing them to us was from Koriston. However, that may also be a false lead as we believe the coffins were transported several times before making their way to Elysium."

"Do you have the driver's name?" asked Caprius.

"I'm afraid not," said Marcus. "All we have are these pocket watches and the name of the shop from where they were purchased. Also, a man by the name of Dallas Moore was who sent these caskets from Koriston. He is your contact. He will meet you at the hotel lounge."

"And, where were the watches purchased?" asked Calista.

"A place called Tillie's Fine Watches on River Street. Here is the address." Marcus handed the note to Caprius.

"This train is headed for Koriston" Confidus said to his son kindly.

"The two of you have your mission," said Vijas.

"Caprius, Calista, you have your assignment. Goodbye, and good luck to both of you," said Confidus.

"And, as we say in the language of elf - Menate' el Demore'," said senator Vijas. Menate' el Demore.' Everyone stood solemnly and shook hands. Then, Caprius and Calista left the boardroom in silence.

As Caprius and Calista sat down in the seats of a car, the last car where the boardroom was had unhooked mechanically from the rest of the train. The train car had come to a stop. Suddenly, from the room of the car, which stood tall, the roof had opened up, and a large hot air balloon had inflated open. After the balloon had grown to its full capacity, from the sides of the disengaged part of the car drew out two propellers. The propellers began to turn faster and faster. A hissing sound and steam from the bottom of the train car drove the car off the train track. It flew higher and higher into the air. Then, the propellers forced the car to move forward, and it flew back to castle Elysium.

Chapter 8

The Train Ride

THE TRAIN WAS BOUND FOR Koriston. Smoke continued to puff out into the clear sky from the steam engine.

Calista sat with her face to the window looking at the distant mountains and reminiscing about things past. She let herself get lost in her memories, not at all concerned with making Caprius comfortable or engaging him in small talk.

Caprius was aware that Calista's mood toward him was quite changed. It was a nine-car train, but there were very few passengers. A waiter came to them presently and said they'd have his undivided attention, given they were alone in their car. The waiter had a mechanical right arm filled with gears and wiring. "Would you care for a refreshment?" he asked. Calista finally turned away from the window, but she avoided Caprius' eyes. Caprius ordered wine and she a cup of tea with sugar. They faded to silence until the waiter returned with their drinks. Calista sipped her tea, but it was scalding hot and burned her lip. She made a small noise.

"Are you alright?" Caprius asked her. She ignored him.

"How is your wine," she finally asked flatly.

"Unfortunately, it's not to my liking." He pushed it to the corner of his tray, but his fingers hit the stem awkwardly and he knocked it over. He and Calista leaped up, and the waiter returned with towels.

"Would you like another?" he asked.

"Actually, would you happen to have the Chateau Rauzan Segla 1729?" asked Caprius.

"No, Sir, I'm afraid not," said the waiter.

"What about the 25?"

"Why, yes, we do. I will get that for you right away, Sir," said the waiter.

"Splendid," said Caprius. He seemed relieved.

"You sure know your wines," said Calista.

"I do enjoy good wine. It's a fun hobby," said Caprius. Now that they were speaking civilly, Caprius decided he needed to humble himself. "Calista, I must apologize for what I said to you days ago. I had no right to say those things. Naturally, you must miss your father very much."

"Thank you. Apology accepted," said Calista with a warm smile.

"How are you enjoying Elysium? Are you liking it here?" he asked.

It didn't take long for them to feel much more comfortable with the other and relax into their conversation. "Yes, I'm enjoying it very much. Your family welcomed me with open arms. You showed me support and your love. And, for that, I thank you. It is very nice here. And, I love the scenery; it's breathtaking. The gardens of Meadow-lie are my favorite place to find peace," she sighed. "I confess, the first few weeks I was in Elysium, I was rather uncomfortable. Living in a strange land, that is, and with people I didn't know."

"You're not a stranger among us, Calista. Our home is your home," said Caprius.

"Thank you, Caprius," she said.

At that moment, the waiter arrived with Caprius' wine. Holding the bottle with his mechanical hand, the waiter poured the wine. "Thank you, my good man," said Caprius.

"As I was saying, the first few weeks I had some difficulty. I had nightmares every night. My thoughts were with my father, but in my dreams, he was tormenting me."

Caprius remembered that time and felt sorry. "Yes, that first week, we heard your screams. We didn't know what was troubling you. And, we still don't know because you weren't able to talk about it. Not even Doctor Finklestein was able to help."

"Actually, he did help. He gave me some sedatives. With some sleep, I was able to feel much better."

"I only hope your problems don't resurface, for your sake."

Calista smiled brightly. "I put the past behind me. I am not bothered by my father's spirit anymore."

Caprius was somewhat puzzled. "I don't quite understand. You say you were tormented by your father, but you loved him and miss him. How does one want to be with someone yet push him away at the same time?"

Calista took a long sip of her tea, which had cooled. "Caprius, my father had a difficult past, one in which he acted in terrible ways. Yet, I still loved him dearly. When I was a little girl, he used to sing me lullabies and tell me bedtime stories. That is a cherished time in my life, when I felt so loved and cared for." She paused. "But, when I became a young woman, his love for me was overshadowed by a sickness, an immoral lust. One night, he had his way with me. The moment I turned sixteen, I ran away. My father had been long since dead, and my guardians cared for me, but I was so tormented by what my father had done, I kept wondering when my guardian would have his turn. There were nights when he'd come by my bedside only to kiss me good night, and I would scream. My nights were filled with terror. And, all he wanted to do was help me, love me. They were good, kind people."

Tears fell from Calista's eyes. "I often wish I'd had the strength to stay and heal. But, I was compelled to go. And, when I ran away, I became a wanderer of Alamptria."

Caprius was silent a moment. He'd had no idea the things she'd lived through. "I am so sorry," said Caprius. He put a hand on her knee to comfort her. She placed her warm hand atop it.

"Years went by, and I found myself living in the city of Koriston. That is when I met the Goncools. One Goncool grew fond of me, named Nigel. By this time, my fear of being with men had faded away, and Nigel became my friend. When, after a time, Nigel and I developed feelings for one another, we moved into an intimate relationship that was caring and made me feel safe. I realized I had found love."

"Why did you leave Nigel or, rather, when?" asked Caprius.

Calista took a deep breath. "Later, I came to understand that the Goncools were plotting against the queen of Koriston. Something about transforming humans into the undead and eternal life. I knew then I was fraternizing with the enemy. Nigel's younger brother Thornin was first in command and oversaw the operation. He was a man whom I had also adored, even developed some feelings for. But, my loyalty was to Nigel, and Thornin knew and respected that. After the Goncools planned to assassinate Queen Amenova, I panicked and went into hiding in Koriston. Nigel and Thornin searched for me, but I'd hidden well. Any time a Goncool went to a pub or an event, I made sure to remain inside. One night, at Gripers Green Dragon Pub, there was a close call; I caught a glimpse of Nigel from a distance. I knew he was looking for me. I saw the look on his face. He missed me. Thornin showed up and comforted his brother with a hand on his shoulder. My heart ached for them both.

"The next day, I learned about their failed attempt on the queen's life and how all the Goncools had been arrested, except for Nigel and Thornin, who must have managed to escape. A trail led the Taughtenslotte army to a house where they found a coffin and a creature resting inside. Disturbed, the creature tried to attack, but one of the Taughtenslottes was quick and destroyed the creature. Then, they burned the small house down. I was across the village and saw the smoke trailing into the sky." She paused.

"A few days later, I learned that the captured Goncools were set to be hanged. And, among them the prince of Elysium. That day, I stood in the crowd watching the hanging. As much as I knew Nigel deserved to be up on the platform with the other Goncools, I couldn't help but feel relieved just a bit to know he had escaped and was probably still alive somewhere. But," she paused, "not long after, I heard a rumor that he'd been apprehended and executed." She grew quiet, her fingers trembling as she rubbed her hands together, as if she were cold. "I'm sure it was for the best," she whispered.

"Nigel was a menace to the world. You know that. But, what can you tell me about the hanging? I still haven't heard the full story of what happened with my brother. He doesn't like to speak of it."

"Yes. It was a most unusual occurrence. Just as they were preparing the prisoners' necks with nooses, your father said something to the hangman and showed him a piece of paper, a letter, I learned later, from Queen Amenova, that stated Andromin should be released. He removed the noose from Andromin's neck amid booing from the crowd. But, deep in the people, I was happy he'd been freed. It seemed he had simply gotten involved with the wrong crowd. He had taken his fate like a soldier, not flinching when the hangman prepared his neck and tied his hands. The more I read and got to know details about Andromin and the Seaton family, the more I felt proud." Calista finished her tea and put the cup down on the table. Her cheeks grew hot. She realized she'd revealed too much.

"Proud of Andromin and the Seaton family? And, this was before you came into our lives. We consider you family despite your not being of our blood… yet, I'm starting to wonder whether you're keeping something from me," said Caprius, staring at Calista directly in the eyes. "Most people might admire or be curious about others, but to feel pride is an intimate emotion, one that means you're taking people personally," said Caprius.

Calista looked around; the waiter was delivering late luncheon to the passengers from a cart and came to them with trays. "Can I persuade you to have a glass of red wine with your meal, Madam?" asked the waiter. "I have the Chateau Rauzan Segla 25, of course."

"Yes, a glass of wine for us both," said Caprius, without taking his eyes off Calista, who was shifting uncomfortably in her seat. The waiter bowed and departed, leaving the two to continue their uncomfortable discussion.

Calista looked at Caprius. He was an honorable person, a good man. She had so many secrets, often she felt as though she would burst for wanting to let some of them out. She yearned to feel that free. But, she also knew she had to tread carefully. She shifted the subject slightly. "After the hanging, I left Koriston and became a wanderer. I was only sixteen, and I was often scared and hungry. When I came upon a small band of warriors who seemed kind, I decided to travel with them. The group's leader was Platasus Cremiss, and he was competent at managing his group, making sure they had food and adequate shelter. He was happy to take me in."

She looked at her fingers, which she was knitting fiercely together. "At first, he seemed all right. We ate together and we slept close to one another. But, I was developing into a woman, and they were lonely. Soon, they made me their plaything. They liked to make crude jokes about me behind my back, fondle my body at any time, interrupt my sleep to touch me or kiss me. They didn't rape me, which they could have easily done, but they had ceased to treat me like an equal. I felt terrible. Violated. My bad dreams resurfaced. When I was alone, which was only when they were off hunting or too drunk to use me, I would weep. I thought about Nigel and how caring he was. I did the right thing by leaving him, but I'd unwittingly delivered myself into a life of slavery. Platisus was deranged. He was a womanizer."

"He's a terrible man," said Caprius.

"Platisus would relieve himself in front of me. He walks like a dog and shits like a horse," said Calista.

Caprius rolled his eyes. His eyes were full of pity. He took her hands in his. "Calista, I cannot tell you how sorry I am," he said. He felt ashamed for trying to pin her into a corner. "You have been through so much pain in your life."

"Yes, I have." She smiled and got a dreamy look on her face. "And, then, one day, the men had decided they'd had enough of simply touching me. They got stirred up and tied me to a tree in order to rape me, one after the other. I tried to reason with them, to beg, but they were like animals. I was sure I would die. Andromin was in the forest and heard my screams. He didn't think of himself or the danger; he leaped in and slaughtered the bastards, one after the other. And, then I was free. I came to Elysium, and now I feel like a complete woman. I have your family to thank for that," she said. She looked down and realized they were holding hands. She dropped his quickly. "Oh, I am so sorry. I didn't mean to…"

"There is nothing to be sorry about," said Caprius. "I took your hands, actually."

She leaned back in her seat. "How much longer before we get to Koriston?"

"I would say less than an hour," said Caprius. Caprius gazed at her. She was so strong and so fragile at the same time. Her hands shook when she took up the glass of wine, but he could see the resolve in her, how the pain and trials she'd endured had marked themselves on her body. He realized she and Andromin had enjoyed a special bond; he just hadn't seen it for what it was until she and Andromin drifted apart.

"Yet, you and Andromin now speak coldly to one another. What has happened to cause such a rift between you?"

Calista tried to balance the consequences of telling Caprius some things without revealing her secret. If she revealed what had happened to damage her good friendship with Andromin, Caprius would understand that. But, sharing that opened the door to more questions, particularly that the man responsible for ravaging his mother before he was born was the notorious Cambrozes Genesis, her father. She worried that information would push Caprius away.

She looked at him, at his strong will, his sincerity. Perhaps he had strength enough to accept her despite what she was. She hesitated, but decided against telling him. The stakes were simply too high. Alienating him could mean being cast out of Elysium.

She said, "I understand that you want answers. Andromin is your brother, and you care for him. But, it's as simple as this: my presence caused problems for Andromin with Fetrona. Fetrona blames me for the problems in their relationship. I see now that Andromin wants me. But, I don't want to be the cause of their dissolution. Fetrona is fragile, and I don't think she would be able to live if she lost him. I'm not interested in being responsible for that, so I told Andromin I cannot be with him for my own personal reasons." Calista began to silently cry. She longed for Andromin every day. It broke her heart not to be with him.

"You speak so calmly, yet you weep. There are things you are not telling me, Calista. I wish you would trust me. It's hard to see you suffer so, and it's awkward for me, knowing you carry more secrets. My father, he also knows that you hold things inside. He said that, on the battlefield of Plamastu, you looked him in the eyes like you wanted to strangle him. That, after he's done you such kindness," said Caprius. His face was taut with worry. "What is it that's eating away at you?"

Calista swallowed, feeling terribly uneasy. "Caprius, please, can we not just leave this alone?" she asked. "Speaking of eating, why don't we eat before our meal gets cold? I'm sure it's delicious."

"Very well. I shall leave this matter alone. But, remember this: I am here for you, and you can be honest with me. Whatever you're hiding, it will not be a burden to me or my family. You can be sure of that. I am your friend. Whenever you are ready to come forth with this, I will be here for you. But, I will not pressure you anymore, Calista," said Caprius. They took the silver covers off their plates and, without much gusto, began to eat the rabbit stew.

Caprius ate little but drank down his wine. His wedding ring clinked against the glass, making a hollow chime. Calista wondered about his wife, Melina. What an impenetrable bond they must have in order to sustain their separation. She wondered whether it was constantly on his mind and if that was why his behavior was so erratic. It would be a long, lonely fourteen years for him. Lantrinon needed Grongone's protection, and until he was old enough, he would stay in Petoshine. Once he was a full-grown teenager, he would be able to handle a sword. "Do you still regret not being the one who escorted Melina to Petoshine?" she asked innocently.

"No. Father made his choice, and he chose Dragus," he said. Then he sighed. "It is what had to be. I only wish there was another way."

"Dragus will take good care of her. She is certain to arrive in Petoshine safe and sound. You can trust Dragus," said Calista.

Caprius' brow furrowed. "Of course, I trust him," he replied, fingers fidgeting on the table, "but she is my wife. I should been the one looking out for her."

"Yes, but can you imagine if something were to go wrong underway? You'd never forgive yourself. You'd never be able to recover from that. And, as a soldier, it might color your judgment."

"On the contrary, I think I would have had an advantage," he said.

"Or a disadvantage. If you land in deep water without a life raft and the current is swift, you might sink to the bottom." She took a breath and let it out slowly. "I know you have the light of Petoshine, but if that flame was ever to burn out and you were alone, then you would die alone." She looked at him squarely. "Imagine what that would do to the rest of us."

Caprius returned her intense gaze and saw a flame of desire there. He began to feel stirrings of it in his own body. "Has anyone ever told you that you are not only beautiful, but also very intelligent?"

"Why, Mr. Caprius Seaton, I do believe you are paying me a compliment. So, which do you prefer: my looks or my intelligence?" Calista asked, batting her eyelashes comically.

"Actually, both. You seem to be the complete package," said Caprius.

"Thank you." She realized they were flirting and felt suddenly uncomfortable. She leaned back and feigned a laugh. "Melina certainly is lucky to have you."

"It's nice to know there is someone else who appreciates me," said Caprius.

She smiled warmly. "How about this: you watch my back, and I'll watch yours."

"You've got yourself a deal," said Caprius. "To your health," he said, raising his water glass. Their glasses clinked together, and they laughed. "You know, I've never seen this side of you before. In fact, I don't think I've even seen you smile, not like this," said

Caprius. "You're always so serious and driven. But, I have to say, a glass of wine, and you're quite fun," he laughed.

"We haven't actually ever had a real conversation before, aside from that unpleasant day at the pub. Our lives have always followed separate paths. You have Melina, and I've got… just my disgruntlements," she said sadly.

"Don't say that. Good things are bound to come your way. When you least expect it, the right person will show up on your doorstep. Elysium has many decent men."

Calista clasped her hands together beneath her chin and rested on them. "Well, I'm looking at one."

Caprius smiled. "Look who's the flatterer now."

"Caprius. Tell me some more about the vim of Petoshine. How is it that this vim works?" asked Calista.

"The vim is a power that it draws from the tower of Castle Petoshine. It immerses a powerful field of energy that is part of a very large Amethyst crystal. This energy is what links my sword of power. I can create a stream of fire or, if necessary, extreme cold. The claymore of power holds fantastic healing power, as well."

"You mean, you can heal wounds?" asked Calista.

"Yes. It can actually mend a broken body. Even heal a body from any diseases. In darkness, it can release a soft glowing light."

"How was this created? By Grongone?"

"It was created by his father, Bremendalf. Well, he actually discovered this power. And, he and the elves created what today is known as the vim."

"What happened to Bremendalf and the elves?" asked Calista.

"Bremendalf was destroyed by Makoor. Bremendalf's mistake resulted in the tragic death of the elves. Today, Grongone remains as the last of the elves."

"I see, such an interesting story," she said.

With a bump, the train arrived in the Koriston station, interrupting the dangerous, rising ardor between the two. Caprius looked out the window at the bustle of people and rush of steam. "Well, welcome to Koriston," he said. "How did you find your journey, Madam?" he asked debonairly.

"Stimulating," said Calista.

"How's that?" asked Caprius.

"I enjoyed our conversation," she said. They began to gather their belongings.

"Do you mean the part when I mentioned how beautiful you are?" he teased.

"No, it was when you admired my intelligence," she said.

They made their way to the exit. "Calista, I have a whole new appreciation for you, and…" he paused, "I think you do for me, as well. But, we should probably leave all of that on the train."

"I've already forgotten our conversation," said Calista, waving her hand.

He reached out and touched her shoulder. She turned around. "But…" he couldn't bring himself to talk about these new feelings that pulsed in his heart. "Never mind. Let's get started on our investigation. Our contact is meeting us in half an hour. That gives us some time to discuss our approach once we get to Tillie's Fine Watches," said Caprius.

"Yes. I think that would be for the best," said Calista. She turned around and disembarked onto the busy platform.

Chapter 9

Tillie's Fine Watches

IN A DARK CORNER OF Raven's Pub, Cynthia Davenport sat with an elderly man who possessed vital information on the Colburn affair. Cynthia was desperate to stop the madman and prevent him from selling his serum to someone who might have been involved with the Goncools. The serum in their hands would be a disaster; they would create an army of super soldiers or even super Droges. She shuddered to think of it. Droges were dangerous enough already. If they were suddenly imbued with super strength, the vampires would have the perfect ally to help them turn Alamptria into a very dark place, one that they solely controlled.

"You do understand that if you pursue this, you may get yourself killed or worse. Colburn could as easily inject you with the serum. You would then be made to serve the Dark Lord," said the man, leaning forward. His eyes glittered in the dim light.

"That's a chance I'm going to have to take. He must be stopped," said Cynthia. "Our beautiful land would be cast into darkness in the hands of Makoor." She paused.

The man folded his fingers together. "Colburn is going to try and sell his serum. Lucky for him, every thug out there will be bidding on it," he said.

"Can you tell me where the auction will be taking place? And, when?" she asked.

He shook his head. "I don't know where and when; though, I can tell you it's going to take a few days. However, I do know someone who knows this information, a downtown local here in Jethro. His name is Kyle Rivers. Heard of him?"

"No, but I will find him. What does he look like?" asked Cynthia.

"He is extremely thin with a gaunt face, white hair, and two front teeth made of gold," said the man. "He usually likes to hang out at Reaper's Strip Bar. Loves the drink. I don't think buying him a beer will get you the information on Colburn, but it'll at least soften him up." The man let his gaze travel slowly up Cynthia's curvaceous frame. "You could resort to... other means to get the information out of him, I suppose."

Cynthia nodded and smiled mischievously. "Sounds like a rabbit with a healthy appetite for bunny," she said. "I guess carrots won't do."

"Well, Cynthia, forgive me for saying, but with that face and body, you'd be able to get him out of his pants and ready to give you anything you wanted in no time," said the man.

Cynthia smirked. "Yes, I can be quite persuasive. I may just need to flash him just one nipple. That way, I'll not only get the information, but I'll also leave with my head held high. This little bunny can hop out of any dilemma." Cynthia put her hands on her hips, stuck out her chest, and winked. "I'll bring my assets." She stood up. "Good to meet you, Rover. I'm off to Reapers." She turned. "Thanks for your help."

"Do be careful, Cynthia!" he called out to her.

***

When Caprius and Calista got to the hotel Karnamoore, they went directly to the concierge and booked two adjacent rooms on the fifth floor. They received their keys, then went into the lounge to wait for their contact. On a nearby sofa, a man caught the eye of Caprius, noting he looked just as he was described to him in the letter Confidus had written, and he was also with a woman, who also fit the written description. Caprius glanced at the man before murmuring, "Where has the time gone?"

"The time will always be with you, Caprius Seaton," said the man, and offered his hand to Caprius. "Dallas Moore, a pleasure to meet you. And, who is this lovely lady?" asked the man reaching for Calista's hand and kissing it.

"This is my partner and agent, Calista," said Caprius.

"Oh, and wife?" asked Dallas, eyeing Caprius' wedding ring.

"No, partner agent," repeated Caprius. "Now that we've gotten that straight, what can you tell us about the caskets you sent us? And, where were those bodies originally shipped from?" asked Caprius.

The man widened his eyes innocently. "They were brought to our post office to be shipped from Koriston to Elysium, care of Confidus Seaton. The slip that was attached was written before the boxes were shipped from Jethro, which is where they originated."

"Did you have any knowledge at all that you were shipping caskets?" asked Calista.

"No, I just move parcels; I don't open them. We take the order, stamp them, and ship them out, that's all," said Dallas.

"What about your driver? The man who delivered the caskets to Elysium? What can you tell us about him?" asked Caprius.

"He wouldn't be any use to you. I sent him to Elysium to deliver the packages. He's just doing his job. He works for me," said Dallas.

Calista pulled a pocket watch from her pocket. "Alright then, what can you tell us about this pocket watch?"

Caprius interjected, "Watches were found with both bodies inside the two caskets."

Dallas took the watch and examined it. He shrugged. "You're asking the wrong person. To me it's just a pocket watch. But, I can take you to a man I know who has a shop on River Street."

"Yes, Confidus said that the address of Tillie's Fine Watches is on Rivers Street. Or River Street. There seem to be two Rivers?" said Caprius.

Dallas sighed with annoyance. "The government here decided to rename the streets, and it's causing everyone confusion. Tillie's Fine Watches used to be on River Street, but that street has been renamed 'Rivers Road.' Another street is now River Street. It was written down for the Council of Confidus incorrectly. People are still adjusting to the switch. And, what's worse is they're both major roads in the city of Koriston. So, you want to go to Rivers Road. And, the address is 467. Not 265, which you've got written down here; 265 is actually a barbershop. It's a good thing we met. I assure you I am correct on this. Your father was misinformed," said Dallas.

Calista rolled her eyes at Caprius and mouthed, "Blah blah blah," which made Caprius smile.

Dallas droned on. "The man you want to talk to at Tillie's Fine Watches is Mathis Wynings. I bought a pocket watch from him myself." He pulled out his pocket watch and showed it to them.

"All right then. I guess our next stop is Tillie's," said Calista.

"Thank you for your time, Mr. Dallas Moore." Caprius winked, handing back the watch. He and Calista shook hands with him and left the hotel.

Caprius and Calista hailed a coach and took it to the address Dallas Moore had given them. In about fifteen minutes, they arrived at Tillie's Fine Watches. "Worth meeting with that bloke after all," smiled Caprius as they entered. The shop was filled with clocks of all shapes and sizes; they were nailed to the walls and covered every surface. Just as Caprius was about to speak to the proprietor behind the clock-riddled counter, every clock in the shop struck three and began chiming. The din was incredible. Calista's hands flew to her ears. Caprius tried to speak, but the owner just shook his head, mouthing "I can't hear you!" The ringing went on for thirty seconds. They had no choice but to wait it out.

Finally, when it ended, they listened to the aftermath in the stillness until the owner, a lanky man with white hair and a long beard said, "What can I do for you?"

"Do you have to listen to this racket every hour?" Calista asked the man.

He smiled. "Every hour on the hour. Doesn't bother me a bit."

"I'd go deaf in here," said Calista.

The man laughed. "We've got clocks of all kinds, mostly European. And, pocket watches galore. Take your pick."

"We are not here to make a purchase," said Caprius.

"Oh?" asked the man.

"We are agents from Elysium on an investigation," said Calista.

"My name is Caprius Seaton, and this is my partner, Calista. We came to ask you a few questions."

"What about?" asked the man. He scratched his chin beneath the mass of white beard.

Calista pulled out the pocket watch. "Is this one of yours?" she handed it to the man.

He examined it closely. After a moment, he said, "Well, I'll be damned."

"Is it yours?" asked Calista.

"Nope, sure is not!" said the man.

Caprius edged closer to him. "Take a good look at it," he said.

"I already told you it's not one of mine," said the man.

"May I ask, what is your name, Sir?" asked Caprius. The man looked nervous and pressed his lips together. "Look, old man, two dead agents were delivered to us in caskets from Koriston, each holding a pocket watch like this one. So talk!" Caprius raised his voice.

"My name is Mathis," he said quietly. "As I said, this isn't one of my pocket watches. But, I do recognize the markings. This is old Telusion, and these markings come from the cult of the undead. Such pocket watches can be found in Plaphorius. But, they aren't made in Plaphorius. They're just shipped there."

Caprius and Calista looked at each other. "From Plaphorius?" Calista asked in amazement. "Are you certain of this, Mathis?"

"I know what I'm talking about. I recognize these markings, and it is Telusion. I've been in this business for over fifty-five years, and if I say it is the dark cult of the undead, then that is what it is." Caprius and Calista were listening to him closely. The old man had their attention. "Okay, look..." Mathis gestured with his hands, "I know about the battle of Plaphorius and that the Elysians destroyed the cult a short time ago," he leaned in and lowered his voice, "but I also know some of these vampires survived. And, I'm telling you, these pocket watches belong to them."

"You said they are not made in Plaphorius," said Calista. "So, where are they manufactured?"

"You'll want to go to Jethro. That's where they are made."

"Jethro!" Caprius and Calista spoke in unison. "But, that's a long way from here," said Caprius.

"I know. But, that's where the pocket watch is from," said the man. He fingered the watch. "Whoever planted these watches on these bodies is giving you a warning: stay away, or you'll be shipped in crates dead just like your other two friends." He held his hands in the air. "I'm not telling you what to do; I know who you are, Caprius Seaton, and I know of the Seatons' powers. But, something tells me that if you go to Jethro, you'll be in a lot of danger."

He went behind his counter and began rifling through some things until he came up with a scrap of paper and a pencil. "The woman you'll want to talk to is named is Enlora Renfield. You can find her in an art gallery called Delvingers. She will know exactly the shop you want to go to. I don't know the shop's name, but she does." He whispered with a smile, "But, I have to warn you, she is very mysterious," he said.

"You've been very helpful," said Calista.

"I have faith in you Seatons. I know what you did in Plaphorius and abroad. But, remember, they know you're coming, and they're prepared for you."

Calista and Caprius walked out of Tillie's Fine Watches, and Calista sighed. "We have to go all the way to Jethro? It's so far," she said.

"I'll check to see if there is a train that goes near Jethro," said Caprius. He looked at Calista. "Why don't you go back to the hotel and relax a bit. If there's a train, I'll buy tickets, and then I'll come back and we can have dinner."

He handed Calista the key to her room, and she hopped into a carriage they'd hailed. As the driver snapped the reins on the horses, Caprius yelled "I won't be long!" Caprius began to walk in the direction of the train station, keeping his eye out for another carriage. One after the other sped by, each full of passengers. He eventually gave up and walked the whole way through the busy streets.

After an hour, Caprius reached the station. He went to a counter that had maps of Alamptria on display. The one he needed was quite detailed. He purchased it from the seller for a shilling and unrolled it at a table nearby. He hunted for Jethro, not having a clue where it was located. He ran his finger over the map's surface, over railroad track markings and forests, until he found it at the outer lying edge. "I see why no train goes there," he muttered. "Bloody well at the edge of the world, this place."

He folded up the map and headed toward the ticket booth. He'd have to buy tickets to Galdington, the furthest village the trains traveled to in the direction of

Jethro. As he walked among the crowd, Caprius caught a glimpse of a familiar-looking man. He tried to remember where he knew him from, thinking hard. Then it hit him; it was Thornin Goncool. Thornin looked up, and the two men locked eyes. Thornin began to run. Caprius ran after him. Caprius dodged people, dog leashes, and baby prams, as he laid chase. He leaped over a bench and skidded around a corner, narrowly missing an elderly couple.

Thornin ran out toward the station's opening where the trains entered. He raced alongside the tracks, Caprius in close pursuit. Thornin turned around at the approach of a train to see Caprius gaining on him. Thornin grinned, took a running leap, and jumped over the track just inches in front of the train. He barely made it, the train tooting its horn in earnest, landing on all fours on the other side. Caprius stopped and, breathing hard, waited as each car sped by. When it passed and went into the station, the Goncool was gone. Caprius punched the air, "Dammit," he shouted. He didn't see that Thornin had hid alongside another train, gone back into the station, and easily boarded another train, the one he'd needed, taken a seat, and picked up a newspaper, as if nothing had happened. He sat back and watched Caprius through a window as his train departed the station.

Defeated, Caprius walked along the rocks between tracks back into the station. He came to the ticket booth and purchased two tickets bound for Galdington. Back outside amid the city's hustle and bustle, he waved at a coach and was surprised when it pulled over. A young couple got out, and he got in. The ride was just long enough for him to catch his breath and think about his and Calista's next steps.

Caprius went directly to Calista's suite. Her door was unlocked, so he went in. She was standing in the living room with a towel wrapped around her. Her shoulders, still wet, glistened. "I thought you'd be dressed by now," he said, moving to the sofa.

"I just got out of the bath," she said.

"Long bath. I was gone nearly two hours."

She smiled lazily and went to the sofa, where her clothes were laid out. She unwrapped the towel from her chest and threw it at Caprius. "Think fast!" she said and turned around. He saw her finely toned body, her curves, and all her beautiful flesh before she slipped into her tunic. "Calista," said Caprius, he teasingly admonished her.

"Oh, come on, it's nothing you haven't seen before," she said pulling her arms through her sleeves.

"Yes, well, Melina—not you," he said. Caprius suddenly felt like a little boy again. Calista was so worldly and had been with so many. He'd only ever known the body of his wife.

"So," she said, flopping down across from him, "did you get the tickets?"

"Yes, I did," he said.

"For what time tomorrow?" she asked.

"Actually, we won't be spending the night here. I got us a train for 8:05 p.m. tonight."

"That's splendid," she said as she fastened her belt buckle. "We can have a leisurely dinner and take our time getting to the station."

Caprius felt suddenly tired, imagining a dinner with Calista. They would flirt, she would look more beautiful by candlelight. "I think because it's so difficult to get a carriage in this town, we should rather get to the station early, have a cup of tea in the lounge there, and dine on board. It's an awfully long trip, so that would at least give us something to do."

"Very well," she said, standing. She zipped up her valise, crossed her arms, and looked at Caprius almost by way of a challenge. "What do you suggest we do for the next two hours?" she asked.

"Calista... I'm a married man," said Caprius softly.

She laughed, a light sweet laugh that made him smile. "I'm glad to say you're not my type. I much prefer fat older men with receding hairlines and bushy eyebrows."

"Glad to say that rules me out," said Caprius. He stood. "There is actually something we must do."

"What is that?" she asked.

"I want to ask the concierge whether he knows anything about Lynin Chiles. Perhaps he left something behind, a clue of some kind."

Calista walked to the door. "All right, let's go."

The concierge was apologetic. "I'm afraid Mr. Chiles departed without leaving anything," he said. Caprius and Calista left.

Chapter 10

The Goncools

THE WOODS OF ELYSIUM WERE dense with snow-covered brush and trees. The escaped Goncools from Zaderack prison found refuge there, and because of the thickness of the wilderness, they built a roaring fire and guffawed over homemade brew one of them had killed a villager for on their way into the forest. They began to discuss their plan of attack against Confidus, the one responsible for imprisoning them.

Just after dusk, one of the soldiers left their base camp to relieve himself. On his way back, he saw a "Wanted" poster for the Goncools' capture. He tore the poster off the tree and chuckled at the rendering of himself and his brothers. He was walking back to camp when he noticed a number of posters nailed to trees. His eyes narrowed; off past a copse of oak trees, all peppered with posters, was a small glowing light. Then, he saw another and then another. They were bobbing up and down. Torches. Several of them. It had to be a band of soldiers hunting them down.

The Goncool peered out from behind a tree. The soldiers were quickly approaching. He stood as still as possible, holding his breath. With the torch in hand, a soldier crashed through the brush and scanned the area. "Nothing here, carry on!" he shouted, moving on. The Goncool kept his spot and was about to run back to camp when he noticed another flame out of the corner of his eye. He slowly turned and saw a different Elysian soldier close by. The Goncool thought he could take refuge behind a larger tree with a hollow trunk, so he began to creep over, when a dead branch snapped beneath his foot. The knight's hand flew to his sword. When the Goncool tried to lift his foot, the branch snapped again. The soldier was lightning fast; with a quick dislodge and swing of his sword, he sliced through the air. A deer suddenly bounded by, and he yelped, startled, and then laughed at himself. While he was recovering from the surprise of the deer, he didn't see the Goncool unsheathe his own sword and bring it down on him until the sword was nearly upon his shoulder. He turned, realized it was a Goncool, and fiercely blocked the blow.

The Goncool pulled back for another swing, but the knight blocked that, too. They pushed each other off, and the knight threw his torch to the ground. "I thought I recognized your face from the posters. Surrender!" growled the Elysian knight.

"Not while I have a sword in my hand, Elysian," sneered the Goncool.

"Then, you shall die, Goncool!" The knight swung his sword and the fight continued.

They held steady until the Goncool's sword nicked the Elysian's armor, and the knight was thrown back by the force. "Hear the crows? They are hungry for blood," said the Goncool, breathing hard.

Moments later, two other Elysian soldiers called out and came running. Now that it was three to one,

one fast swing by an Elysian knocked the Goncool's sword out of his hand. The Goncool fell back onto the ground, and the knight pointed his sword at his chest. "You are under arrest," he said triumphantly.

The Goncool inched his arm down and removed a flask of blood from his hip pouch. "Not if I can help it. I have my salvation," he said. Trembling, he began to drink the blood from the flask.

"What is that?" the knight asked the Goncool. The other Elysian soldiers had arrived on the scene and were staring down at the man, who was beginning to transform. "What is that?" he asked again, terrified. The Goncool's skin was becoming ghostly white and his face twisted into a picture of abject horror. From the back of his body, wings sprouted. He closed his eyes, and when he opened them a moment later, they were glowing red. He had become a horrific vampire.

"Oh, God," whispered the knight whose sword was still pointed at the creature. The soldiers all took several steps back. Trembling, the closest knight swung his sword, which aggravated the vampire. It flew back and hovered in the air, flapping its wings. "Too late, Elysians. I now walk among the dead. All we Goncools share the same fate." With those words, the Goncool flew toward them, knocking some of the knights over. Then, the creature flew off into the distance. The Elysian soldiers got to their feet to watch the creature fly away.

The Elysian soldier sheathed his sword. "We know the rest of them are in the woods. You three, return to Castle Elysium and send more men."

"Yes, Sir," said the soldier.

"That was very brave of you, Gambner. Standing up to that thing," said one of the soldiers.

"It will take more than bravery to capture the rest. Now that we have spotted him, we know the others are nearby. These men will be hard to capture," said the Elysian knight. "They must all be destroyed."

"The word is given. It shall be that. Death to the Goncools!" said another knight.

"We must find them before they consume the blood. For if they transform into the undead, the task will be much more difficult."

"Gambner, this was more than just a vampire," said a soldier.

"Indeed, it was a creature of great power and strength. It has fled to warn the others," said Gambner. "All right, let's move on."

Meanwhile, the creature approached the campsite. As it glided down toward the Goncools, they all looked at him with fear. Before they could run, he quickly resumed his human form. "Barrister, we were specifically instructed not to drink the blood of Makoor until we have Confidus Seaton," said one of his fellow Goncools.

"I had no choice. I had a sword at my throat," said Barrister.

"It will be much more difficult to capture Confidus Seaton if we drink of the blood," said the Goncool Fridel.

"Not to worry, Fridel. We will capture our jailer," said another Goncool.

"I must warn you all. The Elysians are out there," Fridel pointed, "within the woodland, in search for us. I have a plan. We will stay in these woods and let them hunt for us. We will stay well hidden but will ambush the Elysians. We kill four soldiers and take their uniforms. Then, disguised as Elysian knights, we will go to Castle Elysium, confront the king, and capture him.

Confidus is to be brought into the woods. Here, we will give him a full dose of Makoor's blood. Once he is one of us, our mission will be over, and we can consume the blood from the flasks. Confidus will become a devil of the pit, a true follower of Makoor. Then, Confidus himself will inflict his altered state upon all of Elysium." Fridel sat back and dusted off his hands. "We need do nothing more; then, we can go about our business."

"It won't be that easy," said another Goncool.

"I agree with Fridel; just follow the plan. It will work. Once we have those uniforms, the rest will be easier. I know this will work," said Barrister. "But, I am aware that they mean not to simply capture us. My hearing is keen, and I know they mean to kill us all. We are a threat to their society. This is why we must stay sharp and focused."

"What about you?" asked Marlot, a young Goncool. "You're not one of us."

"I will be of much more use in Jethro," said Barrister. "That is where I am going. If Caprius Seaton and Calista Genesis follow every lead that has been left for them, they will end up in Jethro. I have sensed the Dark Lord's wishes. He means to set a trap for them in Jethro. I will be there to take Caprius' claymore of power. Once I have it, I will set forth to Plaphorius, where I will meet Carcass Doom and give him the claymore. And, once again, the Prince of Darkness, himself, will rise," he said.

"Now," he leaned in, "over the hills, there are trenches dug in beneath the great roots of the trees; that is a good spot for a surprise attack upon the Elysians. Once you have the Elysians' uniforms on, you must go to a pub on the border of Elysium, just before the shoreline of the Bay of Begonia. There you will try and obtain any information you can on how to get into

Castle Elysium. The castle will be well guarded. So, I urge you to take great caution. Now go. You have your orders."

"Malfus," he pointed to a Goncool with a rigid face off to the side, "you are to take charge. Everyone else, follow his orders as you would mine. I must go now." Instantly, Barrister transformed himself into the creature of great power and took flight to Jethro.

Chapter 11

Of Absence and Malice - Part 1

AT QUANTUM HEIGHTS, ANDROMIN stood on the balcony of his suite enjoying the view of the winter wonderland below. He took a deep puff of his cigar and let it out into the frigid air in a thin stream. He looked at the cigar. Cigars are fine to wind down with, he thought, but a lovely woman is much more my taste. He took a last puff of his cigar before crushing it into an ashtray already filled with spent cigar ends and walked back into his suite. He flopped into an easy chair and laid his head back. "Fetrona," he muttered. "What has happened to us?" He sighed. "Women. It's harder to live with them than without them." Then, he thought about Calista. How she didn't look at him the same anymore. It made him feel like he'd lost something vital to his life. Hell, he thought. I don't even know her. She's full of secrets. And, she seems to know so much about me, like she's done research. It's not natural.

Andromin tried to talk himself into feeling better, but when he spied the decanter on the sideboard, he grabbed it and poured a healthy drink. Once it hit his lips, he spat it out. "Water? What kind of place is this? This is my holiday!" He set the glass down and pushed it away. "I need a drink," he said, heading for the door.

He went downstairs into the concourse and ambled about, looking in all the shops. When he passed the wine shop, he saw a beautiful woman inside talking to a customer. He recognized her straight away: Mr. Willy B. Pinkles' mistress. Standing beside her was Melina Hampshire's sister, Selena. Not knowing Selena but always operating under the assumption that she would be just as annoying as her sister, Andromin treated her as he did Melina, with the same dismissive scorn. In turn, she disregarded him entirely. It was, for all intents and purposes, he figured, a perfect non-relationship. He tapped on the glass, and when Selena turned around, he stuck his tongue out at her. She frowned and made rude gestures with both hands before returning to her work. Andromin walked away quickly with his head down. He knew Selena would tell Caprius, and his brother would have some choice words for him, but frankly, he didn't care.

He went straight to the hotel lounge and plunked down on a loveseat. He stopped a barmaid carrying a tray of drinks. "Excuse me, I'll have one of those," he said, taking one of the glasses off her tray and tossing her a shilling. Andromin sat back and drank deeply. "This is much better," he said. He sat for a while sipping at this ale and then another. People around him engaged in the theater of their lives, and Andromin placidly watched from his loveseat.

Mr. Willy B. Pinkles entered smiling peaceably and scanned the room. When he noticed Andromin, his smile fell. He approached him and stood before his seat.

"Enjoying yourself, Mr. Seaton?" asked Mr. Pinkles flatly.

"I was until you showed up. And, I had been having such a Quantum moment. Isn't that your motto? 'When seeking life's pleasures... have a Quantum moment?'"

"No need to be rude, Andromin. If sarcasm is what I wish for, I'll talk to my thirteen-year-old son," said Pinkles.

Andromin grinned. "Well, isn't that just your lucky number! If I'm not mistaken, I am sitting at table thirteen. I'm not superstitious, but I do like this spot. This table really does afford one the best view of the whole place. For example, you see that gentleman over there? He's been sitting at that poker table for the past six hours. Arrived just after I did. Now, if I'm right about this, which I know I am, you are about to be taken in. And, you stand to lose a lot more than a few picture frames, a painting, a bottle of scotch, and an awning. So, I'd say if you didn't believe thirteen was lucky before, you should change your tune, because I'm here to tell you your luck is about to run out."

Mr. Willy B. Pinkles looked furtively at the man at the poker table. His nose went in the air. "Thanks for the tip, Andromin. And, may I give you a tip? Try not to make a mess of things while you're here. All I've ever seen from you is your actions are just as bad as your relationships. Hint, hint... Fetrona." Pinkles was riffling in his pockets for his handkerchief and inadvertently dropped a key on the floor.

Andromin decided not to tell him. He looked into Pinkle's face. "Yes, you've made your point. But, now I see two gents I recognize, and as my relationship with them went a little sour some years ago, it might get a bit sticky in here. And, this little bee is out for a sting." As Andromin stood, he spilled his remaining ale all over the table. "Oops, look at that. I seem to have made a mess. Would you mind cleaning that up?"

While Pinkles fumed and turned to summon the barmaid to clean the mess, Andromin bent down to pick up the key. It had Pinkle's room number on it. "I do believe my vacation is about to get much better," chuckled Andromin. "My dear Mr. Pinkles, you're about to get stung in many ways." He made his way over to the two men who had just entered.

"I hate the Seatons. And, him most of all," Pinkles said under his breath. "They think their power and money can let them get away with anything."

Andromin approached the two gentlemen. They were Taughtenslottes from the city of Koriston. "Hello, boys, remember me?" asked Andromin smiling slyly.

"I do recall seeing you years ago, under the most unbearable circumstances. Are you hanging around here now, Andromin?" said the burly one, gulping down his beer. "Because the last time we were together, you were hanging by your neck. What a pity we didn't hang you first. Then, we wouldn't have to sit here and bother with this tedious conversation. You are spoiling my drink." The two Taughtenslottes began to laugh, and the one who'd spoken pointed at Andromin. "Got him good there!" he bragged to his friend.

Andromin calmly took the nutcracker lying on the table beside a bowl of almonds and snapped it around the burly Taughtenslotte's finger. He howled in pain.

Andromin began to sniff him. "Well, my dear Taughtenslotte, you seem to be perspiring. You know you really stink." He continued to squeeze the man's finger with the nutcracker. "Here, maybe this will help wash it off?" He grabbed the man's beer and poured it over his head. Across the room, Mr. Willy B. Pinkles threw his hands in the air before rushing over. The man stood, beer dripping from his thick black hair, causing Andromin to step backwards and release his finger. The man turned and struck Andromin in the face. Andromin grinned at him. "That's the best you got?" he said before driving a fist into his large stomach, knocking the wind out of him. He grabbed the man's arm, turned, and tossed him over his shoulder. The Taughtenslotte landed on top of a nearby poker table, knocking all the chips and playing cards onto the floor, the players all backing up, their chairs clattering to the floor.

In the melee, Andromin took a celery stalk and dipped it into some cream dip, approached the other Taughtenslotte, smeared the dip on the man's face, then popped the celery into the man's open mouth. As Andromin dusted off his hands and walked out of the lounge, he gave Mr. Pinkles a thumbs up. Mr. Pinkles stood still surveying the damage, fuming.

Back in the concourse, on his way to the hotel lobby, he took out the key he had taken from Pinkles. He looked into the wine shop to see Selena and Pinkle's mistress. Andromin decided he would have a little fun. He walked into the wine shop. "Weren't you working in the flower shop before? Were you demoted?" he asked Selena with a huge grin.

"Oh, fuck off, Andromin," said Selena. Andromin walked over to Pinkle's mistress who had her back to him. She was busy writing down some information from the wine labels. "Excuse me, what would you suggest in a good cabernet?" asked Andromin.

She turned around and narrowed her eyes. She licked her lips. "Mr. Seaton, how are you?" she asked.

"You know who I am?" he asked, leaning against the counter and grinning.

"My husband described you to the last detail," she said.

"Your husband?" he asked.

"Yes, Willy and I got married just two weeks ago," she said, flashing a modest ring at him.

"Quick honeymoon?" he asked.

"No honeymoon," she said bitterly. "As soon as we were married, it was 'must get back to work, Christine.' I wonder whether I made a mistake. It's like he just doesn't care."

"So, why stay with him?" he asked.

She rolled her eyes. "He flatters me, says it's good for business that I'm on his arm. And, I live in a luxurious suite. He said he'd take care of me. But, since we've been married, he hasn't paid me any mind at all. Personally, I'd like to get out of the damned marriage."

"Clearly, he's using you. Why don't you get even with him?" asked Andromin, his eyes flashing.

"I don't know," she said frowning.

"I do," said Andromin. He took her slim hand in his. "What if you were to get caught in bed with me?" he whispered. Wouldn't that drive him over the edge?"

She looked shocked, but then her face melted into a slow smile. Andromin toyed with a lock of her hair. "But, it would never work," she whispered, leaning into him. "He always carries the key to our suite. It's only when he is finished working that he comes and gets me."

"Well, look what I have," he dangled the key in the air. "Look familiar?"

Christine took the key. "How in the world did you get this?"

"Pinkles dropped it on the floor," said Andromin. She smiled with glee. "So, how about it? You want to get even?"

"Now?" she laughed.

"Yes, right now. Pinkle's shift should be ending in about forty-five minutes," he said.

"Let's do it," she said. Andromin took her by the hand, and they began to leave the shop. "Wait! We should take a bottle of wine."

"A good idea," he said.

"Hmm, but which one?" she asked, starting to look over the inventory.

"Oh, who gives a damn? It's just a bottle of squashed grapes." Now that he'd gotten up close with her, smelled her floral warmth, he wanted nothing more than her naked body against his.

"You know, I think I'll choose this very expensive bottle of squashed grapes," she said, taking one from a secret spot behind the counter. She crossed the shop floor to Selena. "Selena, I'm leaving early. Would you please put this bottle on my husband's account?" She tossed her long honey-colored hair and left with Andromin, who took the chance to turn around and smirk at Selena before they walked away.

Selena crossed her arms. "Christine, how could you?" she said in disgust.

Just then, a swarthy man strode in and kissed her. "What's Andromin doing here?" he asked.

"More than he ought to. He just picked up Christine," said Selena.

"I'm sure Mr. Willy B. Pinkles isn't going to like that," he said, grinning.

"Brandimoir, when are we going to leave this place?" she asked.

"I have good news. I have found us a place in Morisant. A sanctuary just as you wanted. It is beautiful there. The place is called Bridimar. It is nestled in the hills, and the view is breathtaking."

"When do we leave?" she asked.

"We'll pack tonight and be on the road first thing tomorrow."

"Oh, Brandimoir! Thank you, my sweet." Selena hugged her love tightly, so glad he was hers.

Meanwhile, in Mr. Pinkle's penthouse suite, after quickly drinking down a glass of the opulent wine and playing naughty sex games, Andromin laid in bed with Christine. They had exhausted themselves and fell to talking about life in general; each found the other quite easygoing company, so naturally, they began to talk about their relationships and why they tended to fall apart. "You know this is indeed a very good vintage. What did you do, pull the most expensive bottle you had off the shelf?"

Christine giggled. "Actually, I did. I figured what better way to get even than to run up an expensive tab."

"Yes, but since he is a wealthy man, this may not bother him much," said Andromin.

"He may do alright, but when he sees he was actually charged for six cases of this stuff, he might have to worry about paying his bills for a while," she laughed and lay back on the pillows.

"Six cases?" he said nodding. "You are angry with him!" Andromin sat up on one elbow and looked down at Christine. She had flawless skin over her lithe body. He ran his hand over her and shivered a bit at her curves under his hand.

"How is it someone like you came to be with Pinkles?"

"I was such a fool. I fell for his charm, but he has been using me. That's quite clear now. He's lost all interest." She looked sad, like she'd lost a precious thing.

"Love never lasts," said Andromin. He gulped the rest of his drink and kissed her.

"Wait... I think I hear the door," she whispered. Andromin paused; it was unmistakably Pinkles arriving. He took off his shoes in the front foyer and called out angrily, "Christine! Why in heavens did you not wait in the shop for me? And, what the hell are you doing with such a large amount of expensive wine?"

"In here, darling!" Christine called out.

Pinkles entered the bedroom. When he saw Andromin, he dropped the bottle of wine he'd brought with him. It shattered, and wine gushed onto the floor. "What the hell are you doing with my wife!" Pinkles cried out.

"I'm having a Quantum moment," said Andromin calmly. His hand was on Christine's breast, and he left it there.

"You got a lot of nerve, Seaton," said Pinkles.

"I've got more than that." He leaned down and gave Christine a deep kiss.

"Seaton, you crossed the line here. When your father hears about this-" Pinkles began.

"When he hears about it, he'll say 'well done.' Was it for king and country?" mocked Andromin in a deep voice like his father's.

"Get out of my home. I want you out of here," said Pinkles.

"I'm afraid I'm not decent. You'll have to excuse me," said Andromin.

"You are excused," laughed Christine. "I'm naked too, honey," she said to her husband. "Would you like one last Quantum moment yourself before I leave you?"

"I'll…I'll take you over my knee," Pinkles stammered.

"That would be splendid, darling," she said. "At least it'd be interesting."

"I will deal with you later," Pinkles said. He looked truly rattled, his pudgy face sweaty and pale. "I'm going to the bar. When I come back, Seaton, I want you out of here!"

"That's splendid; you're going to the bar. Have a drink on me," said Andromin. Andromin languidly sat up, stretched, and walked out of the bedroom buck naked, smirking. Before he got to the doorway, he turned. "Oh, by the way, did you lose your key?" he said. Pinkles stormed out of the bedroom, fumbled for his shoes, and slammed the door.

As Andromin dressed in the living room, he smugly congratulated himself on a job well done. He realized he felt much better. "I'm finally enjoying my vacation," he thought before leaving.

Chapter 12

Of Code and Honor

CAPRIUS AND CALISTA SAT UPON seats within the train station. They relaxed and watched the large screens upon the wall transmitting advertisements. As Caprius and Calista waited in the lounge for their train to arrive, a 4 1/2-foot tall balding man with caterpillar eyebrows plunked down in a seat beside Calista. She and Caprius looked at one another and collapsed into fits of laughter.

From the speakers came, "Now boarding on Track K12." Calista decided she would play a little joke on Caprius. "Excuse me, Sir, but I find you very attractive," said Calista to the squat gentleman, who looked terrified that this muscular, doe-eyed woman with long, flowing locks would speak to him. "Would you care to sit beside me on the train?"

The man stammered and began to sweat profusely. He mopped his head with a well-used handkerchief. "Why…why, yes… that…that would be very nice."

Caprius tried so hard not to laugh, he snorted. "Excuse me," he held up a hand. "Allergies."

Now emboldened, the man leaned in. "What's your name, sweetheart?" "Calista," she said, turning her body outward so Caprius could see her batting her lashes.

"My name is Kazoos," said the man.

"What a lovely name," she exclaimed. "I know I've heard that word before; whatever does it mean?"

"A kazoo is a musical instrument," he said.

"Oh, really? That is so very interesting." Calista smiled. "What is that you are reading, Mr. Kazoos?"

Kazoos flipped over his dog-eared book. "It's about the ever-growing need for music in our culture. Did you know that you can tell a lot about a person based on what kind of instrument he plays? For example, if he plays the drums, you can be sure he's aggressive and demanding. Or, if he plays the flute, he's high spirited. Or, if he prefers the violin," he paused, "he's romantic."

"Let me guess, you like the violin?" Calista asked.

"Yes. How did you know?" asked Kazoos.

"Call it female intuition," she said. "So, Mr. Kazoos, which train are you taking?"

"I'm taking the K11," he said.

The boarding call sounded again, "Last call for Track K12. Now boarding!"

"Alright, Calista. That's enough fun. Let's make our train," said Caprius. He stood and smiled sympathetically at Kazoos.

Calista stood and looked sweetly down at Kazoos. "I'm sorry, but we're on the K12. Perhaps another time." She kissed his cheek.

Kazoos looked radiant as she made to leave. "That's alright. It isn't every day a beautiful woman asks me to sit beside her."

"The pleasure was all mine." Calista turned, and she and Caprius jogged to their train and boarded. They were still laughing as they got to their seats, but Calista soon grew pensive. "Poor thing. He was sweet."

"I do think you set his heart on fire," said Caprius.

"Either that or I almost gave him a heart attack," said Calista. "How unfortunate a name. Poor dear," she said again.

"Tell me, what would you have done if he were taking the same train?" asked Caprius.

"I don't know. I guess I would have hoped you'd come to my rescue," she said.

The two continued to chat and banter not noticing that just a few seats over, a man was stealing glances at the pair. It was Nigel Goncool, and beside Nigel was his hideous partner in crime, Vernon Goncool. They both wore similar dark clothing and pretended to read newspapers.

Nigel had nothing but disdain for Caprius, but when he saw his old love, his heart nearly burst from his chest.

"When do we make our move?" asked Vernon, jarring Nigel from his thoughts.

"Later. When the time is right," said Nigel.

Caprius and Calista relaxed and enjoyed each other's company, knowing it was going to be a long journey. "So, I haven't been able to tell you yet, but while I was getting our tickets, I ran into your old friend Thornin Goncool."

"What?" Calista said. "What was he doing there?"

"I don't know. But, something tells me we're going to run into him again," said Caprius.

"Did you try to capture him?" asked Calista.

"As soon as he saw me, he fled. I ran after him, but when I nearly had the bastard, a train came, and he jumped right in front, nearly killing himself. He made it across, and when the train passed," Caprius snapped his fingers, "Thornin was gone."

"How could you lose him?" she asked. She looked down at her hands.

"I don't know. The way he ran, he had an almost inhuman agility..." mused Caprius.

"Is he a vampire?"

"No, I don't necessarily think he is. But, he might be something else," said Caprius. He lowered his voice and leaned forward, his face dark and serious. "I think we are going to have a hard time stopping the Goncools."

"Was anyone with him?" asked Calista.

"No, though I wouldn't be surprised if he were meeting up with someone," said Caprius.

"I will say that Nigel, Thornin, and Lavender Frikiseed were always very close, almost inseparable. It is not likely he was alone," said Calista. "I wonder what in the world Thornin was doing at the train station. Or, where was he going."

"Maybe the same place we are headed," said Caprius.

The thought of running into him gave Calista a terrible feeling. "I don't think I'm going to be able to sleep tonight," she said. "But, I think it's time I turned in just the same." All she cared about at that moment was being alone.

Caprius and Calista walked through the cars to their sleeping compartment. They unfolded their slim berths, where blankets and pillows awaited them, climbed in, and within moments, were both soundly asleep.

Each slept until morning was well underway. They were awakened by the scent of freshly brewed tea and warm biscuits. The train sped through the barren, snow-covered land. Mountains framed the horizon, and the sun was bright. Caprius and Calista took their turns with their morning toilet, then went to the dining car for a light breakfast. Though she had slept through the night, it was a fitful sleep, her troubled dreams all centering around Nigel. But, she decided to let the fresh morning reinvigorate her spirit and give her a new start.

"I'm sorry your sleep was uneasy," said Caprius over cups of steaming Earl Gray. "I can't imagine how hard it will be for you now that you know Nigel is at large," he said.

"I almost feel as if he is watching me," whispered Calista, her eyes red and tired.

"Melina has those thoughts about Fenison Torington. Lately, her dreams have been more and more foreboding."

"I suppose Melina and I have that in common; we both have tormented pasts. Ones that will linger in our memories for a long time," said Calista.

"You know, I never thanked you for being so generous with Melina, letting her confide in you. She opened up to you in a way she couldn't with me. She counts you as a dear friend, you know."

"I am here for her. She is young, and this is obviously very trying for her," said Calista.

"Yes, the fact that you're older makes you something of a big sister for her. She can look up to you, like she does Setra," said Caprius.

"And, Fetrona?" she asked.

"Fetrona is young and… fairly selfish; though, she can be funny and charming. She and Melina aren't that close," said Caprius.

"That seems kind of harsh," laughed Calista.

"It's just that she fancies herself to be very high society and likes to walk about with her nose in the air, but really, she's not that bright and is awfully fond of toilet humor." Calista giggled. "Fetrona has a motto. For high time and sheer fun... bring your drinks to my table. You can almost see it on her forehead. I'm not trying to be mean. I'd just rather Melina spent time with you or Setra."

"I'll try to take that as a compliment," said Calista.

Caprius shook his head. "I just don't understand Andromin's relationship with her. He says how much he cares for Fetrona, but then he'll go off to bed with another woman behind her back. I think he keeps her like some sort of security blanket."

"I don't really know her, but now I feel like I've gotten an idea of who she is," said Calista. "And, at least you said your piece in a refined way. You and your father share that, that quiet elegance, among other traits I've noticed in just the short time I've been in Elysium."

"Yes, we are very much alike. My father said that I look a lot like he did when he was my age," said Caprius.

"And, Dragus?" she asked.

"Dragus is not all that much like my father. I mean Dragus has my father's niceness. He's kind and all. But, my father has more leadership qualities."

"That must be why he was appointed king," said Calista. "He is a strong, honorable man with the stomach to combat any difficulties that come his way."

"Actually, those qualities notwithstanding, my father was appointed king because he has royal blood in his veins. He was related to the slain king Tassidus," said Caprius. "Tassidus never fathered any children, so he was next in line for the throne."

"Well, let us raise a toast to your father. Ruler of Elysium! To Confidus Seaton! Long may he rule!" said

Calista raising her voice as she pretended to be an enthusiastic villager cheering on her king.

Nigel Goncool sat not far away from Calista and Caprius and heard her toast Confidus Seaton. "My friends," he muttered, "your king and society are about to fall." Nigel turned and snuck a look down the aisle, and his eye caught Caprius' claymore glinting in the sunlight.

"Now about us," said Calista, leaning back. "Tell me more about your past loves. Were there any other women besides Melina?"

Caprius felt his past catch up with him all of a sudden. He hesitated. "There… there were a few others. But, it was not really love with them, more like infatuation. Melina is the only girl I have ever really loved."

"And, what about Melina? Was she ever involved with anyone else?" Calista asked.

"There was one other. His name was Fenison Torington. Actually they were together when she and I met," said Caprius.

"You mean you broke them up?" she asked astonished.

"Melina and I fell in love. Fenison was hurt. And, he never really got over it. He was my friend, and I hurt him. You see, Melina and I have a connection. That is why we are meant to be together. But, I am responsible for their break up. And, Melina shares equal guilt."

"I take it you are not friends with Fenison anymore," she said.

"Because of what had happened, Fenison left Elysium and took his own life," said Caprius.

"That's so sad," Calista murmured. She felt suddenly so safe and warm with Caprius, and she knew he felt the same with her, sharing past secrets, trusting her with them. Now, she thought about her dark secret. To make things more complicated, she then remembered one of her many dreams from the night before, one in which she and Caprius had taken part in sexual acts together.

The train went over a bump, and she snapped out of her thoughts and back into the present. "And, as for me... I have been thinking about what you said. About the secret I carry. And, of Andromin. I want to be open with you." She hesitated before continuing. "Do you promise me you will try to understand?" Caprius leaned in. "This isn't easy for me," said Calista.

Caprius took her hands in his and held them gently. "It's okay. You can tell me."

Calista swallowed as she tried to speak. She held back. "No, I cannot," she said.

"I promise you I will understand. You have my word," said Caprius gently.

She let go of Caprius' hands and decided to lay bare her turbulent inner life. Perhaps it would free her. "I'm not the woman you think I am. I dread my past, who my father was," said Calista.

"Go on," said Caprius eagerly.

"I don't know how to tell you any other way. So, I'll just say it," she said. "My father was Cambrozes Genesis." She sighed. "Which makes Andromin my half-brother. That is why, when Andromin tried to get close to me romantically, I pushed him away."

Caprius stared at her, his face registering both shock and scorn. He tried to maintain control, but inside, his stomach was churning. "I'm sure you feel better now," he said icily.

She smiled. "Yes, actually. It's such a relief to get that off my chest."

"I'm very glad for you. But, for me, this changes things." He realized his blood was boiling, made worse by the fact that that horrible man's daughter, the man who terrorized their mother, raped her, ruined her in many ways, was sitting across from him smiling, calmly putting jam on a muffin. "In fact, when this mission is over, I am going to tell my father who you really are. Because of what your father did, my mother was in fear for years!" Caprius lost control of himself. "It took my mother years to recover. Your sick father deserved to die!" he shouted. The other dining car patrons looked over with a mixture of fear and annoyance, and among them was Nigel, who began to grin widely at Caprius' reaction.

Calista broke down. Caprius' voice took on an eerie calm. "I want you out of our castle. You may stay in Elysium if you wish; we can avoid you. But, you are not to have any involvement with my family."

"What about my brother, Andromin?" she said crying.

"Well, you see, we already knew Andromin was the son of Cambrozes Genesis. I found that out a while ago. Which is why he will never be king. But, Andromin doesn't know his own dark legacy, and we, the Seatons, will tell him when the time is right."

Calista continued to sob. "You said you would understand. I thought you would be forgiving." Through her tears, she said, "This isn't my doing. I had nothing to do with it."

"He was your father, and you are his progeny. Apples don't fall far from trees. I should've known something was amiss when you tried to seduce me, a married man, in our hotel. Your father was a sick, coldhearted bastard," said Caprius to Calista. He leaned in close. "And, so are you." Caprius stood and threw down his napkin. "Cry all you want, but I'm leaving. When we arrive in about three hours' time, I expect you to be ready to work and emotionally detached from your feelings. So, pull yourself together," Caprius hissed before returning to their sleeping compartment.

Caprius, upset, didn't do anything more at the time, so upset as he was, at the side of the wall, near the door, he pulled down a switch. In an instant, from the top of the ceiling, a retractable set of beds came down into place. One bed appeared after the other, sliding down. Caprius, knowing Calista would want the bottom bunk, took the top. He settled in for a nap. But, he didn't feel like sleeping or resting. After ten minutes, he decided to watch some entertainment. To the side of the bunk was a built-in remote. It was magnetic, so he pulled on it to grab it in hand and pushed the on switch. From the other side of the bunk, on the path walk, from the side of the wall, came out a sliding bar. Caprius pushed another button on the remote to turn on the TV, and a holographic three-dimensional image came into play. He then pushed another button to remotely angle the image to the side, to his liking.

Shock overtook Calista when she realized what had just happened. Things had been so wonderful with Caprius, her life feeling like it was on track. And, now, because she confided in him, all that was torn to shreds. She stared at the seat in front of her playing and replaying what had just taken place.

She felt a hand on her shoulder. She turned and saw Nigel Goncool standing beside her. Her heart began to race. Nigel sat down across from her, his eyes locked onto her face. "Nigel," she whispered. "But, what-"

"Hello, my lovely. It's been a long time," he said.

She stared at him intently. Emotion flooded her; she felt confused, frightened, and thrilled all at once.

"Nigel, I thought you were dead. What are you doing here?" she asked.

"I am here for you. I heard the shouting, what Caprius said. Calista, I am the only friend you have. And, despite you running off on me, I forgive you. And, I am here now."

"I don't understand." She tried to control her breathing while she put all the clues of the past together. "I heard you were executed. But, I didn't stay in Koriston long enough to find out what really happened."

"And, what did you hear?"

"That you were beheaded," said Calista.

"Actually, it was I who beheaded the executioner, with a little help from Thornin and a few good men who organized my escape. They are now Goncools," said Nigel proudly.

"You never cease to amaze me," she said. "What is it you want from me?" she asked.

"I want to set things straight. Come away with me. I need you. Look what has happened. Caprius knows now who you really are, and he wants you out of his life. You don't need him or his family. You belong with me."

"Nigel, I know of what we once shared. But, I cannot go down that road again," said Calista.

"It will be different this time," said Nigel.

"I don't know," she said shaking her head.

"I heard the way he spoke of your father. Everyone makes mistakes, but to say such slanderous things... are you going to take that from him?" he asked. "Get even with him." Nigel got up and sat next to her. "You have no life in Elysium. I know of your past. And, despite who your father was, I still want you. Calista, I love you. I've always loved you. Come away with me, and leave this life behind. We'll go somewhere far away, you and I." He kissed her on her cheek. She looked at him and gazed into his eyes. They began to kiss.

"Oh, Nigel," she closed her eyes and brought her body to his. She remembered his touch intimately. It gave her goose bumps.

They continued to kiss. "Come away with me," he said.

She pulled away and nodded. They held each other.

"There is something I need you to do," he said.

"What is it?" she asked.

"I need you to get me Caprius' solace claymore. Can you do that for me?" he asked cupping her heart-shaped face in his hands.

"His claymore is right by his side all the time," she protested. "That will be impossible."

"You share a sleeping compartment. You'll do it tonight. When he's asleep. Bring his solace to my compartment. Number 113. I'll be waiting for you," he said. He kissed her again.

"Alright," she nodded. "I'll do it when he's asleep."

"That's my baby." He hugged her and went back to Vernon. "This is going to be easier than I thought. That squabble with Caprius was the best thing that could have happened to us. And, now," he huffed on his fingernails and polished them against his black top, "Calista agreed to turn over Caprius' solace claymore to us."

"Do you believe that?" asked Vernon.

"I believe she will. Kisses can be deadly," said Nigel with a smirk.

Calista spent the next several hours staring out the large window. The landscape was beautiful, but it did nothing to lift her spirits. Finally, Caprius appeared. He sat down opposite her without speaking. Evening was settling in, and a waiter came through the cabin to bring Caprius and Calista their dinner. Caprius ate with gusto. Calista, on the other hand, barely touched her meal. "You should eat," said Caprius. "You need your strength."

Calista didn't respond but thought about Nigel and, further, what she would do later that night to Caprius. He ate and looked out the window, impervious to her. She felt the chill radiating off of him. She knew her chance to be a part of the Seaton family was gone. Her decision was made.

"We should arrive at 3:00 a.m. We'll take a room at the inn to get a few hours' sleep and be on the road by 9:00 a.m."

She nodded imperceptibly, her face to the window. Caprius began to say something but thought better of it. He closed his mouth and walked away.

Eventually, Calista dozed off in her seat, not going back to the compartment she shared with Caprius until the night was well underway and she was sure he was asleep. She didn't want to have to speak with him anymore.

"Calista, Calista, my sweet, wake up." Nigel was stroking Calista's long hair. He kissed her on the lips. "Are we all set for tonight?"

"Yes," she said.

"When you have the solace claymore, bring it to my cabin. Number 113," he said. "And, Calista, I can trust you?"

"I'll knock on your door when I have it," she kissed him goodnight and made her way down the long corridor.

Caprius was breathing deeply on the bottom berth when she entered in the dark. She climbed up to her berth and lay for what seemed a long time. "Caprius?" she whispered.

"What?" Caprius answered.

"Oh. Nothing. Go to sleep," she said, annoyed he was such a light sleeper. She began to wonder how she'd possibly get his claymore away from him if a whisper disturbed his sleep.

She waited more, then tried again. "Caprius, are you asleep?"

"No, I'm not, but I'm trying," he said.

"Sorry," she said. She was very tired and wished she could just get this whole ordeal over with. She knew once she took his claymore, there would be only fear in her dreams that she'd done the most wrong thing of all, despite what he was doing to her.

"Caprius?"

"What is it, Calista?" asked Caprius, annoyed.

She didn't respond and hoped he'd just fall back into his deep breathing again. A few moments later, his breath slowed. "Caprius?" This time Caprius did not answer. She crept out of her upper bunk and landed lightly on the floor like a cat. She reached out and touched the claymore. Caprius sniffed and turned over. His hand reflexively went to his sword, but it fell, limp to the blanket. And, there, Calista was able to slide it from its sheath. She held it and let it catch the moonlight streaming in through the small window. "Goodbye, Caprius. I'm very sorry it's come to this." She opened the door and walked out.

Compartment 113 was at the other end of the train. She walked through the corridors holding the claymore beneath her tunic hoping not to be noticed by any night owls who might be about. When at last she reached it, Nigel opened almost instantly. She wordlessly handed the claymore to him. Nigel smiled gently. "Why don't you come in," he said.

The power of the claymore was at work; while Caprius lay sleeping, his solace dagger at the side of his boot was humming and vibrating, telling him there was danger afoot. The claymore in Nigel's cabin vibrated so loudly, Nigel wrapped it in a blanket. He was gleeful like a child. "The power; it is working!" He embraced Calista and passionately ravaged her. She returned the passion, remembering their love, his body. Yet, once Nigel was satisfied, he sat up. "Get dressed," he commanded her. The solace was humming and vibrating to such an extent he was worried it would awaken those in the nearby compartments.

Alone in the compartment, Caprius sat straight up in his berth. His hand flew to his side. He thought a moment and knew what had happened. "Calista!" He grabbed his solace dagger from his boot and lurched out into the corridor. He moved quickly, not knowing where he was going and trusting only his dagger as his guide.

In Nigel's cabin, Calista reticently began to pull on her clothes. When she looked up, Nigel was pointing a dagger at her. "Thanks for the solace claymore. And, for our little romp. Just like old times. You didn't actually think I trusted you, did you?"

Her heart fell. Again she'd been betrayed, left. "You bastard!" she cried.

"Now, die, little princess," he said and swung his dagger at her neck. Calista quickly stepped back. Nigel thrust the dagger at her again but missed when she jerked to the side and grabbed his wrist. The two struggled, crashing into the walls and knocking things over. Nigel lifted Calista up holding her against the ceiling. Calista swung her right leg, smacking him in the chin. Nigel lost his balance and Calista fell down on top of him. Calista quickly rolled away from him. They both sprang at one another. Calista kicked him in the crouch, and Nigel fell onto the bed. She quickly took the blanket covering him up. Nigel tore through the blanket with his dagger, nearly stabbing Calista as she lunged back. He used both legs to throw her off the bed, and she crashed into the wall. A picture frame tumbled down hitting her head, and she quickly grabbed it. She held the picture frame, smacking it onto Nigel's head as he came at her. With the picture frame around his neck, he swayed the knife side to side. Calista jumped back. Nigel quickly removed the picture frame from around his neck. He growled at her. He jumped at her and she quickly grabbed hold of his wrist that carried the dagger with both her hands. They struggled, holding their hands in the air. The dagger struck the light fixture on the ceiling, cracking it, and the pieces of glass landed onto the floor. The room went partially dark. One light bulb remained upon the ceiling fixture. "I'm going to carve that pretty face of yours!" Nigel swung his arm holding the dagger, and Calista jumped back hitting the wall. "You're running out of room. No place to go. No place to hide." Nigel lunged forward with the dagger as Calista moved to the side. The daggers point struck the wall. Calista kicked his arm and went for the dagger, which was pinned to the wall. She grabbed a hold of it and quickly swung her arm stabbing him at the side of his head, striking his left ear. Nigel screamed as the blade scratched his ear, causing it to bleed. Calista quickly swung the knife again puncturing him in the chest. The blade was not deep. He screamed now holding both hands on her wrist trying to push the blade away. Nigel's hands shook. He was in fear. His eyes widened. He found his strength and twisted her wrist. The dagger fell to the floor. Nigel dove for the dagger head first and grabbed it. Calista was on top of him, and she lunged over him grabbing hold of the frame of the bed on the upper part of the wall. She quickly turned facing him. As he picked up the dagger rising to his feet, Calista held both hands on the bed frame, threw her legs around his neck, and tightened them, pulling him down to the side, tossing him onto the floor, and twisting her body until she was on the floor herself. The dagger, which had fallen to the floor, pierced Nigel's thigh, cutting through. He screamed in agony. He moved to the side on the floor and pulled it out of his thigh. Calista quickly rose to her feet. Nigel rose to his feet. His leg was in pain. He lunged at her, swinging the dagger, and Calista swung her fist at his jaw striking him hard. Nigel spit out his tooth. He swung the blade, but Calista grabbed his wrist. They struggled for the dagger.

Caprius continued his journey down the corridor of the train, following the activity of his dagger. When he heard loud thuds and grunts from what sounded like a woman and man fighting in a compartment, he burst in. Caprius glared at Nigel's sweaty face. "Nigel Goncool," Caprius said. "Why am I not surprised to see you here."

Knowing he was cornered, Nigel elbowed Calista in the chin and grabbed hold of her, pulling her to him. He grabbed hold of the dagger, which had fallen from her hand. He pointed the dagger at her throat and looked at Caprius.

"Back off, Seaton, or she dies!" Nigel shouted.

"Don't listen to him, Caprius! Take your solace claymore and-" Calista tried to say.

"Shut up! You bitch!" said Nigel piercing her throat with the tip of the dagger. "All I want is this piece of tin, and you can have her. You'll find she's very nice in bed."

"Thanks anyway, I'm married," said Caprius.

"What a pity for you," said Nigel. "Her kisses taste like raspberries. She's sweet, inside and out." Nigel peered into Caprius' face. "So, what's it going to be Caprius, the solace or the girl?"

Caprius pretended to consider the option. "Hmm, I don't know. I'm still thinking about it," he said lifting his claymore from the berth.

"You made your choice, now I'll make mine!" said Nigel. Just then, Calista, who was fuming over Caprius not choosing her, who was, she realized, livid from his horrible reaction to her confession, back kicked Nigel in the crotch as hard as she could. He fell to his knees, moaning, and dropped the dagger. Calista grabbed Nigel's hand. She hefted him up and over her shoulder, throwing him onto the floor. She picked up the dagger that he'd dropped, and before he could get to his feet, she stabbed Nigel in the heart. Behind her, Caprius held his claymore of power steady. He channeled his powers and lifted Nigel off the floor. Blood spilled from Nigel's mouth as he tried to ask Calista, "Why?" Before she could answer, Caprius pushed Nigel against the window so hard, he crashed through and dashed to the tracks. Calista ran to the shattered window; Nigel's body rolled over the tracks a few meters from the force, like a limp doll, until he stopped, forever. She turned and, forgetting their recent rift, rushed into Caprius' arms.

Caprius roughly pulled her back looking at her. "You betrayed me," he said.

Calista nodded. She realized that acting emotionally at a time when she needed to be an advocate for

Elysium despite her personal situation was juvenile and could have affected the entire kingdom's future. "I'm so sorry," she whispered. "Whatever is going on between us, that will never happen again."

He pulled her close again and held her in his arms. They stood embracing each other mostly out of the loss of the other. They held on because they knew what they'd had: friendship, feelings of something deeper, trust, those things were gone to them.

Too much had happened for them to try and sleep, so they headed to the dining car to get a drink. Caprius was deeply disappointed in her for betraying him, but he also knew he'd given her good reason to go against him. He took a sip of his grog and clasped his hands together with his elbows on the table. "Tell me, what did Nigel promise you?"

She could barely get the words out. "He promised me that we would have a life together. He lied to me. But, he was convincing; he used our history together to manipulate me, to get me into bed, to make me think we had a future."

"So, you made love to him," said Caprius raising an eyebrow.

Calista shook her head, a few tears falling onto the table. "It was such a mistake. I wish none of this had happened and certainly that I had never taken your solace claymore." Her voice was hoarse, almost broken. "I am so very sorry. There's no excuse." She fidgeted in her seat. "It's just that, when you blew up…" she paused, "you and your father, your whole family, they just mean so much to me. And, now that's all gone."

"I reacted badly. It must have been shocking to you. So, if it pleases you, to be fair, I'll say I forgive you."

Calista sighed deeply. "Thank you," she said, her voice filled with emotion. "And, I will watch your back. No more deceit and no more lies. After the mission is over, as you stated, I will leave Castle Elysium and quietly resign from his majesty's assault force."

Caprius looked down at the table and sipped his grog. They both turned to look out the window into the dark of pre-dawn, there being little more to say. Finally, to break the silence, Caprius said, "At least that's one Goncool out of the way."

A tear slid down Calista's cheek. She brushed it away brusquely. "Eighteen more to go," she said. "I wonder if we'll meet up with any more along the way."

"Seems our chances are best if we encounter them in a group. But, arresting them will be impossible. We're going to have to kill them all," said Caprius. "Will that be a problem for you?"

"No. With Nigel now out of the way, it won't be a problem. My allegiance is to the Council of Confidus. And, I will honor that, so help me God."

Caprius looked at her through narrowed eyes. She seemed to be authentic, and he saw how she was remorseful for what she'd done and that her hasty actions had been beyond foolhardy. But, it was such a dramatic betrayal, he'd need her to prove her loyalty again for him to trust her. He glanced at his pocket watch. "We are approaching the city of Galdington. It won't be long now." Caprius finished his grog and slammed the glass onto the table face down. They quickly got to their compartment, took their things, and then waited in the corridor. Moments later, when the train arrived at Galdington station, Caprius and Calista disembarked.

Vernon Goncool, back in his compartment, prepared his things and wondered what was taking Nigel so long. He was becoming concerned that something had gone awry. Finally, he stepped from his compartment and went to Nigel's. There was no sign of him. The window was shattered, and there was a pool of blood on the floor.

Vernon clenched his fists. He knew Nigel was dead. Vernon ran out of the cabin and through the corridor. He stepped off the train and looked among the travelers until he spotted Caprius and Calista making a quick exit. He followed them but kept his distance.

Caprius and Calista took a simple room at Molly Mable's Inn close to the station. The room available had only one bed. They were so tired and had been through so much, they didn't bother worrying about this. Vernon Goncool held back, and as soon as the pair went up the stairs, he, too, booked himself a room.

Caprius and Calista fell into the bed without any discussion. The night was dark, a shadowed moon in the sky, and soon Calista was woven in upsetting dreams. She saw herself running in the woods. Running from Nigel. She took refuge behind a tree and closed her eyes. Nigel was calling out to her in the sweetest, most loving voice. Yet, she trembled. His voice faded away and all was quiet. When she opened her eyes, a chilled hand came around and grabbed her chin. It was Nigel. The next moment she was back on the train with Nigel in the bunk making love. She felt Nigel penetrate her and gasped, then gasped harder and louder, the pain excruciating, and then with a last push, she gave birth to Nigel's child. She held the baby in her arms. It opened its eyes, and they were bright ruby red. In an instant, she was in a burning village, fire all around her and hundreds of horrid vampire creatures flying in the sky.

She was surrounded by burning corpses; they were closing in. The sky turned crimson red.

Calista woke up screaming. Caprius immediately held her. "I'll be alright. Just a bad dream," she said breathing heavily.

"What did you see?" asked Caprius.

"I saw myself giving birth to Nigel's child. I saw the village burning," she said.

"Which village?" Caprius asked.

"I think it was Jethro," she said. "I have had this dream once before not too long ago. I hope it's not a premonition of things to come." Calista lay back. "The child was a demon child with dark powers. One who would grow up to follow Makoor," Calista whimpered. "My God, what have I done? I only meant to share a night with Nigel. I'm such a fool," she began to sob uncontrollably.

Caprius murmured, "Makoor's followers are growing in size. There are more and more of them every day."

Calista put her hand on her abdomen. "If I am with child…" she paused, "then I must die. This child must not be born."

"Oh, no, no," Caprius murmured. "It was just a dream. You're going to be fine."

But, Calista was beyond herself, locked into her dream state. "If I am to die, then I want you to do it." She grabbed Caprius. "I wish to die by the powers of Petoshine. That is my last wish."

He smiled tenderly. "Yes, I understand. But, we do not know for certain that you are carrying Nigel's child. We will know in time. But, for now, you may live."

"As long as I am alive, I will fight by your side, Caprius Seaton."

"And, I by yours," said Caprius.

Calista was exhausted. She lay down again and, within seconds, fell into a deep sleep. Caprius lay back down as well, and soon, he too fell asleep.

At exactly this moment, far away in the land of Petoshine, within Petoshine Castle, Grongone the great wizard was sitting on his throne in deep thought with his eyes closed. The four Muskata monkey creatures sat on the floor before him in meditation. When Grongone opened his eyes, the Muskatas opened their eyes, too.

"Did you see it?" asked Grongone.

"Yes," said Chooko.

"Tell me," said Grongone, folding his hands together.

"Calista carries a great burden. She had sexual relations with Nigel Goncool and now believes she could be carrying Nigel's child," said Chooko.

"If she is, that child must be destroyed," said Mishka. "For, if it is allowed to be born, then a follower of Makoor it will become."

"Calista must die," said Mravish. "If she dies, the child dies. Then there is no need to worry."

Chooko was angry. "I do not understand," he erupted. "Why did Confidus send Calista on this mission with Caprius? Andromin could have postponed his vacation plans."

"Confidus knew what he was doing. Andromin has too many problems and would not have been a competent partner to Caprius. Calista is a superior warrior. But, now with what is about to happen, I can see this decision may have sent her to her death," said Grongone.

"So, then it's confirmed that the Dark Lord has planted a seed that will grow inside of her?" asked Mishka, tilting her head as she hopped over to Chooko.

"No, no. I for one do not believe it is so. Let us not be hasty," said Chooko. "Grongone, do something?"

Grongone held up his hands, closed his eyes, and opened his mind. He closed his hands, as if to hold air within them, his thoughts entirely on Calista. He slipped deeper into his powers and looked into her womb. He looked deeper and deeper, moving past blood, muscle, tissue, cell. He moved so he was inside and felt her heart beating. He looked again, then opened his eyes. He sighed and smiled. "Calista will bear no child. She is now free of Nigel Goncool. I have seen this with my spirit. Her womb is empty," said Grongone.

Mravish hopped up and down. "I was so worried."

"Then, she may live," said Mishka.

"Yes. Nigel did attempt to plant his seed within her. But, nature has triumphed over the dark forces," said Grongone.

"And, what of the burning village she saw?" asked Chooko.

"That, I'm afraid, is to come. The village is Jethro," said Grongone somberly. "Tomorrow they will enter the village. And, soon, war will enter as well. As we speak, Makoor is preparing his demons for battle upon Jethro. There will be much bloodshed." Grongone slipped back into his powers and was relaying the images arriving to him. "I see that Caprius and Calista are walking into a trap. In her dream, Calista saw Caprius' lifeless body by her side, something she did not tell him. But, she didn't see her own body beside his soon thereafter. She will perish, too." Grongone sat back, his eyes open wide. "I have been blindsided! I did not see it."

"Caprius and Calista must be saved. You must intervene!" said Chooko.

Grongone was shaking his head. "Calista is not a knight master. Nor has the prophecy stated that the daughter of Cambrozes Genesis would become one," he said.

"Are you saying that the prophecy was misread?" asked Mishka.

Grongone glared at the Muskata who dared challenge him. "I know the prophecy," said Grongone. "And, so do you."

"Then, what of Calista Genesis? What is to become of her?" asked Treshka.

"I do not wish to put any more burden upon her. She was not meant to die," said Chooko. "Grongone?"

"I am left with no choice!" said Grongone. He stood and began to pace.

"There is no other way, Grongone?" said Mishka gently.

"Yes, but to have the daughter of Cambrozes Genesis become a knight master with great power? What would Felicia - the Golden Fleece think?" asked Grongone.

The Muskatas began to gather closer around their master's feet, their sweet small voices imploring, their palms facing up in question and pleading. "You either embrace her with the full power of Petoshine or you condemn her to death," said Treshka.

"Caprius cannot save her and fight the battle upon Jethro at the same time," said Mishka.

"If she is to become a knight master, a great ally she will become for Caprius," said Treshka.

"This is a prophecy to be rewritten," said Mravish. "It changes things."

"Yes, but having Calista endure the power, how will it end in the future?" asked Chooko.

"It is a prophecy unforeseen," said Mishka. All the Muskatas shook their little monkey heads quietly.

"I will have to give this matter more thought. There is time," said Grongone. "But, now we must absorb the light of Petoshine. Come, my Muskata friends. We must go now."

Chapter 13

First Knight

CYNTHIA RODE THROUGH THE TOWN of Jethro on horseback. Rain was dumping down, turning everything gray and sodden, but she barely noticed it, her thoughts on the task ahead. The elderly man had had tipped her off that some slug named Kyle Rivers was squirreled away in a little strip bar in a dismal part of town. She needed to find out where the scum would gather to bid on Colburn's serum and give him the tidy profit he was slobbering for. The sound of her horse's hooves on the scrabbled ground below were nearly drowned out by the pouring rain as she made her way to Reaper's Strip Bar.

When she arrived, she tethered the horse to a post and entered. She paused in the doorway, regretting the whole errand. The place was dark, filled with smoke, and stank of sour beer. They began to walk between the rows of tables. Up front was the stage where a beautiful girl, probably not older than her son, was dancing with a pole. The place was packed with scruffy middle-aged men, and as she walked through, she could feel their eyes on her body. "Hey, honey, why don't you set yourself down on my lap," called a man after her. "You look mighty tasty." Cynthia, who had her arms crossed, coolly turned around, eyed him with disdain, and kept walking. She had to look at everyone there to find her man, and she was growing more disgusted by the second.

She paused and scanned the room. "Hey, unless you plan on taking your clothes off, I don't want you blocking my view," said the man behind her.

Cynthia looked at him. "Keep your boy toy in your pants," she said. Just then, Cynthia spotted the man who fit Kyle's description in the corner. She walked toward him.

The man was thin with boney cheeks and long white hair. She stood in front of his table. He took a gulp of his beer and set the glass down with his eyes on her. Cynthia unzipped the top part of her skin tight black outfit revealing the top of her cleavage. "Smile for me," she said sweetly. The man grinned, and sure enough, his two front teeth were gold. "What's up, doc? I'm the bunny you're looking for." Cynthia pulled her zipper down to her belly. "You Kyle Rivers?" she asked him.

"That all depends on what you want to show me," he said, his grin growing even wider.

Cynthia sat on the empty chair beside him. A waitress came by. "I'm buying," she said to him. "Two beers. No wait; make mine a Dykonian soda. A girls got to watch her weight." She leaned toward Kyle. "I want in," she murmured. Kyle's breath quickened and he rubbed his hands on his thighs. "I know you are with Colburn, and I want to bid on the serum."

"It's going to cost you," he said, gazing at her chest.

"When and where is the bidding?" she asked.

"Five hundred. I get my money, I tell you when and where," said Kyle.

"How about I up the price. Instead of five hundred, I'll give you these." She caressed her breasts seductively. "You'll get to see everything. I'll take it all off. Right here, in back," said Cynthia. "You even get to touch," she smiled warmly. "So, where's the bidding?" she asked again. Kyle didn't answer. Cynthia took a deep breath and released a clip at the front of her bra, revealing the soft skin beneath. He looked down and began to reach for her. Cynthia clipped her bra back together and zipped up her outfit to the chest, keeping it open just enough to hold his interest. "Show's over, Kyle." She stood.

Kyle gestured with his hand. "Alright, alright. You can find Colburn at the Sun Myers warehouse. It's just north of Quanta-paloose. The bidding's at noon two days from now."

Cynthia flashed him a gracious smile. She took a big gulp of her soda and set the glass down on the table. She straddled his leg, unzipped her outfit to her belly and stood over him a moment, as if she were going to keep undressing. She waited as he began to look a bit wild in the eyes, then abruptly zipped up all the way to the top. "Hope you enjoyed, Kyle. That's all there is."

Kyle stood in anger, kicking his chair over. Cynthia reached over and yanked out both her swords and held them in front of her. "Careful there, I wouldn't want to accidentally cut something off," she said, staring down at his pants. Kyle glared at her a minute before slowly and painfully leaning over, righting his chair and sitting. "There are rooms over there," she pointed to backstage. "Perhaps you need a few minutes to yourself?

Oh, and you're welcome to my soda." Cynthia slowly backed away before heading for the door.

"Hey, doll, you want a job?" the owner of the strip bar asked as she passed the front. Cynthia walked out of the strip bar without a word.

"I didn't even have to flash a nipple," she said smirking. "I even still have time to get something to eat. I wonder what's good around here," she said. Seeing a restaurant at the end of the block, Cynthia walked toward it and went inside.

***

After claiming two horses at the stables, Caprius and Calista rode over the trails mixed with dirt and snow out of the city of Galdington to the city of Jethro. Keeping his distance was Vernon Goncool, also on horseback. Vernon was furious over the death of his brother and felt not only stricken with guilt for not having been there to prevent it but blind with anger that the two had gotten the better of him. He wanted to the solace claymore and see both Caprius and Calista dead. But, he knew he couldn't be hasty and had to bide his time, so he remained in the shadows until he could give them their due.

The early morning was thick with fog, making it difficult to see more than an arm's length in front of the horses. After Caprius and Calista went down a small hill, they could make out the barest outlines of buildings in the city of Jethro. They continued on, unaware that Vernon was standing on the hilltop behind them obscured by the mist swirling around him and his steed. He made a dark silhouette against the gloomy background.

Calista and Caprius made their way through the gravel-covered main road and looked in the shops as they passed. It was a quaint town, but the people seemed to be deeply affected by the fog. They walked about listless, no one speaking to anyone else. Caprius stopped one man, "I say, my good sir, can you tell me where the local pub is?" The man looked slowly at Caprius but said nothing. Calista nudged Caprius that they should move along. The man looked half-dead and very frail. They waited another moment to see if he'd answer, but he just stood there, his mouth dumbly open a bit. So, Caprius and Calista rode on. "Not a very helpful chap, was he?" Caprius remarked. A moment later, Caprius called out to a woman on a porch rocker. "I say, old woman, is there a pub nearby?" he asked. The woman just rocked back and forth.

"This is very odd," said Calista, shrugging. "I guess we'll just have to find a pub ourselves." They kept on until they finally came upon an old rundown pub beside a church with several large bells in the belfry. The pub's sign was broken. "'The Greasy Spoon,'" Caprius snickered. "That hardly sounds delicious."

There was nothing else around, so Calista shrugged and dismounted. "I guess this place will have to do," she said. They tethered their horses to a post and went in. A few people were sitting at tables with pints of ale before them. They lifted the glasses to their mouths, but no one spoke. Not a word. When the two walked in, everyone slowly turned and stared at them.

"Hello there," Caprius wiggled his fingers to a middle-aged couple. But, they just looked at him with the same sodden expression worn by everyone else.

"Caprius, I think these people are mute," whispered Calista.

"Either that or they're scared of something," said Caprius. They sat at a small table. The place felt less like a pub and more like a funeral home. Caprius suspected he could stick a pin in the man beside him and he wouldn't react.

After at least ten minutes passed, Calista raised her voice. "Are we ever going to get served around here?" Calista began tapping her foot on the floor impatiently.

"Is there a waiter in the house?" Caprius called out. Everyone turned to stare at Caprius. "Well, at least we know they can hear," he whispered to her.

He tried to stare down a few of the people, but their gazes were unwavering. "Mathis never mentioned this place was so dead. I thought the village of Kasheema was dead, but this place has Kasheema beat," said Caprius. A moment later, from behind them, the floor creaked. It was a waiter. Calista continued to tap her foot on the floor. The people were still staring at them. The waiter stood over six feet tall; he had a large belly, receding hairline with long soft orange hair that fell down his broad back, and a scruffy, unshaven face.

The waiter stood by Calista. "Please don't tap your foot. It makes too much noise," he whispered.

Calista stopped tapping. "Sorry," she smiled. "Can we get a menu, please? We're starving!" The man just stood looking down at her. They both looked at the waiter wondering if he would respond. Calista tried again. "Do you have any specials?" she asked slowly. The waiter didn't say anything.

"Alright, let's try this," said Caprius. He spoke carefully, enunciating each syllable. "We would like two glasses of your finest ale and two specials. Do you understand?"

The waiter nodded yes and tried to smile. It took his face several seconds to arrive at the finished product. Before he turned, he said again, "Please, stop tapping your foot. It makes too much noise." The waiter let his smile fall away and walked into the kitchen. Calista stopped tapping her foot. "Well, it seems they only serve one thing, so I hope it's good."

In a corner of the room at a booth was Vernon Goncool. He had a clear sightline to the two and stared unabashedly through the smoke of the cigar he was holding.

After about five minutes, the waiter brought ale to Caprius and Calista. He plunked the glasses down and walked away. They sipped tentatively. "At least the ale is good," said Calista.

"Yes, quite good actually," said Caprius. They savored their ale not knowing when the food might come. After some time, the waiter reappeared with two plates of food. Calista stared at the meal, unsure of what it was. "What is this stuff?" she muttered.

Caprius dipped his fork in. "It tastes like… I'm not sure, but I think it's meatloaf."

Calista lifted a limp brown thing with her fork. "Sautéed with long-stem mushrooms," she said in an arrogant voice. "Oh, come on. This is awful."

"Well, it's the only Greasy Spoon in town, so eat up," grinned Caprius, digging in.

"I'm sorry, but this isn't at all something I want to eat!" said Calista. She was hungry, tired, and annoyed she had to choke down such a dreadful meal. Everyone in the place immediately turned around to look at her. While the pair was occupied by everyone else's eyes, Vernon Goncool stood and left the pub. He was light on his feet, almost as if he were floating.

"Come on, Calista. This is all the food we're going to get for who knows how long. I suspect we're going to need our strength," said Caprius, his mouth full.

Calista pursed her lips. She chewed and swallowed until everything was gone. At that moment, a woman who was eyeing the two of them approached their table and sat down.

"Well, hello there, Caprius," she said.

Caprius' eyes widened. "What are you doing here? Are you spying on me?" he asked.

She laughed. "No, merely a coincidence that we're meeting here. I'm on mission. I had a lead that brought me to this part of town."

"Still, there's more to you than meets the eye," said Caprius.

"Aren't you going to introduce me to your lady friend?" she asked, rubbing Calista's hand.

"Of course. This is my partner in crime, Calista," he said. "Calista, this is… well, I'm very sorry, but I don't know your name."

"Very well, Caprius Seaton. If you must know, or rather if you should try to remember, I am Cynthia Davenport."

Caprius thought for a moment. "Oh, my god. Little Cynthia Davenport. From high school?" he said astonished.

"Yes, well, not so little any more, as you can see," she chuckled.

"Yes, and quite beautiful," he said.

Calista shot Caprius a look. "Now that we're acquainted, Cynthia, you say you're on a mission?" she asked, turning to her.

"Yes, do tell us more about this," said Caprius.

"Of course, but I have to make it quick." She plucked a chair from the neighboring table and sat down. "I'm on a case, which I'm calling the Colburn Affair. A man named Cyril Colburn is in the process of manufacturing a drug to enhance animal intelligence. It also builds strength and stamina. He uses this drug to inject creatures, such as Droges, to give them super strength and hyper-intelligent thinking. If you thought Droges were already dangerous, you wouldn't want to encounter a super Droge. Anyway, if this drug gets into the hands of the vampires, they'll create an army of them. We have enough trouble with the undead as it is."

"This sounds important," said Calista.

"Yes, very," said Caprius. "If this serum gets out, we will definitely have more trouble than we thought."

"What's Colburn's ultimate goal in doing this?" asked Calista.

Cynthia shook her head. "Money. Colburn has arranged a meeting with Alamptria's biggest scums. The highest bidder gets the drug. I just have to wonder what will happen if the drug gets into another set of wrong hands."

"I hope you can stop this from happening," said Caprius.

Cynthia rose from the table. "It's been great seeing you, but I must go quickly," she said.

"Where are you going?" asked Calista.

"North. Just past Quanta-paloose," she said.

"But... that would lead you back to Quantum Heights," said Caprius.

"Yes, it's near there," Cynthia said, shouldering her bag. "I have to dash off. Calista, it was very nice meeting you."

"Nice to see you again, Cynthia," said Caprius, his eyes a bit wide at this new version of the gawky young girl he'd grown up with.

"Perhaps, we'll meet again," said Cynthia before turning and leaving the pub.

Caprius waited another interminable amount of time until the waiter waddled over and gave them their check. Caprius counted out the coins and put them on the waiter's tray. The waiter looked at them, frowned, and shook his head. "Was the service not to your liking, Sir? Did the food not meet your exacting standards?"

"Caprius, just tip him so we can get out of here," hissed Calista.

After Caprius clinked additional coins on the tray, the waiter brightened measurably. "Thank you, come again. I hope your stay was a quiet one," he smiled. While he was reaching down to put the money in his satchel, the church bells beside the pub began to chime for the one o'clock hour. Everyone who had been nearly comatose earlier suddenly became animated, shrieking and holding their ears. Even Caprius and Calista covered their ears against the din and bolted from the pub. Outside, the tolling bells were even louder. When they finally stopped, Caprius said, "At least now we know why they like to keep things quiet."

"Yes, that would explain it. Remind me never to enter this pub again," snorted Calista.

"Because of the food or the church bells?" asked Caprius.

"Both," said Calista. Laughing, the two untied their horses and brought them out to the main road. A man was standing in the center of the road, watching them. Caprius and Calista looked at one another as they trotted toward him. When they were close enough, they finally recognized him. It was Vernon Goncool. Caprius shouted. "Now!" and he and Calista dug in their heels and went at full gallop to run him over and kill him. Not budging from his spot, Vernon calmly unsheathed his sword and held it at the ready. Caprius wondered why the man didn't move, but before he could consider that more fully, he realized something was wrong with his saddle. He was sliding off his horse. The straps had become undone, or, he quickly realized, they'd been cut. Caprius fell off the horse hard onto the ground, directly onto his knee. Calista turned around in her saddle to look at Caprius, but her horse, so spooked by the mishap, bucked and threw her off. She lay on the ground, winded and gasping in searing pain shooting up from her ankle while both their horses galloped away.

Vernon Goncool slowly approached Calista. Caprius tried to stand, but his knee gave way, and he fell back. Vernon edged closer. Caprius dislodged his claymore of power, held it to his knee, and murmured some words. The claymore vibrated and, within seconds, his knee was healed. He stood and ran toward Calista. She was trying to scoot away from Vernon but was clearly in too much pain to move quickly. Just as the Goncool put his sword to her neck, Caprius channeled his powers and sent a bolt of energy through the man's body, causing him to fly through the air and onto his back.

Caprius rushed to help Calista. Her eyelids were fluttering as she struggled to maintain consciousness. Vernon sat up, grinning fiendishly, and transformed himself into a raging, bloodthirsty vampire. Now, hulking and powerful, he charged at Caprius like a lion at its prey. But, Caprius was empowered with his sword, and he charged as well. They hit each other with the extreme force of two blazing stars and fell back, dazed. Caprius immediately got to his feet, swinging his sword. Vernon brandished his, too, and their weapons clashed. Caprius swung wildly and severed the Goncool's right arm. Both arm and sword fell to the ground. Vampire Vernon screamed. Caprius reared up for another swing, but before his sword could make contact, the vampire spread its wings and flew away.

Caprius and Calista watched the creature fly off until it was nothing more than a dot on the horizon.

Calista looked down at the creature's severed arm, the hand still clutching the sword. Seconds later, the arm began to move. It struggled and grew until it had evolved into a complete human form. Caprius seized the brief respite granted by this gruesome transformation to deal with Calista's injury.

"I'm sure it's broken," whispered Calista.

Caprius held his claymore against her ankle. The claymore shined with a bright yellow light and, within seconds, she was able to wiggle her foot. "It's fine," she said incredulously, scratching her head. Caprius helped her up, and they readied themselves for further battle with the newly formed creature.

They turned around and paused in shock. In the sky, over fifty vampires were approaching. "Oh no!" she shouted.

Caprius' claymore began to vibrate and hum violently. "We're in for quite a fight," he said. The vampires landed, creating a circle around the two. There were over a hundred of them—so many that they ran out of space to land on the street and began landing on rooftops and in trees. They salivated and made excited, high-pitched noises.

"I didn't think it would end like this," said Calista, looking at Caprius. "For what it's worth, I'm sorry I wasn't honest with you and your family from the start." She took Caprius' hand and held it tightly against her heart. Then, she held it to her lips. "Let's die with honor," she said quietly.

He realized that, despite everything, he'd been fooling himself. He ached to touch her lips with his fingers, to wind his hand in her hair and smell her clean, earthy scent one last time. All around them, the vampires cackled wetly.

Suddenly, one of them changed himself into human form. It was Thornin Goncool. He walked casually over to them. "Oh, you two. Go ahead and take a final moment for some passion. It is the least I can do for you, given that your death is going to be extremely unpleasant." He smiled graciously.

Caprius and Calista looked into each other's eyes. Just then, in the turbulent clouds swirling above, the face of Grongone, the great wizard of Petoshine, appeared. "Caprius, it is time. The time to endure a greater power has come," he boomed.

Thornin Goncool hunched down, frightened. "What is this?" he asked in a panic.

Seconds later, a great light shined down from the sky onto Caprius and Calista like a perfect beam of sun. Caprius spoke to Grongone privately, inside his head. "No, this cannot be," said Caprius. "She is not a Seaton. Why her?" he asked.

"Yes. Yes. Yes, I know," replied Grongone, nodding.

"Then, I shall do as you ask of me." Caprius looked into Calista's eyes. "Calista, kiss me."

"But, what about—"

"Don't argue," said Caprius, grabbing her around the waist. He brought his face to hers and, as their trembling lips touched, they realized a passion that had been stirring between them since they'd met. They held each other close, their tongues searching, their lips pulsing, and suddenly lightning struck with feverish intensity all around them: the sign of a great power being formed.

"What the hell is going on?" asked Thornin. The other Goncools were petrified. Caprius' and Calista's bodies glowed bright white. Then, as suddenly as it had begun, the storm was over. All light vanished, and the world was engulfed in pitch blackness. When daylight returned, Caprius and Calista stood in glistening new armor, poised and ready for combat. Grongone had disappeared. But, they knew what had happened. Caprius looked at Calista inquisitively, as if to say, 'Are you ready for this?'

She smiled with serenity and power. "I am ready."

The vampires stood hungry and ready to attack. "Put your back to mine," Caprius said, turning around. The vampires edged closer.

Thornin began to laugh. "Oh, your Grongone has deserted you," he minced. He transformed back into a beast and flew up onto a rooftop. From there, he peered down at them. "This is a job for a master." He pointed at them and shouted, "Destroy them! Attack!"

The vampires swarmed Caprius and Calista. Within seconds, it was an all-out war between the knight masters and the vampires. Caprius and Calista swung their swords, slicing apart any vampire who approached them. Calista jumped into the air and bashed her legs into the faces of two vampires simultaneously. She swung her sword, decapitating one, and went on to kill several others.

Caprius brought his sword down through a creature's head, splitting it in two. He dislodged the sword in time to swing it before him, slicing three vampires through their middles. To his side, Calista decapitated another, then another. Then Caprius and Calista turned back to back again and, with their claymores aloft, created an expanding force so strong that the creatures coming at them were blown away as if caught in an explosion. Some of them crashed into the shop windows. One went head-first into a wooden tabletop with such force that his head splintered the wood and came out the other side. He stood with his head still caught in the table. Unable to force his head back through the hole, he went ballistic. Around him, Caprius set vampires aflame. The screaming was deafening.

The creature caught in the table kept trying to break free as he ran scattershot in Calista's direction. Seeing the large, round tabletop with a vampire head stuck through the center, Calista shot flame at it. It was engulfed within seconds. To be sure the vampire wouldn't give them any more trouble, Caprius drove his sword through the creature's face. He got two for the price of one as, yanking his sword free, he accidentally sliced through another's legs. It lay on the ground, writhing. For good measure, Caprius set it on fire, too.

Then came a team of fourteen vampires. Like football players, they ran en masse, their bodies thick and brutish. Just before they were able to reach out and grab him, Caprius leaped into the air, and while aloft, he channeled his powers from the sword to freeze the line of vampires into a wall of solid ice. He landed atop it and slid down, as easily as a skier down a mountain.

Not even aware she was able to do this, Calista extended her arm and, out the end of her claymore, shot a surge of blue electricity so powerful, it penetrated twenty-five vampires, all in some way touching one another, sizzling their flesh into bacon.

"Hmm, that's new!" exclaimed Caprius, amazed at what Calista had done. He didn't stop to celebrate for long as the battle continued to rage: hundreds of vampires amid the many fallen and two soldiers whose powers protected them as long as they were vigilant.

After another half an hour of fierce fighting, Caprius and Calista were soaked in sweat, euphoric from endorphins, and energized for whatever other plans the vampires had for them. The ground was covered with bodies; blood pooled up all around and reflected the coming evening light.

From the relative safety of the rooftop where Thornin Goncool took refuge behind a pile of vampire corpses, he continued to watch, dismayed at the ineptitude of his cult. The last vampires, those who had sustained the fight and were the strongest and boldest, were tiring while Caprius and Calista interestingly seemed to be gaining energy.

Calista cast a flame through the air so big, it engulfed over seventy vampires, sending them withering into dust piles atop one another. The sky was lit up red from yet more fire Caprius sent up that engulfed many more vampires who, too, came crashing down dead. Bruiser vampires trying brute strength came toward Calista, who nimbly sprang into the air. They bashed into one another, and she landed on top of their heads, then hopped to the ground landing on her feet and one hand, her other hand pointing with her sword of power at another faction of remaining vampires.

Every time she and Caprius defeated another one, two, twenty, forty vampires, they let themselves hope the numbers would begin to diminish. They had strength to spare, but at the same time, Calista began to wonder when it would start to wane. They might have been imbued with magic power, but they were still human. She couldn't feel this powerful forever, she knew. As soon as she vanquished another group, she would look up and see yet another standing before her, roaring hideously, their fangs dripping with blood.

Suddenly, the church bells rang out. The vampires screamed and held their pinched little pointed ears. Many of them tried to fly up above the din, and so many of them fled into the sky, they flew erratically and crashed into one another. Caprius and Calista cringed at the noise, but they were more pleased to see how much it bothered the vampires. They took some deep breaths and wiped the sweat from their faces on their sleeves.

Then the noise stopped. The vampires turned on the pair with reinvigorated purpose, as if the knights had been the cause of the noise.

"Had enough?" Calista yelled to them. She beckoned with her left hand. "Come on, show me what you've got."

Caprius muttered, "Don't encourage them, Calista."

"Caprius, seems to me they don't need much encouragement," she said. The creatures reared up and charged. They crashed into Caprius and Calista only to be brutally smacked by an invisible force emanating from their claymores. The creatures flew back, crashing into the walls and windows of the shops. Undeterred, they shook themselves off as would dogs after a bath, then came back for more. Calista and Caprius swung without pause, decapitating each vampire who came before them. At one point, Caprius' aim was poor, and a head bounced off Calista's shoulder, leaving a mark. "Eeww," Calista cried out before instinctively hitting the ground in time for a creature to swoop right down to where she'd been standing. She simply thrust her sword into the creature's face and channeled her powers, which caused the head to burst into flame. As the creature melted and disintegrated, Calista rolled out of the way. She looked up to see nine vampires hovering above her. She sent a lazy flame into the air that spread out like a cross, crucifying the creatures. She dodged the little vampire fireballs that came raining down and ran back toward Caprius just in time to see forty or more vampires flying in circular formation above them like a growing storm.

That gave them an idea. They looked at each other and at the same time, gleefully said, "Fireball!"

They raised their swords and launched a large flame that expanded into the sky and surrounded the formation of vampires like a blazing tornado. Every last remaining vampire disintegrated, and their burning embers fell like rain down onto Jethro, alighting the stores, the houses, and the streets below. People ran outside from the shops and the pub screaming.

Caprius and Calista watched the panicked scene, feeling sorry for the people of this city. But, the crackling of fire and an untamed wind were the only sounds remaining. No more beating wings, no shrieking vampires. Nothing. Their faces lit up by the fires, Caprius and Calista stood looking at the hundreds of dead corpses that surrounded them. They wove through the maze of corpses admiring their handiwork. "Where… on earth… did you learn to fight like that," he finally asked her, his voice incredulous and thrilled.

"I may have learned a thing or two from you," she shrugged, grinning.

The two bantered flirtatiously unaware that remaining on a nearby rooftop was Thornin Goncool staring down at them. Thornin wiped his brow then snarled, his fist clenched, "You may have won this little battle, knights of Petoshine. But, the real war is yet to come." Thornin lifted off into the sky. "Retreat!" yelled Thornin to his remaining few vampires who were in hiding. The ten or so vampires out of the original hundred flew off quietly into the mountains.

Calista and Caprius heard the flapping and spun around with their claymores aloft. They were surprised to see the vampires emerge from behind the main street and fly away in retreat. It made them seem so small and innocuous then, like birds. Thornin and the rest of the

Goncools might have left defeated now, but Caprius and Calista knew they still had the fight of their lives yet to come.

Caprius looked at his partner in battle with a whole new admiration. As much as he did not like the fact that her father had ravaged and terrorized his mother, he was now aware that this woman beside him was the new master knight of Petoshine. His pride in his family was great, but it was clear Calista would be his first knight.

As if she knew what he was thinking, Calista raised her sword in the air, victorious. But, she soon lowered it out of respect, and the two began to walk through the flames. Caprius and Calista nodded to the villagers who watched them as they departed to continue their investigation. It would be a long walk through the city of Jethro. But, they were ready for it.

Chapter 14

The Mists and the Avant-Guard

As Caprius and Calista walked through Jethro, they used their claymores' powers to extinguish the fires that raged all around them. The people were grateful, but as they shook the knights' hands, there was blame in their eyes for their having brought on such evil to their peaceful village.

Aware of the brewing anger, the two knights of Petoshine quickly made their way through the center of the village and continued their journey. They walked a ways until they came upon a teenage boy fiddling idly with some sticks, a bedraggled looking dog by his side. "Let me speak to him," said Calista. She smiled sweetly and approached him. "Excuse me, my young lad, but I was wondering if you could guide us to an art gallery called Delvingers." Calista swept her hair back and smiled again.

The boy looked at Calista like he had found love. His eyes got dopy, and he blushed. "If you're here to see the exhibit, I'm afraid that's not possible. We're closed today, for it is Sunday, a day of rest." He squinted and examined Calista and Caprius. "I can tell you're not from around here or you'd know that."

"Looks like we have come to the right person. You know an awful lot about the gallery," said Calista admiringly. She reached out and brushed a lock of hair out of the boy's eyes.

He looked like he might swoon and started talking rapid fire. "I actually work there. I sometimes work Tuesdays, Thursdays, and Fridays, but mostly just Fridays. That is my long day. And, I get paid two shillings a day. Although, I think I should be paid more because I have been working there for nearly three years now. And, I've never missed a day of work. Oh, except for once. But, that is because I had the measles. But, that doesn't count because it was on a Saturday. And, I normally don't work on a Saturday, so when my employer asked me to come in and I couldn't, it shouldn't have counted as a sick day. I really did have the measles, you know," the boy jabbered.

"My, you're feisty!" said Calista with overly sweet admiration in her voice. Caprius rolled his eyes.

"I'm not a boy. I'm fifteen. I'm nearly a man. My birthday is in August, so I'll be an adult real soon," said the boy.

"What is your name?" asked Calista.

"Shyla. But, don't say it's a girl's name, 'cause it's not. But, you could call me Shy. My last name is Doody. Please, no Doody jokes; I've heard them all before." Again, Caprius rolled his eyes, but he had to smile at the young man. His chatter was growing on him.

"So, Shy, how is it that you started working at Delvingers at such a young age?" asked Caprius.

Shy shrugged. "It's only because my father owns it. He gave me the job," said Shyla.

"Is anyone at the art gallery right now? Anyone at all?" asked Caprius.

"My father is there today. But, no one is permitted to get in. Except me, of course," said Shyla proudly.

"Shy, Calista and I are from Elysium. I am the son of King Confidus. We are here on a mission," said Caprius.

Shyla looked at them suspiciously. "I don't believe you. What would the Prince of Elysium be doing all the way out here?"

"Have you ever heard of the tale of Grongone and Petoshine?" asked Caprius.

"Maybe a little bit," said Shyla. Caprius pulled out his sword of power from his sheath. The boy backed up. "You're not going to kill me are you?"

"No, Shyla, we are not going to kill you," laughed Calista.

"We only mean to show you something," said Caprius. He held out his claymore. "Have you ever heard of the claymores of power?"

"Yes... I have. They are swords of great destructive power," said Shyla. Calista drew her claymore, and with her new powers, she blew an icy frost at a nearby tree. The tree instantly froze into solid ice. "Wow!" The boy exclaimed. Then, Caprius aimed his sword at the tree, shot a flaming torch at it, and melted the ice. Water came pouring down in rivulets, and the tree was unharmed. The boy jumped up and down. "You are knights of Petoshine!" he said.

"So, let's try this again. As I said, we are on a mission, and we could very much use your help," said Caprius.

"What would you have me do?" asked Shyla.

"We need you to get us into the art gallery now. It's imperative that we speak to a woman named Enlora

Renfield. Someone called Melisa who works at the gallery knows her and will introduce Enlora to us. We need to speak with her as soon as possible," said Caprius.

"Well, I would help you, but as I said, the gallery is closed. And, anyway, only my father is there today. Enlora won't be in until tomorrow."

"Could you perhaps, then, take us to see your father?" asked Caprius. "If you do this, let's just say I'll mention to your father that it's high time you got a shilling or two raise. How does that sound?"

"That would be great! Let's go," said Shyla. He started walking quickly, and the two knights followed him. Calista gave Caprius a thumbs up.

Soon they came to the front doors of the art gallery. Shyla opened the door.

"Well, my friend, thank you for showing us to the art gallery.

"There's a small hotel just one block up the street. The Delvinger Hotel," said Shyla.

"Your father owns the hotel, as well?" asked Caprius.

Shyla shrugged. "He's a busy man."

They said their goodbyes, Shyla looking forlorn as he watched Calista depart.

Early Monday morning, Caprius and Calista headed out to Delvingers. They sailed in and went directly to the elegant looking woman there. "Excuse me. My name is Caprius Seaton, and this is my partner, Calista. We are conducting an investigation and are wondering if you can help us."

She smiled gently and bowed her head. "How can I assist the Prince of Elysium?" she asked.

"We are looking for Enlora Renfield," said Caprius.

"Yes, she's here. She comes here to paint portraits. She is in the middle of one now, so I can take you to her, but she greatly dislikes being disturbed when she's at work. I'll introduce you when she's finished," said the woman. "Come this way."

While they followed her, Caprius asked, "May I ask your name?"

"Melina," she said.

"That is my wife's name," said Caprius.

"Yes," she said. "I know."

The last thing Calista felt like talking about was Caprius' wife. "I see you have some wonderful paintings here. Such a fine collection," said Calista effusively.

"Some of our paintings go back as far as the eleventh century. They fetch quite a price," said Melina.

"I should be very happy to have one of these," said Calista.

"I'm afraid they're only for private investors. But, for a more reasonable price, I'm sure Enlora would be happy to paint something for you," said Melina. "On average, it takes her about three weeks to finish a portrait. People come here from all over Alamptria."

"Funny that I had not heard of the Delvingers Art Gallery before. I didn't know such a job in painting portraits existed," said Caprius.

"People hear about us through word of mouth," said Melina. They came to a large room, every wall surface hung with paintings. In the corner by a window sat a tall, thin woman with porcelain skin and dark hair that cascaded down her back. She was concentrating on some detail work on her canvas with a small brush. A fine gentleman in full evening dress posed for her. "This is Enlora," said Melina. "But, please keep your voices down so you don't disturb her. You may speak with her when she is finished."

"Thank you, Melina," said Caprius. Melina walked away and left the knights standing in the room. They watched the artist at work for some time until it became clear they were distracting her and she was getting annoyed.

"Caprius, why don't we look at the paintings," said Calista taking Caprius' arm in hers. They inched their way around the room whispering to one another about the art. After gazing at innumerable paintings, Caprius began to get bored. Luckily, Enlora set her brush down not long after that, sat back, and examined her work.

"Mr. Bradshaw, I do believe it's finished. Would you care to have a look?" asked Enlora.

Bradshaw got off his seat and came around to admire the painting. "It's a perfect likeness," he said reverentially.

"Of course, it is. It will need one week to dry, so please do come back to pick it up then." He kissed her hand exclaiming platitudes and left. The artist began cleaning her brushes in a sink. Caprius and Calista came to her. "That's a very good painting, Mrs. Renfield."

She stared at him sharply. "Yes, it is. And, it is Ms. Renfield. But, you may call me Enlora."

"Enlora, my name is Caprius Seaton, and this is Calista Genesis. We are with his majesty's assault force on investigation."

"Assault force," she said raising an eyebrow. "Am I to be your target?"

Calista laughed. "We would just like to ask you a few questions," she said.

"What makes you think I have the answers?" asked Enlora, patting her brushes in a towel.

"We are aware that you have knowledge of the dark cult and know the marking on pocket watches. A source told us that this pocket watch..." Caprius pulled the watch out of his pocket, "... has markings you are familiar with." Caprius showed the timepiece to her.

She observed the markings closely. "This is Telusion. Markings of the underworld," said Enlora. "The small inscription here is the language of the undead." She handed it back to Caprius.

"Who wrote this?" asked Calista.

"The Dark Lord Makoor," she said, a small smile flickering over her lips.

"And, what of the marking of the two stars with a knife? That's what it looks like to me," said Caprius turning the watch over.

"That is exactly what it is. It symbolizes Makoor's two faithful right hands: Lydia the sorceress and Titanis Clore. The star underneath the two with a burning heart symbolizes Orphius Clore, Makoor's devoted henchman who betrayed him. All of Makoor's followers, thousands upon thousands of them, carry pocket watches exactly like this."

"I am told that these pocket watches are made here in Jethro. Is this true?" asked Caprius.

Enlora stared at Caprius, narrowing her eyes.

"Enlora, is this true?" Calista echoed.

"Yes. It is true," said Enlora.

"Do you know the address to this place?" asked Calista.

Enlora now began to quickly put her painting supplies away. "I know the place and I have the address. But, I don't have it with me. It is written down at my home."

She paused, then smiled slowly. "Mr. Seaton, why not come tomorrow to my home so I can give you that information? And, while you're there, it would be my honor to do a portrait of the two of you. Shall we say 8:00 p.m.?"

"Miss Enlora, thank you for the offer, but we have had to wait two additional days already. Two of our agents have been killed. We are losing precious time. Is there any way we can come to you tonight?"

Enlora paused, staring at Caprius. There was something mysterious and intriguing about her. She smiled, showing perfect white teeth. "Very well, tonight, then," she said. She wrote her address down on a piece of paper and gave it to Caprius, letting her hand linger against his as he took it.

As Caprius and Calista walked away, Enlora stared at their departing backs as if she were a leopard waiting to strike.

When night fell, Caprius and Calista set out on foot to Enlora's house. She lived outside of the village, and as they walked away from the center, the homes grew larger and the landscape more lush. "It is interesting how much she knew about the pocket watches. It is as though she is a part of all this," said Caprius.

"I don't trust her," said Calista. They came to hilltop manor bearing the address she'd written down. They walked through the gate and up the long path to the house. Lying over the grassy knoll to the house was a low mist, giving the effect of a graveyard.

When they got to the front door, Caprius took Calista by the shoulders and looked intently at her. "I think I should do this alone," he said. "It seems she likes me, and I can use that to our advantage. While I entertain her, you go around to the back and try to check out the house."

Calista raised an eyebrow but said nothing.

"I'll give you five minutes before I knock on the door," said Caprius.

Caprius waited, listening to the call of hoot owls. After five minutes, he knocked on the door. He knocked several times. Finally, Enlora came down to answer the door. The door creaked open, and she invited him in. "It is good to see you again, Enlora," said Caprius noticing her gown, which was cut very low in front and touched every gentle curve of her form.

"It is good to see you, too," she said. "Where is Calista?" she asked.

"She couldn't make it. I came alone," Caprius said.

She smiled. "We'll walk this way. I want to begin by painting a portrait of you." She took him to a room at the corner of the house and escorted Caprius to a chair. "I will begin by sketching you on canvas. Then, I will apply the oils." As she said this, she ran her long fingers slowly over her arm.

Caprius looked around. "What a beautiful room. So very many French windows," he said taking his seat before her canvas.

"You enjoy looking into the beautiful surroundings, the darkness of the night?" she asked, picking up her charcoal.

"It is a peaceful winter's night," he said. "You can almost hear the tinkle of snowfall coming into the room." His eye fell on the grand piano in the corner.

"Do you play?" he asked.

"I will tonight, after I have taken care of you," she said. "Whenever I invite someone over to paint his portrait, once I have finished, I always play a melody. It soothes me. For, it will be the last time I shall see him."

"Yes, I would gather in your line of work there aren't too many repeat customers," said Caprius.

Enlora didn't reply but continued to sketch. Caprius tried not to move, but his muscles were seizing up. "I'm sorry, but I need to move around a bit."

She lifted her hand. "That doesn't bother me. As long as you get back into similar position, I can finish. In any case," she said, "I have finished sketching you."

"May I see?" asked Caprius.

She held her arm out to the canvas.

Caprius peered around at the drawing, "And, next, you apply the paint?" he asked.

"Yes," she said and again stared at him as though looking through him.

Caprius found her beautiful, but her face was so still, it was as if made of stone. She dipped her brush in some paint and began applying it to the canvas.

Outside, Calista found a door that led out to the rear garden. It was locked, so she took her dagger and carved around the edge of a small window. After digging into the wood, she was able to pop out the glass, catching it just as it fell from the frame. She put her arm through and easily unlocked the door.

Caprius posed again but became impatient. "Enlora, if you don't mind, I would like to get up and walk around for a bit."

"Please, go right ahead," she said.

Caprius paced back and forth a number of times to stretch his legs. He could see Enlora was not one for idle chatter, so he didn't bother trying. The quiet was actually rather nice. He walked over to the window and gazed out into the night, then turned and went to the piano, striking a few chords, which turned into a tune.

"You didn't tell me you could play," Enlora said.

"My brother Andromin and father are the musicians in the family. But, I know a couple of pieces. Would you like me to play?" Caprius asked.

"No!" Enlora said sharply. She raised her hands and lowered her voice. "Sorry, I only mean to say that we have no time for music. We must finish this portrait."

"Yes, I understand," said Caprius, though he did not. Her behavior was so erratic, it was unsettling.

Caprius returned to his chair, and Enlora picked up her brush. He was becoming concerned that Enlora was so driven to finish her portrait, Calista might not have enough time to explore the house. He tried to converse, hoping it would help him stall for time. "How long have you been painting?"

"Nearly 21 years. I started when I was just nine years old. My father was a painter and I would paint alongside him, simple things like objects. Then, I expanded into portraits. I love painting people. I have even done landscapes. But, portraits are my preference. There is also a great deal of money in it."

"How did you join up with the art gallery?"

"I approached Mr. Doody six years ago. I told him if he would agree to my business proposition, I would give him a cut of forty percent. I told him with his help and my knowledge we could make this venture work out. He saw it as a way to get extra money, and being a sound businessman, he agreed."

Caprius was relieved she was pausing to answer his questions. Clearly, when it came to her painting, she was happy to talk.

Meanwhile, Calista was making her way through the main floor of the house. When she came to the corner room where Caprius and Enlora were chatting, she paused and peered through a crack in the door. Down in the village the church bells began to toll. They were still loud, but from this distance, the sound was manageable.

Caprius heard them, and they brought his thoughts back to the battle they had endured a few days prior. Enlora spoke, interrupting his memory. "There, Mr. Seaton, the painting is finished. You may have a look at it." She stood and gestured to him that he should come by her side.

Caprius approached the canvas and looked at the portrait. He nearly gasped; it was as if he were looking at his twin sitting in the room with him. But, it had a ghostly quality to it, as if his other self had passed away long ago and this was a relic of him in life. "You have really captured the very essence of my soul," he whispered. He turned to her. "But, now I must get that information from you. Where is that watch shop?"

"Come with me to the second floor. The paper with the address is up there," she said. Enlora took Caprius' arm in hers and left the room. Calista, who was in the hall, stepped back into the shadows just as they passed.

Caprius and Enlora walked up the staircase and went into the bedroom. The room was large and luxurious with gilt and scarlet velvet furnishings. Heavy drapes hung over the windows, and it smelled of decaying roses. The bed was the centerpiece; it was large, round, and covered in satin pillows. Enlora opened the dresser drawer. She rifled through some papers until she found the one she was looking for. "Mr. Seaton, I have the address to the clock shop you want," she said.

Caprius reached for the paper, but she pulled it away. "All in good time," she said. She lifted her face to meet his gaze with her own then reached up and softly kissed him on the lips. She took his hand and led him to her bed, laying down and guiding him to lay beside her. She glanced at his solace claymore before quickly returning her eyes to his.

Downstairs, Calista had found a secret staircase that led to the cellar. She was glad she'd taken a candlestick from the kitchen, for it provided her the only light source down there. At the bottom of the stairs was a large empty room. She walked through it and into another room.

Caprius knew he had to comply with Enlora's sexual desires to get what he needed. Somehow he knew if he dashed to her dresser and found the paper among the many papers there, there would be a confrontation that might lead to disastrous results. He told himself this as Enlora pulled her dress over her head and straddled Caprius naked. She brushed her hair back, then took his right hand and, with a silk scarf, tied his wrist to the bedpost; then, with another scarf, she tied his other wrist. She began to undress him.

Calista was perplexed that these cellar rooms should be so very empty. She came to a third room and there was a coffin on a stand. Calista was startled, wondering whether it was a tribute to a dead husband or relative until she opened the lid and saw it was empty.

"My God. Enlora is a vampire," Calista whispered. She held up the candlestick and saw paintings hanging on the wall, all portraits. She understood now that they were victims to Enlora's hunger for blood. Calista's heart seized; she realized Caprius was alone with her and that he was in trouble. Her eyes widened. She threw the candlestick into the casket. It quickly caught fire. Calista ran from the room and had to find her way out in the darkness. She bumped into walls and tripped, but she felt her way along the floor and eventually found the stairs leading up.

She darted to the room where Enlora had painted Caprius' portrait, but the room was empty. Calista quickly took the staircase that lead to the second floor.

In the bedroom, Enlora was straddling Caprius. She slowly began to stroke his inner thigh, moving up and down from his hardening manhood to his boot, up and down. Caprius began to moan and looked at the ceiling. When she was sure he was lost to his ecstasy, she snatched the dagger from inside his boot and held it before her, stroking the blade. Caprius' claymore began to vibrate and hum an eerie song of sadness. So excited by the blade in her hand was she that sharp white fangs grew from Enlora's mouth. Caprius' eyes widened but he said nothing.

Calista, hearing the song of the claymore, ran from room to room. Enlora held the dagger up high, an evil grin on her face. Downstairs, the fire had engulfed the cellar and was making its way up to the first floor. It caught in the corner room where Caprius' painting stood. In seconds, the oils on the painting began to run. In moments, his face was unrecognizable. A flame burst through the painting at the eye of Caprius' face and spread, consuming the entire canvas.

In Enlora's bedroom, a dagger held high above his heart, Caprius struggled to free his hands. Enlora's eyes began to glow red. Calista appeared at the doorway and saw Enlora reach back as if preparing to plunge the dagger into Caprius' chest. Calista quickly prepared her bow and arrow, pulled the string back, and released. The arrow arced through the air. Just as Enlora was about to stab Caprius, the arrow pierced the side of her head. Her eyes rolled backward, and her naked body crumpled onto Caprius, who was too embarrassed and relieved to enjoy it.

Calista ran to Caprius and began to untie him. She had to shove the corpse of Enlora aside, and she landed bum side up. "Is this what you call getting to the bottom of things?" Calista asked Caprius. Calista looked at the lifeless naked Enlora Renfield and began to laugh.

"Sorry, but I was a little too tied up to notice," said Caprius.

Calista sat on the bed. "I'd love to take advantage of this moment," she smirked, "But, I sort of set the house on fire. We should probably go."

Caprius looked at his partner, amazed at how unflappable she was. He opened his mouth to make a smart retort but thought better of it when he realized he hadn't gotten what he came for. "The information; it's on one of those papers on the dresser," he said.

Calista ran over and riffled through the papers. She held one up. "Here we go. No, wait a minute. This isn't the address of a clock shop. Why this is the address of a church."

"Is there anything else on that dresser?" asked Caprius.

"Let me see." She ruffled through stuff. "No. This is all we've got. But, we've got an address. 661 Ainsworth. It has a name on the card. A Sister Mildred."

"Then, that's our contact!" said Caprius.

Calista turned over the business card. "There's a note on the back of the card. It says: 'kill Sister Laura.'"

"So, I see. You know what that means, Calista."

Caprius paced back and forth. "It means Sister Mildred can't be trusted. She's one of them!" said Calista.

"This means if Enlora had failed to dispose of me, or us, she would have made sure that sister Mildred would destroy us."

"But, how? We're knight masters," said Calista.

"There is more to this church then meets the eye, something very foul."

"Do you think that entire church is up to no good, Caprius?"

"No, I don't think so. Sister Laura's life is in danger. What's the name of the church?"

"A St. Basil's Church," she replied. "Caprius?" Calista said in a humble voice. "Sister Laura might already be dead."

"We have to leave immediately. We have to get to Sister Laura. We have to get her to a safe place,"

"Come on, let's go." Calista grabbed Caprius' hand, and they ran out of the room and down the hall. Flames were halfway up the stairs. They ran back up and into Enlora's bedroom. Caprius dislodged his claymore of power and channeled his powers at the wall. In a second, the claymore blew a hole through the stone.

"Come on, jump!" Caprius said. Without hesitation, Calista jumped out of the second-story room and landed in a snow bank. Caprius leaped after her and landed beside her, his face inches from hers. They were both breathing hard. Caprius stared at her for a second, then grabbed her by the back of her head and kissed her.

"What was that for?" she asked gently when they took a pause.

"For saving my life," he said.

"Remind me to do it more often," she said.

They picked themselves up and made tracks through the snow away from the house. Moments later, behind them, the house exploded, flame and embers shooting into the sky like a volcanic eruption. From their safe distance, Caprius and Calista paused and looked back at the burning home. Caprius pulled Calista into a hug. He said into her hair, "Calista, you don't have to leave Castle Elysium. I want you to stay. I reacted badly. Selfishly." Calista smiled, happy in his muscular arms and thrilled to hear him say these precious words.

"Really?" she asked. She was surprised to see that his eyes were wet.

"I feel safer with you by my side," he said, pulling back to look her in the eyes. "Will you stay?"

"I'll think about it," she smirked. "You'll just have to work for it." She touched his cheek. They turned and walked back to Jethro, now warm against the icy night.

Chapter 15

Of Absence and Malice - Part 2

MELINA HAMPSHIRE SAT IN HER bed lying against pillows. As Confidus gazed down at her, she seemed to have a distraught look on her face. She looked at Confidus, feeling his love as he smiled warmly at her. But, as she stared at him, she thought to herself, *'who is this man who looks so fondly at me?'*

"Why not try this. Drink, Melina," said Confidus as he handed her a glass of cold water. Melina hesitated. She felt like she was taking something from a strange man. "It is cold. Just as you like it."

Melina excepted the glass as she took it in hand. She said not a word but drank the water. As Melina pulled the glass away from her mouth, a sudden vision came to her mind. She saw herself in the conservatory of the castle in friendship with people around her. She gazed at Confidus. "I know you," she said. "I see you in my mind."

Confidus put his hand to her forehead, feeling the warmth of her skin. "You're memories are trying to resurface, Melina. In good time, you will remember." Melina finished drinking her glass of water. She handed the glass to Confidus.

"What is that? Over there?' Melina asked. She pointed to an alcoholic drink at the far end of the night table.

"That, my sweet, is a pink lady. But, I don't think you should be drinking that right now. Caprius brought it up for you days ago," said Confidus. "I will leave you to rest now. I'll look in on you later." Confidus turned to Sandra the caretaker. "Sandra, take good care of her. See to her comfort."

"Yes, Your Majesty," she replied. Confidus walked out of Melina's room.

***

Andromin walked through the lobby of Quantum Heights until he got to the seating area, where plush sofas and armchairs awaited visitors and weary travelers. As he plunked down, he noticed the two Taughtenslottes he had encountered earlier, but he ignored them and tried to forget their incident. He rested his head and closed his eyes in an attempt to relax.

Just as he was finally starting to feel comfortable, two other Taughtenslottes arrived and took seats beside their companions. Eventually, they noticed Andromin. "You there! Don't I know you?" one Taughtenslotte asked Andromin, coming over and poking him in the knee.

Andromin opened one eye, then closed it. "I don't think so," he said.

Another Taughtenslotte laughed, "Hey, this is the one I was telling you about,"

"Oh, yes, the infamous Andromin Seaton." The man leaned in. "Can I offer you something? Perhaps a noose?" The four Taughtenslottes laughed.

"Give him a long rope. It's a healthy drop to the bottom of the hotel," said the other Taughtenslotte. Andromin tuned them out and closed his eyes again. He clasped his hands together on his chest.

"You know, I'd bet they sell ropes at the shop here. Perhaps I can help you choose one. I will even offer to buy you one," said one man.

"Buy one for yourself," muttered Andromin.

"You know, they even make ropes of different colors."

"I think his color is yellow," said the man.

"Or pink," said another. "Tell me, Andromin, are you a coward or a delicate flower?"

"I think he's both," said another.

"Oh, look, he has his hands in prayer. He asks God for forgiveness. Have you sinned, Andromin? Are you asking God to redeem your soul?"

"There is no room for him in the Lord's heaven. Souls like his only have a place among the devils," said the Taughtenslotte. Andromin ran his hand through his hair. "Oh, look, the pour soul feels aggravated." The Taughtenslotte stood and pulled out a cigar. "Come on, fellas. I think we have wasted enough time here." The four Taughtenslottes walked away chuckling meanly.

Andromin shook off the encounter and let himself enjoy his rest. After about half an hour, he got out of his comfortable chair and began to walk about the concourse. When he came to a goods shop that sold mountaineering gear, he approached the clerk. "I'll take those two pink ropes," he pointed.

In his hotel room, Andromin prepared the ropes, tying a perfect noose into each. When he finished, he poured himself a glass of grog, sat back in a chair, and planned out his next steps. He finished his drink, took up the ropes and left his suite, making his way down the hall to one of the Taughtenslotte's doors. Andromin looked over the railing and observed the distance from his hallway to the ground: nine floors down. A large crystal chandelier hung in the center of the atrium ceiling. He took the first rope and lassoed it to the chandelier. The other end now dangling was the noose end. When he finished, he went to the end of the hall to wait and watch the Taughtenslotte's door.

People came and went, some noticing Andromin and others walking right by. When finally the Taughtenslotte came up the stairs and walked down the hall to his door, Andromin came from behind and grabbed him by the throat. He pulled him to the edge side of the hallway, pinning the man's arms down as he struggled. With his other hand, Andromin unlooped the rope and put the noose around the man's neck, then tightened it. He turned the man around and held him by his chin. The man's eyes were terrified. "No," he whispered.

"Sorry, but it seems it's you who needs to redeem your soul," Andromin whispered. Then, with no remorse, Andromin threw him over the railing. The Taughtenslotte's neck cracked when the rope tightened and, within a moment, he hung dead. "Hang around much?" Andromin said to the corpse before dusting off his hands and dashing back to his room. Behind him, he heard a woman scream. "So sorry, Selena," chuckled Andromin. "Hope this doesn't give you nightmares."

Andromin returned to his room, and so pumped up with adrenaline, he went for the grog, dispensing with glasses entirely and drinking straight from the bottle. He put away several slugs of it then wiped his mouth. He wanted more revenge.

By now, the hotel staff had been alerted to the death, and they had the body brought down. A number of onlookers had gathered to stare at the dead man.

Unaware of what had just happened, the other three Taughtenslottes, who had gone outside for a smoke, came back into the hotel. They went upstairs to their suites. One arrived to his to see it had been broken into. He went inside with his dagger in hand but didn't see that any of his things had been disturbed or stolen. He stood still a moment trying to figure out what to do next when he noticed the door to the balcony was ajar. He went to it, and Andromin, who had been hiding in the curtain folds, leaped out and pounced on him like a tiger on its prey. He grabbed the man and pulled him toward the balcony ledge. Andromin turned him around so they could see eye to eye. The man was frightened. Without hesitation, Andromin threw the man over. The Taughtenslotte fell down the mountainside, plummeting to his death. "Hope you enjoyed the view, at least," he said, turning around and letting himself out.

Andromin returned to his suite and drank from the bottle heavily. "Two down, two to go," he said.

By now, the two remaining Taughtenslottes had learned of their man's hanging. They did not yet know about their compatriot who had been thrown down the mountainside. They gathered in one of their suites and stood on the balcony. "Andromin Seaton will pay dearly for this," said Harid.

"We could easily turn him in. I'm sure there were witnesses to our conversation in the lounge," said Pulonis. "See how he likes the noose around his own neck."

"No, I have a better idea," said Harid with a sneer. "We will do this ourselves. Have Seaton meet us by the pond."

Pulonis snickered. "What makes you think the coward will come? It'll mean certain death," he said.

"Are you kidding? He'll be there. He wants us dead. But, he's no match for the two of us. And, that will be that," said Harid gleefully.

Andromin left himself only enough grog for a few nips later on. He stood to go to the lavatory. On his way, he noticed through his drunken haze a piece of paper on the floor by the front door. It was a note: "8:00 p.m., the bench at the pond. Come alone. Signed, the Taughtenslottes." Andromin crumpled the note and tossed it into the waste basket. He relieved himself then returned to his chair, closed his eyes, and let his head fall back.

When Andromin remembered what was happening, he looked at the clock: 7:15 p.m. Andromin let his head fall back. A half hour's time went by before Andromin looked at the clock again. He stood and walked out of the suite.

When Andromin arrived at the bench by the pond, he did not see the two Taughtenslottes. He looked around the bench and hopped up and down a few times to stay warm. Before him, the pond was frozen solid. Finally, he heard a voice. "Seaton!" the man yelled.

In the distance were the two remaining Taughtenslottes. He stepped onto the pond and slowly began making his way toward them. He wiped his brow and running nose on his sleeve, then put his hand on his claymore of power. He intently stared at the two, never flinching as they approached. The two men drew their swords and waited. Andromin snickered. "Make me do all the work? That's alright. I need the exercise," he said, closing the gap between them and halting when he was just ten feet away.

"You killed my men. That comes at a high price, Seaton," said Harid. "I would have reported this, but we decided it'd be more fun if we just kill you ourselves." He looked at Andromin's claymore. "But, let's be fair, shall we? No magical fairy powers from you, just skill. Like a real man. Agreed?"

"Agreed," said Andromin. "Like a real man," he repeated. Beneath them, the ice of the pond cracked from their weight. The two Taughtenslottes raised their swords. "Why don't we make this short and to the point," Andromin said amicably. He lifted his sword up high, then brought the tip of it down with fierce power, instantly cracking the ice. The three of them fell through into the frigid water. While the Taughtenslottes choked and floundered, Andromin grabbed one, held his face under water and choked him. The man struggled and reached for his friend, but he was too busy trying to find his way to solid ground. Andromin's grip grew stronger and stronger until finally the man let out his last bubbles of air and died. Andromin let go of the body, and it drifted gently to the bottom of the pond. Andromin burst to the surface and took a deep breath. The other Taughtenslotte was still struggling to get out. Andromin used his upper body strength to pull himself out from the icy water onto the solid ice. The other man was gaining a foothold. Andromin walked to where he was trying to get out. Before Andromin reached him, the piece of ice the man had been clinging to broke off and he fell back into the water.

Andromin held his claymore of power. He channeled his powers and blasted a cold frost from his blade. The water began to freeze. Seconds later there was a thick layer of ice over where the water had just been. The Taughtenslotte, caught beneath it, looked up at Andromin, his eyes seized in sheer terror. Andromin shrugged.

"I never stick to the rules," Andromin said. "Goodbye, my dear Taughtenslottes."

Andromin slowly walked off the pond onto solid ground. He looked back at the pond one last time. The man beneath the ice had disappeared. He sheathed his sword and returned to the hotel.

In the lobby, Andromin was filled with dark thoughts. He felt unhinged and exhilarated. He had committed murder yet suffered no remorse. He looked up; the rope was still hanging from the chandelier. The authorities were questioning people in the lobby, and it wouldn't be long before they questioned the shop staff and found out it was Andromin who had purchased the length of rope.

While Andromin lingered in the lobby, he caught a glimpse of a familiar face. It was a Goncool. He was cheerily whistling his way to his suite and didn't see Andromin. Andromin followed him. The Goncool opened his door and went in. As he was shutting the door behind him, Andromin came out from the shadows and smashed in the door, knocking the Goncool to the floor. Andromin pulled out his claymore of power. The Goncool quickly stood and drew his sword, and in seconds, they were enmeshed in a sword fight in the foyer of the Goncool's opulent suite. The knights fought vigorously, but Andromin was gaining on the Goncool. He fought him out onto the balcony. It was a lovely terrace with a view of the mountains and the setting sun. Neither man was affected by the beauty of the place as they clashed their swords and ground their teeth. Andromin lunged for the Goncool but missed, and the Goncool took that opening to swing wildly, managing to nick the armor on Andromin's chest. But, it affected Andromin not one bit, as he took one swing then another, catching the Goncool with his arm midair. He knocked the sword from the Goncool's hand, which caused him to fall to the ground. He was defenseless at Andromin's feet. Andromin felt the victory in his bones and smiled graciously as he brought the tip of his sword up to the Goncool's exposed throat.

Rather than tremble, however, the Goncool began to laugh, showing his rotting teeth and blackened gums. "Do you honestly think you can win this war? We have men everywhere." The placid evening that had been came under thick storm clouds. Thunder rumbled and there was a flash of lightening, illuminating the crevices of their faces. "I'm going to watch your world crumble and whither into darkness. You think you frighten me pointing that sword at my face? Killing me won't stop the inevitable. Only through the Goncools can you achieve eternal peace." He licked his lips. "Do you know what it is you hunger for, Andromin? It is our blood that will soon flow through your veins. You can try and fight it, but in the end, we will have your soul. Join us." He pulled out a small flask from his pocket. "You know what this is? It is my salvation. Not that which courses through all vampires' veins. But, an extract taken from the Dark Lord, himself." He put the flask to his mouth and drank the blood. Instantly, he began to transform into a horrific vampire. Andromin quickly tried to drive his sword into the vampire's throat, but he wasn't fast enough; the vampire was already in the air, hovering over him. "Too late, Seaton!" he said, his voice high and inhuman. Andromin channeled his powers and propelled fire into the air with his claymore. But, the vampire was faster and dodged the fire with ease. Before Andromin could try to strike again, the creature flew off into the sky, far off in the direction of Mount Drone.

Andromin felt lost and alone. He'd done unspeakable things and almost craved being caught and punished for his crimes, as that would mean the world was still functioning as it should. But, he knew this Goncool had spoken the truth. The mortal world as they knew it was in terrible danger. And, there was nothing, no small amount of murder, that could be done to save it.

Andromin grabbed his things from the room and left the hotel, boarding the first train out. Andromin looked out the window at the wintered landscape, seeing nothing. "I do believe my vacation has ended," he thought.

The waiter approached, bringing Andromin his dinner. He took a bite and made a face.

"Is it not to your satisfaction, Sir?" asked the waiter.

"It tastes like sawdust." He paused to sip his wine and cleanse his palate. "Ah, and the wine has turned!"

"I will get you our best wine, Mr. Seaton," said the waiter, "and a new meal." The waiter walked away.

Andromin felt sorry in a way for the waiter. He knew it was his own fault the food and drink tasted awful. It was because he was rotten through and through, and nothing he did, or ate or drank, or any good thoughts he would have could change things. He thought then about Fetrona. He was always inclined to blame her for their fractious relationship, but he knew he'd never be satisfied with anyone, particularly himself. He looked out again. Darkness had set in, and Andromin sat back, steeling himself for the long trip home.

By the time the authorities would find out that Andromin had committed these murders, something tragic would happen to Hotel Quantum Heights, which, for Andromin's sake, would grant him the privilege of freedom. The authorities would never find out.

Chapter 16

Fallen

An hour later, Caprius and Calista walked into St. Basil's Church. A funeral was underway attended by a small crowd. They made their way up the rows of pews and sat in the fourth row. The woman beside them was sobbing. The priest's sermon was brief, but it enlivened the mourners, and the woman wiped her eyes, crossed herself, and looked more at peace from his words.

"I'm sorry to bother you, Madam, but whose funeral is this?" Calista whispered to her.

She smiled sadly. "It is for my sister. Her life was taken away far too early. She was so young, so vibrant. She was a nun at this church."

"What was her name?" asked Calista, suddenly growing cold.

"Laura Bently," said the woman, a tear falling from her eye.

"Sister Laura? No, it can't be," Calista said. "We came here to talk with her today." She leaned in toward Caprius. "This funeral is for Sister Laura Bently," she said.

Caprius knew what had happened and felt dreadful. Calista laid her hand upon the grieving woman's knee. "May I ask how she died?"

"A foul creature attacked her, a vampire," said the woman beginning to weep again.

"Oh, no. I am so sorry," said Calista. Calista caught Caprius' eye and saw that he knew. Around them, friends and family went up to the casket to pay their last respects. Caprius and Calista joined the end of the line. When they reached her, they looked upon the young woman's face. "I'm so sorry you had to go through this," Calista whispered to her.

After the funeral ended, the casket was taken out, and the churchgoers followed. Caprius and Calista stayed seated.

"Finding the truth just got a lot harder. Come on. Let us follow the procession to the graveyard," said Caprius.

Later, once night had fallen, Caprius and Calista returned to the graveyard. They went to the church and descended the steps into the crypt, carrying a torch to light the way. They walked by all the graves, Caprius holding the torch to each so he could read the markings. He stopped. "Here it is, Laura Bently."

Caprius removed his dagger from his belt buckle. "We must do this to save her soul. Luckily, her coffin is toward the bottom. We can easily put it back in when we're done. Here, can you hold this?" said Caprius, handing Calista his torch.

With his dagger of power, Caprius drew a thin beam of light that cut into the stone wall, making an opening large enough to pull the coffin out. He put his sword down on the dirt floor and pulled on the stone with the tablet. It was heavy, and he struggled, but he gave one last heave and pulled it from the wall. It landed on the ground with a thud. Caprius opened the casket. Calista leaned in with the torch, and in the light, they confirmed that inside was indeed the body of Laura Bently.

He moved her stiff arms to the side, and they cracked. "Sorry to do this to you, Sister, but it's the only way." Caprius tore her shirt open to expose her chest. He took the dagger from his boot and pierced through the flesh and bone. He cut out the heart and set it on the ground. With the powers of the dagger, he set the heart on fire. The heart burst into flames. It burned down rapidly. Then, Caprius drove his dagger into the poor woman's throat. With a twist of the blade, he decapitated her.

They looked down to see that Laura's heart had completely disintegrated into ash. Only bits of blackened and burned cloth remained. "Glad to see you could stomach what we just did, Calista."

"I was actually about to say the same to you, Caprius," she smirked.

"Beautiful and funny. Quite a combination. Here, give me the torch." Calista handed it to him. "Let's get out of here," said Caprius.

They emerged from the crypt into the darkness of night and closed the door. The churchyard was bedecked in white, the gravestones sparkling in the moonlight. When they turned to steal away, they came face to face with the head sister, Sister Mildred. "What are the two of you doing here?" she asked harshly.

"We were paying our respects to Sister Laura," said Calista.

"At this late hour?" the nun said. "You have no business here!" She stuck out her hand. "Give me that torch."

Caprius handed her the torch, and when Sister Mildred's hand brushed against Caprius', a vision came to her. She saw Caprius pulling out the coffin from the wall. She saw Laura's heart taken out and set on fire. She saw him decapitate Sister Laura. The vision vanished, and she was left standing before the two knights. "What have you done," she said, her voice low and full of tremor.

"Nothing, nothing at all. See for yourself," said Calista. The nun opened the door to the crypt. "Good evening to you, Sister Mildred," said Calista. Calista and Caprius walked away casually. They waited for the nun to disappear down into the crypt, then hid behind a gravestone to wait for her to return.

Alone inside the crypt, Sister Mildred went to Laura's coffin. It looked untouched, but on the ground she spied bits of burned cloth and some blood. She bent over with difficulty and touched some of the blood to her tongue with a finger. More premonitions flooded her; she knew Laura's body had been desecrated.

Sister Mildred returned to the churchyard. She looked around, but seeing nothing out of the ordinary, she marched away. Caprius and Calista let the nun get far ahead before following her, their boots making heavy tracks in the powdery snow. They went through the cemetery and into the woods. Calista and Caprius kept the nun in sight but maintained their distance. The stocky nun had good stamina; she climbed a hill that took her deeper into the woods. Soon, she came to a rocky area covered with stones and sprouts of grass. Small shadows moved against the rocks; when the Sister arrived, the shadows sprang to life, snarling and howling. They were Droges. She ignored them and soon came to the mouth of a cave. Without pause, she went inside. Caprius and Calista waited for the Droges to move away, and when the creatures' attentions were elsewhere, the two darted past them and ran into the cave.

Once their eyes adjusted to the dark, they saw the nun in a stiff trot ahead in the distance. The nun passed a section of large stones that surrounded a pit. The pit was wide but not deep, and standing inside of it was the great vampire and Makoor's most vital henchman, Cambrozes Genesis. Genesis wore a long red-silk robe that pooled over the ground.

Caprius and Calista hid behind the stones and looked down. The nun had run in directly to Cambrozes Genesis. "I recognize that man," whispered Calista. "He comes to me in my dreams and tries to comfort me."

"That man is your father, Calista." Caprius took Calista's hand in his and looked her in the eyes. "Do not give in to him. If you do, you will be lost to the underworld."

Down below, they heard conversation taking place. "Something unfortunate has happened. Two knights desecrated Laura's tomb," said the nun.

"What did you see?" asked Cambrozes.

"Visions came to me when I touched the hand of one of the knights and again when I tasted the blood of Laura Bently. Then, I saw it; the knights took out her heart. They burned it and severed her head," said the nun.

"Then, it is finished. Her soul has been saved, and she cannot be among us," said Cambrozes.

"These knights are a menace. They must be destroyed," said the nun.

"Caprius Seaton has received a greater power from Petoshine. My daughter, Calista, has received the same power and is now a knight master. She has gone against my wishes. I have lost her," said Cambrozes.

"You have my sincerest sympathy, great Genesis," said the nun.

"Yes, but now your time has come to fulfill your destiny," said Cambrozes. "Do you willingly give yourself?"

The nun approached Cambrozes and tilted her head. "I pledge myself to you, great one," she said.

"Then, with that, I give you your third and final bite. Let the blood of Makoor flow through you." Cambrozes grabbed her by the shoulders and sank his teeth into her neck. She did not scream but closed her eyes and moaned seductively.

"Let's get them both now," said Calista to Caprius.

"No, wait. Somewhere there is a cult in hiding. And, it isn't in Plaphorius or Mount Drone. We need these two to lead us to them. Then, we will gather our strength, and with our power, we will destroy them all," said Caprius.

The bite to Sister Mildred brought on the Monisar: the transition to the undead. When the transition was complete, Mildred and Cambrozes transformed themselves into horrific vampires. The creatures went deep into the cave, and Caprius held Calista back. "I suspect they have an alternate exit and they'll soon be long gone," he said. "Why don't we return to the hotel and resume our investigation at the church."

"We know sister Mildred is the head of the nuns. If we can get into her office, we may be able to find something," said Calista.

Caprius and Calista turned to leave when suddenly a pack of ravenous Droges was standing in front of them, salivating. They attacked, and Calista swiftly pulled out her sword and fought off the two who had come at her, killing them. Caprius tried to channel his powers to bring flame to his sword, but it didn't work. He tried again—still nothing. The two Droge creatures who had him in their sights pounced on him and bit at his flesh, tearing pieces off. Calista didn't understand and began to panic. "What the hell is happening to our powers?" she shouted. A Droge lunged at Calista, and she decapitated it with a neat slice of her sword. Beside her, Caprius tried swinging his sword at the creatures on him, but the Droge on his arm had the better of him and caused him to swing at empty air. Caprius cried out in pain. Calista turned, driving her sword into the Droge's stomach. She picked off the other Droges who were on Caprius, skewering them and stabbing them through their necks, hearts, and stomachs until they all lay around her partner dead.

Caprius fell among them, his face planted onto the ground. He was badly wounded. Three other Droges since had appeared and stood before Calista. One of them pounced at her, but she sliced it through the chest. Calista didn't wait for the others to attack; she was angry and went after them. Cornered by the cave wall and the rage of the knight, they whimpered and snarled. She put her face down and yelled, "Boo!" The two Droges turned and ran out of the cave. These were not super Droges. Had they been, it would have been fatal. Calista turned and gasped. Caprius was alive but badly hurt. He was drifting in and out of consciousness. She crouched by his side on her knees feeling furious and afraid. She knew it was a sure death to try and walk out with Caprius over her shoulder. If any more Droges were to come and attack, she wouldn't be able to fend them off so encumbered.

The torches on the walls of the cave flickered in the tomb-like silence. Hours passed, and Calista held Caprius and tried to keep him awake by murmuring stories. She mopped at his multiple injuries but was fearing if they didn't get out of this devil's sanctuary and away from whatever other danger lay in store for them, he would die from his wounds.

"I just don't understand it. Why aren't the claymores working?" Calista set Caprius gently down and looked around. "Somehow, we will get through this, Caprius." She brought her claymore of power before her and channeled her powers more strongly than she ever had before. A faint glitter of light came to the blade, but it was far too weak to help her. Calista's hope began to wane, and she trembled. More time passed, and she was at a loss as to how to help them.

Finally, as she was close to trying to heft him out of the cave, despite knowing that meant certain death for them both but not knowing what else to do, she stood and before her came a great sparkle of light. The light transformed into a human spirit. It was Felicia - the Golden Fleece. Calista marveled at her beauty.

"Rise, my child. I am Felicia - the Golden Fleece. I am sorry you have fallen. The light of Petoshine grows dim on this night as an evil has tried to claim Caprius Seaton. All around you is this evil, and it is held in the walls inside a magnetic field. This is why you are unable to access the true powers of your claymores. Without your powers, your swords are only basic weapons, and your bodies are vulnerable like ordinary humans'. If you do not leave soon, Caprius will surely die. And, even you may perish at the hands of the Droges. The only way to save yourselves from the pervading evil of this place is to get out of this cave and into the wilderness, far away from the magnetic field. There, your powers will be restored, and your powers are what will save Caprius."

Felicia took Calista by the chin and looked sternly in her eyes. "Calista, you have been chosen as a knight of Petoshine by the great Grongone. Fulfill the destiny that has been placed before you. But, be warned, you will be at the mercy of the Droges. Good luck, and may the light of Petoshine be with you." With those words, Felicia vanished.

Calista felt instantly more at ease, bathed in the love from the spirit of the Golden Fleece. "All right, soldier, I'm going to take you out of here." Calista hefted Caprius' weak frame over her shoulder and began to drag his body along the ground. She pulled him a long ways over the cave floor, then breathless, stopped to rest. No evident signs of danger were around.

Caprius tried to mutter a few words, but she couldn't make them out. She held him close, his wounds oozing blood and fluids. She knew Caprius was suffering terribly. "Why did we come here?" she whispered to him. They had failed and hadn't been able to follow Cambrozes Genesis to his stronghold, where he would carry out the plans for his sinister plot. Her eyes filled with tears as she held him. She would die if anything happened to him. He was always so filled with passion for life. She remembered when Caprius' father, Confidus, had also been attacked by Droges, and she had managed to save him. But, this was far worse than Confidus' mangled arm; Caprius' wounds were over his whole body. She knew he was dying.

Calista vowed to do everything she could to save him. If he died, the guilt would kill her, too. Calista regrouped her inner resources and began to drag Caprius again through the cave. She dragged him a great distance, nearly to the opening of the cave. As much as her body ached for rest, she pushed on in the hopes that their claymores of power would regain their powers.

She made it to a clearing about twenty yards out of the cave and laid him down. She drew her sword and tried to channel her powers. A tiny glimmer of light came to her sword. "Damn," she said. It was still night, the moon glinting off the rocky terrain and ice. Fortunately, there were no Droges in sight. She pulled Caprius' body up and kept on away from the cave, eventually coming out onto a snow-covered field. She eased up her hold on him, as going over the snow was easier. At the field's edge, she paused, drenched in sweat, and tried her claymore again. Again came a faint glimmer of light, but then a surge of bright light popped out. Yet, as quickly as it had come, it expired. She was disappointed, but at least this was progress.

Dawn was beginning to fade in, and she welcomed the morning light. Sleep was not an option, not with Caprius' life hanging in the balance. The sun emerged and shined down on them. Caprius was coming into consciousness. "Here," she said, scooping some of the pure snow through his cracked and bloody lips. "This will help give you strength."

She ate some of the snow, herself, then brought him as far as she could before she needed to pause again. Again, she tried her claymore, and again, it failed her. Caprius was trembling from cold and shock, so Calista crouched down and buttoned up his coat, reinvigorated to keep going. She dragged him yet further in the snow, finally coming to a wooded area. Calista pulled him around the trees and stopped to rest in a clearing. He looked so frail and helpless. She brushed his hair back from his face and tears dropped on his coat. "Caprius, you can't die. You can't. I love you," said Calista. "You hear me, Caprius?" Caprius was shivering violently now. It was clear he was entering later stage hypothermia, so she got on top of him and held him until she could feel his skin begin to warm. It had been eight hours since the attack. Night would fall soon. They'd neither eaten nor drunk but for a bit of snow, and Caprius' wounds were significant.

Calista reached for her claymore, but rather than pull it out and try it again, she just left her hand there. Then, something extraordinary began to happen. The sword began to vibrate and hum loudly. Calista was ecstatic. "The claymore's power is back!" However, she soon realized the sudden vibration and humming of the claymore meant danger was upon them, and from the violence of the sword's actions, that danger would be extreme.

Calista quickly laid her sword of power against Caprius. With her enhanced powers she drew a yellow light, which surrounded Caprius' body and began to heal his injuries. He opened his eyes and looked right at Calista.

The timing was good, as from over a hillock, Calista spotted a pack of what seemed to be over twenty hungry Droges. She guessed they'd picked up their scent and were tracking them. The Droges came closer. Calista kept her hand steady on the sword. She'd gotten Caprius this far without having the Droges catch up to them, and she'd be dammed if they'd lose the fight now.

Caprius began to stir. Then, he slowly sat up. Calista held the sword of power away from him and was surging the light toward him, channeling her powers yet deeper. Caprius cleared his throat and stood. He slowly drew his sword of power and channeled his powers, immersing himself in the energy. Calista withdrew her sword, amazed to see the transformation. Caprius' body emitted a bright white light.

The hungry Droges had started approaching the two knights, but at the burst of light, they scattered. A few kept on toward Calista, undeterred or perhaps starving. They ran their tongues over their fangs.

Calista turned and aimed her sword at them, pulsing fire and burning three Droges. She shouted at the rest as if they were dogs, "Back! Stay back!" Caprius released his hold on the sword, and the light faded away. He stood erect; his hair gleamed in the late day sun, his eyes were clear, and his wounds were gone. He saw the Droges who were again approaching in a large semi-circle, aimed his sword, and let fly an enormous flame that scorched all the Droges, the trees, and the landscape. Those Droges who could, fled back into the forest; all the others fell over and burned out.

Calista sheathed her sword of power and walked over to Caprius. Caprius sheathed his sword. They paused, staring at one another, then embraced, grateful and relieved to be alive.

"You saved my life, again," said Caprius.

Calista laughed. "You know, you seem to be developing a habit of getting yourself into trouble." She chuffed his arm.

He looked at her with new respect. "It's ok; I know you'll watch my back," he smiled.

"At this rate, I may not be around the next time," she said. "So, you be more careful! You scared the shit out of me!" she yelled in mock anger.

"I will. I promise," he said, grabbing her and hugging her again.

"I guess we better put out the fires," said Calista. "Not the trees' fault we're in this mess."

Caprius and Calista turned, and with their powers, they brought forth an icy frost that doused the trees and put out the fires. They healed the trees and restored the landscape. "We have to get back to St. Basil's Church. We must find something in Sister Mildred's office," said Calista. Now, in the direction of the setting sun, Caprius and Calista began the walk back to the village of Jethro.

They arrived at St. Basil's Church. It was late night. They looked around to find an extension to the church. As they looked around, they came to a window. Caprius tried opening the window by sliding it up. "It's locked!" But, as he looked at the frame in the middle, he saw a small clamp from the inside, which would unlock it. He grabbed his dagger of power. He channeled his powers and drew a cold frost at the top window frame. The top part of the window turned to ice and froze. Within seconds, the frost tingled against the window. Caprius put his dagger of power back to the side of his belt. With the palm of his hand, he broke the icy glass. He turned the knob and slid open the window. "Give me a hand Calista," he said. Calista helped him in. When they both had entered the room, they were relieved. Calista went to turn on the light. "No, Calista. Dowse the light. Use your claymore of power to illuminate a soft blue light." So, Calista did just that. The claymores were lit. "Here's a desk."

"Yes, but is this, indeed, Mildred's office?" asked Calista.

"Let us see." Caprius put his light of power to the desk. There he saw a picture of Sister Mildred. "Yes, this is her office. There's a picture of her here."

"You search the desk. I'll search this cabinet. I'll see what I can find," said Calista. They both ruffled through items and papers. Twenty minutes had gone by, and they'd turned up nothing. "There is nothing but files and books in these drawers."

"I'm done with this desk. There's nothing here," said Caprius.

Calista now opened up the bottom drawer of the cabinet. As she slid it open, there were files. "No. More files," she said. She pulled the cabinet further out to the end. As she looked, her eyes caught a hold of something. There were small boxes of business cards. She looked at a card, which was taped to the box cover. "I found Sister Mildred's business cards."

Outside the church, in a small apartment building across the street, Sister Mildred looked outside her window. As she peered at the church, she looked to her office and noticed an illuminated soft light near the window. Her eyes began to glow a ruby color.

Calista continued to look through the drawer. She came upon another box of business cards. As she picked it up with her left hand, she looked at the card taped to the box cover. Her eyes widened, and she smiled warmly. "I think Sister Laura's death will be justified," she said.

"You found something?"

"Our prayers have been answered," she said. She stood up straight holding the box of cards. She put her sword back in her sheath as Caprius came closer with his light of power. "I have here business cards pertaining to a clock shop in the outer part of Jethro. I am familiar with this street. Braden Clock Works on 267 Londale Road." She smiled warmly, opened the box, and pulled out a few business cards. She put the cards in her pocket.

"This is probably the clock shop Enlora Renfield had information on," said Caprius.

"Precisely," she said.

"Well done, Calista. You certainly make a fine agent," said Caprius.

"We're all done here," she said.

At that moment, the door crashed open, and a vampire creature of ugliness came through, which startled the two knights. Calista immediately used her inner power and drew the full stack of business cards, sending them flying by the hundreds at the vampire. Throwing the box, she drew her claymore of power, and both knights came at the creature. The creature drove her arm into Calista, and she went flying into the cabinet, knocking it over. Calista was dazed as she lay on the floor. She quickly got up to her feet. Using her great strength, she picked up the file cabinet with both hands. Caprius swung his sword, and the vampire creature backed away to the doorway. Calista through the cabinet at the vampire, and the creature was sent flying past the doorway into the hall. Caprius jumped over the cabinet heading toward the creature. As the creature was against the wall, Caprius drove his claymore of power into the creature's stomach. The creature moved to the right, and Caprius' sword drove straight to the wall. The point of the sword hit the wall, cracking the siding. The vampire swung his arm and hit Caprius, sending him tumbling down the hall. Caprius lost his sword, as it was stuck in the wall. Calista walked onto the cabinet, coming down to the hall swinging her sword. The creature took Caprius' sword, pulling it out of the wall, and blocked Calista's swing. Calista and the creature fought swinging their swords. Caprius, who lay away from them on the floor, got to his feet. He was defenseless without his claymore of power, with only the dagger by the side of his belt. Caprius thought quickly. He looked to the wall to see a fire hose inside a glass covering. With his fist, he smashed the glass. He had cut himself. He unwrapped the hose quickly. At the end of the hall, not too far away, was a large crucifix about four feet in length, which hung on the wall. Caprius turned on the water full force. "Calista move!" he yelled. Calista jumped back into the office. The force from the water pushed the vampire creature to the end of the hall. The creature hit the large cross on the wall. Caprius took another smaller crucifix and threw it at the creature. With the combination of water and the cross, the water became holy water. With the power of God driven from the cross and the holy water, the creature began to shrivel and smoke. The creature was driven with rage and screamed. Calista walked out of the office with her sword in hand and watched as the creature had its back against the large cross with holy water gushing at it. Caprius continued to spray the vampire. Minutes later, the vampire creature was nothing more than a shriveled-up corpse. Caprius turned off the water from the hose. The creature fell on top of the smaller crucifix onto the wet floor. The hall was filled with water.

"That was sure quick thinking," said Calista. "But, I don't think the church representatives will be happy with the damages."

"Remind me to make a large donation to the church when we get back to Elysium," said Caprius. Caprius walked over to pick up his claymore of power. He looked at the crucifix on the wall and made a sign of the cross. He walked over to Calista. "Now, we have a clock shop to visit," said Caprius. He began to walk down the hall, which lead to the entrance of the church.

Calista looked at the crucifix and made the sign of a cross. "Sorry, my Lord. All evil must perish." Calista and Caprius walked down the church isle. A large cross hung behind the altar. They walked down the pews and headed toward the doors.

Chapter 17

Down and Out at Quigley's

MELINA SAT IN BED EATING her food, which was laid out for her upon a tray. She still hadn't gotten her appetite back, as she fidgeted with her food. "Melina, you must eat," said Sandra.

"I am not hungry," said Melina.

"Melina, please. You've eaten very little these past days," she said.

"Maybe later on. Not right now," said Melina.

Sandra began to take the tray of food in hand. "Very well. I can't seem to win with you. But, we'll try again later. If Caprius were here, he'd spoon feed you."

Melina got comfortable in bed. "Yes, Caprius," she muttered. "That name is beginning to sound familiar." Melina glanced over looking at the alcoholic drink at the far end of the night table. "Sandra, I want to be alone now."

"Oh, you'd like to sleep. It's no wonder. That's all you've been doing these past days," said Sandra. "I will be back to check on you in an hour." Sandra walked out of the room closing the door.

Melina gazed at the pink lady at the far end of the night table. Then, she turned away and looked at the ceiling. She marveled at its beauty. There were painted heavenly angels upon the golden ceiling. She gazed back at the alcoholic drink. She lifted herself up and sat on the bed. She got to her feet and walked over. She slowly picked up the glass in hand staring at the drink. "Yuck, it is warm," she said as she began drinking it. She took sip after sip. Suddenly, flashes of memories penetrated her mind. She saw images of Caprius. "I know this man," she said. Melina drank down the entire drink. She set the glass down on the night table. Then, she got back into her comfy bed and pulled up the covers. She thought about the man Caprius.

***

In the garden of Meadow-lie, Confidus strolled along the garden trails with Fetrona. He'd become concerned about her wellbeing and thought it wise to take the time to talk to her about her relationship with Andromin. Although Confidus knew her well and had a certain affection for her, he did wonder whether she was right for his son. In fact, Andromin had returned to Elysium two hours prior and told Confidus of his decision to end his relationship with Fetrona. He wanted to let his father know first. Andromin was being cowardly and requested that his father tell Fetrona it was over between them. Confidus didn't want to be the bearer of such news, but he was able to see his son was suffering.

"I don't understand, Confidus. Why did you drag me all the way out here? What is it you had to tell me so urgently?"

Confidus put his hand on Fetrona's shoulder. "Andromin has returned from his vacation."

"Andromin's back! Where is he? I can't wait to see him," she said.

"Yes, well, Fetrona, it seems Andromin has come to a decision," said Confidus.

"I knew it. He misses me," said Fetrona excitedly.

Confidus looked at the ground. He felt dreadful. "Not exactly. My son, as much as he has always loved you, it… apparently it wasn't enough for him."

Fetrona stopped walking. "What did he say?" she demanded.

"Andromin feels like your constant accusations that he's got feelings for Calista have worn him down. He feels nothing but friendship for her, you must know that, but now he feels exhausted from having to defend himself." Confidus paused. "For what it's worth, I can assure you, he's telling you the truth."

Fetrona sneered. "Sure he is." She crossed her arms over her chest. "So, what, he's breaking up with me?"

"Not exactly," said Confidus.

"Then, what's happening here," she asked. "I don't understand."

"Andromin simply feels you two should spend some time apart so you can come to terms with this situation. Until you do and understand that Calista is just a friend, he says the two of you cannot be together. But, if you are willing to give each other time and the benefit of the doubt, then there is hope for reconciliation," Confidus drew in a breath and continued. "He wants you to know you are welcome to see other men. Andromin only wishes for you to be happy."

"Oh, so that's it. It is not Calista, but he wants to see someone else. He's been cheating on me!" Fetrona shouted.

"No, Fetrona, you're not listening. Please try and understand," said Confidus.

At this, Fetrona exploded. "Why is it Andromin couldn't tell me all this himself? Is he such a coward he couldn't face me?"

"No, he did want to tell you. But, he knew his decision would get you upset, and your temper is quite legendary," chuckled Confidus. Fetrona was now steaming, her face red and puffy. "Now, now, dear, you know I'll always care for you and you'll always be considered part of this family. But-"

"I've heard enough! Frankly, I don't think I want to be part of the Seaton family anymore!" she shouted. Fetrona stormed out of the quiet wood, leaving Confidus alone. He felt sorry. She might have had her moods, but over the years, she'd grown on him rather like a daughter.

Hours later, down at Quigley's pub, Andromin sat at a table enjoying drinks, discussing the spread of Goncools over the land. Though they had not exterminated all of the Goncools, they had seriously crippled their forces. This gave the Seatons good reason to feel optimistic. "Yes, now that we've destroyed the Goncools' key members, it will be hard for them to regain their footing," said Andromin gleefully.

Several members of Confidus' council came into the pub and joined the Seatons at their table, taking chairs beside Andromin. "I don't know, Andromin. I think the lot of you is being naïve. You know very well that the other Goncools are just as dangerous. I don't plan to sleep soundly until we have exterminated if not all of them, then at least the vast majority," said Vijas.

"Vijas is right. It isn't over until they have been wiped out. They will be out for revenge now. Who knows what their next move might be," said Senator Marcus, looking pensive.

"Yes, and did you stop to consider those who escaped from Zaderack prison? They should have found their way to Elysium by now. That would have been their first stop. But, where are they?" asked Vijas.

"Hmm," said Andromin . "No sight of them in Elysium," he muttered, ashamed to admit he had forgotten about them.

"Andromin, I'm surprised at you. You're usually much keener at sniffing out the rats," said Vijas.

Andromin didn't like being singled out. He drained his glass. "Yes, you're right, you're right. But," he lowered his voice to a whisper, "my gut tells me we're in for a rough ride," said Andromin.

Vijas began to laugh. "Speaking of rough rides, I think you're in for one yourself, Andromin. Look who just walked in," he said, pointing. Fetrona, her face purple, was headed right for their table.

Andromin turned to look, then whipped his head back around and sank in his seat. "I'll never hear the end of it," he muttered. "Do you think I could sneak out?"

"Too late," said Vijas. Andromin sank lower, trying to hide.

Fetrona came to the table. "Well, well, fraternizing with the men of the senate, are we?" she asked. "Gentleman," she turned to Marcus, "don't you wish to sit with other men, rather than with boys?"

"Fetrona, please," said Vijas. He squirmed in his chair.

"Or, should I say, cowards!" She raised her voice. "That is exactly what you are, Andromin, a great big coward. You couldn't tell me yourself that we were through? You had to get your daddy to say it for you?"

Marcus and Vijas kept silent. "You're nothing but a spineless bowl of jelly!" She began to cry. "You don't even have the balls enough to give me the courtesy of a proper goodbye."

On the other side of a low wall by their table sat a group of men who were listening to the yelling and watching Andromin and Fetrona like a tennis match. These four Goncools were dressed in Elysian uniforms, keeping them well hidden from the Elysian guards. One of the Goncools leaned in to his compatriots. "Gentlemen, I think were about to have our ace in the hole," he said with great relish. The others laughed.

Fetrona went on. "And, to think, when Confidus told me that you were back in Elysium, I actually felt joy!" she said. "Who would have thought that the man I used to love so much would turn out to be such a horse's ass!" She leaned into him, her plump breasts in his face. "I hate you with all my heart," she sneered. Then, she paused and smiled. "My face is up here, idiot! You'll never get to see these again." When he wrenched his eyes away from her bosom, she slapped him across the face and walked away.

When she was well gone from them, Andromin said, "Well, I'd say that went much better than I thought. I actually expected her to be upset." Marcus and Vijas dissolved into laughter.

Fetrona had gone into the other dining room and taken a table for two. She propped up her chin in her hands and waited. When the waitress came to her, she said, "Something strong. Make it a double."

A Goncool had followed her out and came to her table. He leaned over. "You know, beautiful, he's not worth it. You deserve far better," he said running his swarthy hand down her neck.

Fetrona glared at him and grabbed his hand. "You think so? What do you think of these?" She put his hand directly on her breast and threw her head back. "You're darn right I'm worth more." She brought her head up and looked at him with a sultry gaze. "Are you more?"

He bent down and put his mouth up by her ear. "The name's Godfrey Miles."

She took his hand in hers. "Fetrona Nightly."

"And, what a pleasure it would be if you were," he said. Without taking his hand away, he sat beside her. They began to talk, their heads getting closer and closer together. Finally, she decided it was time to preserve the rest of her secrets. She stood.

"Going so soon?" he purred.

"Perhaps, I'll see you at Confidus Seaton's masquerade ball tonight," she said.

"Masquerade ball? Yes, of course. What time did that start again?"

"It's at 7:00 p.m. sharp at Castle Elysium. Do you have a costume?"

"No, but if I can't find one, I may just come as I am."

"I'm sure that would be just fine. Good day, Mr. Godfrey." Fetrona walked out of Quigley's Pub.

Godfrey made haste back to his table. "Gentlemen, we have a masquerade ball to go to. And, Confidus Seaton will be in attendance." Godfrey took a big gulp of his grog and grinned.

Chapter 18

Time and Time Again

CAPRIUS AND CALISTA WALKED THROUGH a run-down part of Jethro until they arrived at Braden Clockworks. The businesses on either side of the shop had closed down. Braden's was quite small, its sign torn through the center and faded so it was nearly illegible. The only giveaway that the shop was still in operation was that the clocks in the window were merrily ticking away.

When they entered, they went directly to a young woman dusting the small clocks that arrayed the front counter. Behind her sat a man on a stool polishing the glass of a pocket watch.

"A good day to you, Sir. Good day, Madam," said Caprius.

"'Tis a good day if I make a sale. A far better day if I make several. But, today is just another day." The man looked over his spectacles at Caprius. "Unless you are buying?" asked the man.

"I'm sorry, but we're not," said Caprius.

"Then, as I said, today is just another day. I'd be happy to make one sale," the man said. "So, how can I be of service to you?"

"My name is Caprius Seaton. I am with his majesty's 'Holy Council of Sacred Deeds.' This is my partner, Calista Genesis."

The man gasped, lost his balance, and fell off of his stool. "Well, agents! What a nice surprise." He chuckled awkwardly and furtively looked around. "I truly didn't expect the pleasure of your company," he said as he stood and dusted himself off.

"Are you all right?" Calista asked.

The young woman did not offer to help; she only watched as the man struggled to regain his composure. "Papa, you should be more careful," she said.

Caprius raised an eyebrow, then pulled out the pocket watch. He handed it across the girl to the man. "Does this belong to you?"

The man examined the pocket watch silently. He looked at the two soldiers, let his eyes trail down to their swords, and sighed. "Yes, this belongs to me. At least it did at one point. But, I guess it's yours now."

"You manufacture these pocket watches here, do you not?" asked Calista.

He hesitated. "Yes," he said and looked down.

"What can you tell us about the markings?" she asked.

"They're just markings," he shrugged. "What do you mean?"

"Whom do you work for?" asked Caprius. He was getting tired of all the back and forth.

The man got off his seat and put his hands on the counter. He righted his posture. "All right, if you must know, I work for the people of Plaphorius. They come to me, and I give them what they want. I'm not involved in anything. I just do my job. I don't ask them any questions and keep my business to myself. They tell me where to put the markings, so I keep my mouth shut and do it."

"You realize you are working for the undead, the underworld," said Calista angrily.

"Yes, I know. Look, it may be morbid and unethical, but they pay well. I have a business to run and a family to support," said the man. "When you're paid as much as I am, you don't ask questions, you just do the job."

Calista leaned over the counter and squeezed the man's fingers. "Ow, that hurts!" he yelped. Calista released his fingers, and he shook his hand out, the two of them glaring at each other.

"If you don't want to feel any more pain, you'll tell us what we want to know," said Caprius.

"I don't know anything," said the man. "I told you all I know."

"Two of our agents have been killed and shipped to us in caskets filled with soil. Do you know anything about that?" asked Calista.

"No, I don't," he claimed, but his face betrayed him. They knew he was lying.

"Our last agent to be seen, Lynin Chiles, was headed to this shop. Have you heard of anyone by that name?"

"Can't say as I have," smiled the man pertly.

"Protesting while your face tells us the truth is only going to make this hurt more," said Calista grabbing his fingers and squeezing so hard tears came to the man's eyes. The man's daughter stood like a statue.

"We've got lots of time," said Calista. "You're just going to have to try harder. Calista twisted his fingers again, and his face contorted. The girl continued to stand there, looking on dumbly. "Don't stare, my dear. It's embarrassing to your father," said Calista.

"All right, all right, I'll tell you what I know," said the man. Calista released him. "Lynin Chiles was here. But, he didn't stay long. Like you, he asked me about the pocket watches. The watches are Telusion. Markings of the undead. I told him the same thing I'm telling you. But, there is something else. I… I can't tell you much about it, but I can show you. It is something from the undead, something that might be very useful to your investigation. It's in the back room," he said. His smile had fallen.

"Fine. Bring us there," said Caprius.

"Lana, can you prepare the blood work for them," said the man over his shoulder. "We'll be there in a couple of minutes." The girl went into the back room.

"What is this blood work?" asked Calista.

"It is pure blood extract taken from Dark Lord Makoor himself." The man's demeanor shifted suddenly; he became chatty and congenial. "Now, generally, when a vampire baptizes you with its own blood, you become one yourself. But, this blood extracted from the Dark Lord is extremely potent. We're talking about super vampires."

"Interesting," said Calista. She glanced at Caprius and raised an eyebrow.

"Let me take you to the back and show you the samples I've got. Come with me," said the man. Calista and Caprius followed.

In the back room, two stools sat at the ready. Caprius and Calista slowly walked toward the stools looking at one another curiously. Caprius shrugged before they both sat down. Before them was a counter with two flasks filled with blood. "This is the blood I was talking about. From the Dark Lord himself," said the man.

Calista and Caprius examined the flasks. "How many of these do you have?" asked Calista.

"I only carry a few. The main shop that produces this carries a larger supply," said the man.

Calista was confused. "But, what would a clock maker want with this?" she asked.

"They're for me and my daughter. Makoor has promised us eternal life," said the man, smiling slowly.

"Have you taken it?" asked Caprius holding up one of the flasks.

"No, no," he waved his hand and chuckled. "They need us here at the clock shop. If we had, we would have killed you both by now. But, we'll take it eventually," said the man.

"How soon can you take us to the main plant?" asked Calista.

"Oh, soon, really soon. In fact, sooner than you think," said the man cheerily. He looked across the room at his daughter, who was standing by the wall. Without a word, she nodded and yanked on a lever by her shoulder. The floor beneath Calista and Caprius opened up, and they fell through. Above them, the floor sealed shut, leaving them in darkness. They tumbled down quite a ways. Both of them had the foresight to pull their claymores out and aim them down beneath them, creating a cushion of air that helped them land gently. When they did, they stood up and realized they'd landed between spikes that would have skewered a wild boar. "What on earth…" started Calista. She didn't bother to finish her sentence. She and Caprius used their claymores as torches. Once they were lit, the two were able to see that they were down at the bottom of a gorge. Calista poked around their surroundings; she opened a few cabinets full of supplies and saw some large sacks.

Caprius touched the top of one of the spikes. "Youch!" he exclaimed, putting his finger in his mouth.

"I don't want to think about how much it would have hurt if we'd fallen just a few centimeters to the right or left," said Calista. "I see why he didn't mind being so candid with us all of a sudden."

"Sure, he figured he'd drop us in here and we'd turn into shish kabobs," Caprius said, joining Calista at the wall. She pointed to a row of large sacks leaning against the cave wall a ways down. "I hate to say what I think these are."

"May as well have a look at them," said Caprius. He knelt down and untied the one closest to him. When he pulled up the sack, he took a step backward. "Lynin Chiles," said Caprius. His shoulders slumped.

"That confirms our suspicions, then," said Calista gently. "And, who is the other?"

Caprius untied the other sack to reveal the man's face. "I don't know this person. He is not one of ours."

"Probably an innocent bystander," said Calista. "And, the last one?"

"I don't know who this is either." They both looked at the dead for a while. Suddenly, the sound of footsteps was coming from the tunnel ahead. "Quickly, hide," Caprius whispered, "behind the rock." Calista and Caprius extinguished their claymores and darted behind the large rock. The footsteps came closer and closer. Through a crack, they saw a large hunchback emerge from the tunnel and approach the three bodies. He hefted the first body up over a shoulder and slowly walked down the tunnel. When they could no longer hear his footsteps, the two knights came out from the rock and lit their claymores. "That man no doubt delivers the bodies," said Caprius.

"But, to where? And, to whom?" asked Calista.

"To whomever is in charge of this operation. And, wherever that is is where we are going," said Caprius.

"But, we can't just follow this man," said Calista. "He'll notice us eventually no matter how many rocks we're able to hide behind."

Caprius thought for a moment. "I know, we'll get rid of these two bodies and get into the sacks ourselves."

"And, we'll be delivered directly to the kingpin himself," said Calista, grinning.

"Precisely!" said Caprius. The two set to work pulling the bodies from their sacks and hiding them behind the rock. They quickly slid into the sacks as the man was returning. "I'm glad he's so big," whispered Calista. "At least we can hear him coming."

Caprius and Calista stood completely still and held their breath.

When the man came to the bodies, he stood in front of them scratching at his bald head. He paused a long time, then said, "Na, can't be. Man, I need some sleep." He picked up Caprius' body and put it over his shoulder. Calista heard the footsteps trailing off as he walked down the tunnel. She waited what seemed a long while. Her muscles began to cramp. She wondered whether the man had discovered the body he was carrying was still alive but figured she'd have heard some kind of tousle if so.

Finally, the man returned and flung Calista over his shoulder. He tromped away, whistling tunelessly. She thought about Caprius and hoped they'd be brought to the same place.

It was very uncomfortable being bumped and jostled; at least, thought Calista, where the hunchback was walking was lit up by torches. He finally came to a stop. She heard the gentle whinny of a horse and realized she was being put in a carriage. He threw her down. She felt wooden boards and what she assumed was Caprius in the sack beneath her. "Oof," she said inadvertently when she hit him. Calista rolled off Caprius, landing on the carriage floor. The man stood there for a moment, "What was... no, couldn't be."

The man got into the driver's seat of the carriage, yanked the reins and drove off. The carriage came out of the cave and up onto the street. Caprius and Calista lay still, not saying a word, not even to one another. After what felt like about half an hour, the carriage went up a drive to a large house on a hilltop. The man paused the horse, hopped out, opened a creaky iron gate, got back in, and they kept on.

When they arrived to wherever they were, he got out and threw one of the accompanying bodies over his shoulder. Caprius waited; a door opened then shut. Once he was sure they were alone, he sat up, clambered out of the sack and nudged Calista. "Let's go. We are here." Calista struggled out of her sack, too. Both freed, they jumped from the wagon.

"Where do we go now?" Calista asked.

Caprius unsheathed his claymore of power and held it before him. "My claymore senses danger from within."

Calista brought out her sword, as well. "Yes, I sense it, too," she said. They walked toward the door, which was the rear door of the house. When Caprius had his hand on the doorknob, the door flew open, and there stood the hunchback.

"Who the hell are you?" he asked. Calista grabbed the man's collar with both hands and aggressively turned his back toward Caprius. Caprius cracked him in the head with the hilt of his sword, knocking him out cold. Calista staggered under the man's weight until she dropped him in the doorway. She and Caprius stepped over his prone body into the house.

They prowled through the house going from room to room looking for clues. They turned up nothing. "Look for a door to the basement," whispered Caprius. Calista opened a door off the kitchen; a flight of stairs lead to the basement.

"Caprius, here," she whispered. Caprius ran over and they walked down the stairs cautiously holding their swords of power aloft.

In the basement, they went from room to room. They came to a door, and their claymores vibrated wildly. Inside was another flight of stairs leading down. The house had ended; it seemed they were now in some sort of cavern, as the walls were made of roughly hewn rock. At the bottom, there was earth on the ground, and stalagmites and stalactites poked into the air from all over like teeth.

As they went further in, they realized they were going deeper underground. The top of the cave was high up, and there was no light. They lit their claymores and let the blue glow lead their way. As they progressed, their swords hummed indicating the danger was coming closer.

Finally, they saw a light. They kept on toward it until they came to what seemed to be the end of the cave; it was a cliff overlooking a giant gorge below. Torches lit up the whole space and a small gathering of what appeared to be vampires in human form was taking place. They seemed to be praising their leader, a horrific fifteen-foot tall creature standing in the center. The creature had before him the sack with the dead body inside. Calista and Caprius bent down and peered over the cliff's edge. The vampires gently took the body out of the sack and lay the body before the great creature like an offering. They spoke words of worship to the great Makoor, praising him. Then, the creature bent down and, as if it were a feather, lifted the body up, holding it out in front of him. The next moment he sank his teeth into the neck of the corpse and held there, his eyes rolling back in ecstasy, until the body was fully drained of its blood. The dead man, who seemed to only have perished just before this ritual, instantly shriveled and aged, leaving him only a saggy layer of flesh atop bones and skull. The creature finished his meal and dropped the wasted body on the ground.

"Shall we make our presence known?" asked Calista.

"Yes, let's do that," said Caprius. He noticed that to their right was a staircase carved into the stone. He motioned to her to look at it and grinned. She knew he wanted to make a dramatic entrance. Their swords in hand, they jumped and channeled their powers to pull a force from their claymores, which gently brought them to the ground. They landed in the center of the vampires.

The creature backed up with his hands before his face. When he recovered, he said, "How nice of you to visit; I am Volsar Goncool, and you two knight masters are about to meet your doom."

"I remember you, Volsar," said Calista. "But, it is you who is gravely mistaken. For, today is the last day of your conquest."

"My conquest is only beginning. It is a shame we did not exterminate you earlier before you became a knight master, Ca-lisss-ta. But, no matter. We will take care of you now. Kill these humans!" he yelled to his vampires. Without delay, the vampires transformed into horrific vampire creatures and leaped in to attack the knights. Calista and Caprius swung their swords in arcs before them and, one by one, drove their swords into the creatures' chests. Once the creatures were speared, the knights channeled their powers to ignite the vampires, centering the fire at their black chests. The fire quickly spread to engulf the creatures. They screamed as they burned.

"See you next time," said Volsar. He spread his wings and flew into the air. Calista aimed a large flame at him, but he swerved and it missed him. She drew a far larger force from the claymore that propelled her into the air so she came face to face with Volsar. Calista knew she only had one opportunity to kill him, so she swung her sword with all her might, but she was already falling and missed. She let her claymore guide her back to the ground as she cursed her poor aim. Volsar was watching her and laughed. But, he was so busy scorning her, he didn't see the top of the cave and smashed into it, sending rocks and earth tumbling to the ground. Likely injured but still too inhuman to mind the pain, Volsar flew out of the opening, went up through each floor of the house, and crashed out through the roof and into the icy night sky.

There was no time to think about how they'd lost Volsar Goncool, however, as the vampires on the cave floor continued their vicious attack. Calista, newly aggravated, swung her sword and cleanly decapitated one. The head tumbled to the ground, transforming back into human form, but fortunately, one of his fellow creatures pounced onto the head and crushed it. The skull cracked, and blood gushed onto the ground. Caprius, not trusting that it wouldn't transform, drove his sword into the creature's face, then backed up and sent a large flame from his claymore onto three vampires who were in fast approach. Calista met his fire with her own and the two flames collided, causing the vampires to burst into a bonfire. The two knights held steady until the vampires were nothing more than ash. When all was quiet, with only the sound of torch fire flickering, they knew they'd bested this cult for good. Except for Volsar. "He got away," said Calista angrily.

"We'll get him next time," said Caprius.

From behind them, a woman called out. "Help! Get me out of here!" The pair turned around and saw a woman locked in an animal cage. They ran to her; it was Tilly Croft, a knight from Elysium.

Caprius and Calista were thrilled to see her. "Tilly, we thought you were dead," said Caprius.

"I'm not dead or undead. I'm very much alive and glad to see you. I knew after I sent the pocket watch with the body and the note I wrote to Confidus asking him to send a knight master, he would," said Tilly.

"You sent the bodies?" Calista and Caprius spoke in unison.

"Not exactly. They made me put the bodies into the caskets and fill them with dirt. Normally, these creatures get Droges to do their dirty work, but since none were around, they forced me to do it. The note and the pocket watch I slipped into the casket and covered with dirt. I knew the pocket watch would lead you to this place."

"I see. So, then they delivered the bodies. Well done, Tilly," said Calista.

"I still don't understand why you were not killed or infected by the blood of Makoor," said Caprius. He eyed her suspiciously.

"Eventually, they would have. But, while they still had grunt work to be done, they kept me around." She smiled and put her hand on Caprius' arm through the bars. "Okay, guys, we've had our little reunion. Now, how about getting me out of here?"

"Stand back, Tilly," said Caprius. He concentrated and blasted the lock with the power of the claymore. Tilly threw open the cage door and hopped out.

"We successfully destroyed the cult, but my fear is it was far too easy," said Calista. "Was this their main fortress?"

"No, I don't think so. This was but a small cult. There are many more," said Caprius.

"Then, our work is finished in Jethro," said Calista.

Caprius cut her off, "But, Volsar Goncool remains at large, and the main fortress of these creatures is yet to be discovered. It isn't just Plaphorius or Mount Drone. Somewhere out there lies the answer."

"I did manage to overhear something about their boarding a train. But, I don't know where they're going," said Tilly.

Caprius checked his watch. "If we run, we have just enough time for us to catch the last train."

"Actually, since we can't do anything else here now, we could go to Quantum Heights. Tonight is their 10-year anniversary. We should be in attendance," said Caprius.

"Then, let's go. We'll see if we can get some horses to take us to Galdington," said Calista.

Tilly sighed. "I personally can't wait to sit on a real chair and get a drink," she smiled.

"Agreed. But, we nonetheless need to remain vigilant; some of the Goncools are still at large, and they're dangerous. We need to keep one eye over our shoulders at all times," said Caprius.

"Now, that's an interesting visual," said Calista, making the three of them laugh.

Caprius, Calista and Tilly walked up the stairs. When they got to the back entrance of the house, the hunchback was lying on the ground, his head bitten clean off, likely the work of Volsar Goncool.

"Oh, there are four horses harnessed to the wagon. I should have my hearing checked. I only noticed three when I was in the sack," said Calista.

"In the sack?" asked Tilly looking suspiciously first at Caprius then at Calista.

"It's a long story. I'll tell you all about it on the way," he said.

They unfastened the horses, mounted, and rode off to Galdington.

Chapter 19

Masquerade/The Power of the Golden Fleece

ALAMPTRIA'S FINEST IN THEIR MOST elaborate costumes were gathered at the castle. The masks and disguises made the guests indistinguishable from their true identities. People in painted faces, feathered headdresses, and vibrant dresses and cloaks sailed about the room enjoying the festive music, food, and drink. The four Goncools dressed as Elysian soldiers were trying to identify which of the masked guests was Confidus Seaton. They didn't pause to enjoy themselves as they were focused on their mission. A scantily-clad woman passed by a Goncool offering up a tray of hor d'oeuvres, but he brushed her rudely aside.

Godfrey tapped a man on the shoulder. "Excuse me, you wouldn't happen to know what Confidus Seaton is wearing, would you?"

"I'm afraid I have no idea," said the man. "Good luck in finding him." Godfrey and the Goncools continued their search. The party grew in attendees and in enthusiasm. Soon, the hall was packed with people, making it harder to search for Confidus. Yet, at one point, a hefty woman came away from the bar area. "Mr. Godfrey! Mr. Godfrey!" she called out before cornering him. "It is Fetrona Nightly." Fetrona removed her mask.

"Well, Fetrona. How good it is to see you, my dear," said Godfrey.

"Are you enjoying the party?" she asked.

"Well, yes, it is splendid, splendid indeed," he said. "And, how are you coping? Getting over Andromin?"

"I'll be all right. I'm a strong woman," she said.

"I'm glad to see you're handling things well," he said. "You wouldn't happen to know what Confidus is dressed as, would you, Fetrona? I would like to have a word with him."

"Why, yes! He's dressed as an Egyptian Pharaoh," she said, "with a golden mask and staff."

"Do you know where I might find him?" asked Godfrey.

"I can take you to him. Follow me," she said. The four Goncools walked with her. One of them furtively held on to a flask he'd had in his pocket that was filled with Makoor's blood.

Just then, Fetrona sighted Confidus. "There he is, over there!"

"Thank you, Fetrona. You've been most helpful. I shall never forget it," said Godfrey. He made to walk away.

"Well, don't leave me here, silly. I'll take you right to him," she said.

Before they could walk any further, an Elysian soldier along with six other guards approached the group. "Hold it right there," he said sternly. "Why are you four dressed in scout uniforms at this ball? Didn't you read the memo?"

"Sorry, Sir, I don't believe we received it," said a Goncool.

"And, there certainly is no drinking on the job. Give me that," the Elysian knight reached for the blood-filled flask from the Goncool's hand. The Goncool held tight, but the soldier wrestled him for it, and the flask fell to the ground, spilling over the floor. The soldier looked at the blood pooling up on the floor aghast. "All right, I am taking the four of you in," he exclaimed.

Another soldier stepped to the front. "Wait a minute, Sir; I knew there was something suspicious about these four. There were four Elysian scout uniforms reported missing and four knights were found hanging from the trees in the woods. Sir, these are Goncools!"

"You are under arrest," said the head Elysian knight. The Goncools quickly drew their swords, but with the flashing lights and jaunty music, their aim was off and they missed. A fight quickly commenced. Once the guests standing near them realized this was real and not part of the party, they ran off screaming. Confidus turned to see the fight. Godfrey broke away from the pack and ran off toward Confidus with his sword raised high. Confidus stood, frozen, as if he didn't quite comprehend what was happening. Just then, a brave guest intervened by knocking into Godfrey; the Goncool fell to the floor in front of Confidus. The soldiers quickly rushed to him and apprehended him, lifting him to his feet.

Confidus peered at the man's face. "He is a Goncool, Your Majesty," said the Elysian knight.

"Well done, gentlemen. Take him into custody," said Confidus. Fetrona who had come to stand by Confidus' side was trembling and confused.

The three other Goncools who fought the Elysian knights had been killed in the fight. The Goncools' plan to turn Confidus into a deadly vampire had been foiled. The guards searched Godfrey, finding his flask containing Makoor's blood. They took him out of the ballroom.

He was escorted through the people by three guards. Suddenly, Godfrey broke free. He ran down the castle hall, chased by the guards, out of the castle and into the garden of Meadow-lie. Godfrey ran until he found himself at the back entrance to the basilica. In the garden, Setra Helmsly was taking to Felicia - the Golden Fleece. Setra wasn't the type to be attending the masquerade ball. She was more interested in speaking to Felicia, as she was concerned about Melina. The guards spotted Godfrey climbing an iron fence. He nimbly tumbled down into the garden. Setra was startled as Godfrey came by. The Golden Fleece new exactly who this man was. Suddenly, the Golden Fleece's eyes brightened and glowed white. Electric shocks shot out from her eyes and landed on Godfrey, sending pure electricity through his body. He shuddered, was jolted, and then collapsed on the ground dead.

The guards made it over the gate and found his body. Felicia looked to them as she always did. The Elysian knights picked up Godfrey's body and carried him away. Setra, who was distraught over what had happened, watched Felicia metamorphose back into the statue she was and left the garden.

Chapter 20

Inferno

BEHIND SOME BUSHES JUST OUTSIDE Quanta-paloose, Cynthia spied on some brutish looking men entering the Sun Myers warehouse. She watched the parade of misfits and thugs until the last one entered and the door closed behind him. Cynthia stole to the side of the warehouse, where she spotted a window ajar. She lifted the window and crawled in, dropping down to the wooden floor quietly like a cat. She took stock of the place in the dark, assessing shadows. Then, she crept to the door, slowly opened it, and went into the hall. A light was coming from a room at the hall's end. She made her way down the hall; there was a wooden railing at the front of a small balcony of sorts that looked down over a large room. Peering around the corner, she saw the thugs gathered around in chairs. She couldn't see who was speaking, but she knew it was Colburn giving his opening speech. "Now as you can see, gentlemen, I have here two small snakes in these tanks," said Colburn. "As you can see, while they are both separated, they seem wild and eager to get at one another. Luckily, they are separated by glass. These snakes are not poisonous. So, now I inject one of these snakes with the serum, and now the other. Oh, this little critter bit me. But, as I said, they're not poisonous. Now, as you watch closely, the reptiles will start to manifest momentarily." And, as they watched, the two snakes began to grow in size. In minutes, they had grown from two foot snakes to twice their size. As they stopped growing, they noticed the snakes' behavior. "As you can see, they not only grew twice their size, but you notice that they are now quite tame. And, they seem to be getting along."

Cynthia noted the circumstances in the room below: dozens of barrels were grouped in clusters on all sides of the men. She turned around and saw that behind her was a stairwell; she crept down the stairs, trying to walk lightly. When she was three steps from the bottom, the stair beneath her foot creaked. She froze and waited, but the men were guffawing among themselves and didn't seem to notice. She let out her breath and made it to the bottom.

Cynthia crouched down as she went into the room and hid behind some barrels. She assessed the barrels' locations and came up with a plan. Slowly, she tipped over one of the barrels and let the wine spill out onto the floor. Then, she did the same to another. She went over to the other side, sliced into a slat of another barrel and carefully tipped it over. Colburn was speaking on a podium, gesturing wildly about his serum. Colburn picked up one snake from the tank, as if it was his pet. "There, you see, it is quite tame and in my control."

"Look at the size of that thing," Cynthia muttered.

Colburn raised his voice into something deep and menacing. He was a bald man with a stone face. His eyes were dark and grim. Among the men, Cynthia noticed, was a Goncool. Beside Colburn was a lantern on a barrel. Cynthia scuttled behind the various barrels until she was close enough to see the black gnarled hairs on the backs of Colburn's hands. She slowly lifted a lid off the barrel before her, then scooted to the one beside and did the same.

"Did you hear something?" one man asked another beside him. Cynthia knew her luck was running out. She put one hand on each barrel, muttered a few words of prayer, and shoved the barrels over. The wine spilled onto the floor and ran toward the men. The men turned at the sound and saw the flood of wine and Cynthia standing there holding two barrel lids.

"What the hell!" someone yelped.

Cynthia smiled. "Hello, boys" she said.

"Cynthia Davenport," said Colburn. He smiled cruelly.

"What, you're not going to welcome me to hell? That's right, sadly, you're in your own crematorium. You won't live to see your super snakes do much more than burn to the ground." Cynthia reared her arm back and jettisoned one of the lids through the room. It cut the air like a knife as it sailed over the men's heads. Cynthia's aim was excellent; the lid smashed into the lantern, shattering the glass and toppling the candle onto the floor. The wine had pooled up, and when the candle fell, the wine erupted into giant orange flames. The barrel lid hit a man in the head before crashing to the floor, and he fell silently into the fire unconscious. The fire raced along the wine and crawled up the podium, igniting Colburn. Cynthia leaped into the room and flipped over another barrel onto the floor. A man began to run toward her. Cynthia stuck out her foot and kicked the barrel at him. He tried to jump over the barrel, but he slipped on it and came crashing down onto the floor. The man, too, was slowly overtaken by the flames.

The fire was spreading rapidly. The Goncool, who had been quietly sitting toward the rear of the group of men, darted to the podium and grabbed the vials of serum. Colburn, now fully engulfed, ran about in circles, screaming. In the mayhem, Cynthia was able to race out into the same stairwell and make it outside. She slammed the door behind her, grabbed the smaller of her swords and brought the blade down onto the handle, hard, breaking the lock from the outside. Cynthia ran toward the bushes, knowing she didn't have much time. The fire had engulfed the entire warehouse. She got to the tree where her horse was whinnying and pacing about nervously, untied him, and mounted. She looked up a last time at the warehouse and saw a man climbing out of the second-story window. Her heart sank when she saw the pouch in his hand. "He has the serum," she said. She dug her heels into her horse and galloped after the man, who landed on the ground and begun to run. In the last hour, a thin blanket of snow had fallen, and she was grateful she could see his tracks. The man got to his horse and sped off into the forest. But, Cynthia was after him.

***

The train Caprius, Calista, and Tilly were waiting for entered the station. As it slowed, people were already standing up and preparing to board. All around them, their fellow passengers were chattering excitedly about the upcoming festivities at Quantum Heights. The train stopped, and those who had just arrived into the station disembarked. As the three prepared to enter their car, they noticed that the last two cars of this passenger train were freight; loud sounds of whinnying horses were coming from them.

Finally, they boarded and relaxed in the dining car. It was after 9:00 p.m., and as the train sped through the territories, none of them talked about how their disappointment that the mission had come to an end. For despite having destroyed the cult, they knew there were bigger issues to deal with, primarily where the vampires' lair was situated. They might have uncovered the plot at Jethro, but Volsar Goncool had escaped and gone into hiding. "Do you think Volsar flew to Mount Drone?" asked Calista.

"He might have. Unfortunately, it's over for now. In any case, at least we now understand that all the vampires in the cult carry these watches, though they don't need them to tell time; their instincts inform them of when night falls, which is for them obviously imperative, as the sun disintegrates them."

"When we were in the cave of the cult, I noticed piles of dirt and a number of wooden caskets. That was from where they delivered those bodies. The deliveries were obviously meant to be a warning to us that we needed to stop sending agents, or those we did send would be returned dead," mused Calista.

Tilly's back seemed to be going up. "Calista, we know that already. I'm the one who was following their orders and helped send those bodies, remember? And, I was the one who sent you that pocket watch? If it hadn't been for my thinking, you never would have discovered that vampire cult," said Tilly.

"Alright, and if it hadn't been for us, you would be dead or undead," said Calista, frowning.

"We all certainly played a part," said Caprius smiling at the two women. "I just wish we had destroyed Volsar and Cambrozes."

"Yes," said Calista. She looked down at her hands.

"You don't still have warm feelings for your father, do you?" asked Caprius.

"No, I do not." She stiffened and sat up tall. "I am now a knight master of Petoshine. My allegiance is to the vim and the great Grongone. There is no conflict within me. If it must be that I will kill my father, then that is what I will do. I know now he is an evil man."

"Evil, yes. But, he is no man, and whatever humanity he might have ever had is gone now. Now, he is a creature of great power. Only together can we destroy him," said Caprius.

"Then, that is what we shall do. Destroy him together when the time comes," said Calista.

"Wait a minute, Cambrozes Genesis is your father? And, you're a knight master of Petoshine?" asked Tilly dumbfounded. "I was wondering how you were able to do those things with your sword, like throwing flames of fire."

"You know, I could use a fine glass of grog. I need something to warm me up," said Calista, rubbing her arms. She turned around to look for a waiter.

"Wait a minute. Don't go off the subject. You have some explaining to do. I just heard Caprius say that Cambrozes Genesis is your father," said Tilly.

Caprius sighed. "I said all of that in full confidence. Tilly, now that you know the truth, this conversation doesn't leave this table. No one needs to know of Calista's past," said Caprius.

Tilly was aghast. "Caprius, this isn't right," she said.

"Tilly, please," said Calista.

"She's had a hard life. And, that notwithstanding, Calista has earned her status of knight master. She saved my life," said Caprius.

"Yes, twice," Calista held up two fingers.

"So, please, let's just keep this between ourselves," said Caprius.

Tilly shook her head and glanced meanly at Calista. "Fine, but I don't understand this at all," she said. "That someone with her history could suddenly be a knight master possessing the vim of Petoshine. It's ridiculous."

"It's a very long story," said Caprius. "So, for now, let's just enjoy the fact that we're in comfortable seats, with drinks soon to be in front of us, and we can rejoice in our health."

A waiter stopped by the table. "Your timing is excellent, my good man. A round of grog for us, please?" said Caprius.

Tilly was glowering. "So, tell me, Calista, how in the world did you become a knight master?"

A man approached their table. At first they didn't look up, thinking it was the waiter again, but once he began to speak, their hearts froze. "Yes, Calista, how in the world did the daughter of Cambrozes Genesis betray her father and follow the vim of Petoshine?" Without another word, the man turned to Tilly and fired three shots from his pistol into her chest, killing her. Tilly slumped over on the table. "Lavender Frikiseed," said Calista. She leaped up, and her and Caprius' hands instantly went to their claymores.

"Tut tut," he clucked with a fiendish smile on his face. "Hands off your claymores, or you'll both be dead like your friend here," said Lavender.

Calista checked Tilly's pulse. "She is dead," she said. "You didn't have to kill her."

"Oh, but I did. I wanted to show you both that a bullet is quicker than a blade," said Lavender. "So, if the two of you want to stay alive, you'll do exactly what I say."

"What do you want, Frikiseed?" asked Caprius.

"What do I want? What do you think I want, moron?" Lavender pointed the gun at Calista. "Take it out, Caprius, real slow. And, put it on the table. Or your lady friend here dies." Caprius slowly took out his claymore of power from his sheath and placed it on the table. "Now, turn the sword's handle toward me." Caprius did as he said. "Push it here." Lavender picked up the claymore. "Now, you, up!" he said to Calista. Just then, the waiter approached with drinks. When he saw what was happening, he jerked backward, spilling the glasses on his tray.

Lavender pointed the gun at the waiter and shot him. The waiter dropped to the floor. "The drinks are on you," he chuckled, then pointed the gun again at Calista. "All right, Calista, my sweet; you're coming with me. This way." Calista glanced quickly at Caprius before walking down the aisle in front of Frikiseed. "And, you, don't get any ideas, or you'll have her blood on your hands."

Calista walked toward the front of the car with Lavender's gun at her back. They went through the doors into the next car, then through that car and into another. At the table, Caprius sat quietly, trying to devise a plan for getting her back. After enough moments had passed, he jumped up and followed them.

When Lavender and Calista arrived at the front of the train, only the engine remained. They went into the engine car. "OK, stop here," he said. "Now, unhook the train from the engine," said Lavender nudging Calista with his gun. Calista unhooked the first car, and they separated. She watched regretfully as the train separated from the engine where she stood alone with

Lavender and the conductor, who she was sure would soon be dead, too.

As Caprius walked through the aisles, he noticed the train was slowing down. He knew instantly that Lavender had unhooked the cars and made his getaway on the engine. He thought a moment, then as the train lost its momentum and stopped, he bolted toward the back. He passed through each car on his way to the last, people turning in confusion, not only at the stopped train, but also at the knight with no sword sprinting through.

When he came to the first freight car, he opened the door and saw the horses. The conductor turned around to see Lavender pointing his gun at Calista. "What the hell is going on?" he asked.

"Just shut up and keep going," said Lavender.

"Is that one of those new guns?" asked the conductor nervously.

"No talking from you," said Lavender. The conductor turned around and, with shaking hands, kept the train moving on course.

The train continued to travel up into the mountains. Calista stood by the wall never removing her eyes from Lavender. "Since you're undoubtedly going to kill us both," said Calista, "you could at least reveal the hiding place of the vampire nest. It wasn't in Jethro; the cult there was too small. It has to be somewhere we'd least expect it," said Calista.

Lavender laughed. "Calista, you are right. There will be no hero rescues here. You're on your own. So, of course, I can let you in on my little secret." He leaned in and whispered. "We're going to the nest right now." He cackled.

"What do you mean; we're headed for... oh, no. You're planning on striking Quantum Heights?" asked Calista, astonished.

"Wouldn't you know that we've been nesting in the hotel basement all along! Slowly multiplying. In..." he checked his pocket watch, "exactly twenty minutes, if not sooner, all the civilians vacationing there will be undead. We can't be stopped!" grinned Lavender. Then, his face darkened. "By the time we arrive, it will all be over."

Caprius had gotten into the freight car, where he saw horses.

Calista was dumbfounded. She became angry. "All those innocent people," she whispered. Her hand instinctively crept down to her claymore of power. Lavender nudged her arm away with his gun. "Ah, ah, keep your hands off your claymore. And, you, driver, look at me!" The conductor who was trying to see what was happening behind him spun back around to the front. "Wait, come back," said Lavender. "I want you to take the lady's sword. Do it!" Lavender yelled. The man leaned over and took Calista's sword. "Now, open your window and throw it out." He did as was told. All three watched the claymore bounce off the rails and sink into a snow bank before they sped out of sight. "Now, then, my good fella, you have overstayed your welcome. I have no more use for you." Lavender fired at the conductor and killed him. He crumpled onto the floor.

"How many people have you killed?" asked Calista.

"Do I hear judgment in your voice, Calista? How many of my kind have you killed? No matter, though. I'm about to kill you, and we can stop the cycle right here."

As Lavender raised his gun, Caprius was racing on horseback, trying to catch up to the train's engine. He galloped as fast as his horse would go over the snow-covered ground. As he rode, sweat and tears clouding his vision, he saw Grongone's face in the clouds above. Grongone used the vim of Petoshine, and threw it down to Calista's claymore of power nestled in the snow. The tip glowed blue. Caprius looked into Grongone's eyes before the blue light caught his attention. Caprius slowed his horse to retrieve the sword. He held out his hand and channeled his inner power. The sword began to vibrate and shake, its blue glow strengthening. Caprius sped up, leaned over, and forced the sword into his hand. Grongone's face disappeared from the clouds. Caprius picked up speed and soon saw the engine on the tracks.

Calista saw over Lavender's shoulder a small figure. As it approached, she could see it was Caprius on horseback. She began to inch back toward the controls.

She purposefully made a frightened face and looked out the side window. Lavender followed her, and in that instant, she lunged at the controls and pulled down the emergency brake. The engine screeched to a stop. Both Calista and Lavender fell over from the abrupt motion; startled, Lavender fired as he went down. Calista jumped on top of Lavender, and they struggled for the gun. When the train stopped, Lavender cracked Calista hard across the face and pushed her off of him. He took his gun and pointed it at her.

"Poor pathetic, Calista," said Lavender aiming at her heart. Just as Lavender was just about to squeeze the trigger, a claymore of power burst through Lavender's back and out through his stomach. A red glow appeared from the sword, which ignited a flame.

The fire spread throughout Lavender's midsection. He looked down at his body, in shock and perplexed. "But, how…" he began before Caprius, who had boarded the engine car, yanked the sword out of Lavender's body. Calista accepted her claymore of power Caprius held out to her, channeled her powers, and blew a force of energy at Lavender, sending him as a blazing torch flying out of the engine car and onto the snow.

They sheathed their swords and smiled. "It's over," said Caprius. "We did it."

Calista returned to the controls. "Not yet, I'm afraid. Lavender said that the vampire's nest is in the basement of Quantum Heights. We have about ten minutes before the entire hotel is infested with vampires."

Caprius swallowed. "My God. Under our noses all this time." Caprius ran his hand through his hair. "We have to get to the hotel. When we get there, we will have to burn it down."

Calista chuckled ruefully. "Mr. Willy B. Pinkles is not going to like that."

"He'll like that more than becoming a vampire, I assure you," Caprius said. Caprius joined Calista at the controls. He put his hand gently atop hers, and together, they pulled the lever up slowly until the engine began to pick up speed. Soon, the engine was moving at a good clip over the tracks.

***

The Goncool who Cynthia was chasing had arrived at the Quantum Heights hotel. Cynthia was approaching the grand hotel. The Goncool opened the doors and headed for the basement. Cynthia entered the hotel doors. As she looked to the distance, she saw him enter a room. He went down the stairs to the basement.

Cynthia walked in and heard the thumping of footsteps going down the stairs. The Goncool arrived in a large basement hall. There, he saw other Goncools, vampires, and Droges. Cynthia came down the stairs, slowly opened the door, and glanced in. She hid, spying on them. She saw the creatures of the underworld. The Goncool was talking. Cynthia knew she was outnumbered by many. She knew that approaching them was suicide. She squinted her eyes and drew her hand across her hair. "Shit. I'm too late," she said.

***

The train picked up speed until it was storming at full capacity across the tracks. They drove across a long bridge that stood one hundred and fifty feet over the sea. Ahead were the mountains of Morbid, smaller mountains near the Moldavian Sea. The sky above was thick with storm clouds, but the moon shown through, creating an eerie white glow over the snowy mountains. The engine traveled over the bridge and was soon again on land. "Calista, get down. We're going to make a dramatic entrance!" said Caprius. They threw themselves onto the floor. The engine went right through the train station, careened off the tracks and slammed into the Hotel Quantum Heights. The impact caused the engine to flip over onto its side, but Caprius and Calista hung on. The engine slid on its side through the hotel lobby, throwing sofas and tables into the air, people screaming and running, expensive vases shattering, water and flowers flying every which way. Paintings hanging on the walls came crashing down. The engine kept on through the marble room, crushing the concierge desk and a ghoulish vampire who had come up from the nest. Its skull was bashed in, and blood splattered everywhere. Finally, the engine came to a stop. Cynthia heard the crash. She knew her mission to destroy the serum was foiled. But, she managed to destroy Cyril Colburn. For that, she was satisfied. She went back up the stairs. She arrived at the hotel lobby to find a train had crashed through. She observed the fire. Calista was lying on top of Caprius, their bodies pressed against each other. She could feel his heart beating inside her own body. Though she wanted nothing more than to stay with her body on his, Calista turned away from Caprius at the smell of hot wires. In an instant, a fire sparked in the engine, and the engine burst into flames. The concierge desk close by caught fire, and the fire caught on all the splintered wood spread throughout the lobby. Calista crawled out of the engine and Caprius followed. They stood on top of the engine by the doors, the engine on its side. They noticed that a number of vampires, in anticipation of their big event, had come up and were shaken by the blast. "We have to get off the engine! It's going to blow!" Calista yelled. They jumped down and unsheathed their swords in preparation for combat, then ran into the adjoining hall, blowing out flames with their claymores as they went. Spotting a spiral staircase, they noticed Cynthia watching.

"Nice to see the two of you," said Cynthia.

"Did you stop Colburn?" asked Calista.

"Colburn is dead. I burned down the warehouse. But, a Goncool escaped with the serum. I chased him to Quantum Heights. They're down stairs. They're plotting they're next move," said Cynthia.

"Cynthia, Calista and I have to go downstairs. We have to destroy them."

"There's something big transpiring down there. There's a large coffin, vampires, and Droges. It's too much for me to handle," said Cynthia.

"It's far too dangerous for you. This calls for the powers of Petoshine," said Caprius. "You get out of here, Cynthia. Your job is done. Let's go, Calista." Caprius and Calista ran down the stairs to the basement. Cynthia looked around to see fire everywhere. The entrance to the hotel was blocked and in flames. She began to walk quickly up the stairs.

Caprius and Calista entered the basement hall. They slowly approached the vampires and the Goncool. "Well, well, well, if it isn't the knight master Caprius and the infamous Calista. So nice of you to join us. And, you have the claymores of power. I have been expecting you."

"It ends here, Goncool," said Caprius. Caprius and Calista noticed a coffin in the center. Beside the coffin was Lydia the vampire sorceress.

"Get them!" The Goncool yelled. Suddenly, the Droges ran with swift speed. These were super Droges. The vampires readied themselves. Caprius and Calista swung their swords. They were slaughtering the Droges. A quick swing of the sword, and Calista gutted a Droge. Another swing and Caprius severed a Droge's head. The fighting went on. Calista was knocked with great force, sending her flying into the vampires. The vampires grabbed hold of her. One of them grabbed her claymore of power from her. "Stop!" the Goncool yelled. Caprius saw that Calista was at the mercy of vampires. Caprius backed off. "Now that I have your attention, Caprius, walk toward me." Caprius slowly walked toward them holding his claymore of power. A Droge who was near Caprius growled and snarled. The Droge walked with him. "All I need is one claymore of power. I have one. Calista, my dear, in case you get any ideas…" he paused. "Take off her arrow pack and throw it over there. And, get rid of the bow." They threw the arrow sack and bow across, landing by the door.

Meanwhile, Cynthia was walking the stairs. She stopped and thought about her friends. "No, I can't leave them. I have to go back," she said. She ran down the stairs. In the basement, the coffin was opened to find the corpse of Titanis Clore. Lydia stood by the coffin holding the sword of Petoshine.

"Once this ritual is complete, and my powers bring Titanis Clore back from the dead, he will embrace the powers of Petoshine. Give him the ultimate power and strength. Then, not even Grongone's power can destroy him." Lydia began her ritual. "You, Caprius Seaton, will not interfere. Or, we will rip off Calista's arms," said Lydia.

Caprius smirked. He recalled the words of Grongone. "All right, Lydia, you win. I won't interfere. Go ahead with your ritual."

***

Melina Hampshire stood by the night table holding the empty alcoholic drink. She saw the images of Caprius in her mind but could not put the pieces of the puzzle together. It had been clearly stated to her who Caprius was to her, but she could not see it. "Why can't I get the entire picture of who Caprius Seaton is?"

***

Lydia began the ritual. Words of devil worship were spoken. From within Lydia came great power. The claymore of power began to glow brightly. There were great electrical shocks from the sword of power. The shocks transferred to Lydia and to Titanis Clore. The basement hall lit up in great light. Clore's body began to draw energy. The power of the claymore intensified.

Clore's body began to twitch, as if coming to life. Lydia began to feel weak. She could not give out her power anymore, and she stopped. The entire basement went dark. There was silence. Suddenly, Caprius drew a light from his claymore. The hall lit up. Lydia began to feel sick. She put her hand to her chest. She gasped for air. Her face began to show a blue color. Her hands changed to blue. There were bright blue veins on her hands and face. She struggled to stay focused. Then, she let out a last utter and fell to the floor dead.

***

With Lydia's death, as Melina stood holding the empty glass, she suddenly felt light headed and dropped the glass. The glass shattered on the floor. She felt a sudden up lift, as she felt the weight upon her mind lift. The vampires' connection to her had vanished. Her mind was clear of who she was. "Caprius," she said smiling.

***

The Goncool looked down at Lydia. He then looked at Titanis Clore, who was lifeless. Suddenly, arrows shot across the room striking the vampires through the heads. The large Droge beside Caprius was confused. "Doesn't that bring tears to your eyes," Caprius said to the Droge. Caprius swiftly drove his sword through the Droges jaw and into its brain. He dislodged his sword, and the Droge fell dead. Calista was free from the vampires and retrieved her sword of power. She ran toward Caprius. At the doorway stood Cynthia holding Calista's bow and arrow. The Goncool lay on the floor dead with an arrow through his skull. The Droges were dead and the vampires destroyed.

"We have to get out somehow. The fire is spreading," said Cynthia.

"Up we go," said Caprius. The knights ran up the stairs. They came to the lobby to take the circular stairs up, and the train exploded, sending fire and steel fragments into the air. Just as the fire came up the staircase, they jumped, landing on the second level. They found another set of stairs leading to the next floor. The fire spread hungrily, following the path of the stairs behind them.

"Up the staircase!" Caprius said to Calista and Cynthia. They ran up the staircase, setting the stairs beneath them on fire. Extending over the whole front façade of hotel were giant French windows. When they arrived on the fourteenth floor, three vampire creatures appeared at the top of the staircase and began to come down to meet the three knights. Caprius sliced the first one through its middle, and the two parts tumbled down the stairs and crashed into the wall. Calista decapitated the second vampire. The head tumbled lightly down the stairs, but its body was heavy and smashed into Calista, causing her to step back and nearly lose her balance before she was able to shove the body away and down the stairs. Now that she and Caprius had reached the fifteenth floor, there were no staircases. Cynthia was surprised by two vampires, and drew both her small swords, slaughtering them. They ran through the hall, and vampires approached them by dozens. As they passed through the hall, Caprius and Calista set the walls ablaze, creating a tunnel of fire. The vampires attacked ceaselessly, and the three knights came at them swinging. They sliced off head after head and sent body parts every which way. At one vampire, Calista swung but missed, and the vampire leaned in and shoved her against the wall. He came to her and held her aloft against the wall by her neck. She still had her sword and jabbed it into the creature's side, channeling her powers and setting the creature on fire. Though it was engulfed in flames and melting, the disintegrating creature held on to her as it screamed in pain mere centimeters away from her face. She grimaced and blindly swung her sword, slicing off the creature's hand from its wrist. She fell to the floor beside the remains of the vampire, it smoldering and stinking as it turned into a pool of vampire flesh. Calista ran to Caprius. He was hacking away at a vampire, and she got in the way of his sword. Her reflexes saved her as her blade met with a clang. "Watch where you're swinging that thing!" she said. They had no time to share in the joke, though, as they each had to contend with yet another vampire. They swung their swords in tandem, decapitating them simultaneously. "Why don't we just run right through them!" said Calista. So they did. With their claymores outstretched, they bolted down the hall, slicing at any vampire who came to close. Soon, the clutch of creatures was behind them, seething and snarling like rabid animals. With some distance separating the knights from the creatures, Caprius and Calista turned around to face a mass of them, channeled their powers, and threw large flames from their swords at the group, engulfing the creatures with fire. The hall burned like an inferno. Caprius, Calista, and Cynthia turned and ran. At the end of the hall, they came to another set of stairs. They ran up several floors to come to a staircase leading to the twenty-third floor.

At the top, two vampires stood waiting for them. Goncools. These Goncools had consumed Makoor's blood. Caprius and Calista slowly walked up, their swords dripping with vampire blood. The Goncools gazed down at them. "Careful, you're dripping," Caprius nodded to Calista's sword. "We really should try not to make such a mess," he said, trying to keep a straight face.

"Right, we don't want to damage the hotel. Mr. Pinkles wouldn't like that," said Calista.

"Enough of your stupid banter. I'm going to enjoy watching you die," said one of the Goncools. "And, I'm going to make your death as unpleasant as I can, Calista. You killed our dear brothers. And, for that, you will pay," said the Goncool. "You may think it's easy to destroy us; after all, you bested our forces in Jethro, but those were merely inexperienced members of the undead. We are Goncools. Masters at swordplay. You will feel our wrath."

"Stop squawking. Why don't you show us what you've got," said Caprius. Caprius and Calista looked at each other, then ran up the stairs to meet them head on. The four of them swung their swords. Down from another hallway, vampires approached.

"I'll take care of these guys," said Cynthia. She slowly walked the hall to meet them.

With every swift stroke Caprius took, the Goncool was quick in defense. They clashed swords with every swing. The Goncool put his hairy, sweaty face right up in Caprius' face when their swords crisscrossed each other. He pushed Caprius, who had to hop down a few steps. Cynthia swiftly swung two swords a sliced the vampires. "You know, I'm just toying with you," said Caprius to the Goncool, who looked like he was enjoying the fight and feeling confident he would soon best the Seaton.

"Your skills are no match for me," laughed the Goncool.

Caprius spryly hopped back up the top steps to resume their fight. They swung and blocked each others' swings. Again and again. Calista was fighting fiercely, as if she was gaining power the longer they fought, similar to her inaugural vampire battle as knight master. The Goncool was growing weary and was backing up from the fury of her swings. They came to where the staircase curved, into the landing, in front of the large French windows. Through the windows, a reflection of them swinging swords was cast upon the glass. Calista lunged around the corner but missed, and the Goncool swung but only managed to knick her armor-covered thigh. The Goncool leaned in. "Why not join us?" he said shyly. "The Goncools could use you. You must realize your father belongs to us, which means you are destined to follow him down the dark path of immortality."

Calista shrugged and smiled apologetically. "I don't listen very well," she said.

"One day, you will realize that you are only prolonging the inevitable. Let me stop your tormented mind. You may not see it, but I can open your eyes. Only when you have tasted the blood of Makoor will you know that I was only trying to help you. Lower your sword. Come to me, Calista. All it takes is one bite. And, you will see that my word is true," said the Goncool.

Caprius glanced over and could see Calista's intensity falter. "Don't listen to him, Calista!" said Caprius raising his voice.

"Never fear, Caprius. Bite this, Goncool!" she said as she jammed the claymore toward his face. The Goncool was fast, and he blocked the sword and pushed her off. Their fight took on a new ferocity. They struck at one another's' swords, swinging again and again, neither backing down. Beside her, Caprius swung his sword, and the Goncool tried to back away. But, he was not fast enough. Caprius' blade went clearly into the Goncool's stomach. The Goncool looked down, touched the blade, and looked at Caprius. He began to laugh. He stared Caprius in the eyes, then jammed the blade deeper into his own abdomen.

Caprius realized the Goncool not only felt no pain, but was also not in any way injured. That meant all this fighting was for nothing. Some of the Goncools were impervious to being killed. The Goncool snarled and growled at Caprius and swung his sword. But, Caprius ducked, grabbed the handle of his sword and pulled hard, throwing himself back and tumbling down the stairs. From the floor, Caprius looked up at the wounded Goncool. He had his hands on the gash and was healing himself, the open wound closing before Caprius' eyes. Soon, he was completely revitalized. "Ha, you can't destroy me. I have taken the blood extract from Makoor, himself. Can't you see? It is useless. I'm a Goncool! The vim of Petoshine is no match for my powers. That is why you must understand, my friend, that the Dark Lord will soon control all of Alamptria."

"You are indeed full of surprises. But, now, it's time to die Goncool." Caprius channeled his powers to his claymore, and his eyes glowed white. The Goncool spread his arms, and with his sword in one hand, he swooped down, swinging his sword. As the Goncool came down, Caprius held out his sword; the Goncool lunged into the blade, and the blade pierced his chest. The Goncool gasped hunched over. Immediately, Caprius dislodged his sword from the Goncool's chest, quickly swung over, severing the Goncool's head. The head and body toppled down. Caprius observed the dead Goncool.

Around them, Hotel Quantum Heights blazed, the firelight vibrant against the darkness of the night and the glow of the moon. The fire had spread more than half way up the hotel. Caprius ran up the stairs to help Calista. Cynthia had fallen behind fighting her own battles. Calista and the Goncool continued to fight. Caprius stepped in, making it two against one. They both swung their swords, and the Goncool had to decide which strike to block. He ended up missing both, and when he lurched from the momentum, Calista kicked his abdomen using such force, the Goncool crashed backwards through the giant window. Shattered glass flew everywhere. The Goncool plummeted through the earth, landing three stories down on top of a balcony. He hit the ground on his back and lay there in a daze. Just outside of the east wing of the burning hotel, Caprius' friend, Nero Fergus, was also fighting off vampires with his sword. A skilful sword fighter himself, Nero decapitated one of the creatures and hooted in triumph as the head toppled, fell to the ground, and sank into the snow up to its grotesque eyeballs. Beside Nero, not too far away, stood the hot air balloon. Caprius and Calista, seeing how they could escape the hotel, leaped through the opening in the broken window and made it easily down to the balcony, with their swords of power cushioning their landing. The Goncool stood, and Caprius ran toward him to attack. As Caprius swung his sword and missed, the Goncool swung hitting Caprius' jaw. As Caprius was falling back, he whisked his sword to cut the Goncools arm at his side. The Goncool immediately healed his wound, and Caprius fell to the concrete floor. The Goncool with his sword over his head, swung down, missing Caprius as he rolled. They looked at each other from a distance. Caprius was struck with an idea and reached for his Graffel gel tool, switched the button to electro shock, and shot a thread across, which wrapped around the Goncool's body nine times, shocking him. The surge of electricity began to eat away at the Goncools body and flesh. The blue shocks sizzled and smoked, eating him away. The Goncool was in agonizing pain. But, with a sudden surge of power, the Goncool broke free of the thread, disengaging the shock. The Goncool ran toward Caprius. Caprius rose to his feet, only to be pushed against the balcony railing. The two pushed against each other with Caprius' back at the railing. As they rolled, the Goncool now had his back against the railing. Pushing their swords against each other, the Goncool took his other hand, grabbing Caprius from below at his crouch. The Goncool swung him over his head, and Caprius was thrown over the side of the tower. Calista yelled "No!" Calista ran toward the Goncool swinging her sword. The two clashed their swords and fought. As Caprius was falling, with quick thinking, he reached for his Graffel gel tool and shot a thread that lassoed onto a stump on the rail of the balcony. The thread being gel-based, acted like an elastic band, tossing Caprius up. Caprius swung to the side, swinging on top onto the balcony railing. As he climbed over the railing, he ran toward Calista, who fought the Goncool. Caprius saw Nero, as he slew the last of the vampires. "Way to go, Nero; now get to your hot air balloon!" cried Caprius. "Now!" Nero, not at all surprised to see the knight covered in blood and floating down to the ground on magical powers, gave Caprius a thumbs up. But, in a moment of inattention, the slain vampire rose again and grabbed him. He drove his fist into Nero, gutting him in one fell swoop. Nero collapsed to the floor, his entrails spilling from his body. Caprius cried out, "No!"

The Goncool who had gone through the upstairs window and was resting on the balcony floor got up as if nothing had happened and laughed. Enraged, Caprius and Calista swung their swords, but the Goncool fought back easily. Caprius had pushed the Goncool back hard to crack the railing of the balcony. They fought, the three of them, hard and long. Calista slashed the creature's thigh at the artery, but he simply touched it and healed instantly. They resumed their fight, swords striking fiercely so fast and hard it was difficult to tell who's sword was whose. The knights were losing steam, but they didn't dare let up, for the Goncool wouldn't stop until they were both dead; this much they knew. Then, without any warning, the Goncool made a horrific face and shrieked, then choked on his own blood coming up his throat. It took Caprius and Calista a moment to understand what was happening. They backed up and realized a sword had come out through the creature's neck from the back. It was Nero. Nero collapsed onto the floor. He fell back, drained from his last heroic effort. Calista wasted no time. She drove her sword into the Goncool's chest, channeling her powers. Caprius then drove his claymore of power into the Goncool's face. Their swords burst out fire, and the Goncool was instantly set ablaze. They held their swords momentarily into its body, watching the fire engulf him. They retracted their swords and the Goncool ran screaming toward the end of the balcony. He broke through the loose railing and fell down the mountain side to his death.

Caprius and Calista ran to Nero and knelt down. Caprius elevated Nero's head on his knee. "Nero," said Caprius humbly, "I cannot believe-"

"That was just such a brave thing you did," said Calista. "Standing up to that Goncool."

Nero tried to breath. "You're, you're out of danger," Nero gasped.

"Yes, thanks to you," said Caprius.

"Now, go my friends. Take the balloon and save yourselves." The knights looked back at the hotel; the fire had spread throughout the whole building. Nero took his last breath, shuttered, and died. Caprius put his friends head down gently. He and Calista both stood up and gazed down at the poor lifeless Nero.

"We have to get off this mountain and away from the hotel," said Calista.

"Yes, it's what Nero wanted. He was such a good man. To the balloon, quickly!" said Caprius. They ran to it and climbed into the basket.

"Can you fly this thing?" asked Calista.

"I hope so. Now's a good time to learn how, anyway," said Caprius trying to figure out the leavers. Calista looked back behind them and felt the heat of the fire on her face.

"Whatever you've got to do, do it faster!" she said.

"I'm trying! I think I've got it!" said Caprius. The balloon slowly began to rise, but instead of taking them out of danger, it was drifting them directly toward the hotel. Caprius tried some other leavers, and the balloon lurched even closer to the fire.

"Caprius!" Calista cried out. Caprius tried another combination of leavers and suddenly, gently, the balloon began to sail away from Hotel Quantum Heights. "Caprius! Look over there. It's Cynthia." And, indeed it was. She was trying to escape the towering inferno. Calista and Caprius cried out to Cynthia. They tossed her a rope, which hung from the basket. Cynthia ran toward the edge of the balcony. "Get under her, Caprius!" Cynthia jumped off the balcony edge and grabbed the rope. As Cynthia held on, she pulled herself up. The balloon drifted off. She climbed the rope onto the basket. Caprius and Calista helped her in. She was now safe.

They gripped the railings, unsure of how the wind would carry them, but once they were a ways away from the hotel and gaining height, they relaxed. They turned around to look at the blazing inferno of Quantum Heights in the far distance, now just a dot of orange light against the dark mountains. "Poor Mr. Willy B. Pinkles. And, the treasury board isn't going to like this either," said Calista.

"Yes, but now Mr. Pinkles has his own personal crematorium," Caprius laughed. "And, here he was worried about my damage to the hotel, which," he added a bit more soberly, "in the light of things, now seems fairly insignificant." He quieted. "So many lives lost."

"You want to give me back my bow and arrows," Calista said to Cynthia.

"Cynthia, I feel like you are a part of this team. Would you like to come and live with us in Castle Elysium? You are welcome to stay with us."

Calista smiled. "Well, I'd like that very much. But, I have an adopted son back at Jethro," said Cynthia.

"How old is he?" asked Calista.

"He is sixteen years old," she replied.

"Well, he is most welcome to come live there, too. We would be happy to have you both," said Caprius.

"I don't know what to say except thank you," said Cynthia.

"You're very welcome. There is only room for three in this basket. Once we touchdown in Elysium, we will get a bite to eat. And, you and I will go back for your son. I just want to get Calista home," said Caprius. Calista smiled warmly.

"I'm curious, Caprius, how did you know Lydia's ritual wouldn't work?" asked Calista.

"Well, you know, Calista, I remember something Grongone once told me. The powers of Petoshine can't be used to harness the dark powers of Makoor. It is used for good. And, when Lydia used the vim against her own powers, I knew it would destroy her. The dark cult doesn't know that. And, when you threw your bow and arrows toward the door, I was hoping a certain someone would come to the rescue."

"Oh, so you knew I was going to come back for you," said Cynthia.

"I had a hunch," he said. Calista sat in the corner of the basket and closed her eyes.

"Yes," nodded Caprius. "You should get some sleep. We're doing fine now, going in the right direction. We are over the sea. By morning light, we should arrive in Elysium."

As the three of them relaxed, now observing the view of the towering inferno, there was a sudden down fall of the hot air balloon. As Caprius and Calista held tight to the basket they stood in, suddenly, the hot air balloon took a good drop. Cynthia looked up to notice flame. "The balloons on fire!" yelled Cynthia. The bursting flames from Hotel Quantum Heights had set the top side of the balloon ablaze.

"We're going down," said Calista.

"Were dropping faster now," said Caprius. Then, the sea beneath them began to twirl and create a funnel. The water rose to great height and twirled around the hot air balloon. As they looked into the wall of twirling water, they kept falling. Grongone's face appeared in the sky. As he looked down at the knights, he showed great concern.

"What do we do?" said Calista concerned. Down, down, down they went. Suddenly, a great light emerged from beneath them. There was some sort of force, which took hold of the hot air balloon and brought it down gently. The basket had settled down gently onto a surface, and as the balloon had collapsed and hung to the side burning, from the top, a hatch began to close. The three knights watched the roof close with a clang and observed their surroundings. It was dark. And, now lights began to turn on everywhere at the sides. This was a very large cargo area. The knights got out of the basket. They began to walk. From a distance, a man stood with a staff in hand, helping him walk. Caprius smiled.

"Death does not permit you to lie sleeping. Rise and embrace the vim," said the man. As Caprius looked at his pointed ears, he knew who he was. "One does not stay dormant when he is struck down. Rise and fight young knight masters!"

"Who are you?" asked Calista. "What is this place?"

" You have entered flight gazer Petoshine. I am the sword of justice—the song of the whooping crane that strengthens your mind. I am the last of my kind," said the elf. "The light of Petoshine will guide you to be the sword of peace. My name is Grongone."

"It's nice to see you again, Grongone," said Caprius. Grongone bowed his head.

"You saved our lives," said Cynthia.

"Some lives are worth fighting for, Cynthia," said Grongone.

"You know who I am," she asked surprised.

"My dear, I know everything. I must say you all fought bravely. It is time for you to embrace the vim. And, you Cynthia Davenport, it is time for you to become a knight master." Cynthia smiled. "Come my friends. We will have refreshments and induct Cynthia in a knight's blessing." The three knights followed Grongone. As they walked through the great hall, they entered a room where they were given refreshments. After a well-deserved rest, Cynthia was inducted in a ceremonial blessing and given the gift of the power of a claymore. Grongone put his hand upon Cynthia's forehead, charging her with the power of the vim. "Cynthia, I strengthen you and I embrace you with the powers of the vim." After embracing the vim, Cynthia got off her knees and accepted her claymore of power. "Now, my friends, before I take you all to Elysium, we must collect Cynthia's adopted son, Henry Hudson."

Deep beneath the waters of the sea of Valgeroth, the flight gazer Petoshine emerged from the waters. As the gazer rose, the waters cascaded down from the ships surface and shot across the heavens.

***

Caprius sat back in his cushiony chair upon the flight gazer. He felt conflicted. Calista was the direct descendent of a deranged man who followed the dark forces of Makoor. But, he also knew she was the light of Petoshine and a knight master with great skill, who defeated the dark forces and certainly would again. But, he wondered if he'd imagined it or whether it was real. That look in her eye when the Goncool tempted her, tried to entice her to join her father. Would she one day be so tempted to follow the dark path of immortality and work against Petoshine? Or, was her soul pure, and she would help defeat the evil that had befallen the land of Alamptria?

***

The knight masters had arrived at Castle Elysium. Caprius entered his bedroom suite. As he looked around, he could not see Melina. He noticed the glass door by the balcony open. He walked out to the balcony to see his beloved Melina standing there. There, by the sunrise, she stood looking at him. She was dressed in a beautiful white gown. She smiled warmly at him as she quickly walked over. "Caprius, my love," she said to him. They held each other close. Happy of Melina's memory return, he hugged her with great emotion. There figures shown against the sunrise. A brand new day had begun.

THE END

Visit online at: www.richardavalicek.com

Made in the USA
Middletown, DE
14 November 2015